P9-DWF-849

3 7814 00168 4761

DISCARDED
BAKER CO. LIBRARY

AUG 2 8 2003

LAKER
Laker, Rosalind.
New world, new love
26.99

Baker County Public Library
2400 Resort Street
Baker City, Oregon 97814
541.523.6419

DEMCO

Laker, Rosalind.
New world, new love
                26.99

NEW WORLD, NEW LOVE

Recent Titles by Rosalind Laker from Severn House

THE FRAGILE HOUR
THE SEVENTEENTH STAIR
TO LOVE A STRANGER

NEW WORLD, NEW LOVE

Rosalind Laker

BAKER COUNTY LIBRARY
2400 RESORT
BAKER CITY, OREGON 97814

This first world edition published in Great Britain 2002 by
SEVERN HOUSE PUBLISHERS LTD of
9–15 High Street, Sutton, Surrey SM1 1DF.
This first world edition published in the USA 2003 by
SEVERN HOUSE PUBLISHERS INC of
595 Madison Avenue, New York, N.Y. 10022.

Copyright © 2002 by Rosalind Laker.

All rights reserved.
The moral right of the author has been asserted.

British Library Cataloguing in Publication Data

Laker, Rosalind, 1925-
    New world, new love
    1.   French - New York (State) - New York - Fiction
    2.   Love stories
    I.   Title
    823.9'14 [F]

    ISBN 0-7278-5911-0

Except where actual historical events and characters are being
described for the storyline of this novel, all situations in this
publication are fictitious and any resemblance to living persons
is purely coincidental.

Typeset by Palimpsest Book Production Ltd.,
Polmont, Stirlingshire, Scotland.
Printed and bound in Great Britain by
MPG Books Ltd., Bodmin, Cornwall.

LAKER
(Rosalind)

To Mary and Richard for friendship
and all the laughter

AUG 2 8 2003

One

It was a crisp and golden New York morning in early spring. Daniel Lombard would always remember it as the day he saw the Frenchwoman for the first time. He had come out of the mercantile office on an East River wharf, his business completed, and was lingering on the steps when he saw her.

Maybe it was her wide-brimmed yellow hat, bright as a little sun, which had first caught his eye and caused him to focus on the curiously haunting beauty of her oval face. She was among the passengers clustered along the bulwark of the newly arrived tall-masted American ship, the *Ocean Maid*, all taking in the busy scene below while waiting to disembark.

There was much to see. Wagons and carts and carriages coming and going, stevedores rolling hogsheads of wine, shifting cargo or loading the noisy, clanking cranes. Everywhere passengers were arriving and departing, many trailing porters in their wake. Prevailing over all was that peculiar dockside odour blended of tarry ropes, spices from the Dutch East Indies, stale fish, sacks of corn and salt-encrusted timbers.

Earlier, through the window of the mercantile office, Daniel had seen the customs officers and other officials going aboard. Being an importer of silks, he was always interested in ships, and he had asked a clerk where the *Ocean Maid* had been on her voyage.

'She's home at last after lying in embargo for several months with other of our ships at the French port of Bordeaux, Mr Lombard,' the young man had replied. 'All because of an upstart ruling by that unpredictable Revolutionary government there! Now at last Captain Hooper has been allowed to return

1

home and has brought with him an assortment of people escaping the guillotine. That Revolution is nothing more than a bloodbath now. New York is flooded with these émigrés. Some have started up their own businesses and they even print their own newspaper in French.'

Daniel knew from his sister's letters that it was the same in Charleston and he shared her compassion for these unfortunate people. After all, as she had written, their own French Huguenot ancestors had been forced to flee to the New World to escape religious persecution little more than a century ago and now for another reason a similar desperate flight from France was happening all over again.

'Are there many of these émigrés in Boston where you live, sir?' the clerk asked.

'Not compared with the number of those arriving here.'

'You'll soon see a crowd collect,' the clerk continued. 'As word spreads that there's a ship in from France, émigrés already here come rushing to the quayside in the hope of finding people they know on board or, at the very least, news of family and friends.'

The clerk's words had proved right. Quite a little crowd was gathering on the wharf, all shouting up to those on board, and more were clustered around the foot of the gangway to question those stepping ashore. Daniel strolled forward, tall and broad-shouldered, his gaze still fixed on the Frenchwoman, and came to a halt at the back of the crowd.

He was a striking-looking man, not conventionally handsome, but his face was strong-featured, the nose chiselled, the black brows straight over sharply intelligent grey eyes, and he had a wide, well-shaped mouth that was warmly sensual. Twenty-eight years old, he had the easy, self-assured air that comes from success and position. Having long been exasperated by the fashion of wigs and powdered hair, he wore his black hair groomed in the latest short, brushed-forward style. He also favoured the new, highly fashionable slim-cut coat worn with tight doeskin pantaloons and high polished boots instead of knee breeches and buckled shoes, which fashionable men had reserved for evening attire. His top hat had the high, narrowing crown and the slightly curving brim that made all other headgear appear thoroughly outdated.

On board, Louise de Vailly was unaware of being studied. Holding her hat brim between her thumb and index finger, she shook her head regretfully at those calling up to her, being unable to give any of them the information they required. In the crowd some of the women were weeping in disappointment. Then Louise felt an impatient tug on her sleeve from her fifteen-year-old sister.

'Come along, Louise. I want to get off this horrible ship and you're missing our turn at the gangway.'

'Yes, I'll be glad to get ashore too, Delphine.'

It had been a hard voyage lasting the customary six weeks with overcrowded quarters and extremely rough weather. There had also been very little food, which had been no fault of the captain, for the Revolution had resulted in widespread famine in France and he had had great difficulty in getting any supplies. Louise picked up her bundle of belongings, which was all she had been able to bring away with her, and followed her sister, similarly burdened, who set off ahead of her down the gangway.

Daniel had a better view of the newcomer now. She had the finely moulded facial bones of the well-bred Frenchwoman, her complexion devoid of the thick cosmetics that many of the aristocratic émigrés, men and women, continued to use as if still at the Palace of Versailles. Instead her skin had a healthy tint from the ocean air and seemed to glow. Her green eyes were large and long-lashed and her luxuriant hair a rich chestnut. She held her head high, her chin tilted, and he had the impression that whatever hardships and terrors she had endured in the past her courage was not diminished and she was prepared to face whatever this new country held in store for her.

Around her long throat was a scarlet ribbon, symbolic of the cut made by the guillotine's blade. He had seen that worn by other émigrés, both as a sign of having been bereaved by the guillotine and as a mark of respect for the victims. As her gown and cloak were black and in spite of the cheerful sunshine colour of her hat, which she had tried to sober down with black ribbons, he judged her loss to have been personal.

Louise was halfway down the gangway when the heel of her shoe slipped and she grabbed at the side-rope to steady herself. Instantly her hat, released from her hold, was snatched away by the wind and went sailing off into the air.

'Oh!' She made a vain attempt to catch it. Then to her relief she saw it make a full circuit over the water and with a swirl of ribbons land some distance away on the cobbles of the wharf. An urchin ran to snatch it up just before the wheels of a wagon rolled over it.

She stepped ashore to a barrage of fresh questions from those waiting, some delivered in a hostile manner from fellow countrymen and women not of the nobility, but who could tell that she was from her speech. She knew only too well from similar encounters on board how angry and resentful many hard-working, previously loyal people had become towards the aristocracy, whom they blamed rightly but indiscriminately for being the cause of the Revolution. Privately she sympathized with them. They had had to flee for their lives too, and she knew herself how agonizing it was to leave one's homeland when it was not by choice.

It took time before she was able to make her way through to where her sister was waiting for her, the errant hat in hand. There was no sign of the boy.

'Here you are, Louise.' Delphine, whose own pale straw hat had been fastened all the time by a flattering bow under her chin, handed it over to her. 'The little thief was about to run off with it, but that gentleman stopped him.' She indicated Daniel with a smiling nod. He had drawn away, but had paused to look back at them. 'He speaks excellent French and we had a useful little chat. He warned me that we should watch out for thieves and charlatans of every kind.'

Louise inclined her head towards him. 'Thank you, sir,' she said appreciatively in English.

'My pleasure, ma'am.' His voice was deep and articulate.

Briefly she felt herself held by the intensity of his penetrating gaze before he raised his grey top hat and continued on his way.

She turned back to her sister and spoke briskly. 'That should be a good omen! A kind act from an American citizen as soon as we land. Now let's go.'

After putting on her hat again, she heaved her bundle more securely on to her arm and they set off along the busy wharf. Ahead a cart was being stacked with bulging white canvas sacks, but suddenly some began to slide off again. There were shouts of alarm as one burst asunder on the cobbles, spilling nutmegs everywhere in a wafting wave of their fragrance. The carter and stevedores and bystanders rushed to gather them up, for their value on the market was tremendous and quite a few went unseen into pockets. The sisters had to skip and skirt the rolling nutmegs before they reached some hackney carriages. Most had already been taken and were on the move, but they managed to secure one just in time.

As soon as they were seated Louise gave the coachman an address she had been given by Captain Hooper during the voyage. When writing it down for her, he had pointed out that it was some time since he was last in New York, but it was a respectable lodging house and he saw no reason why it should have closed in his absence.

In all, he had been helpful to his passengers. She knew he had been aware of not paying her nearly enough for the pearl earbobs she had sold him, but the transaction had supplied her with necessary currency. Not only did she have dollars in her purse now, but also some English golden guineas. They were still legal tender in America even though now in 1794 it was nearly eleven years since the last of the British troops had left the country's newly independent soil.

Captain Hooper had also chosen not to question the travelling papers that she and Delphine had presented upon boarding his ship, for he must have guessed that they were of dubious origin. Again, when he had seen that a French warship was

5

coming alongside not long after the *Ocean Maid* had set
sail, he had taken the precaution of sending all his French
passengers below and replied to the shouted demand that he
only had Americans on board. For all that, Louise knew she
would always be grateful.

As the dock gates were left behind, Delphine could hardly
sit still in her excitement. 'Now we're really here, Louise! Isn't
it wonderful to know we're safe at last?'

Louise agreed, her feelings running deep, and momentarily
she had to fight against the dark shadows of the past before
casting a thoughtful glance at her sister. Delphine had had a
bleak time of it in recent years and had missed all the pleasures
that would have been hers if circumstances and the terrible
Revolution had not changed the whole course of their lives.
Louise hoped to find ways to make it up to her in time to come,
although not with too much indulgence, hard as that might be,
for Delphine with her volatile nature could be headstrong and
foolish at times.

Yet weighing against that was the courage the girl had
shown during the long months they had been in hiding from
the revolutionaries and again during their desperate escape.
There was also her warm heart and her deep need to be loved
at all times. Louise knew she was her sister's only anchor. For
herself she had only one overwhelming resolve in this new
country, which was that never again would she allow anyone
or anything to take her freedom from her.

At first the district beyond New York's harbour was
mainly industrial with factories and workshops, tanneries
and slaughterhouses, smithies noisy with ringing blows on
anvils, whirring machinery and shouting workmen, some of
whom were emerging raucously from one of the many taverns.
But before long, after the carriage had passed an old fort in the
distance that was flying the Stars and Stripes, the city opened
up into streets lined with trees, some still not in bud, others
tinted with fresh young green. Some of the houses were of
wood, but most were in grey stone or russet-red brick. Now
and again there would be a row of tall, narrow houses with

interesting gables that hugged each other as if there was no room to spare. Louise guessed these had been built at the time when the Dutch had dominated the city they had called New Amsterdam.

On all sides there was traffic, every kind of vehicle on wheels from the elegant to the humble and any number of riders on horseback. The sparkling air seemed vibrant with prosperity and opportunity. Louise drew a deep breath in anticipation of the future.

Both sisters took eager notice of the fashions. It was a long time since they had seen so many well-dressed people, although as in any city there were the poor as well as the beggars in rags to be seen. Most of the women's skirts were still full over petticoats, although there was a definite trend towards a slimmer line with those more aware of fashion. The majority of men were wearing tricorne hats and flared jackets with their knee breeches, as had been worn for many years, but here and there were those who had taken to the new style of well-cut coat with tight pantaloons that had suited so well the stranger on the wharf.

Now and again Delphine inhaled deeply the aromas that drifted from street stalls where hot snacks were being sold, the traders shouting encouragement to buy.

'How delicious!' she exclaimed ecstatically. 'I'd forgotten there was still good food in the world.' She had spoken in English and her command of it was fluent, Louise having coached her daily when they were in hiding and again on the voyage. As the coachman took them into a long wide street, she leaned forward to question him. 'Where are we now?'

He looked back over his shoulder at her, his ruddy face creasing against his high collar. 'This is Lower Broadway. You have to be in the money to live here.'

Delphine almost sprang out of her seat as she looked eagerly from side to side. 'This is where Maman's cousin lives! I wonder which house it is.'

Louise wondered too as she viewed the large mansions. All of them had gleaming windows and recessed entrances with well-polished brass doorknockers or bell-pulls. She had the address tucked in with her belongings and would look at it later. She had been a child when a quiet young man from the New World, named Theodore Bradshaw, had swept Cousin Madeleine so completely off her feet. It had been a surprise to everyone, for she had had so many suitors whom she had refused. Although the couple had toured Italy and Greece to view the antiquities for a year after the wedding, he had eventually taken her home to New York.

Soon along this splendid street, as in the other streets they had passed through, there were many shops and coffee houses, establishments for chocolate drinking as well as reading rooms, bookshops, taverns, pastry cooks and jewellers. Here and there were stables and harness makers. Brass plaques on some of the fine buildings indicated the presence of lawyers, insurers and bankers. Louise spotted a library and promised herself a visit. She was interested to see that although all the shops had brightly painted trade signs extending over their doors, not all displayed their wares in the windows as in Paris and also in London. She mentioned it to Delphine, whose quick reply was sharp-edged.

'You forget I know nothing of that! I never had the chance to visit Tante Violette in England after she married there. You were the one privileged to dance about in London, Paris and Versailles. I was always at home.' Then she forgot old grievances at the sight of a particularly fashionable woman getting into a carriage. 'Oh, look! Her coat is apricot silk and there are matching plumes on her hat!' She turned eagerly to Louise. 'When shall we have something new to wear?'

'We'll see about it tomorrow,' Louise promised willingly. Except for the gowns they were wearing, which had been kept for this day of arrival, the few garments they had with them had suffered through being washed in buckets of sea water. As soon as they had an outfit each in which to present themselves to prospective employers, she would find work for herself and a suitable place for Delphine. She was lucky in having her jewellery still in her possession and a piece could be sold when money was needed. She also had in her safekeeping a few fine pieces that Delphine had inherited but she was determined that these should never be sold. It was her fervent hope that with better times her sister would be able to wear them, which was something she had never had the chance to do at home.

As Delphine continued to chatter happily like a child about all she was seeing, Louise smiled, pleased to see her sister so merry after all they had been through together. Although thin from their recent poor diet – Louise was aware of her own gown loose on her – Delphine was still exceptionally lovely with her piquant, almost elfin looks and her curling, copper-red hair inherited from their late mother.

The carriage turned into a narrow side street and Delphine's exuberance waned as it drew up outside a moderately sized, tawny brick house, the woodwork in need of a coat of paint.

'Do we really have to stay here?' she protested sulkily. But Louise was already getting out of the carriage. The door was opened by a plump, middle-aged woman, a white frilled cap on her tightly curled grey hair.

'Good morning, Mrs Ford.' Louise handed over a message that Captain Hooper had written for the woman. 'We have just landed in New York from the *Ocean Maid*. Captain Hooper suggested we should seek accommodation here.'

'Oh, he's in port again, is he?' She read the message through before regarding the sisters on her doorstep with narrowed, assessing eyes. 'You both speak English? Good! He has remembered that I don't deal with folk who can't understand me.' Her glance swept Louise up and down. 'You're a widow, ma'am?' She paused before attempting Louise's surname. 'De Vailly? Is that right? And you're with your sister?' Her glance went to Delphine. 'Miss de Montier?'

'That's correct,' Louise replied.

'Well, I've only one room left, but it should suit you.' She led the way upstairs. There was a reassuringly clean aroma of beeswax and newly washed floors.

The room shown to them was small but adequately furnished. Louise paid two weeks' rent in advance as requested. In turn Mrs Ford offered the use of the laundry tub in the basement and, for a little more money, hot water in the bathhouse. The sisters accepted eagerly the chance to bathe away the effects of their voyage. Afterwards Mrs Ford had ready for them a simple meal of cold ham and other meats with salad and crusty bread. Neither Louise nor Delphine in their hunger could remember enjoying food more.

When they went upstairs again to their room Delphine thumped herself down on the edge of the bed as she took up her protest once more. 'This accommodation is so cramped! I still don't see why we couldn't have gone straight to Cousin Madeleine instead of coming here.'

Louise shook her head firmly. 'Not until we've established ourselves with our own apartment and full-time work. We're not going to be a burden to anyone, even though I know she would welcome us gladly for our own and Maman's sake.'

Delphine sighed at her sister's attitude, but said no more. She made up her mind to call on their first cousin once removed by herself if circumstances became intolerable. She'd endured enough hardship and privation to last a lifetime and wasn't going to prolong it unnecessarily if an opportunity was there for the taking.

Louise was eager to get her bearings and, after getting directions from Mrs Ford, she and Delphine went out into the city. Their first call was at a banking house, recommended by Captain Hooper, where she deposited her jewellery in a box for safe keeping. The banker himself was able to advise her as to which jeweller would give her a fair price whenever she should wish to sell a piece. Afterwards they explored a little, walked as far as Trinity Church and sat for a while in a park, watching the New Yorkers go by. On the way back to the lodging house they passed the Tammany Museum, where a notice outside announced its latest attraction, a full-sized replica of the guillotine complete with a decapitated wax victim. Both sisters shuddered and hurried by. In the next street Louise bought two newspapers, a New York edition and another printed in French.

When Delphine was in bed and asleep Louise sat down to read the newspapers by candlelight, trying not to disturb Delphine's sleep by rustling them when she turned a page. In the American edition there was news of the war in Europe, for after the universal horror at the regicide of Louis XIV at the guillotine, the British and their Allies had taken up arms against France. There was also a section that listed work vacancies and another that advertised the skills of those looking for work.

She encircled three adverts that looked promising. Although she had learned in conversation with Mrs Ford that most émigrés were making use of whatever talents they possessed, she still was amazed when she read the advertisements put in by her fellow aristocrats, in which they offered their individual skills. The men had become dancing masters, riding and fencing and archery instructors, gardeners and teachers of mathematics and various languages. As for the women, they were now seamstresses, embroiderers, makers of beauty preparations, wig-dressers, weavers of fine ribbons and, like some of the men, singing and music teachers.

Louise knew from many of the noble names that in the past they would have been waited on hand and foot by a horde of servants, never having to reach for a fan or even put on their own shoes. She admired them for their efforts in new and difficult circumstances.

Turning to the French newspaper, she caught her breath at the list of those at home in France who had most recently gone to the guillotine under the Reign of Terror, as the latest wave of savage murder was called, instigated by the tyrant Robespierre. It was in just such a list that she had found the name of her own husband and, only a matter of days before, that of an uncle, three cousins of whom she had been extremely fond and several close friends. Through the slowness of travel the list she was reading now was already old news and many more names would have been added to it by now.

She put both newspapers aside and gazed unseeingly down into the moonlit street below. At least her parents, although they had both died far too young and tragically, had been

11

spared such an horrific fate, her mother in giving birth to Delphine and her father five years later through a riding accident. That was when she was fifteen, so her father's only brother became her and Delphine's guardian.

Count Henri de Montier was a stern, well-intentioned man, long-established at the court of Versailles, who enjoyed an extravagant lifestyle such as had never appealed to their father. He was a widower with no children of his own, but had made up his mind unyieldingly how to deal with his two new charges. He had arrived at their home, the Château de Montier, in time for the funeral and afterwards talked to Louise on her own.

'I'm taking you back to Versailles with me. Your father has provided you and your sister with large dowries and neither of you will have any difficulty in making a good marriage when the time comes. You are also an heiress in your own right, Louise. Your father's hobby of studying those ancient law books from your great-grandfather's collection, which I remember filled many shelves in this château's library, enabled him to invoke an old law in his will. It ensures that this property and rich estate will always be yours and never your husband's unless you should choose to sign it over to him. We shall leave here tomorrow.'

At any other time Louise would have been overjoyed at the prospect of balls and parties and entertainments presided over by the lovely Queen Marie Antoinette herself, but she was presently too steeped in grief at losing her father.

'Not yet, Oncle,' she said haltingly, her throat still sob-strained, her handkerchief tear-sodden in the pocket of her skirt. 'In a while, but not yet. In any case, Delphine is only five. She wouldn't like to be away from home in strange surroundings.'

Although Louise had been only ten herself when their mother had died, she had become instantly protective towards her newborn sister and that had never changed. Her uncle gave an impatient snort.

'Don't talk nonsense, girl. Delphine will stay on here with her nurse until she is of marriageable age, as you are now. The present châtelaine is running the household efficiently and your late father's bailiff has kept the estate in good order. However, I shall send a bailiff of my own to take full charge of the land, a capable man by the name of Jacques Droux. We don't want the peasants taking advantage of your father's demise to become lax in their toil. In fact, to my mind, he was far too easy on them.'

Louise had been looking down at her hands in her lap, clasping them tightly. Now she raised her head, steely determination in her clear green eyes.

'I'll not go anywhere without Delphine!'

The count remained unmoved. He knew how to crush rebellion, whether in a horse or a woman. 'If you do not agree to do as I say, I shall put you in one convent and Delphine in another. Is that what you'd prefer? I'll not ask you again.'

It broke her. She could never let her sister go among strangers on her own and this man's will was of iron. Her parting with Delphine had been agonizing. The child had wept and screamed and clung to her. Louise, also in tears, had tried to comfort her.

'I'll do everything I can to bring us together again soon. And I'll write often. You'll write to me too, won't you?'

Her last view of her sister that day had been of her breaking free of her nurse to run after the coach, her face tear-streaked and her arms outstretched.

Louise sighed at the memory. Now they were both in an alien land and all they had known lost for ever. In that moment she felt a terrible upsurge of homesickness for the contented days at their country château, before she ever left for Versailles – in those years before France descended into chaos.

Before undressing, she took off the scarlet ribbon from around her neck. Another widow on the ship had given it to her, but she would not wear it again. Neither would she use her title any more, which was why she had not given it with her name to Mrs Ford, for it belonged to the past, together with private and agonizing memories of rape, brutality and deceit that she had been forced to endure. As for her wedding ring, that had gone long since in desperate circumstances, and it was her mother's that she wore.

She had also finished with mourning black. Nothing could ever make her forget those dear to her who had gone, but for Delphine's sake she had to make tomorrow a new beginning and the way to more secure times.

Two

B efore breakfast next morning Louise had decided against the employment vacancies that previously had most interested her. One had been for a hairdresser – and she was deft at dressing her own hair and her sister's rebellious curls – the second a post for a governess and the third that of a housekeeper. But she had come to the conclusion that it would not be wise to work away from Delphine for the time being and they must find employment under the same roof.

Since her escape from France, Louise had held no false pride about the status of whatever work she might have to take, but she wanted employment that would interest her. If it should be in a trade that she could learn to master, there would be possibilities for advancement. She realized that opportunities for an ambitious woman were as limited in this country as they would be anywhere else in the civilized world, but she intended to keep her eyes and ears open for any chance that came along. As for Delphine, her oft-stated aim was to make a good marriage with a rich man, but that was no more than a dream in their present circumstances.

After breakfast Louise returned to their room with borrowed pen and ink and a stick of red sealing wax to write a letter to their aunt in England, leaving her sister chatting to Mrs Ford downstairs. She sat down at the little table and began to write. Violette, her late father's sister, had married an Englishman over thirty years ago and Louise had visited them in London during the early years of her marriage to Fernand de Vailly. He'd let her go on her own, having no interest in going himself, and she'd had a happy, carefree visit that stood out in her memory. She knew that Violette would be bitterly disappointed that she and Delphine had not sought refuge with her, but this letter would explain the circumstances.

When Louise eventually put down her pen she sealed the letter using her own seal with its family crest, one of the few things she had been able to bring with her from home. She was glad to be on her own for a little while. As she had written to Violette, when planning their escape from France, she had expected that they would get across the Channel to England by fishing boat as so many other émigrés had done, but fate had intervened and brought them to the other side of the world instead.

Her thoughts ran back to the day at Versailles when that great angry mob had come from Paris to swarm through the palace gates. Just before they had broken into the palace itself and had come roaring for blood up the staircase, she and some other ladies of the court had been elsewhere in the great palace and were cut off from the royal family's presence. They could do nothing but wait in an agony of suspense until their worst fears were realized. Through a window they glimpsed that hideous procession as the King and Queen and their children had been taken off to Paris, the heads of loyal soldiers carried triumphantly on pikes ahead of their coach like banners.

It had been a signal for many aristocrats to get over the borders into neighbouring countries without delay, for nobody knew what would be happening next, but her one thought had been to get home to her sister. It had been a hazardous journey made in a working woman's clothes that a maidservant had found for her. She had set off on a horse from the palace stables, but it was stolen one night while she slept under a tree. All the time, she avoided entering any taverns or hostelries, fearful that she might be spotted as a noblewoman and murdered by peasants fired up by the Revolution. Her money soon ran out as suspicious farming folk charged her exorbitantly for whatever food they could spare. Eventually she arrived home on an old nag for which she had exchanged her wedding ring. In spite of her bedraggled appearance Delphine had recognized her from a window and come running joyfully to meet her.

The countryside around was quiet enough at the time, but there was a change in the atmosphere. When she rode around the estate the morning after her homecoming the peasants, some of whom she had known all her life, barely answered her when she spoke to them and looked away when they saw her riding nearby. Only Pierre, the former bailiff, a conscientious fair-minded man, was the same as he had always been towards her, knowing it was no fault of hers that he had lost his authority to the bailiff, whom her uncle had installed over him. Delphine had written that the workers had come to hate the ruthless intruder, who had cut their wages and brought them close to starvation, but those letters had been intercepted and Louise had never received them.

'I thought you didn't care,' Delphine said, 'because you never commented on what I'd told you in your letters to me.'

Louise shook her head despairingly, still shocked at learning that Jacques Droux had been stabbed to death with a pitchfork only days before her return. 'Naturally you would have assumed that was the case, just as you thought I didn't want to see you when I never came home after those first early visits. But I will try to put things right.'

She had reinstated Pierre immediately and restored the workers' wages to the previous level. The accounts had shown her that the murdered bailiff must have pocketed the difference taken from them, for there was no record of the pay cut in the books. She had hoped by her actions to undo the damage done in her absence, but years of brutal treatment had taken its toll on her estate. The seeds of the Revolution had already been deeply sown in the small corner of France that meant so much to her.

With a sigh, Louise rose from her chair, took her cloak and hat from a peg, Delphine's as well, and went downstairs with her letter. Their first call was to the post office, where Louise sent her letter on its way. Even if Violette replied by return it would be many weeks before she could hope for its arrival.

By the end of the first week in their new land they had explored the city extensively. Louise treated this time as a vacation before starting work, during which they bought fabric from one of the city's markets, and made themselves new gowns. Louise also altered the black silk gown in which she had landed, adding a row of small scarlet bows down the front of the bodice and using braid in the same bright hue around the neck and sleeves, finally banishing its mourning look. They also retrimmed their hats with roses, which they had made themselves out of coloured ribbons. Later they would have new headgear as well, but Louise considered that would be an extravagance for the time being. In any case she liked her yellow hat, which Delphine had made for her when they were hiding from the revolutionaries, even though its over-bright colour was due to a misjudgement of the amount of natural dye required.

They had one frightening experience when they emerged from a shop on Pearl Street to see an advancing procession of shouting demonstrators swarming towards them with banners, the Tricolour and the Stars and Stripes held high and fluttering side by side. Nearly all were wearing the scarlet Phrygian caps that had come to symbolize the Revolution to Frenchmen and foreigners alike. Delphine cowered back, terrified of being seized, and instinctively Louise put her arms around her. An elderly man, standing nearby, noticed and guessed their nationality.

'There's no need to be afraid, ladies,' he said reassuringly to them. 'This is just a band of hotheads who want President Washington to go to war on the side of France against Britain and her allies. They argue that the French helped us during our revolution, but they forget we weren't murdering our own people.'

'Is the President considering aid?' Louise asked in surprise.

'It's my guess that he won't. He has enough to do building up this new nation of ours. Tomorrow you'll probably see another demonstration against supporting France. We like to air our opinions in this country. It's what freedom is all about, isn't it?'

'Yes, indeed,' Louise agreed firmly, thinking that nobody held to the principles of freedom more than she did herself. She continued to keep her nervous sister close to her until the marchers had gone by, although none had looked in their direction. It was the first of many similar demonstrations they were to see, but neither was alarmed by them again.

After several days of walking about the city to apply in vain for work together, it was Louise's yellow hat that eventually gained employment for her and Delphine on Broad Street with a milliner named Miss Sullivan. A sharp-faced businesswoman with elaborately dressed fair hair, she eyed Louise up and down, knowing French chic when she saw it. But it was the hat that intrigued her.

'I notice that the straw of your hat is plaited in a most unusual way,' she said, trying not too show too keen an interest. 'May I examine it more closely?' She held out a hand, expecting it to be removed for her inspection.

Louise smiled, making no move, for she sensed the woman's eagerness. 'It's a traditional pattern from my home district in France and to my knowledge not to be found anywhere else. My sister made my hat as well as the one she is wearing, which is a variation on the same pattern. I was first taught the skill by an old nurse and passed my knowledge on to my sister.'

'So, you are both able to make them!' Miss Sullivan thought swiftly ahead to the summer, when such flattering hats would be in demand. A stock could be built up in good time before the warm weather set in. 'Has either of you ever made any other kind of millinery?'

'We have both altered hats of felt and other materials to suit us.' Louise did not add that it was when she and Delphine had found a collection of old ones in a box in the attic after her homecoming and worked on them for fun.

Miss Sullivan paused for a few moments as if considering carefully before making a decision. 'I think I can offer you both a place each in my workshop.' After stating what their wages would be, she added, 'You may start on Monday morning. I supply clean aprons and caps. Be sure that you're here promptly at seven o'clock.'

But Louise was not ready to accept yet. She had seen that she had the upper hand as far as the straw hats were concerned. 'I should like to know what bonus we would receive on each French-styled straw hat that we make.'

Miss Sullivan was taken aback, but she did not want to lose the two young women's skills to a rival milliner. Negotiations followed, Louise standing firm, and she left the shop satisfied with the extra that would be added to their low wages, which the milliner had promised would rise with time and satisfactory work.

That same day they found a small apartment of two rooms furnished with a few usable pieces that included a cupboard and a table with two chairs. The rent was moderate as it was in a poor area of the city, but it was still within walking distance of their new employment. Delphine complained bitterly about its humble location, but Louise pointed out that it had the advantage of an indoor water pump and a privy that they would not have to share in the tiny courtyard at the rear of the house.

Together they scrubbed and cleaned their new accommodation from floor to ceiling, Delphine moaning about what it was doing to her hands, until Louise was satisfied with the result.

Before long Delphine began pestering Louise again about calling on their cousin, but without effect. They were in a market, getting a few items that they needed for their new home.

'I want to see Madeleine as much as you do, Delphine,' she said, picking out some china plates from others that were cracked. 'Probably more, because I remember her from early childhood and was very fond of her. She came to see Maman not long before you were born. It was on the eve of her sailing to this country with her husband and I was allowed to hold their baby, Mary Anne, who was about six weeks old then.'

Delphine's mouth set stubbornly. 'All the more reason for me to meet her now.'

Louise paid for the plates and two battered but still serviceable cooking pots. 'Not until I feel we've really established ourselves. Then we can visit Madeleine with our heads high and she won't feel that she has two dependants landing themselves on her for their keep. Not that she would see the situation in that light, but since we have our health and strength I couldn't put her under that obligation without just cause.'

Reluctantly Delphine accepted the situation for the time being, understanding her sister's independent attitude, but still exasperated by it. They returned to their apartment loaded with purchases that were all mundane, except for four fine wine glasses that had been a bargain Louise had been unable to resist. As yet they had been unable to afford wine, but she had made up their mind they should have a bottle to celebrate Delphine's sixteenth birthday, which would be very soon.

On Monday morning they presented themselves at Miss Sullivan's shop. She introduced them to the four other workers and the two apprentices. The workshop had plenty of window light with two large tables and a stove to heat the steaming irons. Louise was relieved that although the women were not exactly friendly neither were they hostile in any way. Before long Delphine and the apprentices, being the same age, were chatting together in whispers, talk being discouraged by Miss Sullivan, except about a task in hand.

Hurrying to the workshop one morning neither Louise nor Delphine paid any attention to a hackney carriage passing along Broad Street on its way to the docks. Daniel Lombard was at the start of his journey home again. It would take him northwards by coastal vessel to Boston, which he preferred to travelling the long distance by road. He was thinking how successful the trip had been this time when suddenly he spotted the unmistakable yellow hat.

'Slow down!' he instructed the coachman quickly, leaning forward in his seat as he watched to see where the Frenchwoman and her sister were going. It could only be to work at this early hour. He had thought of her any number of times and even looked for her wherever he had happened to be, always hoping that all was going well for her. Then he saw both the young women disappear into the side door of a shop. As the carriage drew level the hanging sign showed that it was a milliner's.

Relaxing once more against the leather upholstery, he told the coachman to take up pace again. Now he would know exactly where to find her the next time he was in New York and it would be as soon as he could get here again. No woman had kept running through his thoughts after so brief a meeting as she had done.

As the carriage continued to carry him on his way he snapped open his gold watch and took note of the time. There was still over an hour before the ship sailed. Just long enough to manage another meeting.

'Stop here, coachman!' he ordered. 'And wait!'

He sprang out of the vehicle and hurried the short distance back along the sidewalk until he reached the milliner's shop. It was not open yet and he hammered on the door with the gold head of his cane. Miss Sullivan, who was in the showroom overseeing the dusting by her two assistants, raised her eyebrows at such impatient rapping and went to the door herself.

Daniel entered immediately and looked quickly about him. 'I realize this is an early hour, ma'am,' he said at once, 'but I'm about to take ship for Boston and wish to buy my sister a new hat in the latest style before I leave.'

In the work room Louise had settled down to making yet another straw hat. Delphine's task was the complicated hand-weaving of the straw itself. When suddenly Miss Sullivan appeared in the doorway it was to beckon urgently to Louise. At the back of the showroom she explained her reason.

'There's a new customer in the showroom. He wants to be served in a hurry as he's sailing up the coast very shortly. The hat is to be a gift for his sister – or so he says.' Her caustic tone conveyed disbelief as to the identity of the recipient, for men often bought hats for their mistresses, wives always coming to choose their own. 'He's selected a few, but can't make a decision unless he sees each one worn by someone with chestnut hair. So I thought of you. Take off your apron and cap.' She handed Louise the expensive hat she was holding. 'Start with this one.'

Louise guessed that the milliner must be expecting the customer to spend lavishly as she was giving in to his whim. She made herself ready and smoothed her hands over her hair before putting on the hat. It was of cream felt, trimmed with an abundance of ostrich feathers shaded from pale green to deepest emerald, its wide brim tilted high on one side, which set off the face of the wearer. She had once worn such hats at court and with total confidence she swept into the showroom, making an entrance as she had done so often at Versailles in the past. The customer was seated, hat and cane in his hand, but he rose to his feet at once.

'This is very obliging of you, Madame de Vailly. We have met before, as perhaps you will remember.'

She had recognized him instantly with that all-encompassing look to his penetrating eyes, lit brilliantly now by his broad smile. 'I do remember. You kindly intervened on the day I lost my hat.'

'My name is Daniel Lombard.'

Miss Sullivan gave a little cough. She was quite pleased that the customer seemed acquainted with Louise, but she did not want the sale to be lost in chit-chat. 'This is one of my most fashionable hats, sir. Perfect for this time of year and exactly the style worn by ladies of high society today.'

He sat down again, crossing one long leg over the other. Louise displayed over a dozen hats for his approval, during which he enjoyed watching her. This lovely woman had an unconsciously sensual grace in all her movements, which held his attention far more than any of the hats. Finally he asked her advice as to which he should choose, much to Miss Sullivan's annoyance at being ignored. Louise suggested the first one, which she had liked best. She put it on once more for his final approval.

'Yes,' he said decisively. 'That's the one.'

Miss Sullivan stepped forward. 'Where is it to be delivered, sir?'

'I want it shipped to Charleston.' He stood up, ready to leave, and as Louise took off the chosen hat, he added to her, 'I hope we shall soon meet again.'

'Bon voyage, Mr Lombard.' Her smile was polite, but without encouragement. She left the showroom, aware of his eyes following her, and went back to the workshop. On the East River wharf it had registered with her that he was a very good-looking man and at close quarters he had a dangerous sexual attraction of the kind she wished to avoid at all costs. She'd had a surfeit of men's approaches at court. She had stemmed them then and intended to continue here in the same way.

Although it was early days yet at Miss Sullivan's, Louise had become very interested in the millinery work, determined to learn everything she could about the trade. She did not find making the straw hats arduous, although it had been hard on the hands until she had made fingerstalls for her sister and herself. Neither did she mind being kept to the straw work, because all the time she was able to observe closely the cutting and steaming, the shaping and sewing of the designs being produced in felt, velvet and silk. She could see how easily she could acquire these skills. All the designs used were from England, the days long gone when France's elegant Queen had set the fashion for the rest of the world to follow. But Louise had ideas of her own that she would have liked to follow, and sometimes sketched them out in the evenings.

After working a full month at the milliner's Louise made a decision that she knew would please Delphine and announced it as she put a new sketch away. 'I think we're established enough now for us to pay a call on Madeleine—'

Her words were cut off as Delphine gave a shriek of delight, springing forward to hug her exuberantly. 'Oh, yes! When?'

'Next Sunday afternoon.'

'That's wonderful!' Delphine whirled around the room, seeing an end to living in this hateful place and visualizing a splendid social life opening up before her. She would have called by herself long before this if she had been able to find the address in Louise's belongings, but perhaps her sister had been aware of her intention and memorized it before throwing it away.

Louise was as happy as Delphine when they set off for Lower Broadway, but not for the same reason. From the day of arrival she had been longing to see Madeleine after all these years, as one of her own kin in a land of strangers, and she remembered her cousin's husband as a pleasant kindly man. Anticipation soared gloriously in her as they reached the steps leading up to the shining crimson door of the grey stone mansion. Delphine lifted the brass knocker and thumped it twice. After a few moments a butler opened the door.

Louise spoke. 'I am Madame de Vailly. Please inform Mr and Mrs Bradshaw that their cousin and her sister are here from France.'

'Madame, my regrets, but Mr and Mrs Bradshaw no longer live here.' The butler, an émigré himself, had spoken in French, his cultured tones showing that in the past he would not have been opening doors for others, but would have had them flung wide for him. 'The house changed hands over two years ago and there is a new owner living here now.'

Louise had turned pale with disappointment, but Delphine panicked. 'But they are still in New York?' she demanded frantically, her voice high-pitched.

'One moment, please.' The butler left the door open and crossed the wide hall to enter a room. He returned after a few minutes. 'Mr Johnston would be pleased to receive you.'

They were shown into the presence of the present owner, a portly, middle-aged man who greeted them courteously and invited them to be seated. When he had satisfied himself that they were genuinely related to the Bradshaws he went to his desk and wrote down their new address.

'Did you know that they moved away from here through tragic circumstances?' he asked as he handed the folded paper to Louise.

She was alarmed. 'No, what happened? I've had no communication for a long time. It wasn't easy in France to get letters from abroad, with all the upheaval there.'

'Then I'm sorry to have to tell you that their daughter died of the yellow fever, which does occasionally strike the poorer areas of New York and other cities during the hot summer months, sometimes causing a dangerous epidemic. Nobody knew how she could have caught it, for there was only one other case reported that year and that was on the outskirts. Both parents were devastated. Understandably, Mrs Bradshaw could not endure to stay in this house any longer without their beloved child, which is why they moved five hundred miles away to Boston.'

Outside in the street again Louise, deeply distressed by the tragic news, put the address into her purse. 'Poor bereaved Madeleine.' She shook her head sadly. 'And Theodore too. What a terrible loss! I'll write to them this evening and send our condolences.'

'Yes, of course,' Delphine said quietly. 'Mary Anne would have been my age now if she had lived.' She fell silent as they walked along. Then suddenly she burst out bitterly, 'Boston of all places! Why did they have to go so far away? Now we've no chance of seeing them for goodness knows how long!'

Louise said nothing, but it was one of the times when she despaired of her sister's self-centredness. That evening she wrote to Madeleine and Theodore. She despatched the letter next day.

Madeleine answered as soon as she received the letter. Her warm invitation to visit could not have been more eager. She was longing to see them both without delay. Louise wrote back to explain that it would be a while yet before that was possible. The correspondence, which Louise had begun long ago in continuation of her late mother's custom, was resumed as if there had never been any time between.

Three

W hen Louise went to the stock room one morning she found that there was very little hat-straw left and she reported it to Miss Sullivan.

'I should have ordered a fresh supply last week,' the woman answered irritably, 'but it slipped my mind. You can go to Pomfret's horse market for me. Mr Pomfret has always been able to supply me with the superior type of straw that I require.'

Louise was glad of a chance to escape from the work room for a short while. The trees were full of their young green foliage and the sunshine itself seemed caught among the branches. Her step was brisk and it did not take her long to reach the horse market, which she had passed many times. Its cobbled yard stood open to the street and smelt sweetly of hay and, more pungently, of horses, harness and dung, all familiar to her from the stables of home. It was always a hive of activity and today was no exception. On all sides men were examining horses and arguing prices, whether they were buying or selling. A handsome carriage pair, glossy as polished mahogany, was attracting keen attention. She was unable to resist wandering into the stables and there she went slowly past the stalls, patting the necks of the horses with a few words for each.

'Madame la Marquise de Vailly!'

Surprised, Louise spun round to see who had called her by her title for the first time in this country. A man, entering the shadowed interior, his back to the sunshine, broke into a run and rushed towards her, his coat-tails flying. She recognized him with a happy cry. It was Alexandre de Clement, an old friend from home!

'Alexandre!'

'So, it is you, Louise!' A moment later she was being embraced by her friend from childhood and whirled around in the air before being set on her feet again. 'When I caught a glimpse of you from the yard I couldn't really believe that you'd be here in America.' He stood back, his feet set apart and hands on his hips, and laughed with sheer pleasure at their reunion. Strongly built and russet-haired, with a square, good-humoured face, his happy grin seemed to stretch from ear to ear. 'I should have expected you to be with your aunt in England. Not here!'

'That was my original intention.'

'Is Delphine safe too?'

'Yes! She and I escaped together. And tell me that Blanche is with you!' Louise looked eagerly beyond him for the sight of his wife. The three of them had grown up together, Alexandre at a neighbouring château and Blanche the daughter of the local doctor in the nearby village.

'Yes, she's well and happy, but not with me in New York today. As you will remember, she never liked city life. She's upriver on our farm not far from a town called Troy where we live now with our little daughter, Henrietta.'

'You have a child!' Louise was delighted with the news. 'My congratulations! How old is she?'

'Just two and a half years. She was born in New York, but I nearly lost Blanche after the birth. Her recovery took so long that eventually a doctor suggested country air. That's why we moved away from here and, thankfully, she began to get well again. Sadly, we're not able to have any more children, but we're grateful for our little Henrietta. It's only business that brings me to the city once or twice a year. Do you have any news of Blanche's parents?'

'Only that they left for England quite early on. I should think they're safe. I never saw their names on any guillotine list.'

'Thank God for that!' he exclaimed with relief. 'Now, tell

me, how is Fernand? You didn't say he was here with you.'
When she shook her head wordlessly he guessed her husband's
fate and glanced about impatiently. 'We can't talk any more in
this place. There's a chocolate house just along the street. Let's
go there.'

When they reached the marble-floored establishment there
was a variety of hot chocolate drinks from which to choose,
all served in silver pots with fine porcelain cups and saucers
and a plate of sweet almond cakes to each table. Louise chose
hot chocolate with cream and Alexandre a bitter one with a
dash of brandy in it. Although the place was busy they were
lucky enough to get a table in an alcove, which gave them the
chance to talk quietly.

They had not seen each other since he and Blanche had
come to Versailles to visit her while staying in strife-ridden
Paris shortly before the final eruption of the Revolution. He
had been arranging his grandmother's funeral and attending to
her affairs. Then they had gone south to see to the old lady's
country estate and Louise had heard no more from them.

'So tell me about Fernand,' he began. 'What happened?'

'He was in Paris when the mob took the King and Queen
from the palace. Whether he came looking for me afterwards
I don't know, because I left Versailles that same night. I
had to get home to Delphine, not knowing what was happening there.'

'That couldn't have been an easy journey,' he stated bluntly.

She made a dismissive little gesture. 'Others had worse. As
the months went by I had no word from him, but then neither
of us knew where the other was. I wrote to him at the Palace
of the Tuileries. I thought he might be among the courtiers
with the royal family, but no reply ever came. Life was very
quiet for Delphine and myself during the many months when
we were at home in the country.'

'How did you pass the time?'

'I dealt with the estate, saw to the accounts, and sorted
the wheat from the chaff among the servants. Delphine's
governess had been having an affair with a swindling bailiff,

whom my uncle had installed, and I had reason to believe she had intercepted some of my sister's letters to me. There were also others I no longer trusted, so I dismissed them too.'

'What about entertainment? There were always so many social happenings in the past.'

'Sometimes friends called, but life was subdued, none of us knowing what might happen next. Most of us were hoping, as so many of the country-born aristocracy did, that we could keep things stable for the peasants and ourselves. I made use of my father's library, reading for hours, and I taught Delphine all the dances that were so popular at Versailles. Even as a little child she loved to dance. I also coached her in English as she has a natural ear for languages. She is still very musical and practised playing her flute every day. Somehow it meant a great deal to me to hear her music in those worrying times. Then the horrific news reached us of the execution of the King and then the Queen, as well as the terrible trials taking hundreds to their death at the guillotine.'

'An obscene mockery of justice and still the present orgy of slaughter goes on!' he declared angrily, his fists clenched before him on the table. Then he drew breath. 'But I interrupted you, Louise. Please continue.'

'When our servants heard that the death sentence was also being imposed on many that served the nobility as well as the nobles themselves, they became frightened of staying with Delphine and me. All, except a couple of stable hands, left en masse overnight, and we were alone at the château. Then not long afterwards a guillotine was erected in Bordeaux. That was far too close for the stable hands, who left in panic, taking all our horses with them.'

'The thieves!' Alexandre exclaimed bitterly. 'So Madame Guillotine was erected in Bordeaux too, was she?'

'It happened in so many places.'

'During the time you and Delphine were at home were you threatened in any way?'

'We had a stone thrown through a window from time to

time. It was an old newsheet, wrapped around one such missile, which finally told me of Fernand's execution.'

Alexandre, although he had not liked her husband, shook his head at the senseless slaughter. He thought to himself that life had not been easy on Louise. He remembered how dazzled she had been by Fernand's charm, unable to see him for the man he was, but it was understandable. She'd been so young and inexperienced in the ways of the sophisticated world of Versailles in which she had been plunged, lonely, bereaved and homesick. It was no wonder that at sixteen she had believed herself to be in love with Fernand. She had not realized that as an heiress she had been the target for many mercenary young noblemen, and in her uncle's haste to get her off his hands his choice of a husband for her had been a bad one.

'Do you know if your Oncle Henri managed to escape?' he inquired.

She sighed. 'He was executed a few days after the King. I lost a close friend about the same time, as well as cousins of whom I was very fond. Somebody did bring me all that terrible news. I was still wearing mourning for them when I landed here.'

'So how did your escape come about?'

She gave a smile of protest. 'I want to hear why you and Blanche decided to settle near Troy and everything else you have to tell me.'

'Afterwards.' Then he added jokingly, 'You know I'll be in trouble if I can't answer all Blanche's questions about you when I get home.'

'Then I'll be brief. I realized that the time had come to get away and I made a simple plan that Delphine and I should dress inconspicuously and go into Bordeaux to find a fisherman I could bribe to take us across the Channel to England. I didn't know then that a watch was being kept on all boats and escape had never been more difficult.'

'I've heard that many would-be émigrés were caught that way.'

'In any case,' she continued, 'time had run out. On the eve of our leaving home my loyal bailiff, Pierre, came pounding on the door to tell us to gather a few belongings and go with him at once as we were in great danger. Fortunately we had made bundles of what we could take, hoping to look like laundry maids, and so we were able to leave within minutes. Revolutionary soldiers arrived a short time afterwards and a search for us began. It's thanks to our kind rescuer hiding us behind a false wall, that we're alive today.'

'How long were you there?'

'Two months.'

Alexandre whistled through his teeth. 'It must have seemed like two years!'

'We were thankful to be in a safe place as the soldiers were everywhere. Then two were billeted on Pierre and his wife, which meant we had to be silent as mice whenever they were in the house. We had a candle and played cards. We danced for exercise whenever possible, and I taught Delphine how to make hats for us both out of straw, which Pierre's wife dyed for us.'

'So how did you eventually get away?'

Louise gave a soft laugh. 'We were smuggled in a hay cart into Bordeaux, where one of my father's old employees, whom Pierre had contacted, kept us in his attic for another month. He worked in a government office and when he heard the *Ocean Maid* was being released from embargo he managed to get travelling papers for us. I believe they were forged, but I never knew for certain. They were closely scrutinized by guards before we went on board, but they let us pass.' Louise sat back in her chair, relieved her account was over. 'Now Delphine and I are working for a milliner and all is going well.'

'Thank God for that!' he said with feeling.

In his turn he explained that he had realized early on that France was falling into chaos and his one thought was to get his pregnant wife to safety. 'We stayed for a while on my grandmother's estate not far from Marseilles, where we were lucky enough to get passages on a foreign ship. I'd brought enough gold with me to establish us securely here. My only regret is that our daughter won't be growing up at my old home. I had the happiest childhood there that anyone could have. As you know so well, I had inherited it only three months before my grandmother died. Blanche and I had no idea when we left for Paris that we would not see our château again for some years.'

Louise, distress clouding her face, reached across the table and put her hand over his. She had been dreading this moment when their conversation would turn inevitably to his home. 'I have some bad news to tell you, Alexandre.'

His face stiffened. 'What happened? Was it looted?'

'Worse than that.' Her clasp tightened. 'It was burned down during the time Delphine and I were hiding in Pierre's cellar. Pierre said that the soldiers broke into the wine cellar and went on a drunken rampage.'

Alexandre looked down at her hand, automatically returning her clasp. 'Blanche and I have always thought of our time here as a transitory period before going home again one day to our roots.' He was silent for a few moments. Then he raised his head and looked at her. 'At least I've heard the news from you, who spent almost as much time in my home as Blanche and I did in yours.'

'You still have your grandmother's estate.'

He shook his head. 'Neither Blanche nor I would ever have wanted to live there. Before we left the property, I sold it all to a neighbour who had always wanted my grandmother to sell the land to him, since his own ran alongside its boundaries. I told him why I was taking my wife out of France, but he was undeterred by the unrest at the time, believing that everything would settle down again. How mistaken he was!' He looked down unseeingly at her hand, frowning thoughtfully. 'So, my château has gone to ashes. I didn't know I was burning my boats completely in bringing Blanche to the New World.' Again he sat in silence, coming to terms with the destruction of his hopes of ever returning home, and she felt full of pity for him. Then resolutely he raised his head and spoke on a brighter note, not aware that sadness still lingered in his eyes. 'Now that's enough about the past. How soon can you and Delphine visit us? Blanche will be impatient to see you again.'

'And I to see her and Henrietta. It can't be yet, but it will be as soon as possible.'

Alexandre walked back with her to the horse market, where they parted affectionately with promises to keep in touch. Then he left to go about his own business and she to find Mr Pomfret. Although she ran most of the way back to the shop, Miss Sullivan was still furious that she had taken so long over her errand.

In spite of her insignificant position in the workshop, Louise continued to be highly ambitious. Unlike Delphine, who resented every day there, she welcomed the chance to learn everything about the millinery trade. She had soon found that Miss Sullivan was receptive to her suggestions as to how the straw hats could vary in shape and trimmings. It led to her taking part sometimes in making the other millinery, which she enjoyed, and it also brought about a slight increase in her wages. Delphine made no attempt to hide her boredom, and was often slow in finishing a task. Louise began to fear that she would be dismissed once the stock of straw hats was deemed sufficient.

By now the two apprentices had mastered the intricate straw-weaving and Louise saw a chance to get Delphine work that should be of more interest to her. All the hats sold by Miss Sullivan were in the height of fashion, abundantly and elaborately trimmed with flowers, feathers and fancily tied bunches of ribbons, which she ordered regularly from a supplier.

'My sister is skilful at making flowers and trimmings out of silk ribbons and other materials,' Louise said to the milliner when the opportunity arose. 'She made the pink roses on her straw hat.'

Miss Sullivan had noticed that they were exceptionally

well made and thought immediately of the money she could save if Delphine's work kept up to that standard all the time. 'Very well. I'll let your sister show me what she can do.'

Delphine took up the new work without enthusiasm, even though it appealed to her artistic nature and the milliner was pleased with the results. It was all so different from making pretty things for her own pleasure. She hated every day in the workshop more and more, feeling as confined as a bird in a cage, and was sure she would start screaming aloud if it went on much longer. At least when she and Louise had been hiding in Pierre's cellar there had always been the hope that the next day they would get away, which had kept her spirits up. But at the present time she could foresee no end to her present daily grind.

It cheered her when in celebration of her sixteenth birthday Louise bought two tickets for a play at the John Street Theatre. They wore their best gowns and Louise had obtained good seats. Delphine was consumed by excitement. She had as much pleasure from seeing the bejewelled and elegantly dressed patrons in their boxes as she did from the performance itself. Afterwards they had a little celebratory supper at home. Throughout the next few days Delphine was often lost in thought, her hands falling idle in her lap as if the magic of the evening was still with her, and she was reprimanded several times.

It was an overcast morning in early May when Miss Sullivan looked up from her rosewood and ormolu desk to see Daniel Lombard enter her shop. Swiftly she went to meet him, anticipating another good sale.

'Good day, sir. Did your sister like the hat that I shipped to her?'

'The hat? Oh, yes. She was very pleased with it, but I'm not here for another one today. My reason for calling is that I should like to have Madame de Vailly's address.'

Miss Sullivan was taken aback and her brows arched. 'I couldn't do that without her permission and I think she would be unlikely to give it.' Louise's cool farewell to him on the hat-buying day had not escaped her notice.

'Then allow me to ask her myself.'

'Out of the question! I have a rule that my employees cannot interrupt their work for any social reason.'

He roamed restlessly around the showroom. 'Come, come, ma'am, there's no need for anyone's work to be interrupted. You can give me the information easily enough. Let's have no more prevaricating.' His glance fell on some gauzy stoles and he picked up one at random, which shone delicately with silver threads, and tossed it on to her desk, knowing that it would be expensive. 'I'll take this.' Then, as he drew some golden dollars from his pocket into his gloved palm in readiness to pay, he added crisply, 'And so where does the widow live, ma'am?'

Previously, when Louise had displayed the hats for him, he had noticed that she wore a wedding ring. Although she had come to America on her own with her sister, he wanted confirmation that she did not have a husband in France or elsewhere in exile.

'You've made the most irregular request, Mr Lombard.' Miss Sullivan did not want to antagonize him now, or else he might change his mind about taking the stole. She hated to lose a customer who chose what he wanted without asking the price. She was well aware that his purchase was a sop to her protests, but she felt her dignity demanded a final show of reluctance. 'It is against my principles.'

She saw him pick up another gauzy stole, sparkling with gold threads this time and double the price of the first, and she caught her breath slightly.

His sharp glance shot towards her as if she had spoken. 'Well, ma'am?'

'I've been thinking,' she said without further hesitation. 'As you are already acquainted with the young widow, it is a different matter. I'm sure Louise would have no objection.' She hoped he realized that she had given him a bonus in letting slip the Frenchwoman's Christian name in case he did not know it already.

'Thank you, ma'am. I look forward to doing business with you again.'

He departed with his purchases, which at his request she had packed separately, the pink-striped boxes tied with ribbons. Miss Sullivan went to the door and peered after him through the glass panel. He was not a man to be thwarted, she thought, and considered him all the more dangerous for it.

BAKER COUNTY LIBRARY 37
2400 RESORT
BAKER CITY, OREGON 97814   AUG 2 8 2003

Four

That evening Daniel had no difficulty in finding the address he had been given. It was in one of the old Dutch houses. He entered the dingy hallway, thinking he would have plenty of stairs to climb, but instead he found Louise's name on a door at his right hand. He drew off a glove and knocked. A most appetizing aroma wafted out as Delphine opened the door to him. In her surprise she did not speak.

'Good evening, mademoiselle,' he said with a smile, before looking beyond her into the candlelit room. Instantly he was reminded of paintings of Dutch interiors. The walls were panelled, the floor black and white tiles, and an old red tapestry rug, which in its heyday would have graced a fine Dutch table, had been hung across the window as a curtain. Louise, a striped apron tied around her waist, was stirring a cooking pot on the range, the glow of the fire flickering over her face and creating a golden nimbus about her figure. She straightened up as she saw him, the spoon dripping in her hand.

'Mr Lombard!' she exclaimed in a startled voice.

He switched to speaking in French. 'I apologize for arriving unannounced, but I arrived back in New York today and wanted to invite you and your sister to dine with me this evening.'

Delphine spun round on her heel to look eagerly at Louise. 'Do let's accept!'

Louise put down the spoon and came across to the doorway. Her face was flushed, but whether it was from annoyance or the heat of the range, he did not know.

'Thank you, but no, Mr Lombard. It was kind of you to think

of it, but our dinner is already prepared.' Her tone was adamant in her polite refusal. She had nothing against him personally, except that she was wary of the penetrating look she met in his eyes, which seemed to be seeking out the very depths of her. 'Displaying the hats for you in Miss Sullivan's showroom was part of my work. There was no need for you to feel under any obligation to return a courtesy.' She stood ready to close the door.

'That's not the reason I came. I wanted to see you again.'

Delphine intervened quickly, glad of a diversion on this evening, which otherwise she and Louise would spend on their own. She gave him a dazzling smile. 'Then since you are here and our meal is ready, do stay and eat with us. You're very welcome, isn't he, Louise?'

Louise hid her exasperation with her sister, her upbringing and the rules of hospitality making it impossible for her to say other than, 'Then please come in and sit down.' She indicated the table with two chairs in the shadows. At the range she lit a taper through the grill and took it across to give a flame to the table's candlestick.

As Delphine laid a third place, Daniel brought forward a wooden stool for himself. There was no cloth, but the table was scrubbed white and although the crockery did not match, the cutlery was silver and very fine. He guessed the sisters had salvaged it before leaving home in their flight from France.

Delphine poured some red wine from a flagon into three engraved glasses. These were too delicate to have been carried in the bundles that the sisters had brought ashore and must have been bought locally. He thought how very French it was that the two of them, obviously existing on the most meagre means, had not been able to consider drinking wine from coarser containers.

'We hadn't treated ourselves to wine in New York before the other evening,' Delphine explained. 'Which is why we have some now. It's from Madeira and very good, We couldn't afford the French wine, but I suppose the problem of importing it at the present time has made it soar in price.'

'It has indeed. What was so special about that particular evening?'

Happily Delphine told him about her birthday celebration as she cut up chunks of a long, freshly baked loaf, which she said Louise had made from a French recipe.

Louise served the cassoulet straight from the cooking pot. There was little meat in the rich sauce, but he found it as delicious as the aroma that had drifted from it, and he guessed she had used some of the wine in it.

'Where did you learn to cook so well?' he asked her appreciatively, accepting another chunk of bread to go with his second helping.

Louise smiled ruefully. 'Through necessity and the help of an old book of recipes that I found when Delphine and I were without servants before we escaped from France.'

'Whereabouts was your home?'

'Just a few miles from Bordeaux.'

He would have liked to ask her how she and her sister had escaped, but since she had not offered any information, it would be tactless to ask questions. In any case it might be painful for her to recount it, stirring up sad memories. He had been reading in the newspaper only that day that under the present reign of the terror the guillotines were not able to cope with the number of victims and other gruesome methods were being used in wholesale slaughter.

'I've never been to Bordeaux,' he said. 'Although, as a boy, I was once in France with my parents. It improved my command of the language, which was sometimes spoken at home.' A fondness for France warmed his voice as he spoke of visiting Paris and Rouen and other parts of the country.

'You crossed that terrible Atlantic Ocean just for a visit!' Delphine threw up her hands dramatically. 'I'm determined never to set foot on a ship again!'

'My parents' reason for taking me to France was to introduce me to our Huguenot roots.' Daniel smiled. 'It's said that all Huguenots know their ancestry. Mine had fled here to the New World in the last century when Louis XIV began prosecuting

Protestants for their religious beliefs. So, my forebears settled in South Carolina, as did many other Huguenots at that time. I was born in Charleston and my sister, Elizabeth – for whom I bought the hat – and her husband still live in the family house that my great-grandfather built. Did you know that when Marie Antoinette was imprisoned, there was a plan in the offing to smuggle her out of France and bring her to safety in Charleston?"

"We have never heard that!" Louise exclaimed, both she and Delphine showing their surprise. "If only that could have happened!"

"Sadly time ran out," Daniel said gravely.

Louise shook her head in deep regret. "She was such a brave woman and didn't in any way deserve her fate."

In spite of herself, Louise was becoming more relaxed in his company. Conversation with him was easy. They found that they shared a deep appreciation of music, and Delphine offered to play her flute for him when their meal was over.

When he asked them both how they had settled down in surroundings so different from all they had known in the past, it was Delphine who answered first – and forcefully.

'I've never been used to being shut in all day, working my fingers to the bone! I hate it! I know lots of exciting things are happening every day and night in the city, but we never get the chance to see anything or go anywhere, except that one and only visit to the theatre. At home I'd have gone to Versailles with Louise if our uncle hadn't prevented it in the first place and afterwards her husband put obstacles in the way. Then came the Revolution, which ruined any last chance for me!'

It was a bitter tirade. Daniel turned to Louise, whose weary look showed she had heard it all many times before. 'Do you feel the same about this new life of yours?'

'No,' she answered without hesitation. 'But then I had a surfeit of balls and parties and great occasions, all the excitement that Delphine missed, and which I hope she'll have the chance to enjoy one day on a more moderate scale. I'm determined that we should make a success of our lives here.'

'Well said!' Daniel said admiringly. In his turn he told them that his business was importing silks from India and China. 'I used to get wonderful French silks from Lyons as well, but the Revolution has put an end to that source for a while. I came to New York this time to inspect a cargo of silks from Delhi before shipping them on to my warehouse in Boston.'

'What drew you to the silk trade?' Louise inquired with interest.

'I suppose it was to be expected, since my ancestors were silk weavers, but I started my career in my father's business, exporting raw cotton from the South to the mills of Lancashire in England and other destinations. I often visited my uncle's cotton plantation in Alabama to get to the basics of the whole process. After my father died from a heart attack, never having overcome his grief at losing my mother, I kept the business on for a while and expanded it, but it was never what I really wanted to do every working day of my life. So I decided to sell up and make a change.'

'Why did you decide to go as far north as Boston?' Delphine questioned.

'There were several reasons.' He did not elaborate, but went on to talk of Boston itself and its history, which held Louise's interest. But Delphine, quickly bored, broke in to ask him about fashionable life there, which she did want to hear about, and he answered her questions readily. She became quite starry-eyed as she pictured the balls and soirées and parties he described for her benefit.

'We have cousins in Boston. I wonder if you know them?' she said eagerly. 'Mr and Mrs Theodore Bradshaw.'

'Yes. I'm acquainted with them, but not closely. Our paths cross at local gatherings. He is prominent in local politics and she devotes herself to charity work. I shall look forward to telling them I've met you both.'

The meal had ended, but after Louise had cleared it they sat on at the table with the last of the wine, there being nowhere else to sit. Delphine gave a short recital on her flute, the sweet music dancing around the room as she stood with her back to the window-hanging, which glowed ruby-red behind her in the candle glow. Daniel applauded her enthusiastically when she sat down again.

As the evening went on, none of them noticing the clock, he recounted some amusing incidents, taking particular pleasure in making Louise laugh. She had a way of tilting her chin, exposing her long white throat, her eyes half-closed with merriment under her long lashes, making him yearn to put his lips to her smooth skin and kiss her beautiful mouth.

When the time came to leave he hoped that she had forgiven his brash acceptance of her sister's invitation to him, but as she must have guessed, it had been a chance to get to know her better that he had not been able to resist. Yet did he know her any better? A slight melting of her coolness had not given him an insight into the mysterious depths of her. He was uncertain whether she would accept an invitation for her and her sister to dine with him the following Saturday evening, but he tried his luck after thanking them for their hospitality.

Louise, seeing Delphine's undisguised excitement at the invitation, felt obliged to accept for her sake, but as she closed the door after him she was uneasy. He was too vibrant and powerful a man to let into their lives. Then she reminded herself that after he had entertained them he would be going back to Boston, their brief acquaintanceship at an end.

Daniel, making his way back to the City Hotel, knew that, even more than before, Louise was going to dominate his thoughts and everything he did until he saw her again.

The following evening Delphine opened the door to a messenger boy from the hotel. He handed two striped boxes to her and left again. She had recognized them instantly as being from Miss Sullivan's shop.

'Look, Louise! This one is for you. There's a note for each of us!' She read through hers quickly. 'These gifts are a token of appreciation from Mr Lombard for our hospitality.' She tugged at the ribbons and let the box fall to the floor as she ran with the silver-threaded gauze stole to the mirror. There she draped it about her shoulders. 'It's beautiful and so expensive!'

Louise sat down and read her note from him before opening the box slowly. Then she let the stole with its glittering gold thread remain unfolded in its box on her lap. She felt as if Daniel was closing in on her.

After work on Friday Louise made preparations for the following evening with Daniel, certain she was going to enjoy the occasion in spite of her misgivings, for it would be a great treat to be in more sophisticated surroundings after such a long time. She took from the closet the black silk gown that she had trimmed with the scarlet bows and braid. Now she removed these trimmings, putting them carefully aside for re-use, and cut the neckline into a décolletage. Then she took her sister's silk gown, which was a deep blue, needing nothing added or taken away, and again cut the neckline deeper. The sleeves of both gowns were fashionably elbow-length already and nothing had to be done to them.

'We can wear our lace shawls to hide the gap when we want these gowns for day wear again,' she explained to Delphine, who made a deprecating grimace.

'But those old gowns are so dull for a special invitation.'

'I haven't finished yet. I promise you that when the evening comes you'll be well pleased with your appearance. Now be patient.'

Next morning Louise went out during the short break Miss Sullivan allowed for a midday snack and collected from the bank a sapphire necklace, which Delphine had inherited, and her own parure of a diamond necklace, chandelier earrings and bracelets. She carried the leather cases unobtrusively in an old canvas bag.

As Louise had expected, Delphine was enthralled by her own appearance when she was dressed and ready, the sapphires glowing around her throat. She could scarcely tear herself away from her distorted reflection in an old mirror to fasten Louise's necklace for her.

'These sapphires match my eyes! I wish I could wear them

every day,' she said, patting the necklace proudly as she returned to her reflection.

Louise was amused. 'I don't think Miss Sullivan would approve of that!'

Daniel came himself in a carriage to collect them. They emerged in their cloaks, for the evening was wet and windy, both wearing the gauze stoles draped over their heads, for which they thanked him.

'I've been looking forward to this evening so much,' Delphine declared excitedly when they were seated and the carriage was on its way to the City Hotel. Recently built on the West Side of Broadway, five storeys high with its entrance flanked by expensive shops and its own elegant coffee house, it was New York's first grand hotel and it had become highly fashionable to dine at this new and expensive venue.

'I hope it lives up to your expectations,' Daniel remarked with a grin.

'I know it will!' she declared exuberantly.

At the hotel their cloaks and stoles were taken from them. In the golden aura of candlelight and the dazzle of jewels, Delphine was aware of heads turning as they were shown to their table. She felt as proud of her sister's diamond-sparkling appearance as she did of her own.

'Was Versailles as grand as it is here, Louise?' she asked eagerly as soon as they had taken their seats.

Louise smiled to herself at her sister's naivety, but did not show it as she answered, not wanting to cause her any embarrassment. 'The palace had many lavishly beautiful rooms, but I'm sure this dining room could have taken its place somewhere in that vast building.'

Her tact was not lost on Daniel. He had observed both sisters closely over dinner at their apartment and seen how caring and protective Louise was towards Delphine. He wondered how long it would be before she woke up to the fact that her sister would always be a source of trouble, forever scheming for her own ends. He'd once loved a woman of Delphine's character and knew the signs, which he had been too blind to see at the time. If it lay in his power, he would not let Delphine destroy Louise's chance of happiness.

He knew himself to be in love with Louise. Maybe he had been since first sighting her in that yellow hat. Yet in spite of her softened attitude she remained totally self-contained, an invisible guard between her and any slight intrusion by him into her private self. She did not seem to realize that her very reserve was a challenge to him, holding out the promise of undiscovered depths that he longed to explore.

As she merrily explained something to her sister about the tradition of French kings always dining publicly, his gaze under lowered lids dwelt appreciatively on her, his thoughts running swiftly towards his intense desire for her. He wanted to bury his face in her gloriously burnished hair, to caress and to know every part of her lovely body, for he was able to see enough of her pearly breasts in the low-cut gown to make his hands ache to enfold and arouse them. Although she would still be mourning her late husband, he knew that nothing could deter him in his pursuit of her. He meant to have her eventually, however long it took. There was no barrier he wasn't prepared to break down when the time was right.

At that point, just as Louise was turning her head to speak to him, waiters brought the first course and he was saved from her seeing the stark passion in his eyes.

During the several courses, he noticed how Delphine kept glancing around the room with an entranced gaze. He supposed she was imagining how it must have been to dine in that brittle world of Versailles that had gone for ever. Louise saw deeper than that and felt the chill of concern. Delphine was promising herself that one day she would come and go in such grand places, no matter what it cost to achieve her aim.

In spite of the formality of the evening, the three of them conversed as freely as when they had eaten together in a humbler setting. Delphine scarcely knew what she ate in her exhilaration at being in such a splendid setting. She was fully aware of the keen glances cast in her direction by men, young and not so young, and she sparkled flirtatiously with Daniel.

In contrast, Louise quietly enjoyed each course, even though none was up to the French standards she had known in the past, but the wines had been well chosen by Daniel and were quite excellent.

After they had finished dining they went through to a large salon for the serving of tea, one of the English customs that had lingered on. Before sitting down Louise paused to look at a framed etching on the wall. It showed the new capital of Washington. Daniel came to her side.

'That's how it will look when all the buildings are finished,' he said, studying it. 'It was New York's loss when the Government moved to Philadelphia. Yet it's right that the country should have a fine new seat of government, designed with an eye to space and beauty, as well as a grand house for the President and all who take the presidential oath after him. But the circles of high society here have missed all the splendid social occasions that centred on him and Mrs Washington, which is why the present flood of French aristocrats has been like manna from Heaven to them.'

Louise turned to look at him with a soft laugh. 'Is that true?'

He grinned. 'Indeed it is! To have the names of dukes and duchesses and other titled personages on a guest list means a great deal to certain people. It shouldn't be long before you're swept up in the whirl.'

Delphine, standing by them, was suddenly filled with hope. She would enjoy being fêted. Maybe the future was far brighter than she had hoped.

Before the week was out Daniel took them to a concert and then on Saturday evening to a ball at the exclusive Belvedere House, bringing a business acquaintance as a partner for Delphine. His name was Harry Turner, a pleasant young man, but too intellectual for Delphine and she found his conversation tedious. But when they danced in the beautiful octagonal ballroom she was in her element, starry-eyed as the chandeliers spun overhead.

When the evening had ended and Daniel had brought the

sisters home again, he suggested a Sunday carriage ride into the country the following afternoon. Even as Louise began to shake her head Delphine pushed impishly in front of her.

'Yes, we'd enjoy that very much, Mr Lombard.'

'Call me Daniel, please.'

As soon as he had gone Louise let her clenched hands rise and fall in exasperation. 'Why did you accept, Delphine? I told you I didn't want to extend our relationship with him beyond this evening! He's been thoughtful and generous, but enough is enough.'

'I'm not turning down anything that is fun!' Delphine retaliated defiantly. 'Where's the harm in a carriage ride? And I'm sure it will lead to another invitation.' Her tone became self-pitying. 'Remember, I've never known anything like this evening. It was all quite wonderful. Daniel will be gone again soon enough.' She managed a catch in her whining voice as if close to tears. 'Surely you don't wish to deprive me of what little chance I have to enjoy myself socially?'

Louise frowned impatiently, recognizing her sister's appeal as emotional blackmail.

'You know I don't want to deny you anything within reason, but we're getting too deeply involved with Daniel.'

Delphine laughed with a hint of maliciousness. 'You are, don't you mean? He'd like to be alone with you, I can see that! So just be thankful that I'm always present.'

Sunday dawned warm and sunny. In the afternoon, Daniel arrived, driving a pretty little cream-coloured carriage with the black top folded down and a pair of dappled greys in the shafts. He drove the sisters out of the city into the May-bright countryside. It was the first time they had been out of New York since their arrival and both enjoyed the change. There were forests and hills and isolated farmsteads as far as the eye could see, with the sparkle of a river here and there. Everywhere the dogwood trees were in bloom, spreading their pale blossom across the landscape like a soft cloud.

The afternoon ended with coffee and slices of sweet raisin

bread in the City Hotel's own coffee house. To Delphine's delight Daniel produced three tickets for a play opening.

'I hope you've no other arrangements made,' he said.

Louise was aware of her sister's frantic glance, which begged her not to refuse him. She hesitated briefly, forcing herself to accept the situation for this last time. 'No, we haven't, but you're doing far too much for us.'

'I could never do that.' His eyes were serious.

The play was excellent and they had the best box, which the President and Mrs Washington had occupied whenever they had patronized the theatre. During a light supper afterwards, Daniel spoke of taking them to a ball at Rousselot's before he left New York again.

'When you have so much business in this city, why don't you live here?' Delphine asked flirtatiously.

'The heart of my business is in Boston.'

'But you'll never stop coming back to see us, will you?' Delphine insisted. She did not want him deterred from inviting them out by what she considered to be Louise's stupid failure to encourage him.

He grinned, having no illusions about her query. 'You can be sure of that.'

When they arrived back at the apartment, she thanked him for the evening as Louise turned the key in the lock. Then, as Delphine went in, Louise turned to say goodnight to him.

'Don't go in yet, Louise. This is the first chance I've had to talk to you on your own.'

She guessed what was coming and was quick to forestall him. 'Before you say anything, let me speak first. I've enjoyed your company, but I need to live my own life, which was impossible for me in the past. To be free as I am now once seemed an impossible dream, and I don't intend to lose my total independence for any reason. I hope you understand.'

'I do,' he replied, his eyes narrowed.

'I'm so glad.' She felt relieved. 'I felt it only right to speak frankly.'

'I agree. It allows me to speak with equal frankness and say that you're only postponing the inevitable.'

Startled, she gave an incredulous little laugh. 'You're very much mistaken!'

He ignored her words as if she had not spoken. 'The day I saw you on the ship as you waited to come ashore was a turning point in my life. I'm finding it harder to leave you every time, not just when I go back to Boston, but each time I bring you home again to this dreadful place.'

'You are saying far too much,' she protested firmly. 'I'll bid you goodnight and go in now.'

'Wait! When I return to Boston again in ten days' time it's likely to be the end of the summer before I can come back again. At least say you will write to me.'

She shook her head quickly. 'No, Daniel. I've explained why already. I only write to three people – my childhood friend living near Troy, my aunt in England and my cousin in Boston. I'm sure Madeleine will gladly pass news of Delphine and me on to you whenever you should happen to meet her.'

'Louise!' he exploded in total exasperation, seizing her by the shoulders. Bringing her hard against him, his powerful arms went around her, his hand cupping her head, and he almost lifted her off her feet as he buried her mouth in his in a violently passionate kiss as if he would never release her. Against her will her resistance melted, long-suppressed desires searing through her softly pliable body as his strength and warmth encompassed her. She clung to him, exulting in her wild response, all else lost to her. But even as she drifted towards the abyss she regained her sanity and stiffened fiercely in his embrace.

He was breathing deeply as he loosened his arms and she thrust them away from her with both hands, her eyes locked with his.

'Nothing has changed!' she declared breathlessly, dismayed that he had roused her dormant sensuality with such burning force.

'Time will tell,' he said quietly.

'You mustn't come here any more! I don't want to see you ever again!'

He was astounded by her vehemence. 'I hope you don't mean that.'

'I do! My life is my own! You want to change and disrupt all that I came to find here in my new country.'

He answered sharply. 'That was never my intention.'

'Maybe not at first, but it is now!'

'Since when has love created a prison?'

Her face set angrily. 'More than you could possibly know! I want none of it!'

'You're making a terrible mistake.'

'No, you're wrong. I made a dreadful error once and I don't intend ever to let anything like it happen again!'

'Who was it that set you against loving?' he demanded. 'Your husband? A lover?'

She shook her head fiercely. 'It's not love itself, but its consequences. I want to be unfettered by it for the rest of my days! I have no place in my life for you, Daniel!' Her whole attitude conveyed her implacable determination to end their relationship. 'So please go! Now!'

She could see he was infuriated by her rejection, his face taut, the skin straining over the bones of his face, and he took a step back from her. 'Very well, Louise. But it's not goodbye. I shall hope that when our paths cross again one day – as they will – that we'll find ourselves on better terms. I bid you goodnight.'

He went quietly out of the house, which disturbed her far more than if he had slammed the main door after him in a final departure. She stood for a few moments with her eyes closed, aware that she was trembling in every limb. Although he had spoken of love, she assured herself that she would soon fade from his mind. A man such as Daniel, who emanated power, wealth and virility, could have his choice of women anywhere. Faithfulness was not an attribute she could associate with him.

Turning with effort, she went slowly into the apartment.

Delphine, her face scarlet with temper, stood waiting for her.

'I heard!' she hissed accusingly. 'You've sent him away! How could you?'

'I don't want to discuss it now or at any other time.'

She looked so pale and intense that for once Delphine respected her wish, choking back all she had wanted to say. But she displayed her rage and disapproval by flouncing about as she undressed. Then she climbed into the wall-bed and turned her back on Louise without saying goodnight.

Louise barely noticed, only thankful that her sister had not made more of a scene. In bed she found it impossible to sleep, her thoughts going back to her marriage. She had been so happy in those first blissful weeks after their wedding in the Royal Chapel at Versailles. Fernand had been a wonderful lover, awakening her senses to delights previously unknown and finding in her a loving, highly passionate woman. But after a while he tired of her. The man she had married so joyfully revealed himself as brutal and uncaring, only greedy for her money to settle his never-ending gaming debts; and gossip spoken maliciously in her hearing kept her informed about his latest mistress.

In the early days of their marriage she would gladly have signed over her inheritance to him, but it had not become hers until she was twenty-one. By that time she had long since become wise enough not to make such a move, able to see that her fortune would run through his fingers like sand and eventually leave them both penniless. It was not that the money itself held any great importance for her, but she had responsibilities in the care of her sister, the upkeep of the Château de Montier and the family estate, with a great number of peasants dependant on her for their shelter and employment. She also foresaw that as a last source of funds Fernand would have had no hesitation in selling her beloved home, which was something she would never allow.

She turned restlessly on the pillow. Now her home and her fortune had gone anyway. Her name and Delphine's would be on a French list banning them and all other émigrés from their homeland for ever. All her efforts not to think too much about the past had failed in these sleepless hours, just because Daniel had stirred her sexually to a pitch that still tormented her in the darkness.

Five

It was almost dawn before Louise slept. When she woke later than usual she found her sister still in bed. Without any sign of the previous night's animosity, Delphine complained that she was feeling ill.

'Then stay in bed today,' Louise advised, feeling the girl's brow. It was not unduly hot, but it was so utterly unlike Delphine to claim sickness that Louise accepted that she was not well. 'I'll explain to Miss Sullivan and I'll do some of your tasks during the midday break to ease the situation.'

She left Delphine half-asleep with her pillows freshly smoothed and hurried off to work. All through the day she remained anxious about her sister and was thankful when it was time to go home again. She burst into the apartment, throwing her cloak aside, but stopped abruptly at the sight that met her.

Delphine, her expression radiant, stood in the bedroom doorway, her hair arranged in a more adult style and wearing her blue silk gown.

'You're well again,' Louise stated flatly, relieved but wary as she sank down on to a chair. 'You've been up to something, I can tell. What is it?'

Delphine flung herself down on her knees in front of Louise and caught hold of her hands. 'I've so much to tell you! And I'm so sorry I pretended to be ill this morning, but it was the only way I could get some time on a weekday to myself. You must promise not to be cross with me, but I couldn't face another day in that old hag's shop.'

'So what have you done?' Louise asked wearily.

'It all started on the evening of my birthday when we went to the theatre. Afterwards I found myself longing more than ever for something exciting to happen in my everyday life. Then Daniel came like a rescuer into the drabness of our daily routine, taking us here, there and everywhere. Then last night you sent him away and it was the last straw. But at least he had made me realize that there is fun to be had if the right door opens, and I want to go on enjoying myself every minute of every day for the rest of my life.'

'Nobody can do that, Delphine.'

'Not working for a milliner, but what about dancing away the hours?'

'What are you talking about?'

'This morning after you'd left I got up and dressed my hair in this new style. Do you like it?' She did not wait for a reply. 'Then, when the hour was right, I set off for the best dancing school in New York and charmed Monsieur Rousselot himself into employing me as an assistant teacher and dancing partner to his pupils!' She sprang to her feet and whirled around triumphantly before stopping abruptly to face Louise again, her skirts still swirling about her. 'Don't say no, I beg you!'

Louise had heard of Monsieur Rousselot's highly respectable establishment before Daniel had mentioned it as the location of the ball he had hoped to take them to. She also knew of the Frenchman's reputation as a master of the dance. It was not only from what she had read and heard about him in New York, for not long after her marriage he had replaced the former dancing master in instructing newcomers to Versailles in the latest dances. 'Why didn't you tell me what you planned to do?'

'I was so afraid you'd stop me from applying just because you couldn't keep an eye on me all the time. Especially as it was Daniel who unwittingly put the thought of it in my mind.'

Louise smiled ruefully. 'You must think me an ogre.'

'I don't! You're the best sister in the world!' Delphine hugged her in quick reassurance before drawing back to fling out her arms imploringly. 'So, what do you say?'

'When can I see Monsieur Rousselot?' Louise inquired with a smile.

Delphine flung back her head and laughed in her delight. 'I said I hoped that you would call on him this evening.' Then she paused uncertainly. 'There is only one small complication. He says I must have some fine gowns as he has such a rich clientele and his standards are very high.'

Louise thought of her jewellery. There was a ring she could sell. 'If I approve of the conditions you shall have whatever you need.'

The dancing school was in a fine mansion on Broadway, almost opposite the City Hotel. Louise guessed that the dancing master must have found American investors willing to back him in his enterprise, for she doubted that he could have set up on his own in such style. It was like entering the private residence of a rich aristocrat and she and Delphine were escorted up a splendid staircase to the ballroom.

Monsieur Rousselot came forward to meet them, using a silver-topped cane as tall as himself, which was ornamented with ribbon streamers. He was a slightly built, thin-faced man with a pointed nose and protuberant blue eyes, his face painted with a black beauty spot just at the corner of his mouth. His white wig was immaculately curled, his cravat a waterfall of lace, and he was dressed in an embroidered satin coat, knee breeches and white stockings with silver-buckled shoes. Before greeting Louise he followed the Versailles custom of matching the depth of his bow to her rank. 'Madame la Marquise de Vailly, I am greatly honoured.'

'It is a pleasure to meet you, Monsieur Rousselot,' Louise replied, thinking how strange it was to hear her title used again. 'Although I was never your pupil at Versailles, I watched many of the dance entertainments that you devised.'

'Ah, the great days of France.' He sighed nostalgically. Then he waved a graceful hand in an encompassing gesture as they entered the ballroom, leaving Delphine to follow behind. 'As you can see, I've done my best in the decor to recreate the atmosphere of Versailles that you will remember so well.'

She had already noticed that there had been an attempt to capture something of the Palace's beautiful Hall of Mirrors, where she had danced so many times in the lovely light of more than three thousand candles. This clutching at the past made her uneasy, but she could understand that people who had never seen Versailles would take pleasure in imagining themselves to be there at his weekly balls. It was probably the secret of his enormous success and for that he was to be commended.

She paused to look around her. The ballroom, although large, was barely half the length of the original and, instead of tall graceful windows balancing arched mirrors on the opposite wall, there were mirrors on each side. Gilded, high-branched candelabra on plinths, similar to those she remembered, were spaced to double the glow of the candle flames in their reflection. A pair of crystal chandeliers, instead of ten twice the size, were suspended from a ceiling painted with mythical scenes.

No lessons were in progress, but musicians were gathering on a carpeted dais in readiness, including a lady harpist. A stately-looking woman, no longer young, with a patrician profile, she wore a scarlet ribbon around her neck, her hair powdered, and her full-skirted gown was of black silk. Louise had recognized her instantly.

'As you can see, madame,' Monsieur Rousselot was saying, 'there is an orchestra at the evening sessions for my advanced adult pupils. You will have heard of the balls that are held every Saturday, when a buffet supper is served in the room that lies through those double doors. These attract New York's highest society. For those wishing to improve their dancing at the same time, I have my best instructors, men and women, who unobtrusively give guidance in the steps.'

'Would my sister be present?'

'No, not for some time to come. She is a natural dancer, but far from being up to my standards yet. I shall teach her to be more than competent in all the finer aspects of the art of noble dance, even to the delicate angle of a fingertip and the pointing of a toe. Perfection is always my aim.'

Louise thought to herself that it would do Delphine good to aspire to such high achievement or else her enthusiasm might wane. 'There will be no problem with silk gowns for my sister.'

He hesitated. Nobody knew better than he did what it was like to arrive in this savage land without money and this would mean an immediate outlay. Yet he was within his rights to insist on correct attire as he paid higher than average wages to allow for the expense. 'Three at least for afternoon classes, madame? Plus two gowns of cotton or muslin for morning and during my tutoring of her?'

'She shall have them.'

'You need never be concerned about your sister when she advances to adult classes that include gentlemen and – later when her dancing is perfect – to partner at the balls, because a chaperone is always present. I also ensure that my young ladies are taken home afterwards by carriage under strict supervision. I will not have my establishment tainted by any breath of scandal.' He indicated the lady harpist with a graceful sweep of his hand. 'This evening our chaperone is the Comtesse de Valverde. I taught both her nieces at Versailles. You are already acquainted with her?' He had seen Louise and the countess exchange smiles of recognition.

'Yes, I am.'

He escorted her across to the dais. Hortense de Valverde stepped down from it at once to greet Louise emotionally and kiss her on both cheeks. They had never been close friends, always on formal terms, but the sight of a familiar face in alien surroundings meant a great deal to them both. The dancing master left them together and Hortense's face saddened as she mentioned Louise's widowhood.

'We were grieved to hear of the Marquis de Vailly's fate. A fellow émigré gave us the news.'

'I trust your husband is safe?'

'Yes, he is here in New York with me. Our three sons and their wives and children have taken refuge in England, but we hope for a reunion in our beloved France one day. Are you alone in New York?'

'No, my sister is with me.' Louise beckoned Delphine to join them. The Comtesse greeted her warmly.

'I shall introduce you both to our circle,' she declared animatedly. 'We have all kinds of social gatherings. Not like the old days, of course, but nonetheless enjoyable. I'm holding a card party next week and I want you both to come.'

They talked a little more, exchanged addresses, and Hortense wrote down the name of an émigré seamstress for Delphine's new gowns. Then the sisters left as the first of the evening dancers began to arrive.

The next day Louise took a ring to the jeweller she had dealt with previously. Afterwards three lengths of silk were purchased and a couple of sprigged cotton lengths for two other gowns. These were left with the recommended seamstress, who took measurements and a note of Delphine's wishes as to style and trimming. Then an order was also placed with a cobbler for three pairs of dancing pumps. During the time everything was being made, Delphine worked out a week's notice with the milliner. Then the morning came when, in a high state of excited anticipation, she set off for the dancing school in her new sprigged cotton.

Normally Louise never watched the clock during her working hours, but her thoughts kept going to her sister as they had done when she had believed her to be ill. She was the first to leave the workshop at the day's end. At the apartment she found that Delphine had arrived home just minutes ahead of her and was changing out of her silk gown.

'How did it go?' Louise called out eagerly, hanging her yellow hat on a peg.

Delphine, looking happy, emerged in her petticoats and performed a few dancing steps across the room. 'I'll soon be wearing out my new pumps if I have many days like today.' She promptly seized a broomstick and inverted it as she went into a lively impression of Monsieur Rousselot thumping his cane in emphasis, mimicking his slightly querulous voice.

'Poise! Poise! Poise, mademoiselle! Spine straight, head high! No affectation, *if* you please! Dip the body and listen to the nuances of the music. Dip again!'

Louise laughed. 'Yes, I can picture him doing that. How long did he coach you?'

'From the time I arrived at eight o'clock until noon.' She replaced the broom. 'I was on my own with him except for the comtesse, who played the pianoforte. Then in the afternoon somebody else played for him and I could hear music for the classes in two other salons. I had to practise alone in front of a large mirror.' She glanced down at her feet and giggled. 'If my toes don't fall off from fatigue I'll be the best dancer in New York before long.'

Louise was extremely relieved that all had gone well. 'I'm sure you will.'

Delphine darted across to the table. 'There's a letter for you here from England. On the way home I asked again at the post office and it was handed to me. It must be from Tante Violette.'

Eagerly Louise broke the seal and read the letter aloud as they sat side by side. Violette had been overjoyed to receive the letter from America and, in answer to Louise's query, she was in good health, but sadly her dear husband was far from well and bedridden. She wrote of her anxiety through months of not knowing how her two nieces were faring in France, there having been so many terrible tales by word of mouth and in the newspapers. She had hoped daily for their appearance on her doorstep and, although she was thankful they were safe, she was stricken with disappointment that they were so far away. Could they not take ship for England without delay? She knew there were dangers on the high seas through the war with France, but surely they should be safe on a neutral ship and she would gladly arrange payment. She sent her deepest affection and would eagerly await a reply.

Louise turned to Delphine, feeling she should give her the chance to voice an opinion on the offer. 'What would you like to do?'

'Stay here,' Delphine replied without hesitation.

Louise nodded thankfully. She regretted having to disappoint their aunt, but she was relieved that her sister did not want to make the change. They were both starting to put down roots in this new freedom that was theirs.

Delphine had viewed their aunt's offer in an entirely different light. The social round that Louise had enjoyed when on her visit to England would be nonexistent with their uncle lying ill. They could even end up sharing the nursing and that would be unendurable. What was more, as she had once said to Daniel, the last thing she ever wanted was to go on board a ship again, the nightmare of the rough voyage from France was still with her.

On the evening of Hortense de Valverde's card party Louise and Delphine were astonished to find that she was living in an apartment as fine as any she would have had in France. They soon learnt that it had been loaned to her by a wealthy American silversmith of French Huguenot descent, Richard Hoinville, who owned a great deal of valuable property in New York, and he had been equally generous to a number of other émigrés in various ways. The tables had been set up in one drawing room and, in another, Delphine joined those of her own age group. Although most of the guests were émigrés from the French court, Louise did not know any of them. But since as many as 6,000 had lived at the great Palace it was not surprising.

'You are going to be partnered by Mr Hoinville this evening,' Hortense told her, showing her the card table where she would sit. 'He is such a knowledgeable man and will be able to tell you anything you want to know about this country.'

When Richard Hoinville arrived, Louise was dismayed to see that Daniel was with him and they seemed to be on good terms. Although she was out of earshot, she could tell by the way Hortense greeted them both that Daniel was known to her. After a few words Daniel was left talking with some other people and Hortense led Richard across to where Louise was standing. He was tall and in his mid-fifties, straight-backed with well-cut features and shrewd blue-grey eyes, a look of reliability and steadfastness about him.

'Two good players should be at the same table,' Hortense said after the introductions, adding that she knew Louise's skill from past card parties at Versailles.

He and Louise smiled at each other. 'I'm honoured, Madame de Vailly,' he said in a voice as deep as a baritone's, bowing to her.

Hortense beamed on them both. 'You'll have worthy opponents in Mr and Mrs Hammond,' she added, seeing the couple coming towards them. 'As you know full well, Richard.'

'I can see it's going to be a very pleasurable evening,' he replied, a twinkle in his eye as he smiled again at Louise. She realized he was preparing her for the Hammonds.

They were a middle-aged couple, he a prosperous, self-satisfied banker, and she a comfortably rounded woman, handsomely gowned and bejewelled, with darting, inquisitive eyes that did not want to miss anything. She began at once to talk proudly about her five sons, who were all successful and married, and to number her grandchildren, who – in her loudly spoken, unassailable opinion – were all highly intelligent, better-looking and infinitely more adorable than anybody else's and, if still babies, exceptionally advanced for their age. Then her voice dropped to a depressed note as she referred unenthusiastically to her only daughter.

'Margaret is sixteen and at the moment she is with the young people in the other room. Unfortunately she is a shy girl and is far too much on her own with her books and her painting. So different from the boys when they were that age.' She gave an exasperated sigh as they took their places at the card table. 'She didn't want to come this evening, but I insisted. Before supper I'll see if she's tucked herself away in a corner as she usually does. Then I shall rout her out of it.'

Louise was relieved that Daniel had not yet seen her and was at a table quite a distance away, but his presence disturbed her. She seemed to sense his every movement. Then, as she was sorting the hand she had been dealt, he must have glanced over his shoulder, for she was suddenly aware that he had caught sight of her. For a matter of seconds she could feel his gaze boring into her.

It was halfway through the evening when double doors were opened into the supper room. As it happened, there was no need for Mrs Hammond to rout out her daughter as she had threatened. Just as people rose from the tables Margaret appeared, looking flushed and happy, with Delphine at her side. She was fair-haired and narrow-faced, taller than Delphine, and somewhat colourless, but she had fine hazel eyes. Glancing about the room, she sighted her mother and hurried across to her, bringing Delphine by the hand.

'Mama! I'd like you to meet my new friend.'

Louise guessed that Delphine, with her charm and vivacity, had probably coaxed the girl into joining the card games. Then, with a burst of kindness the like of which she showed now and then, she had kept Margaret under her wing, almost turning the girl's head with her friendliness. Mrs Hammond's pleasure at this unexpected development increased further upon hearing that Delphine was sister to the aristocratic Frenchwoman to whom she had been talking. It was a friendship to be encouraged.

Leaving the Hammonds with the two girls, Richard drew Louise away to the buffet table. 'Let's get away from that couple for a while,' he said with a chuckle.

When they had made their selection from an array of dishes, they went with their plates and glasses of wine to two chairs set slightly apart from the rest. Daniel did not come near and sat elsewhere with others in the supper room.

Richard asked Louise how she passed her time and nodded approvingly when she told him about her work. Then, knowing that he had lived through all the upheaval of the War of Independence and remembering Hortense's advice, she asked him about its aftermath.

'I always want to learn more about my new land.'

He looked pleased. 'That's the right attitude. Well, the need for reform was acute and many injustices under British rule had to be swept away, but I'm not alone in regretting that severance from Great Britain did not come peaceably. What's more, old ties are strong and our history has roots deep in the past. It's why so many British customs linger on and it will take another generation to make the people of this country feel truly American.' He smiled wryly. 'But now at least we have the freedom to make our own mistakes with nobody else to blame.'

She looked down unseeingly at her supper plate. 'Freedom is what I came across the ocean to find.' Then she met his clear blue-grey eyes again. 'I've heard it said that none of us at Versailles knew that we were dancing blindly all the way to disaster. Many courtiers and landowners never went near their country estates, only drawing incomes from them and not caring that the peasants went hungry. I doubt if any of the nobles ever glanced out of their coaches at the poor and destitute begging at the palace gates or did anything to alleviate such desperate need.'

His gaze sharpened on her. 'But you did.'

She stiffened defensively. It was an automatic reaction. At Versailles she'd had to conceal her charity work from Fernand for so long that even after all this time it was like having a close secret unexpectedly probed. Quickly she recovered herself.

'Not enough. It was never enough.' She spoke with despair. 'When my sister and I left France, conditions for thousands of people were so much worse than ever before. Starvation was rife. I long for the day when the cry of *Liberté, Égalité* and *Fraternité* will take on its true meaning in France.'

He regarded her seriously from under his brows. 'Spoken like a patriot. But the excesses of the Reign of Terror are beginning to sicken people here and there's a swing of opinion towards supporting the British in the war against France. Do you still consider France to be your country in spite of the horrific crimes being perpetrated there under Robespierre and his fellow tyrants?'

She showed surprise that he should ask. 'Love for one's homeland can never be erased! Although I'm here to stay, there are times when homesickness nearly tears me apart. After all, nothing can change the beauty and landscape of France itself. What's more, I have enough faith in my fellow countrymen and women to believe that one day justice and mercy will defeat the present evil regime.'

'Tyrants always fall eventually,' he agreed, nodding his head. 'History has shown us that.'

'It's very hard to lose one's home and be banished from one's own country.' She did not realize he could see her anguish in a darkening in the depths of her green eyes. 'But I like to think I'm becoming more of an American citizen every day.'

'Well said, ma'am.'

It was when they were about to return to their card table, players having started to regather, that she saw Daniel facing her. He stood framed in the entrance of the drawing room, his feet apart in a stag-like stance as he waited for them. Louise steeled herself as they approached him. He was frowning.

'Ah!' Richard said jovially. 'Here's someone for you to meet. Daniel Lombard can tell you all about Boston as well as the Deep South. He and I have been business associates over several years.'

'I know Mr Lombard already,' Louise said quickly.

'Do you indeed? Splendid!'

Daniel's cold eyes pierced her, his mouth unsmiling. 'Good evening, Louise. I hope you're well.'

'Thank you, yes.' Her whole body seemed to shiver in awareness of his proximity and, by the way he was looking at her, she was certain he knew it.

'I'll escort you home at the end of the evening.'

'That won't be necessary. I've made arrangements.'

'A hired carriage? That can be dismissed.'

Richard, observing them both, sensed the thinly veiled friction between them and intervened smilingly. 'No, not a hired carriage, Mr Lombard. I'm taking Madame de Vailly home myself.'

Daniel inclined his head, not taking his eyes from her. 'In

that case I can leave you in safe hands, Louise. Enjoy the rest of the evening.'

He went back to his table. Louise let out a deep breath, tension ebbing from her. She was grateful to Richard for his timely offer.

In all, they won three games, but by a trick of the cards lost the last one. When the evening was over and guests were gathering in the hall ready to leave, Richard offered Daniel a lift in his carriage as well, but he refused, saying that he would walk back to the hotel, needing some exercise after being seated the whole evening.

'I'm sorry you won't still be in New York next week,' Richard was saying to him as Louise and Delphine came into the hall after collecting their shawls. 'But we should be able to cover all the details at the meeting tomorrow morning.'

'I'm sure we shall manage it.' Then Daniel said goodnight to the three of them and left without looking back.

On the way to the apartment, Richard invited Louise and Delphine to dine at his home one evening during the forthcoming week. 'I'm giving a dinner party for three émigré doctors, who have recently arrived in the country. One of them is an unusual, idealistic young man. His name is Charles Noiret. He's not letting the grass grow under his feet and has already established his own practice. I think you'll find him interesting.'

Louise accepted only for herself. The Hammonds had invited Delphine for the same evening. It made Louise realize that at last she was entitled to some life of her own and the time had come for her to stop concentrating on being wholly a guardian and nursemaid to her sister.

Six

C harles Noiret proved to be as interesting as Louise had been told he would be. Although there were already a number of guests gathered at the Hoinville residence when she arrived, she picked him out intuitively. He stood with his back towards her, gesticulating vigorously in some deep discussion with two other men, who – as she discovered later – were local doctors. His plum velvet coat had seen better days, his shoes were polished but well worn, and his thick, unruly fair hair was tied back by a bedraggled ribbon.

He spun round on his heel with an unassailable jauntiness as Richard spoke to him and she looked into a smiling brown-eyed, high-browed face, the mouth mobile, and the cleft chin decidedly stubborn. As the introductions took place he made a sweeping bow of unnecessary depth that made her think of a schoolboy doing his best.

'I hear you've not been long in this country, Dr Noiret,' she said as he faced her again. 'But you've made a niche for yourself already.'

'Indeed I have,' he answered enthusiastically with an almost boastful pride. 'All thanks to Mr Hoinville for granting me a loan at a low interest. He's also lent me one of his horses on which to make my calls until I can afford to buy one of my own. My surgery is down near the docks in an old house that needed plenty of repairs. I've had that done and the whole place scrubbed and whitewashed as well as installing some necessary furnishings. Fortunately I had my surgical instruments with me when I escaped from France and so I was saved that expense.'

She smiled, liking him. 'So, if that's your location, I can tell you're not aiming to make a fortune with rich patients.'

'*Mon Dieu*! No!' He shook his tousled head vehemently. 'There are more than enough doctors ready to wait on them! To date, among other patients who have come to me, I've some of our own countrymen and women unable to afford medical aid elsewhere.' He tilted his head to one side, eyeing her mockingly. 'You're welcome to view my premises if you're not too proud to let your skirts brush past the poor.'

She knew he was challenging her. 'Every weekday I work in a milliner's shop from seven in the morning until seven at night. But if Sunday afternoon is convenient I'll call on you then.'

His eyebrows shot up and he made his ridiculous bow again. 'On the strength of that promise I shall escort you into dinner.'

In all there were ten guests with Richard at the head of the table. Louise was seated at his right hand, with Charles beside her, and the conversation was lively. The other two émigré doctors were older, serious men, one of them accompanied by his wife and spinster daughter, who had escaped with him. The other doctor was a bachelor, proud that, as he spoke a little English, he had obtained a position at the New York Hospital. Louise, hearing his efforts as he demonstrated his knowledge of the language, hoped his patients would be able to understand him. Charles, on the other hand, spoke it fluently, having had an English tutor in his boyhood. As dinner ended, Richard rose to his feet and raised his glass in a toast.

'To our great President.'

Everybody stood and drank the toast. Louise could tell that it was always customary at Richard's table and she approved, for from all she had heard and read of George Washington he deserved the respect and affection of his people.

Delphine had made her own plans for Sunday with Margaret and her parents, which left Louise free to go on her own to the address Charles had given her. Although her apartment was in a poor area, it was superior to the rough district where Charles had established himself. All the houses looked in need of repair and rubbish littered the streets. The shining brass plate on his door shone like a piece of gold in its incongruous setting of poverty and decay. To the side of it was a stone mounting block left from the house's grander days. She tugged the bell-pull, aware of being watched with curiosity by those lounging in their doorways or sitting at their windows. Some barefoot boys had stopped kicking a ball made of rags to stare at her.

Immediately, from within, footsteps came running and the door was jerked open by Charles in his shirtsleeves and wearing a bloodstained apron. 'You've come at just the right time!' he exclaimed with relief. 'I need help! I've a patient here with a knife wound!'

She threw off her cloak and followed him at a run into his surgery. The patient, a burly-looking fellow bare to the waist, lay strapped on to a high-legged, leather couch, blood flowing from a single horrific slash across his chest and arm. Charles hurled a clean cloth at her. 'Apply pressure here!' He indicated the spot. 'As hard as you can! I have to stitch him up without delay!'

Without a second's hesitation she obeyed. Charles took needle and thread to begin his work. The patient was barely conscious, but he uttered a dreadful-sounding howl as the needle entered his torn flesh and would have jerked upwards if the leather straps had not held him down. Then his head lolled to one side as he became totally unconscious. His breath stank of ale and brandy, the tattoo marks on his arms indicating that he was a seaman, and it was her guess that the knifing was the result of a drunken brawl. Although he was oblivious to all that was going on, Charles spoke to him now and again as the stitching proceeded.

'Hold on, Ben! I'm not going to let you die yet.'

Louise had to change cloths many times as each became blood-soaked, throwing them into a bucket. When the stitching was done Charles padded and bandaged his patient. Then Louise unfolded a blanket, drew it up to the seaman's neck and tucked it in around him.

'Well done, madame!' Charles said admiringly, offering her a bowl of water in which to wash the blood from her hands and arms. 'Many women would have fainted away at that gruesome sight. You've helped with something like that before.'

'Not exactly. There was a convent not far from Versailles where I went as often as I could to help in the nuns' charity work. Mostly it was assisting at births – so many abandoned women and young girls turned to the nuns for help – or else I fed the sick and dressed any injuries.' She looked across at the patient as she dried her hands. 'What happened?'

'There was a fight outside one of the taverns and he suffered the worst of it. Four of his shipmates dumped him here and went charging off again to search for his attacker.'

'If they find him it could be extra work for you.'

He shook his head grimly. 'Not in the mood they were in. It would be a gravedigger's task.' Then he noticed the state of her dress. 'Those bloodstains! Your gown is ruined! I should have thought to give you an apron.'

'There was no time to waste. Every second counted. That seaman's life depended on it.' She was glad to reassure him. 'My gown is muslin and will wash.'

'That's a relief.' He went to bend over his patient and looked at him closely while feeling his pulse, before adjusting the blanket again. 'I managed to get some brandy into him to dull the pain and he'd already drunk enough ale to sink a ship, so he couldn't have felt much. But he will suffer from the wound when he comes round and he's lost a lot of blood. Fortunately he seems to have the strength of an ox and that should help him pull through.'

'Perhaps you'll get more seafarers after this one's recovery, being so near the docks.' She sat down in the chair he had drawn forward for her.

'I've had a number of them already.' He took a bottle of Madeira and two glasses from a cupboard. 'Apart from accidents at sea, which need proper attention when a ship comes into harbour, they pick up all sorts of diseases in foreign ports and pay generously for any treatment that helps them. I get stevedores and other dock workers, who usually want to pay in goods they've stolen from the cargoes, but I always insist on money.' Grinning cheerfully, he sat down on the opposite side of his desk. 'Those fees go towards financing treatment for patients who have nothing. The same system worked when I was in practice at home in Calais.'

'You sound like Robin Hood in the English legend.'

He threw back his head in laughter. 'Not I! I'm just practical. The penniless sick have the right to be healed and I use the best available method. If I were in luck, sometimes in Calais I'd be called to a prosperous merchant's house and that would help to fill up the coffers too. I'm counting on the same happening here to let me clear myself of Richard's loan.'

Louise raised her glass. 'To Ben's speedy recovery.'

'I echo that.' After drinking the toast he put his glass down and went again to his patient, his frown showing his concern. His long, capable fingers sought out Ben's pulse once more before returning to carry on their conversation. He had drunk two glasses of wine to her one when suddenly the patient uttered a deep-throated groan. Instantly Charles was on his feet. 'He's regaining consciousness. Now I must get him to drink plenty of water. Luckily I've some fresh-drawn from the pump.'

She went to his side. 'Can I help?'

'No, you've done more than enough this afternoon.'

Just then the front door crashed open and there came a thumping of heavy boots along the hall as Ben's shipmates returned. As they burst into the room, demanding to know how he was and angry that his assailant had eluded them, Louise seized the moment to make an unobtrusive departure. Charles signalled that he would see her again soon.

She was careful to keep her cloak wrapped around her to hide her bloodstained gown. It was as well that Delphine was with the Hammonds because she was in no mood for an hysterical display of concern.

It was now early summer and the straw hats at Miss Sullivan's shop were selling well. She was fully aware that the variety of shapes and colours suggested by Louise had greatly extended her market. Her stock began to dwindle quickly and soon the straw hats were sold as fast as orders could be fulfilled. Those in the workshop were glad of the overtime and even Louise, who was now working on the more elaborate millinery, had to break off to help when demand exceeded supply.

At Monsieur Rousselot's dancing school Delphine had advanced under his intensive tuition and was given her first class of pupils. To her great disappointment they were all aged three to five. At the end of the first day she complained bitterly to Louise.

'I can't cope with little children. I don't even *like* them! They wouldn't pay attention and kept running off the floor to their nursemaids, who sat in a row along the wall gossiping together. When I called the class to order the children either bawled their heads off or else stood there as if petrified and wet themselves.' She stamped her foot like a child herself when Louise responded by laughing. 'It's not funny! I didn't work as hard as I have done to end up with a bunch of babies. You know I never even liked playing with dolls when I was little and I've no time for any of them.'

'Hasn't it occurred to you,' Louise said, trying to compose her face, 'that Monsieur Rousselot could be testing your patience? After all, when you advance to older children and adult classes you'll have plenty of pupils who'll seem to have two left feet and no sense of rhythm. Your patience will be tried enough then.'

Delphine looked doubtful. 'Do you think that's what he had in mind?' Then, always dramatic in her actions, she threw up her hands helplessly. 'Then I'm finished! I'll never get those infants to learn anything and I've two more batches of them coming tomorrow. My career is over!'

Louise shook her head. 'Don't lose heart so easily. I've an idea that should help you. After we've eaten dinner we'll get the sewing basket out and I'll tell you what to do with your classes.'

Delphine found that by smiling at her pupils, using quiet tones, and by handing each child a flower from a bunch which she and Louise had made together, they were soon coaxed into forming a ring and pretending to be flowers as well. After a while even the shy ones stopped hanging on to their nursemaids' skirts to join in the dancing games. All the crying that was done took place when it was time to go home again, including the stamping of little feet in temper, but that was the responsibility of the nursemaids. Thankfully, Delphine closed the door on them.

But she had made a beginning. Although there were days when she could have screamed at times with impatience, she kept a smile glued on her face and had the satisfaction of having an orderly class when Monsieur Rousselot happened to come into the room.

'They were all turning in the wrong direction, but some were managing the steps quite well and the rest were bobbing up and down to the music. As always, I'm left a nervous wreck!' She collapsed with exaggerated exhaustion into a chair.

'Persevere,' Louise advised firmly. 'I'm certain you'll advance from that age group before long.'

Her words proved right. Soon Delphine was teaching the young adults' class, both boys and girls. There were budding romances, but these were watched out for and quashed by the girls' own chaperones. Delphine had begun to take everything in her stride, but the highlight of her days was the time she spent at the Hammonds and when free of work she was rarely at her own home, except to sleep.

Louise had begun to see Charles every Sunday afternoon. They would set out from home at the same time to meet along the way. He had given her a key, which meant that if he were delayed through dealing with an emergency she would wait at his house until he returned. Neither of them had any money to spare and often they would take a picnic to a grassy stretch that overlooked the river or enjoy the ocean's air from a promenade. Sometimes she sat before him on his horse and they would leave the city behind and go out into the countryside. Otherwise they chose a park with shady trees where she would sit beside him as he lay full-length on the grass. They told each other their hopes and dreams that they had never told anyone else, which meant a great deal to them both.

When their outings were over for the day he would cook omelettes in his kitchen for them both or else she would provide supper at the apartment. They had grander fare when invited to Richard Hoinville's mansion, but enjoyed their simple meals together just as much, never running out of talk or laughter. Once she asked him why it was that he, who had done so much for the health of the poor in the past, had been forced to flee France.

He made a comical grimace. 'It made no difference to the Revolutionaries that I was the black sheep of the family. I shared the same blue-blooded lineage as my arrogant brother at Versailles and that was enough to condemn me.'

Although Louise still saw Hortense de Valverde from time to time, she much preferred gatherings, such as at Richard's house, where, often with the exception of Charles and herself, everybody else was American. Émigrés were too prone to talk about the past and lament at length the grandeur that had gone for ever. Sometimes she wondered if in trying not to look back she was attempting to shut out a deep-seated dread that something from those awful days of the Reign of Terror could still reach out to her. She had not forgotten an old nightmare about her escape, although mercifully it had never returned. Once or twice she had been tempted to discuss it with Charles, but had decided against it as being too trivial.

To Delphine's joy the day came at last when Monsieur Rousselot told her she could assist him at one of his classes. She found herself in the role of partner to a motley collection of people in the familiar steps of the various minuets, gavottes, gigues and the contredanse among many others. Her determination never to be demoted to the infants again made her uncharacteristically considerate and encouraging, and always with a smile, no matter how clumsy the dancer.

Her ambition was to partner at the evening balls, but these

were discontinued until the autumn when the heat began to blast down on the city and many left with their children for homes in the country. The classes quickly depleted until Monsieur Rousselot lowered his prices for the summer, which brought in pupils from less affluent families. Then Delphine was invited by Mr Hammond to go with his wife and daughter to spend a month in the country with his cousin and his family.

'You'll love it there,' Margaret enthused. 'Picnics and hayrides and summer parties. I've always been too shy to enjoy it in the past, but with you it will all be different. We'll have such fun!'

Delphine thought uneasily that Margaret was becoming far more outgoing than her parents suspected, always keeping a demure attitude in their presence. She knew Margaret's parents considered her a good influence on Margaret and she hoped the girl wouldn't do anything foolish that would put an end to the social life she was having with the Hammonds. The new invitation was tempting, but she could not risk losing her post at the dancing school. If she could count on meeting a rich young man in the country, she would leave. But the Hammonds, although very comfortably off, were not in the very wealthy circle in which she wanted to marry.

When Louise was told about the invitation, she suggested that Delphine should ask the dancing master if he could spare her from the classes for a week. 'There's no harm in asking and he knows how hard you have been working. I'd like you to have some country air. Charles says there are all sorts of sicknesses about, now that the weather has become so exceptionally hot.'

The next morning when Delphine arrived for work she was told to go immediately to Monsieur Rousselot's office. He waved her to a seat, but before she had a chance to speak he rose from his desk, came round to the front and perched his weight on it.

'I had some serious news brought to me this morning,' he began. 'Two cases of yellow fever have broken out in the city.

I've been told that this will send even more people fleeing out of New York and my classes will dwindle to nothing. I believe it's some years since there has been more than a handful of cases, but it is a contagion that seems to strike fear into everybody.' He sighed. 'It means reducing the number of my instructresses. As you were the last to join my establishment, I'm afraid you have to be the first to leave it. But,' he added to soften the blow, 'you may return in the autumn when the danger is past. To compensate, I will allow you to partner at the balls. You have been here long enough to know that your ball gowns must be elegant and not in any way flamboyant.'

Delphine looked down at her hands to hide her glee. How lucky she was that this had happened! She would be able to spend the whole month with Margaret after all. Composing her face into a regretful expression, she looked up at the dancing master again. 'Naturally I shall miss teaching my pupils, but I shall look forward to coming back in the autumn.'

Louise helped Delphine to pack, folding the silk gowns carefully. They had bought a large, battered old trunk for almost nothing and Delphine crammed it with all her clothes, saying she would need everything. Louise was thankful her sister was leaving the city and would be out of danger. Cousin Madeleine's tragic bereavement was very much in her mind. For herself she had no qualms. She had nursed those with fevers at the convent and had long believed herself to be immune to infections. It was with relief that she waved Delphine off with Mrs Hammond and Margaret in their carriage.

By the time Delphine had been gone for almost a week Louise was becoming more used to the apartment being so quiet; even Sunday was to have a different routine. Normally they went together to morning service at Trinity Church before Delphine set off to lunch with the Hammonds while she went to meet Charles.

When Sunday morning came Louise awoke with a bad headache and had to rest longer in bed before it eased enough for her to get up to wash and dress. She was unable to eat any breakfast, a wave of nausea sweeping over her, and she wondered what she had eaten that could have upset her. Once, as she turned quickly, she became so dizzy that she almost fell. She would just have to rest today. Charles would surely come all the way to her. At least when he came he would fetch some physic from his surgery to help her.

An hour later she had collapsed on to her bed, shivering violently with fever, her headache almost unbearable. She slept and woke again to shooting pains in her head. Although desperate for a drink of cold water she did not have the strength to move until she remembered that her door was locked and when Charles came he might think he had missed her along their route.

Slowly, stopping to rest in exhaustion on the way, she crawled on her hands and knees across to the door and unlocked it. Sweat was pouring from her and it took her even longer to get back on to her bed. She realized how ill she was and the thought crossed her mind that if Charles had an emergency to deal with she could lie there and die, for there was nobody in the rest of the house who would realize anything was wrong.

Whenever she managed to lift her head to look at the wall clock, she cried out involuntarily in pain. The hour when she should have been meeting Charles came and went, the day creeping on until she realized he was not coming. By that time she was drifting in and out of the many strange shapes and colours floating all around her and it was a relief to slip away through their patterns into oblivion.

It was at that time that Charles finished an exhausting day after an interrupted night's sleep. He had been called out twice to what he had diagnosed immediately as yellow fever. Although he had no previous experience of the contagion he had read about it and discussed the symptoms and treatment with an American doctor at one of Richard's gatherings. He was told that in the last bad epidemic in New York, which happened many years ago, those afflicted were moved out of the city into hastily erected canvas shelters to avoid the spread of it.

'A sensible precaution in some ways,' Charles had acknowledged, frowning.

'That's what has been done during epidemics in the South, where the hot and humid climate fosters an outbreak. It can spread like wildfire. There's no cure. Bloodletting is all that can be done. The terrible thing is that there have been occasions when a suspected victim of the fever, becoming ill in the street, has been stoned by panic-stricken crowds to drive the poor creature out of town.'

'What of the sick in the tents?'

The doctor hesitated. 'I regret to say they die like flies and, most of the time, so do any family members who've had the courage to go with them.'

'What of medical aid to ease the suffering?'

The doctor hesitated. 'There are always one or two of our profession who will risk their lives in a hell of pestilence.'

It was obvious to Charles that this doctor would never be one of them. The conversation had been in his mind when he had left his Sunday morning breakfast at the summons of a wild-eyed little boy.

'Please come, doctor! Two of my brothers are very sick. One's turned yeller and Mom don't know what's wrong!'

He had grabbed up his medical bag with his herbal potions and pills and followed the child into the next street. He found both boys suffering the early symptoms of yellow fever, with painful heads, vomiting and shivering chills. One already showed a more advanced stage, with the first yellow in the skin, which came from the affected liver. He knew there was no hope. He had to tell the woman what the contagion was and she turned ashen. But she straightened her shoulders.

'I shall do my best for my boys,' she said bravely, tears swimming in her eyes. The fact that her five siblings were used to sleeping together in the same bed made him despair of the other three boys' chances of escaping the contagion, but he told the mother to keep them away from the two sick children.

'Where's your husband?' he asked. 'He must help you swab the patients with cool water to get their fevers down.'

'He's far away on a whaling ship, but my spinster sister lives along the street and she'll help me. We'll manage. We'll have to, because nobody else will come near, as it's the yellow fever.'

He nodded. 'I'll look in later. The potion I gave you should ease the patients' head pains.'

By the end of the morning he had attended three other cases of the dreaded fever and two suspected ones. Then he was called to a fatal case when a man dropped dead by the dock gates. He had great difficulty in getting the body moved, as everybody was afraid to come near. Charles was left in no doubt that he was dealing with a serious outbreak of the contagion even if it was not yet an epidemic.

He pondered over how it had come to the city. Was it by ship? That seemed the most likely conclusion. Heat in itself could not create the contagion. Why was it more prevalent in the South? What was there that hibernated the fever until it burst forth? It was something he'd like to investigate in time.

On the chance of being called out again he wrote a note to Louise, telling her what had happened and instructing her to leave immediately, adding that he would contact her soon. He pinned it to his door and returned to his desk again, writing out a report on his yellow fever cases, being duty-bound by the authorities to do it. He had almost finished when a woman came to see him. She was big and strong-looking, with straggling grey hair tucked up under a linen cap, and clad in a faded multicoloured dress.

'You'll be wanting my 'elp now, Doctor,' she said, folding her arms in front of her ample waist. 'I knows more about t'yeller fever than anyone.'

Charles sat back in his chair, quill pen in hand. 'How is that?'

'I nursed my pa and ma and the whole family through t' great epidemic of thirty-odd years ago when people was dying everywhere. Cooled down the fever and drove it out. So, I'll nurse for you now, but you'll 'ave to pay me.'

He was interested in spite of himself, having used the same

method with certain fevers in France. In spite of her rough manner and unprepossessing appearance, her cap and apron were clean as well as the nails of her work-worn hands. On a closer look he judged her to be no more than fifty, but a hard life had left its mark on her features. As for her speech, her tongue was caught up in an English dialect that he found difficult to understand. 'What's your name and where are you from originally?'

'I'm Joan Townsend and I was born in Suffolk, England. I came to this country when I was a girl. Don't say I sound as if I'm just off t' boat, because everybody does and I wouldn't change even if I could.'

'Very well. Tell me where you live, Mrs Townsend. If nursing is needed anywhere, I'll let you know.' He would have returned to his writing, but she sat down on a chair like a hen settling on eggs and arranged her skirt neatly.

'I'll wait,' she said calmly, linking her fingers together on her lap. 'And you can call me Joan.'

Losing patience, he was about to order her out when there came a hammering on his door. He went to open it and found a distraught young man on his doorstep.

'It's my wife, Doctor! She has a high fever! And she's turned a yellow colour!'

Charles hurried back into his surgery and again grabbed up his medical bag.

'You see,' Joan stated complacently, rising to her feet. 'I'll come with you.'

'No!' he roared, losing patience with her. 'You'll leave now!'

He set off at a swift pace with the young man, whose home was not far away. He found the young wife as her husband had described and hoped it was not too late to save her. He ripped away the heavy bedcovers that had been piled on top of her to drive out the fever.

'There's no need for these blankets! She must be cooled down. Get some cold wet cloths for her forehead.' He gave the same instructions as he had in the homes of other patients that day. 'I'm afraid it's yellow fever. Get her to drink as much clean well water as possible. She will be extremely thirsty.'

He had great faith in the qualities of good water for flushing impurities out of the body, a theory not supported by any of his profession known to him. But then, neither did he believe in bleeding a patient for almost everything. As he left the young wife's sickroom, her husband, his expression desperate, caught at his sleeve.

'I've heard that one of those terrible fever camps is to be set up outside the city. They won't try to take my wife, will they, Doctor?'

Charles answered calmly. 'It's not officially an epidemic yet. But if it is declared, I shall go with my patients to the isolation tents and tend to them there.' It was a decision he had made when he had first heard of the outbreak elsewhere in the city.

When he came out of the house, Joan was waiting for him expectantly. He gave a nod. 'Very well. Go in and help that young husband. He's out of his head with worry.' He shook a warning finger at her. 'And don't disregard any of the rules I've laid down with him for the treatment of his wife.'

She grinned, showing gaps in her teeth. 'You'll find I'm worth my weight in gold.'

It was five o'clock when he reached home after checking on the patients he had seen earlier. The note was still on the door with no sign that Louise had been there, but he knew she would have taken notice of his warning.

He felt tired, but he made himself a meal and would have gone to his desk to record the new case if he had not started wondering about Louise. Perhaps she had not come at all, something unexpected having happened. He wanted to see her and if today should be the start of an epidemic it would be many weeks before he could meet her again. If he went to her home now he could talk to her at the window from a little distance away, because for all he knew of the contagion the infection could be hanging about his clothes.

Going out to the stable, he saddled up his horse and rode

off. Before long he drew level with her living-room window. Still in the saddle, he reached out with his riding crop and tapped on the glass. When Louise did not appear he tapped again without result.

On her bed Louise, her head clear for a few lucid moments, heard the tapping. Somebody was at the door! She must get there and ask for help! In her confused state she had no thought of Charles. Forcing herself to sit up, she cried out again at the pain that the tremendous effort sent shooting through her head. Rolling herself from the bed, she fell sprawling on to her face and lay there unable to move.

'Help me!' she croaked from her dry throat. Then she drifted once more into enveloping darkness.

In the street, Charles tried tapping on the bedroom window just in case she was dozing. Then, disappointed at not finding her at home, he swung his horse round and started back the way he had come.

But he had not gone far when he decided that he should have left a message in case he was too busy tomorrow to make another visit. Riding back again, he dismounted and took a pad and a stub of pencil from his pocket. Outside the door of her apartment he set the paper against the wall and wrote. Then he bent down to push it under the door, but a wooden draught-excluder, fastened by some previous tenant, gave no space for it. Without hope, he tried the door and to his surprise it was unlocked. This was not a district in which to invite intruders.

'Louise?' he called out as he entered. There was no reply and he put the note down on the table where it would be easily seen. It was as he was turning to leave that his attention was caught by the rumpled end of a quilt lying on the bedroom floor. Curious, he pushed the door wider and then he saw her. In a rush of fear, he dropped to one knee beside her, turning her limp body towards him. Her eyes were closed and her luxuriant hair tumbled about his supporting arm. He had seen enough cases that day to know just what the danger was. Somehow he must get her home with him, but there were too many people about outside for him to take such an obviously sick woman on his horse. The cry of *Yellow Fever*! would go up, and that could result in a general panic. He and Louise could be pelted with missiles to drive them out of the district, as had happened to others in the past, and he would not risk any further harm coming to her.

Gathering her up, he laid her gently on the bed. 'I'm leaving you for just a few minutes, Louise,' he said, even though she did not hear him.

Outside, he looked one way and then the other along the street. Women were gossiping in doorways, others sat with their men outside the nearby tavern and children were playing everywhere. Taking his horse, he went along to poor-looking stables, where the only vehicle for hire was a rickety old cart. It would be a rough ride for Louise, but he had to get her to safety. His horse snorted and reared its head, nostrils flaring at being harnessed up, only used to a rider, but Charles patted its neck and spoke encouragingly until it quietened down. Then he led it back to the house.

In the apartment he ripped the linen from Delphine's wall-bed and carried the mattress out and dumped it in the back of the cart. A bundle of pillows and another of sheets followed. Those watching him were used to people taking their belongings in flight from a creditor or a landlord wanting overdue rent. By the time he appeared with a long roll of blankets, those around had lost interest and none noticed the care with which he laid this final bundle down. Then he locked the apartment behind him and set off on foot, leading the horse.

The cart lurched drunkenly over the ruts in the street, shifting its cargo from side to side, but Charles did not risk stopping to check on his new patient until he turned down a deserted alley. To his relief as he drew back the blanket, Louise opened her eyes for a moment and murmured his name before her lids closed again.

Seven

For five days Charles fought to save Louise's life, Joan giving him able assistance. When he was out, visiting other patients, Joan seized the opportunity to give Louise a spoonful of a concoction from a bottle she kept hidden in her apron pocket. It was mainly herbal, but as it had a couple of ingredients in it that her old grandmother had advised for any life-threatening fever, she was certain that Dr Noiret, with his decided notions about clean water and his other strange ideas, would throw it away if he found out about it.

Yet she knew from past experience that, if the contagion was in its first stages, her concoction helped people to recover. Although it had been too late to save the young wife and three other of his patients, Louise was holding her own and Joan thought that with a few more doses she had a good chance of pulling through.

Every day Joan marvelled to herself over the diligence of the young French doctor, whose face was constantly wrenched by anxiety over Louise and who, in spite of his physical tiredness, never turned anyone away or failed to go to a house where he was needed.

The fever had been declared a minor epidemic. Through some quirk of fate it had not claimed more than one more person in the two streets where it had first been reported. Instead it had located itself fiercely in the district near the docks. With so many important commercial interests at stake, an isolation camp was hastily erected at a safe distance from the city and the evacuation of the sick from the infected area began to take place. Louise, although thin and bedridden, was through the crisis of her fever. Lying in an upstairs room, she heard the first rumble of wheels as the evacuation began. As the only doctor in the area, it had been Charles's responsibility to organize it.

When he came into the room, a travelling bag slung over his shoulder and his medical bag bulging with extra supplies, she tried to keep a smile on her face.

'I'm leaving now,' he said, grinning cheerfully for her benefit. 'But I know you'll soon be completely well again.'

Although she had been prepared for his departure, it tore at her heart to see him go. His earlier reassurance that if he had been going to catch the fever it would have happened already held no weight now that the time of parting had come.

'I'll be looking forward to our Sunday afternoons together when you're back again,' she managed on a light note.

'So shall I. Then we'll make up for lost time. As I believe you're no longer infectious, Joan will soon take you to Mr Hoinville's house. Everything has been arranged. He'll see that you're cared for until fully recovered. Then Joan will come to assist me at the camp.' He took her hand, kissed it and then her brow. 'Au revoir, Louise.'

'God be with you,' she said in a choked voice.

His gaze lingered long and warmly on her before he clamped his tricorne hat on to his head and went from the room to clatter away down the stairs. Joan, who had tactfully kept her distance, even though they had spoken in French, as they usually did on their own, came into the room when the front door banged after him.

'Help me to the window!' Louise implored, pushing aside her bed cover. 'I want to see him leave.'

Joan almost carried her to the window, for her feet dragged weakly. Then she looked down into the street, but he was not expecting to see her and did not look up. She saw him set his hands on to the back of a cart full of sick people and leap up on to it to sit with his legs dangling. Even as she watched, he turned to comfort a sobbing child.

Three days later Joan brought the horse from the stable to

the mounting block by the house. Then Louise, supported by the woman's strong arms, took each stone step slowly until she managed to sit sideways on the saddle.

Joan looked up at her almost accusingly. 'I hope you realize how much t' doctor loves you.'

Louise met her eyes. 'I do,' she replied quietly.

It was true, she thought, as the woman began to lead the horse at a gentle pace. She and Charles had formed a bond between them that was more than friendship; a warm love that would stay the rest of their lives. But they each had their own paths to follow. Whether those paths should ever merge to become one was something only the future could reveal.

To shorten the journey, Joan led the horse through narrow streets. She also wanted to avoid being seen by the guards, who stopped anyone leaving the infected area, other than those on the sick carts, which had to keep to a specific route.

By the time they reached Richard's home, Louise was totally exhausted, no longer able to sit upright on the saddle. Joan pulled her down from it and she would have collapsed if she had not been held. She did not know they were being watched from a window or that their arrival had resulted in immediate activity within.

Joan half-carried her through a side gate and followed a path by the side of the house until they came to an open doorway. They descended a short flight to a basement laundry room where footsteps had scuttled away at their approach. The woman continued to support Louise in her arms as she looked about her. The household washing had been interrupted by their arrival, but a hip bath stood ready with hot water and a stack of towels on a chair beside it.

'Take off all your clothes, ma'am,' Joan ordered, even though she had washed and ironed them herself in readiness for Louise that morning. 'As t' doctor said, you mustn't go into this house wearing anything from his place.' She shrugged her shoulders to disassociate herself from his strange theories as she knelt down by the hip bath and poured some cold water into it from a brass jug that stood ready. She swirled it about with her hand. 'It's ready.'

When Louise was safely in the hip bath, Joan dropped the discarded clothes into one of the steaming tubs. Then she washed Louise's hair vigorously, fingers hard on her scalp, before drying it with equal ferocity.

After Louise had dressed again in a set of garments that had been waiting for her, she sank down on a bench, her legs giving way again. 'You will give my letter to Dr Noiret as soon as you see him?'

'You can trust me.'

'I do, Joan. Thank you again for your good nursing and for all else you have done for me.'

The woman shrugged carelessly. 'You was just another case of fever to me. The rest of it I did for t' doctor.' She picked up a bell that had been left on an ironing table and handed it to Louise. 'Ring it as soon as I've left and someone will come.' Then she thumped back up the steps and disappeared from sight without a backward glance.

It was Richard himself who came when the bell sounded, a manservant following him. 'You must be exhausted,' he said with concern. 'I was watching from a window when I saw how you nearly fell to the ground.'

'I'll be stronger soon. I don't want to impose on your kind hospitality for too long.'

'You are not to worry about that or anything else. Now I'm going to see you to your room.'

The manservant carried her up the short flight into the house and then to the head of a sweeping staircase. In a large bedroom, a maid was waiting in attendance.

'I feel overwhelmed by all that is being done for me, Richard,' Louise said gratefully, once she was seated.

'It's a pleasure to help you get completely well again. Now rest. Just ask for anything you want.'

Later that day, when Richard came again to see her, she was in bed. She guessed that he would remark on the barely touched supper tray beside her and forestalled him.

'I'll do better tomorrow.'

He glanced at the tray before he returned her smile. 'I'm sure you will, but I didn't come to check up on you. I've something to tell you, now that you have rested. Until I received Dr Noiret's message two days ago, I thought you were in the country with your sister.'

'Why did you suppose that?' she asked in surprise.

'I heard it from Daniel Lombard. He had been looking everywhere for you. Finally the milliner told him where she believed you had gone, which set his mind at rest.'

'Why was he back in New York again so soon? He'd told me that he wouldn't be returning until the early autumn.'

'That was his intention, but he'd made this special trip with the best of motives. He wanted to take you and your sister out of the city and away from the danger of infection.'

'Is he still in New York?'

'No, he departed again as soon as he had brought me the news of you.'

After Richard had left her room, Louise thought over all he had told her. She was relieved that Daniel was no longer in the city, otherwise he would have found out that she was here. Another fraught scene with him was beyond her strength at the present time. She felt subdued by the knowledge that he had risked the danger of the yellow fever epidemic to take her and Delphine to safety.

Every day, tempting food was served to Louise in her room and gradually she began to regain her strength. Richard came regularly to see her just to chat, or else they would play chess or backgammon. Before long she was able to dine with him each evening in the small dining room in which he dined when alone. Above the fireplace there was a portrait of his wife, the artist having captured her delicate, almost ethereal beauty. She thought it no wonder that Richard had never found another woman to take her place.

At table they talked of Charles. No news had come from the camp, but all the time she could picture him in that tragic place, going from patient to patient, never sparing himself.

'Why didn't you leave the city when this outbreak of the fever first occurred?' she asked Richard one evening when they had left the table for the drawing room and sat with porcelain cups of tea, which she had poured from a silver teapot.

'As a boy I had the yellow fever, or something close to it. Nobody was ever sure, but it seems to have given me a certain immunity. As a result, not even the heat of summer can drive me out of New York. I have a rural home, but I prefer to go there on my own in the fall, when the trees are ablaze with colour and summer activities are over, all the neighbours having gone home to the city again.'

'That sounds idyllic.'

By the end of nearly three weeks of convalescence Louise felt well enough to return home. She announced her decision after coming indoors from her daily stroll in the tree-shaded flower garden that lay at the back of the house. Richard, who had been reading a newspaper, put it aside and left his chair to protest at once.

'It's too early! You're still convalescing and I gave my word to Charles that I'd keep you here until you had completely recovered your health.'

'You've been very kind and I'm extremely grateful, but I'm well again.'

He gave in reluctantly. 'At least you can go home with the good news I've just read in the newspaper. It is believed that the epidemic is on the wane at last.'

'That's truly wonderful news.'

'Now I must tell you another of Charles's requests that has been carried out. Everything in your apartment that might still have held the infection has been taken away and burnt.'

'By whom?' she exclaimed.

'I know someone who controls much of the manual work in the city. He sent in a couple of men prepared to take the risk for a suitable payment, and afterwards some women went in to scrub the whole place clean.'

She could scarcely believe what she was hearing. 'So, I'm going home to two empty rooms!'

'Not at all! Everything removed has been replaced. I have relied upon an advisor at the shop to supply it all as economically as possible. We both know Charles's funds are limited. I hope it will all be to your taste.'

'In the meantime, he is in debt to you.'

'It's of no consequence.'

'I shall repay every dollar,' she stated determinedly. 'Please give me all the receipts.'

Richard took them from his desk and gave them to her. Shortly afterwards she went home in one of his carriages with a hamper of food and some wine, which he had insisted that she take with her. Charles had returned her key to her before leaving for the camp, but it was with some trepidation that she turned it in the lock.

To her relief, the furniture in the first room remained untouched, except that she could see it had been recently scrubbed anew, as had the old black and white tiled floor. Even her old pots and pans had a fresh shine to them and she could tell that the crockery had been washed too, for it had not been replaced in exactly the same way on the cupboard shelves. But there were new drapes at the window and the red rug that had hung there was gone. In the bedroom there were also new drapes in a similar blue to before. Thick, more comfortable feather mattresses had been placed both on her bed and in her sister's wall-bed, but the sheets and covers were her own and had been laundered before being neatly stacked on a chair.

Abruptly she rushed to the closet and flung the door wide, fearful of finding it bereft of her clothes, but again the infection had been washed out of them and nothing was missing. Her shoes showed signs of having being immersed in water. Her yellow hat had suffered the same treatment, leaving its brim wavy and beyond repair.

That evening Louise wrote to Delphine, telling her all that had happened. She wished she could have written to Charles, but as yet there was no contact between the city and the camp. She felt tired and soon went to bed. Her last thought before sleeping was that now life was returning to normal it should not be long before Charles was home again.

Louise was pleased to find four letters waiting for her at the post office when she went next morning to send Delphine's letter on its way. She took them to a nearby park and sat on a bench to read them. None was from Delphine, but that did not surprise her, as she knew how all else could be forgotten when her sister was enjoying herself. Yet there was one from Mrs Hammond, saying that their visit of a month in the country would be extended for as long as the slightest danger of infection remained in the city. She closed by saying that the girls were having a happy time and her own social round was quite exhausting. Louise thought of Charles, whose round of another kind held the true meaning of the word.

The next letter was from Madeleine, full of concern for her and Delphine, another from Blanche being on the same anxious note. Louise made up her mind to write and reassure them both without delay. The last was from her Aunt Violette, which was mostly a medical report on her sick husband, who was growing weaker every day. Louise recalled her time with them in London and how the couple had been so much alike in enjoying life to the full, still unfashionably in love with each other. She wished so much that she could visit and help Violette at such a stressful time, but a whole great ocean stretched between them.

Putting the letters away in her purse, Louise left the park and went to the bank, where she had a banker's draft drawn up to settle the debt owed to Richard. After delivering it at his mansion, she set off again to see Miss Sullivan. As soon as she entered the shop the woman sprang up from her desk, her eyes icy, and rushed forward to grip the door open as if Louise would be leaving again immediately.

'How dare you come back here!' the woman screeched. 'Not a word from you for over a month! Not a message! At least you could have let me know that you were dancing off into the country with your sister! And all the trouble I had with Mr Lombard demanding to know your whereabouts as if I were hiding you somewhere. He had the audacity to stride past me into the work room and question everybody there. That's when one of the girls remembered that you had said something about your sister going to the country and you packing for yourself. Then we realized where you had gone.'

'She misunderstood me. I did the packing for my sister. I've been ill with the fever.' She noticed how the milliner instinctively recoiled. 'But I'm perfectly well again now. I could have sent word when I was convalescing, but I wanted to explain personally. If it's possible, I should like to return to work.'

Miss Sullivan, mollified, gave a slow nod and released the door for Louise to shut it. 'In that case I'm prepared to reconsider your appeal. There's scarcely any business at the moment, so many people out of town or scared to go anywhere that isn't absolutely necessary, but I want to build up a good stock for the fall and winter. The new fashion plates have come from London. I'll show them to you now.'

She was glad to have the Frenchwoman back again, for she had a skilful touch and imagination that outstripped her two best milliners, competent though they were. Louise, studying the London designs, was pleased to see that large hats, always the most flattering, were still shown, although with more restrained trimming, and there were smaller hats as well, which showed the direction in which fashion was moving.

The epidemic was declared at an end. Those who had survived the camp began to come home, but they were pitifully few in number compared with all those who had gone there. Louise began to watch for Charles, knowing he would come to her immediately, and expecting every knock on the door to be his. When it came, she rushed forward to open it and saw Richard standing there, his face grave.

'What's happened?' A sick dread plummeted down into the pit of her stomach. 'Is it Charles?'

He nodded, closing the door after him. 'I received the tragic news this evening and I've come at once to tell you.'

'The fever? When did it happen? Early on?' Her voice was a strangled whisper.

'No.' He led her across to a chair and sat down opposite her, taking both her hands into his. 'It happened today in the exodus from the camp of the last survivors. I'd sent his horse for him to ride home and he was already in the saddle, intending to be the last to leave. Then he saw that help was needed in moving a cart carrying convalescent women and children. He dismounted to put his shoulder to the cart with the others, but the man beside him slipped as it jerked forward and they fell together, the heavy wheel crushing Charles's chest. He died instantly.'

She stared at Richard, her eyes wide with shock, all colour drained from her face. For a few moments she sat immobile, her back very straight. The power of speech seemed to have left her. Then a great heart-wrenching sob burst from her and she bowed her head, her whole body shaking, and thumped her fists up and down on her knees as if her grief was beyond her strength to bear. All the time her tears fell unchecked on to her green skirt, making darker spots in a pattern of their own.

Richard found her terrible grief all the more harrowing for her silence after that one great sob and, remembering the utter desolation of his own bereavement, he knew that at the present time she was beyond comfort. Yet still he made an attempt.

'My dear young woman, try to take consolation in knowing that even if Charles had foreseen his death, he would still have gone to the camp to try to save the lives of others.'

At first he thought she had not heard his words, but eventually she gave an almost imperceptible nod. He had to strain his ears to hear her words.

'I know, and I shall always love him all the more for it.'

He was surprised. 'I knew you were close friends, but I hadn't realized that your feelings for each other went beyond friendship.'

She stood up slowly as if in a trance. Drifting across to the window, she looked out as if she expected to see Charles coming along the street. 'You don't understand,' she said in the same barely audible tones. 'I doubt if anyone could. Now so many things have been left unsaid. So many years lost.'

The relationship she had shared with Charles had been unique. They had both been aware of the love developing between them, but had been content to let it follow its own pace, both unsure where it would lead them. She had never felt closer to another human being and doubted that she ever would again. Yet they had never kissed, biding their time until the moment came. She drew her fingertip lightly across her brow as if the touch of his lips might still linger there from their last moments together.

Richard came across to her side. 'Would you like to come with me now and stay for a while as before? At least you'd not be on your own.'

She took a handkerchief from her pocket to wipe her eyes, although her tears continued to flow copiously. 'Thank you, but no. I need to be alone. It was thoughtful of you to come as quickly as you could to tell me.'

Reluctantly he left her. A week later he escorted her to the funeral. At Charles' graveside she threw a single white lily, symbol of the France into which they had both been born, on to his coffin.

Eight

News finally arrived late in September that set all the émigrés rejoicing. Louise rushed immediately to buy a newspaper, in which she read that at the end of July the tyrant, Robespierre, had finally been deposed and he and his confederates had been executed on the guillotine, where he had sent so many innocent people to their death. The Reign of Terror was at an end!

Her joy was in knowing that Justice had raised its head again in France. By now her homeland would be readjusting itself after years of turmoil, with a new government in power, who – judging from the newspaper's report – would be concentrating on winning the war against France's enemies. There would still be no return for any homesick Frenchmen and women listed in France as émigrés, for only those who had supported the Revolution were wanted there. In any case, all who had fled were mostly like herself in having had all their income and property sequestrated. There was nothing to go home to any more, no matter how those like Alexandre longed to return.

Delphine returned from the country in mid-September, Mrs Hammond having been extra cautious about coming back to the city too soon. As soon as Delphine entered the apartment she burst into tears and flung her arms around Louise in an emotional embrace. 'I could have lost you through that terrible fever!'

Louise, almost crushed, released herself breathlessly. 'But here I am, fit and well!' She paused. 'All thanks to Charles.'

Delphine drew back soberly. She had received the news of his death in a letter from her sister and was deeply sympathetic.

Before leaving for the country, she had seen how very fond her sister had become of him. 'I was so sorry about what happened.'

Louise nodded. As yet she could not talk of Charles, the pain was too great. 'I'll make some tea,' she said briskly, 'while you tell me about your stay in the country.'

'It was all right for the first four weeks, but nothing went right after that.' Delphine removed her shawl as she went into the bedroom to look at the new drapes and tidy herself.

It was always a special occasion when they had tea, which was expensive, and today Louise was marking her sister's return. She had the teapot and cups on the table when Delphine emerged. 'What happened?'

'We had lots of parties and good times, and on the whole Margaret behaved herself fairly well.' Delphine sat down and took the cup handed to her. 'But when our visit was extended she seemed to go mad. It was as if she felt she'd been reprieved from losing the freedom that we'd both been enjoying.'

'What happened?'

'She started bribing a servant to bring her bottles of wine, just because Mrs Hammond doesn't approve of intoxicants, and we drank it at night in our room. It was a poor wine and I hardly touched it, but Margaret would often end up vomiting.'

'Didn't that cure her?'

'No! Once at a party she became publicly tipsy on champagne. Her mother was furious! Naturally the woman no longer thought me a good influence and declared I was responsible for Margaret's behaviour, because I'd influenced her with my French ways. But there's more. Margaret had started flirting as if she'd never seen a young man before. Although previously she had done plenty of slipping away at parties for kisses, she started climbing out of the window at night to keep trysts with one or another of them.'

'Did you go too?'

'Yes, but not through choice. I'm never going to damage my chances with a rich man by losing my virginity through a fumbling by a stupid youth in the dark!' Delphine tossed her head in contempt at the idea. 'I was afraid Margaret would allow too many liberties if I wasn't hovering around, but perhaps she did in the end. Yesterday Mrs Hammond found her in the hay with one of the grooms. It was the last straw.'

Louise raised her eyebrows. 'What a disastrous turn of events!'

'Margaret hates me now as much as her mother, because she believes I told on her for being in the hayloft. But I didn't know where she was!' Then she shrugged cheerfully. 'But I don't care. Tomorrow evening will be my first at a Rousselot ball! Are my new evening gowns here?'

'They were delivered yesterday.'

'Just in time!' Delphine rushed into the bedroom to try them on.

The sisters settled down to a routine that was singularly peaceful after all the past traumas. Richard arranged a trip to his rural home to let them see the full glory of the autumn trees that made breathtaking canopies of scarlet and crimson, bronze and gold and brilliant yellow. Louise, her face upturned in wonder as she wandered under the branches, raised her hands to catch the occasional leaf that came fluttering down. She wished so much that Charles could have been with her. They'd never had the chance to share an American autumn together. So much had slipped away from them.

Delphine was not in attendance at all the Rousselot balls. Turns had to be taken with other female instructors, but as winter began to take hold, she noticed gleefully that when an extra one was needed, she was picked out more often than anyone else. Whenever she caught sight of her reflection in the ballroom mirrors she was in full agreement with those who complimented her by saying she was as light as thistledown when she glided about the floor.

It was a grey damp day when Louise suggested to Miss Sullivan that a single, richly coloured hat should be displayed on a stand in the window where the small panes prevented a clear vision to passers-by.

'A lighted candle-lamp placed on either side of it from opening to closing time would make it eye-catching to those going by in carriages as well as those on foot,' she concluded.

Miss Sullivan made a show of uncertainty as she always did before agreeing to Louise's latest idea. 'Perhaps you're right. But I leave the choice of hat and its arrangement to you.'

Louise changed the display hat every day before opening time, always choosing those in such sumptuous hues as Pompeian red, various shades of vivid green, King's Blue and acid yellows. The duller the day the more brilliant the hat. She added the swirl of a gauze stole around the base of the hat-stand or a cluster of ribbons and sometimes a large ostrich feather to enhance the hat itself. Carriages did draw up, increasing custom, especially on very wet days when customers were few and far between.

Early one morning, bright with winter sunshine, she was dressing the window when she saw Daniel go by in a hackney carriage from the direction of the harbour. He did not glance towards the shop and over two weeks went by with no other sign of him.

She was beginning to think he must have returned to Boston again when a shadow fell across her early one morning as she set a purple velvet hat on its stand. Glancing up, she saw Daniel standing there, looking hard at her through the window. Then he turned and stepped back into the carriage that was waiting for him. She realized that he had been unable to resist seeing her just once before his departure from the city.

There was light snow in time for Christmas and the street cleaners turned their brooms to keeping the streets and sidewalks clear. On New Year's Eve Louise dined with other guests at Richard's house and Delphine was at Monsieur Rousselot's for a grand ball. It was an hour before the old year gave way to 1795 when Delphine happened to glance towards some late arrivals at the ballroom. Her attention was caught by a young man, still with a boyish look about him, who had arrived with a party of friends about his own age. His fashionably cut hair was the colour of ripe wheat and, although he was only moderately good-looking, his straight, thin nose and strong chin came from a good bone formation, while his skin held a suntan that could only have come from some distant clime. He had a confident, self-assured air and must have been entirely aware of his fine physique as he stood, tall and square, to await Monsieur Rousselot, who was already crossing the room at his customary elegant pace to greet him and his companions.

Delphine, trapped with a partner in a lively minuet, had to keep turning away from the newcomer as they followed the intricate steps. Then, suddenly, as she rotated back once again, he turned his head and saw her, the glitter of impatience fading from his deep-lidded, very blue eyes. He raised his eyebrows appreciatively, showing that the sight of her was an unexpected pleasure. It was in that instant she fell in love.

Louise was home first and in bed when Delphine came bursting into the apartment, her face flushed and excited.

'I've so much to tell you!' she exclaimed, bouncing down on to the bed. 'I've met the man I'm going to marry! Not that he knows it yet!' She laughed in her exhilaration. 'His name is Pieter van Dorne and he's Dutch, but his home is in Banda in the Spice Islands. Where are they? I didn't dare show my ignorance.'

'The Dutch East Indies.'

'Oh, yes, I remember. He's twenty-two and his family has a nutmeg plantation. He's been here six months, learning all there is to know about the import side of the family business, which will be his one day.'

'How did you hear all this about him?'

'From Pieter himself during the one spare dance I had in the whole evening. And after he followed me home! When I left the ball with that miserable old chaperone I didn't know that he intended to come after me in his carriage. As soon I had entered the house he rushed in after me. We've been talking in the hall for nearly an hour. He wanted to know all about me, as I did about him.' She bounced up and down on the bed again. 'Say you're deliriously happy for me!'

'I'll have to meet him first,' Louise pointed out with a smile.

'So you shall. He wants to call on you next Sunday afternoon.' She leaned forward, supporting her weight on her hands, her face eager. 'On the day we landed here in New York, do you remember how that sack of nutmegs split on the wharf just in front of us? I think it was an omen! Do you recall what you said?'

Louise shook her head. 'It can't have been anything important.'

'But as I see it now, it was! You quoted an old saying about the wealth of Dutch plantation owners in the East Indies, because nutmegs are in such demand worldwide.'

'Oh, yes. *When a nutmeg tree is shaken, golden guilders fall from it.*'

'That's right! It means that not only is Pieter the most beautiful man I've ever seen, but he's as rich as Midas! A combination that I've always wanted.'

Louise sat up, linking her hands around her drawn-up knees. 'So, you're in love for the first time,' she observed dryly. 'Is it with the man or his money?'

'Don't tease! The man, of course! But it's wonderful to know that he's rich too. And I'm not just in love for the first time. It will be for ever!'

Louise thought to herself that, in addition to everything else that Delphine had attributed to him, he was also much travelled and was almost certainly worldly wise, but she would not make any prejudgements. She also knew better than to warn her sister at this point against letting her heart run away with her. Seeing Delphine so dazzled, it could have been herself at the same age after her first meeting with Fernand.

But Pieter van Dorne did not call on Sunday afternoon, through no fault of his own. New York was gripped by a savage blizzard that brought the whole city to a standstill. For three days the snow fell ceaselessly and then as abruptly the sky cleared to an icy, translucent blue and the city stirred into life again as householders and street cleaners shovelled and swept the snow from doorsteps and sidewalks. A message from Pieter confirmed that he would be calling the following Sunday to present himself.

He arrived exactly at the appointed time. Louise met him with a completely open mind and welcomed him to their home.

'I'm honoured to meet you, Madame de Vailly.' His Dutch accent was very pleasing, his smile revealed good white teeth, and his expression was interested and animated as he looked about the room with a boyish enthusiasm, taking in every detail. 'It was lucky that this street of old Dutch houses escaped the fire that once swept through this part of the city. Some ancestors of mine came from Holland to settle in New Amsterdam many years ago. Their surname was the same as mine. Perhaps they lived in this very house!'

'I've often wondered about those who first made a home under this roof.' Louise shared his interest. 'That would have been long before it was divided into apartments.'

'From now on, think of those people as my forebears,' he suggested exuberantly.

Louise was amused. 'It would certainly bring them to life in my mind.'

During the afternoon, Pieter volunteered information about his parents, his brother, Jan, who was two years younger than himself, and the family home. It was for Louise's benefit, Delphine having heard it all before at their first meeting, although she still gave him her rapt attention.

'Mademoiselle Delphine has told me about the château you both had to leave in such dangerous circumstances,' he continued. 'I'm hoping to visit France one day when everything is back to normal. Before the Revolution my father did a great trade in exporting our nutmegs there. I'd like to re-establish it before I go home again.'

'That could be quite a while yet, with France at war,' Louise pointed out.

'I'm in no hurry to leave these shores.' He looked across at Delphine and they shared a private smile.

Louise took the opportunity to ask him about Banda and the Spice Islands. He responded willingly.

'Banda itself is a busy little place with ships coming all the time for cargoes of nutmegs and cloves from the various plantations.' He obviously enjoyed talking about his birthplace. 'There is a volcano, but it's been inactive for as long as anybody can remember.' His voice took on a low, almost caressing note. 'Exotic flowers bloom everywhere and we have the most wonderful sunsets. All the colours that come with the trees in the American fall are there in the same rich depth, turning the sea to the same hues before the night comes quite suddenly, melting everything to a warm, velvety darkness, with the sky more full of stars than anywhere else on earth.'

A few moments of silence followed. Louise found herself wondering how many times he had cast that spell over women as he conjured up those scenes of beauty with the same soft words. That boyish appearance of his was deceptive. Beneath the surface there was nothing naive about him.

'You are quite poetic, Mr van Dorne,' she said.

'It's impossible not to be when describing the islands. I believe them to be the most beautiful in the world.'

Louise thought to herself that he must have been asked about his birthplace countless times since coming to this country and was probably genuinely homesick when he spoke of its wonders. 'Tell us more,' she requested.

'Well, I know how much you and Mademoiselle Delphine would like to see the turtles when they've just hatched out from the sands of the beach and, tiny though they are, go scurrying towards the sea. As for the island people, they are fine-looking, wear colourful clothes and know how to enjoy themselves. They like to race their long narrow boats, often twenty-six oarsmen in each, and afterwards they dance and sing far into the night.'

'It sounds like paradise,' Louise remarked admiringly.

'It is to me,' he admitted.

The day ended with Pieter taking them to supper at Belvedere

House. As soon as Delphine was home again she turned eagerly to Louise.

'What do you think? Isn't he interesting? And fun to be with? Surely all he said made you want to visit the Spice Islands?'

'I should love to see them,' Louise agreed sincerely. 'I'm sure they're as beautiful as he described.'

'But it will be a long time before he'll be going home again,' Delphine smiled with satisfaction. 'He has to go to France first.'

Louise regarded her quizzically. 'Do you mean that spending the rest of your life in the Spice Islands doesn't appeal to you?'

'I didn't say that,' Delphine declared happily. 'It's all far into the future anyway. In the meantime he is enrolling in Monsieur Rousselot's adult classes for the very latest dances, and I'll be there to assist.'

'I suppose Pieter will be at the balls too?'

'Yes, when I'm there. I'm going to ask Monsieur Rousselot if I can attend them all now that I'm one of his best teachers.'

Delphine put her request to the dancing master next morning, but he refused, saying that she was already allotted more attendances than the other teachers. But she did not tell Louise of his refusal, thinking it would suit her to have some Saturday evenings to do as she pleased. Pieter had already spoken of hoping to see her other than in her sister's company or at the dancing school.

Her scheme did not work out well at first. She had to make the pretence of going to the Saturday evening balls when she was not required there. Fortunately nobody noticed her slip into one of the practice rooms, where she either danced in front of the mirror for her own benefit or read a book. Her ride home with the chaperone and two other dancing teachers was not queried and so each time she escaped a cold late-night walk in the dark. Then, if Louise happened to ask her about the evening, she was careful to say that Pieter had been unable to come due to some other engagement. In this way she was able to prevent anything untoward coming to light in any later conversation her sister might have with him.

Whenever Pieter took the three of them to the theatre or some other entertainment, it seemed all too familiar to Louise. She was reminded of when Daniel had escorted them both, although her role was now that of chaperone to her sister and she was still not easy in her mind about the Dutchman. Maybe she was just being over-protective, but after so many years it was a habit hard to dispel. She reminded herself that Delphine's experiences with Margaret in the summer had shown that she knew how to keep level-headed in a difficult situation. What was more, whenever Delphine made up her mind about something, she could be as stubborn as a mule, and keeping herself intact until marriage was the strongest motive in her life.

As soon as Delphine had let Pieter know that on certain Saturday evenings she was only at the dancing school to practice, he swept her into his own social circle at parties where the people she met were far more exciting to her than any she had met before. He taught her to gamble and she became adept at cards, often winning, but he would foot her losses if her luck ran out. She was always careful never to take too much wine or to let Pieter delay in taking her home, for if Louise suspected, there would be terrible trouble and she could foresee these wonderful evenings coming to an end. She had sworn Pieter to secrecy and he had been only too willing to oblige. She lived for his kisses and caresses, but she was resolved that there should be nothing more before a wedding ring was on her finger.

It was an evening early in April at one of the parties, when gaming was in full swing, that Daniel came from a neighbouring room, where he had been playing cards. He was astonished to see Delphine and looked around for Louise, only to find that she was not there. A short conversation with a friend gave him the information he required, and he took a long look at Pieter van Dorne before he left. Neither she nor Pieter knew that they had been the focus of his attention.

During the interval of a play at the St John's Theatre, Louise stayed seated in the box, giving Pieter and her sister the chance to stroll the passageways and have a little time to themselves. She had just flicked open her fan against the heat of the candlelights that illumined the stage and the auditorium when the door reopened. She thought they had returned sooner than expected, but as she turned her head she saw it was Daniel who had entered.

'Good evening to you, Louise.' He took the chair next to her. 'I haven't seen you for quite a while. Last time it was a mere glimpse through the milliner's window.' His handsome mouth parted in a grin. 'With those panes of glass between us there was no danger of my getting another rebuff.'

She ignored his jibe, remembering how he had come to New York during the epidemic. 'I've never thanked you for making a special journey at the time of the yellow fever,' she said evenly.

He shrugged as if it were nothing. 'I feared that as virtual newcomers to this country you would underestimate its danger. Since then, of course, I've heard from Richard all that happened.'

She was afraid he might mention Charles and spoke quickly. 'Are you enjoying the play?'

He regarded her thoughtfully, as if light chit-chat between them was a waste of time. 'I've seen better,' he answered casually. 'Incidentally, I saw Delphine and Pieter van Dorne in the passage. Neither of them noticed me. By the manner in which they were gazing at each other, they looked like a newly betrothed couple. Is that the situation?'

'No, not yet, but I believe a betrothal to be in the offing.'

'Indeed? Do you approve?'

'I want my sister to be happy,' she answered, not wanting to discuss her doubts with him or anyone else. As always when he was near, she was uncomfortably aware of his intense male presence, which seemed even more powerful in the shadowed interior of the box. In a moment of fantasy she thought that, if he should touch her, sparks would most surely fly up from the contact. 'How do you know Pieter's name?'

'Through being in the import business myself. Pieter van Dorne is a fortunate "Nutmeg Lord", as these Dutchmen are called in the trade. He's heir to a great plantation and has your pretty sister in love with him. His only misfortune is in having a father who rules his family and his plantation like a despot. It's an old saying that money isn't everything.'

Louise looked at him sharply. Was he giving her some sort of warning? But already he was asking her if she had seen Richard recently. 'Not since I dined at his house three weeks ago,' she answered. 'He is a good friend.'

'I agree. I was there yesterday.' Daniel rose to leave. 'It's always a pleasure to see you, Louise. Enjoy the rest of the play.'

The door closed after him. When Delphine and Pieter returned they found her deep in thought. They were hardly in their seats before the curtain went up again.

The following evening after supper Louise chose a moment to talk to Delphine about Pieter, for Daniel's few words had had the effect of strengthening her private misgivings. She had also noticed how secretive her sister had become, whereas in the past she had always been so open and confiding. 'I don't mean to pry,' Louise began, uncertain how Delphine would react, 'but has Pieter spoken directly of marriage to you?'

Delphine smiled smugly. 'Many times.'

'If he has proposed, why haven't you told me? And since you're in my care, shouldn't he have spoken to me first?'

'He will do when it's time to make everything formal.'

'Do you mean he hasn't actually asked you yet?'

'He will when the moment is right.'

'What makes you so sure?'

'Pieter wrote to his father the day after he met me, telling him that he'd found the girl he wanted for his wife.' Delphine dived down between her breasts and produced a wide ring on a ribbon. 'He told me when he gave me this token of his undying love. It's his own ring from his little finger, but as it's too large for me to wear, I'm keeping it close to my heart.' She kissed it and let it drop back again out of sight, her face radiant. 'When some more money comes through from his father, he intends to buy me a beautiful betrothal ring. That's when he'll ask your permission to marry me.'

Louise felt the grip of dismay, remembering what Daniel had said about Pieter's father holding the purse strings, which was an easy way to keep a wayward son on a leash. 'Don't bank on everything going just as you wish, Delphine,' she implored. 'Promises can be broken so easily.'

Instantly Delphine's good humour vanished. 'You don't like Pieter, do you?'

'I didn't say that. He's very pleasant, as well as good company, and he has a quick sense of humour, which I enjoy. There isn't a thing against him that I could name. But you should remember that he's not his own master yet and no doubt he has obligations to his father and his future inheritance.'

'I have to admit that's true,' Delphine said sullenly. 'His father sends him fresh instructions with every nutmeg ship. Pieter knows that sooner or later he'll be told to return home.'

'Does he want to leave here?'

'No, of course not! He's still determined to go to France and says that we'll be married before we go.'

'That seems to endorse his wish to make you his wife.'

'Don't have any doubts about that!' Delphine gave back heatedly. 'The fact is that, even though I love him with my whole heart, I wouldn't want to go to France with him. Not because it would be difficult for me to regain entry there, because under a new name all would go well.' She drew her chair closer, her expression troubled. 'I've never told you this before, but I've a terrible foreboding that, if ever I set foot on a ship again, I'll drown at sea. I'd rather have gone to the guillotine than let that happen to me.'

Louise took Delphine's hand into both her own. 'I know you were badly frightened during that storm on the *Ocean Maid* and so was everybody else.' She recalled vividly the wildly swinging lanterns, the screams of women as the great waves crashed over the ship, and Delphine huddled like a terrified child in her arms as water swirled under the cabin door. 'But we came through it safely, as you would on any other ship. The weather isn't always bad on the sea, as you should know. Next time you could cross the ocean as if sailing on the proverbial millpond.'

Delphine shuddered. 'It's not just the voyage to France that worries me. If the day ever comes when Pieter wants to go back to Banda, just think what that would mean for me! A voyage around Cape Horn and then on again almost for ever! There's only one solution open to me.' She cheered up visibly at the thought of it. 'I've had it worked out from the start.'

'So tell me.'

Delphine's confidence had returned. 'It's so lucky for me that Pieter is set on restarting the French trade, because it gives me the extra time I want. I think he was in his father's bad books when he left home, and this coup would reinstate him in the old man's eyes. So after we're married and living in a grand mansion on Lower Broadway he can go to France on his own and then return to me. That's when I'll persuade him to stay here and take full control of the importing of the van Dorne nutmegs, leaving his brother to care for the plantation.'

Louise shook her head. 'No, no, Delphine! That's only a daydream. The time will come when he'll decide to go home, no matter what you say. If you love him enough, when that day comes you'll have to conquer your fear and go with him.'

Delphine's eyes flashed angrily and she sat back in her chair. 'If he loves me enough he'll stay. I don't want to live anywhere else in the world but here!'

'Then the only advice I can offer is that you bide your time.'

'As you did with Charles!' Delphine retorted furiously. 'Much good it did you!'

Louise, her face stricken, raised her arm swiftly and struck her sister hard across the cheek. Then abruptly she sprang to her feet, her chair falling to the floor with a clatter, and turned away, her shoulders bowed, her face in her hands.

Delphine stared at her, stunned that for the first time in her life Louise had hit her. She put her fingers tentatively to her reddening cheek. She was not angry any longer, only filled with remorse at her own thoughtless cruelty. Standing, she addressed Louise's back in a faltering voice.

'I'm so sorry. Please forgive me. I didn't mean to be so cruel. You know how thoughtless I can be at times.' She rested her hands lightly against Louise's shoulders. 'Don't hate me, even though I deserve it.'

Louise lowered her hands and with tears in her eyes she turned slowly to face her sister. 'I don't hate you. I never could, no matter what happens.'

Thankfully, Delphine threw her arms around her and the two of them embraced tightly. Louise, her face still full of pain from the thoughtless barb, hoped desperately that Delphine with her romantic dreams would never experience the wrenching heartache that was still hers.

Louise decided that when summer came they would visit Madeleine and Theodore in Boston. There was no reason why her path and Daniel's should cross there, but if that did happen it would be a passing incident, as when he had come to the theatre box.

Louise was enjoying a musical evening at Richard's house when Delphine arrived at the dancing school for the ball, where she was to meet Pieter. Monsieur Rousselot had restricted the number of times she was allowed to dance with him, having told her sternly that no guest had the right to monopolize her as had happened previously. She did not mind, for it added deliciously to her anticipation in the glances they exchanged and the amusement she shared with him in the comically yearning expression he conjured up from across the room. It was always an exciting moment when he took her hand to lead her on to the floor, the pressure of his gloved fingers conveying all sorts of messages to her.

This evening he was late. Delphine kept looking towards

the door. Two of the dances that should have been his went by and she began to be anxious. What could have delayed him? When she sighted one of his gaming friends she swept across the room in a whisper of rose silk to speak to him.

'William, have you seen Pieter? He should have been here two hours ago.'

He looked startled and then uncomfortable. 'Didn't you know, Delphine? Surely he told you?'

She felt herself turn icy cold with dread, all colour draining from her face. 'Told me what?' she demanded in a harsh whisper.

William drew her to one side, out of earshot of anyone else. 'He's sailing on the van Dorne ship tonight. It was a last-minute decision after he received a final ultimatum from his father to return home when the vessel docked yesterday. The old devil was going to cut him off without a guilder if he didn't return on that same ship.'

Delphine's whole face felt stiff. She could hardly voice the question she felt compelled to ask. 'Was it because Pieter wanted to marry me?'

'No. Pieter's time here was already up when he met you, and after that he continually ignored a paternal order to return home that came with every one of his father's ships. Ever since this final letter, Pieter has been busy packing and clearing up business matters.' Pitying her, he decided a harmless little lie would ease the blow that had been dealt her. 'I'm sure Pieter told me he had sent you an urgent message to inform you of his departure.'

'It must have been for me to join him!' she declared fixedly, her eyes still wide with shock. 'Louise must have kept it from me, knowing my terror of the sea. I don't care if I do drown as long as I'm in Pieter's arms! He'll be watching and waiting for me. What time does the ship sail?'

'Half past eleven.'

She grabbed the young man's arm. 'There's still time! Take me to the docks now!' When he protested she shook her head frantically, not listening to anything he said. 'Now!'

He could see she was bordering on hysteria and thought it wise to do as she wished. It was Pieter's responsibility, not his. She ran ahead of him down the curved staircase and he followed, calling for his carriage. As it bowled along on its way to the East River docks, she sat staring unseeingly through the window, talking more to herself than to the embarrassed young man, who was regretting that he had allowed himself to become entangled in this nightmare situation.

'The captain can perform the marriage ceremony,' she was saying. 'You will have to tell my sister what's happened and where I've gone. Pieter will be so thankful to see me. It's much better for us to arrive married at Banda, a fait accompli if his father should raise any objections. But there shouldn't be any lasting difficulty. There isn't a man I can't charm if I've a mind to it.'

William decided that she was mad. Rambling on as she was, it seemed certain that Pieter's desertion had turned her brain. He snapped open his gold watch, able to see in the passing lantern light that sailing time was only minutes away. She did not look in his direction, but spoke as if he was the one needing to be reassured.

'Pieter won't let the ship sail without me.' Her voice was still strange. They passed through the harbour gates, the coachman stopping only for William to enquire from which wharf the van Dorne ship would be sailing. Then on they went again, the wheels rattling over the cobbles. There was plenty of activity everywhere in the lantern light, the vessels looming large as they passed by. When they reached the van Dorne berth Delphine leapt out of the carriage only to stand staring in disbelief at the ship sailing away in the moonlight. Then, before William could stop her, she hurled herself with a piercing scream into the water.

Nine

Delphine did not take long to recover physically from her ordeal, but mentally was a different matter. William and a sailor had dived in to save her, and others had come to help them get back up on to the wharf. Then the sailor had kicked over a barrel to throw her limp body across it, face down, and pump the water out of her in the time-honoured way of the sea until she coughed and spluttered as it gushed from her mouth. Louise had just returned home when William arrived, carrying her sister in his arms, wrapped in his coat, her wet hair streaming down like dark copper silk with a single strand of seaweed entangled in it. As he was leaving again, neither he nor Louise noticed that Delphine overheard him tell Louise of the lie he had told her.

As the days went by Delphine, listless and apathetic, went for hours without speaking, only ever answering in monosyllables. Louise became increasingly anxious about her. Such silence was distressingly unnatural in a normally garrulous girl, and there was no question yet of her returning to work.

Adding to the change in her, Delphine had stubbornly taken over all the household chores and the marketing, whereas previously she had always been reluctant to do her full share. It was as if she needed to be busy every minute to keep from remembering. Although she was up first every morning to prepare breakfast and always had a meal ready when Louise came home, she scarcely touched food herself and became visibly thinner until the simple clothes she wore daily began to hang on her. Monsieur Rousselot, who had been told that Delphine was unwell, sent word to ask when she would be returning. Delphine only shook her head at the letter and let it drop on to the table.

'I never want to dance again,' she said dully in the longest sentence she had used to date.

Louise was at a loss to know how best to help her recover her spirits. Previously there had been rarely a day when Delphine had not played her flute, but now it lay neglected in its box and was never touched. Louise decided that the only solution would be to get her away from New York, with its painful memories. There were plenty of other cities, maybe even Washington itself, where already people were buying some of the newly built properties, and there should be plenty of opportunities for her as an experienced milliner. It would be exciting to live in the very heart of this new nation. By selling one of her most valuable pieces of jewellery, she could even finance a small dancing school for Delphine. But for the present she would accept Alexandre and Blanche's long-standing invitation to stay with them, which would give Delphine the chance to fully recover in the country air.

She went to see Monsieur Rousselot on Delphine's behalf. He was understanding and expressed his hope that Delphine would soon be well again, but it was a different matter when Louise gave Miss Sullivan notice of her departure. As she had expected, the milliner was furious that she would be leaving on the brink of the summer season, no matter what the reason.

'This time there will be no coming back when it suits you!' the woman declared fiercely, handing over Louise's wages. 'Goodbye to you.'

Quite unexpectedly Alexandre came himself in answer to the letter that Louise had sent, turning up on the doorstep with a beaming smile. 'I've combined a business trip with the pleasure of escorting you both back to the farm with me,' he announced, hiding his private shock at Delphine's emaciated appearance, having last seen her in France as a healthy, pretty child. 'Blanche can hardly wait for your arrival. She's been baking and preparing ever since your letter came, and so, if you're ready and packed, we'll leave tomorrow.'

Louise had withdrawn her jewellery and her small amount of savings from the bank and had only to hand the apartment keys to the landlord. She had also said farewell to Richard and to others whom she knew would miss her, with promises exchanged to keep in touch. A stallholder from the market had bought the furniture and all else that she had thought pointless to take with them. With their clothes and possessions packed into two trunks and a wooden box, they set off with Alexandre for the country, leaving New York behind them.

The voyage on a sloop up the great Hudson river took over twenty-four hours and was a holiday in itself to Louise, although Delphine spent most of the time in the cabin that they shared, showing no interest in anything. The weather could not have been better – very warm, with a soft breeze – and when Louise was on deck with Alexandre, or eating a meal with him by a saloon window, she was enthralled by the passing scenery. It was a panoramic vista of lush foliage, thick forests ancient as time, clustering blossoms in a variety of colours, mountain slopes and sheer rocky precipices. When the sloop called in at one of the small towns along the way there was the chance to buy moccasins and beadwork from women of one of the tribes whom Louise thought of as the true-born Americans. Their quiet dignity and the proud, straight-backed stance of their men, waiting a short distance away, filled her with admiration.

When the time came to disembark, it was late morning on a day full of sunshine. Waiting for them was a horse and carriage, brought by a strongly built man, whom Alexandre addressed as George. He was a freed slave and one of several farmhands whom Alexandre employed.

'My pleasure, ma'am,' George said when Louise thanked him as he handed her up to sit beside Alexandre, who had taken the reins. Delphine said nothing when he assisted her. He had been quick to load up the luggage and sat on one of the trunks as they set off for the farm, which was only a mile away and encompassed many acres of pasture, cropland and forest.

As they drew near the farmhouse, Blanche came running to meet them, her flower-printed skirt billowing about her. Her delicately shaped face with the lustrous brown eyes and high arched brows, which gave her the look of being perpetually amazed at life's goodness to her, was alight with joy. Some tendrils of her blue-black hair danced from their pins as she approached, her arms outstretched in welcome. Louise sprang down from the carriage without waiting for George's helping hand and rushed into a shared embrace, both of them almost overcome by their reunion, and they kissed each other on both cheeks in the French manner.

'You're here at last!' Blanche exclaimed thankfully as they drew apart to laugh together in their happiness. 'I can't begin to tell you how much I've been longing for your visit.' She turned eagerly to Delphine and kissed her too, seeming not to notice a lack of response. 'How wonderful to have you here! I want so much for you to feel at home with us.' She stepped back and flung her arms wide in exhilaration. 'You are both more welcome than the flowers in May, as we used to say to each other in France long ago.'

Arm in arm with Louise, Blanche led the way up to the farmhouse while Delphine followed behind with Alexandre, who pointed out various landmarks to her, undaunted by her lack of interest. He and his wife had been well prepared by Louise's letter for the state she was in and they both intended to do their best for her.

Louise studied the farmhouse with interest as they approached. It stood on a rise, giving it a fine view in all directions. She had expected it to be a log cabin, having glimpsed so many along the river banks, but this was a large single-storey house, built of wood, its clapboards white and the door a cheerful red, as were the window frames and shutters. A shady veranda encompassed it on all sides.

'What a charming house!' she exclaimed.

'This wasn't our first home here,' Blanche explained. 'There was just a little log cabin when we came, but as soon as the land was in order, Alexandre had our new house built on this site.

It gives a view of the river and I love it.' Then she spotted her daughter's face at one of the windows. 'There's Henrietta! She was too shy to come with me to meet you, but that won't last. She is used to people constantly coming on business or socially.'

Louise waved to the child, who promptly disappeared, but as they took the steps up to the house, Henrietta had come to the door. She had the confidence and self-assurance of the much-loved child and she stared up at Louise, her eyes more golden than brown, her piquant little face pink-cheeked and framed by a cloud of russet hair that matched her father's.

'Bonjour, madame,' she said, her words singularly articulate for her three and a half years, and she held out her hand. 'Come with me. I'll show you to your room. It's very pretty. Papa has painted it pink for you.'

Louise was enchanted by her and took her proffered hand. 'How kind of you, Henrietta, but first of all I'd like you to meet Delphine.' She had hoped her sister would at least smile at the child, but Delphine only glanced at her and then away again.

Louise let the child guide her to the bedroom while Blanche took charge of Delphine. It smelt of new paint and new fabric, the gauzy white drapes at the window still crisp in their folds. There was a door that opened to the veranda, as had every other room in the house. Through the window she could see an orchard and beyond that was a wide stretch of woodland.

'You live in a beautiful place, Henrietta,' Louise said as she removed her hat and cloak. 'Do you have many playmates?'

'Betsy is my best friend.' Henrietta had perched on the edge of the bed, swinging her legs to and fro. 'We share her baby sister and my pony and the cat and five new kittens and my duck and my toys.'

'Where does Betsy live?'

'In the cabin that was our home once. George is Betsy's papa and Maria her mama.' Then the child's eyes widened in delight as Louise took from her tapestry bag the doll that she had bought in New York. 'Is she for me? *Merci!*'

'What name shall you give her?'

Henrietta slithered down from the bed to hug the doll to her and kiss its painted wooden face. 'Sophie! It's such a pretty name.'

At that point George appeared with a trunk balanced on his shoulder. Henrietta, although she had been prattling away in French, immediately switched to English. 'Where's Betsy? I want to show her our new doll!'

He lowered the trunk and smiled at her as he set it down by the wall. 'You'll find her in the kitchen.'

The child went running off, followed by George on his way to bring in the rest of the luggage. A few minutes later Blanche appeared in the doorway. Louise, tidying her hair in front of the mirror, turned towards her.

'You're bringing your daughter up to be bilingual and, even more important, unselfish,' she said admiringly.

'We're doing our best. Alexandre is determined that none of the bad old ways of the French aristocracy shall contaminate our lives here.'

'How wise you both are!'

'Let me show you the rest of the house. Delphine is coming too.'

Delphine followed them through the pleasant rooms, all simply and comfortably furnished, and they ended the tour in the large kitchen. There Louise met George's wife, Maria, a good-looking woman, also a freed slave, who helped Blanche in the house. Her baby, only three months old, was asleep in a home-made basket cot in which Maria carried her to the farmhouse every day.

'Luckily Lily is a good baby and doesn't interfere with my work very much,' she said to Louise.

Blanche, leaning over the cot, glanced up over her shoulder with a smile. 'We love having a baby in the house again. Henrietta and Betsy will have this little one to play with them too later on.'

'Where are the girls now?' Louise asked.

She nodded towards the window. 'They're outside with the new doll.'

Louise looked out and saw the two children, one head as dark as the other was coppery, changing the doll's frock for another out of a basket of tiny clothes.

Blanche gave a little laugh. 'They'll play for hours there, but don't think it's always like that. They're like two squabbling kittens sometimes. Now it's time you and Delphine had some refreshment after your journey. I can see that Maria has everything almost ready.'

The light and delicious meal was served in the dining room, where the wallpaper had a design of green leaves on a white background, which gave it an airy, open-air look, aided by the sunshine penetrating the slatted blinds. Delphine scarcely touched the food and sat silent the whole time. Blanche would have shown her concern, but having been forewarned, she made no comment.

Louise was surprised to find how many of her titled countrymen and women had settled within the vicinity. Some had bought farms, others had started their own small businesses in Albany and Troy, the two nearest towns, just as they had done in New York. As a result, Blanche and Alexandre's social life was far more active than she had ever expected, and her friends were a welcoming host and hostess whenever they entertained.

Although it was a peaceful area, Alexandre had never been easy in his mind when he had had to leave Blanche on her own for any length of time, for peddlers and tramps often came to the farm door on their travels. Not all of them were to be trusted. There had been cases of rape and it was for that reason he had taught her how to handle a gun. Now that Louise was under his roof he thought it advisable to teach her to shoot too. He was a patient instructor and she was quick to learn, having a steady hand and eye. Before long she excelled at hitting the target that he set up.

To Louise's intense disappointment Delphine remained locked in her room whenever there were visitors, no matter how merry the gatherings must have sounded to her in her isolation. Few people ever saw her, although, knowing of her presence, some included her in their invitations, but she was adamant in refusing all of them. She also retained her silence as one week and then another went by. She was still only picking at food and seemed to get thinner every day.

Blanche undertook many of the lighter chores, as with any other farmer's wife. Yet not once had Delphine offered to help her hostess, even ignoring Louise's suggestion that she could at least collect the eggs or feed the hens. Instead, while Louise churned butter or gave their hostess a hand making cheese, skimming milk or tending the herb garden, Delphine went off on walks by herself, often staying away for hours. At first her lengthy absences had caused alarm, but it soon became apparent that it was only solitude that she sought. In the end it was George, who all unwittingly was instrumental in instigating her recovery.

She was coming back to the farmhouse one afternoon when she paused by the stables to take some grit out of her shoe. George, who was in charge of the horses among his other tasks, happened to see her as she was putting it on again. He came out of the tack room with Blanche's saddle, which he had been polishing.

'You ride like the other ladies, don't you, Miss Delphine? I ask, 'cause Mrs de Clement's mare, Séraphine, hasn't been ridden for several days and needs some exercise.'

Delphine was on the point of refusing abruptly, although she had always loved horses and riding, perhaps even more than Louise. Then she thought how much farther she could get away from the house if she rode, and all else it might do for her. 'Yes, I'll take her out for a while.'

As soon as she was in the saddle, Delphine experienced again the almost forgotten pleasure of being able to set off on a splendid horse to ride wherever she wished. Séraphine was frisky at first, being as glad to be out as Delphine was to have charge of her. They went off at a canter, the glossy brown mare and the thin rider, whose almost claw-like hands held the reins expertly, but as if they were a lifeline.

Every day Delphine went riding and became as fond of

Séraphine as she had been of her own horse, which she had ridden so often through the French countryside. Blanche was pleased that her horse had given the girl some interest, and both she and Louise noticed how her appetite improved. Soon Delphine regained her lost weight and even put on a little more. She had begun conversing again and during dinner in the evenings she told what she had seen and where she had been that day. Once she had ridden into Troy and bought some hair ribbons, and another time she had followed for several miles the travellers' road that led to Albany and beyond, saying how some soldiers, drinking outside a tavern, had cheered her as she went by.

Louise felt that Delphine's recovery was surely complete when she heard her playing her flute on the veranda, where Henrietta and Betsy, not minding that Delphine always ignored them, sat side by side on a step listening to her.

Louise decided that it was getting close to the time when she and Delphine must draw their stay to an end. Blanche happened to overhear her asking Alexandre's advice about her idea of settling in Washington.

'You can't go yet, Louise!' she exclaimed in dismay. 'It's far too soon. At least stay the rest of the summer! In fact, I don't think you have a choice.'

'I wish you would stay,' Alexandre endorsed. 'It's like old times, with the three of us being together, and the extra time should prepare Delphine fully for taking up her life again.'

'I'm easily persuaded,' Louise admitted gratefully. 'Until the end of the summer, then. It will give me time to write some letters of enquiry and finalize my plans.'

Delphine came into the house soon afterwards. She had been galloping Séraphine across the pastures and had jumped three high fence rails that had stood in their way. Blanche had seen her from the window, not for the first time, and met her in the hall to express concern.

'I don't want to spoil your pleasure in riding Séraphine,' she said gently, 'but I'd like you to ride her at an easier pace. I'm so afraid you will take a bad fall if she suddenly baulks at a fence or if you fell together and were both injured.'

Delphine's face twisted with misery. 'If that's how little you think of my riding ability, I won't ride her ever again!'

Even as Blanche protested that she had no wish to ban her from the saddle, Delphine bolted to her room. In spite of entreaties outside her locked door, she did not appear for dinner, replying that she was not hungry. In the morning she slipped out of the house while the others were at breakfast and went walking alone as before.

Blanche wept. 'I've undone all the good that's been achieved. But I was only considering her well-being. I haven't mentioned it to you before, Louise, because I kept hoping I was mistaken, but I think Delphine is pregnant.'

Louise caught her breath. 'Can it be?'

'Just think about it,' Blanche advised, her face distressed. 'Was Delphine's wretchedness due entirely to heartache or was it more? Then there's the extra weight she has gained. What's more, I fear all the recent galloping and jumping has been to cause a miscarriage.'

'But she's had no morning sickness!'

'She could have gone in and out of her veranda door unseen and none of us would have heard her in the outside privy.'

'How blind I've been!' Louise paced the floor, a hand to her forehead. 'Why ever didn't I grasp the situation? So that's the reason you said I really had no choice when you spoke of us staying on here?'

Blanche nodded. 'It's so fortunate that you are both staying with us at this time. Delphine can have the baby here without any outsider knowing about it. All scandal can be avoided. You've already planned on starting afresh in a new place and, as an émigré, Delphine can appear to be a young widow with her baby. There will be nothing to sully her good name.'

'You have thought everything out, Blanche.' Louise, although still uncertain, was deeply touched by her friend's wish to protect Delphine. She knew Blanche hated subterfuge as much as she, but Delphine as a single girl with a baby would be shunned everywhere. All her dreams of marrying well would be at an end, quite apart from the stigma of illegitimacy her innocent child would bear all through life. The future would be bleak for both. 'I'll talk to Delphine when she comes back later.'

That afternoon Louise and Blanche were busy in the dairy when Maria suddenly burst through the door. 'Come quickly, ma'am! You too, Madame Louise! I just came back from the wash house with the laundry and found Miss Delphine lying in a faint on the kitchen floor!'

Louise was first out of the dairy, kicking off the wooden pattens that kept her feet above the damp stone floor, and ran out into the sunshine, up towards the house. Blanche, who had been about to skim a bowl of cream, dropped it accidentally in her alarm, but kicked it heedlessly out of her way, splashing cream everywhere and leaving her pattens in her wake as she followed Louise at speed. Both of them feared they would find Delphine miscarrying.

Sensibly, Maria had kept the children out of the way and Louise and Blanche were alone as they flung themselves down on their knees beside the unconscious girl. There was no sign of blood, but a strong smell of alcohol. Louise, raising Delphine's head on her arm, looked at Blanche in bewilderment.

'She's drunk! Completely senseless!'

Blanche reached under the kitchen table and brought out an empty bottle of her husband's home-distilled spirit. 'Look at this! Not a drop left. We'd better get her to bed quickly. She's going to feel very ill indeed when she comes round.'

It was late evening when Delphine began to moan as she recovered consciousness. Louise, sitting by the bed, grabbed a bowl and held it for her just in time as she vomited violently over and over again. On the opposite side of the bed Blanche watched her with pity before summoning Maria, who took away the used bowl and left a spare one in case it should be needed. Delphine fell back again on to the pillows, her face drained white. Louise took a damp cloth and wiped her sister's trembling mouth.

'We know you're pregnant, Delphine,' Louise said quietly. She groaned. 'Haven't I lost the baby?'

'No. Did you suppose an excess of alcohol would do it when galloping Séraphine and taking fences with her failed to work?'

'It's what I hoped,' Delphine answered in a weak voice. 'I remembered one of the assistants in the millinery workshop telling of her sister drinking gin and jumping off the kitchen table for a miscarriage.'

'Is that what you did?' Blanche asked, aghast.

'I couldn't find any gin, but I knew Alexandre's spirit was very strong, so I took a swig of it between jumps.' Then Delphine gulped noisily. 'I'm going to vomit again!'

Both Louise and Blanche tended to her until eventually she fell into a deep sleep. They had not questioned her again. Throughout the night, Louise went to see that Delphine was all right, once giving her a drink of water.

'I want to tell you about Pieter,' Delphine muttered, bleary-eyed.

'In the morning,' Louise said quietly. 'Go back to sleep now.'

Throughout the following day Delphine felt too ill to talk or rise from her bed, but the following evening, in the last rays of the evening sun, she and Louise sat down side by side in wicker chairs on the veranda. Then out came the account of the stolen Saturday evenings, the hectic parties, the gambling and, after Pieter had given her the ring and sworn to marry her, how she had finally surrendered to him. It was here that Delphine closed her eyes on private memories, seeming to feel again his exploring fingers and travelling lips that had awakened her naked body to such ecstasy.

Louise had listened without comment, looking ahead at the descending darkness of the night, which came so quickly on this side of the world. All the time she was wondering why she had been so foolish as to put such trust in her sister's declaration that she would allow no pre-marital intimacies.

She remembered her doubts about Pieter and recalled Daniel's words, which had been a warning after all.

A veranda lantern, which had been lit earlier, took on life and shed its glow over the sisters where they sat between the golden squares of the lighted windows. Louise finally turned and looked at her sister. 'I can understand how it all happened. Blanche has thought out a way to save this situation.'

Delphine, whose head was lowered, listened without comment to all that her sister had to say. Then slowly she looked up again, her eyes dark and tragic. 'I loved Pieter as I'll never love anyone else again. I had no fear when I threw myself into the water, because I wanted to drown. I didn't know then that I might be pregnant. It was because I could not face the future without him.'

'This will sound like a platitude, but it's still early days to get over such a love as you felt for Pieter.'

Delphine, shaking her head, looked at her sister almost in pity. 'You don't understand. Pieter drained away all my capacity for loving when he deserted me in that cowardly way. If he had told me the truth, terrible though it would have been, I could probably have come through it without any harm to my heart in the end. Now he's left me hating him as much as I once loved him.' She thumped her fists on the chair arms. 'I don't want his horrible baby! I wish I could cut it out of me!'

Louise reached out and stilled the pounding fists, speaking sharply. 'Don't say that about the baby!' She realized that Delphine's misery had been festering away inside her ever since the Dutchman's betrayal, changing her vibrant enthusiasm for life into a dangerously embittered outlook. 'Your child didn't ask to be conceived and has a right to love and care. I'll do everything in my power to help you.'

Delphine jumped to her feet as if all her patience was lost and she set her teeth as she glared down at Louise. 'I shall loathe this baby as much as I loathe its father!'

Then she flounced into the house, banging the door after her.

Louise sat on for a few minutes, deeply distressed. Delphine had always been highly emotional, needing love as much as she needed air to breathe, and as yet it was impossible to estimate just how much damage had been done to the balance of her mind.

When Blanche talked to Delphine a few days later, she was unaware that she did no better in softening the girl's attitude to the coming baby. Intensely maternal herself, she found it impossible not to find joy in the prospect, whatever the circumstances, especially as she felt she had mapped out a way for Delphine to make an unblemished future for herself and the child.

'If you don't want to face the outside world under the pretence of widowhood,' she said kindly, 'you are welcome to stay on here and make your home with us.' She patted Delphine's hand encouragingly. 'Think about it.'

She failed to notice Delphine's shudder at such a future.

'I believe I persuaded Delphine to think more kindly about the baby,' she said to Louise afterwards. 'It's a beginning, and once she has the infant in her arms, she'll forget all the animosity towards it that plagues her now.'

Louise tried to be as optimistic, but failed to be convinced. In some ways Delphine had become a stranger and it was no longer possible to assess anything about her.

Ten

Surprisingly, Delphine became more placid as the summer months passed. She no longer went far afield, but kept within sight of the farmhouse. She would wander by the hay fields, where the grass had grown almost man-high, and through the vast cornfields, which were turning harvest-gold. It was as if she had resigned herself to the situation in a way that delighted Blanche, who was busy making baby clothes and new bed covers for the cradle that Alexandre had brought down from the loft. She might have been the expectant mother herself, the pleasure she was taking in getting the layette ready. Delphine, out of boredom, embroidered some of the little garments and Blanche took this to be another good sign.

Delphine did not go to the barn for the harvest supper, but unbeknown to the others, she sat on the veranda with her flute and picked up the lively tunes that were being played for the dancing. All the time she hugged her secret plan to herself. It made the time she was spending at the farm just bearable.

A cold north wind had stripped the last of the autumn leaves from the trees and thick ice had formed on the river before intense black clouds heralded the first snow. It descended ceaselessly for several days and after that the frozen river became the highway, sledges passing to and fro as normal life resumed.

In spite of the bitter weather the farmhouse was kept warm and snug with blazing fires. Long icicles hung from the roof and held a diamond glitter whenever the pale winter sun broke through. Those were the days when Louise and Blanche joined in snowball fights with the children and Alexandre built them a snowman taller than himself.

Delphine's labour pains began on a morning late in January when a heavy fall of snow reduced visibility to a hand in front of the face. It meant that the local midwife could not reach the farmhouse, so Blanche and Louise made ready to deliver the baby themselves. It was about midnight that Delphine began to scream her hatred of Pieter and what he had done to her. Her labour was long and agonizing. It was not until the next evening that her son gushed into the world and let forth a strong cry of protest.

'You have a lovely boy, Delphine,' Blanche said joyfully, about to put the baby in her arms, but instantly Delphine turned her face away.

'I don't want him! I never will!' Then she gave a bitter cry. 'Send him to the Spice Islands!'

Blanche, not noticing Louise's signal that she should draw back for a few moments, went swiftly to the opposite side of the bed, unable to believe that the sight of the child would not bring forth instant mother love. 'Just look at him, Delphine.'

Delphine's lids were tightly shut in distaste, but as Blanche lowered the baby towards the pillow, she sensed the movement and as she raised herself slightly her eyes flew open. For a second or two she looked into the face of her son, her pupils widening in horror.

'He looks like Pieter!' she shrieked hysterically. 'Take him away! I never want to see him again!'

She collapsed back on to the pillows. Her face, already white, took on an almost death-like hue. Louise cried out in alarm, seeing a spreading bloodstain.

'She's haemorrhaging!'

Delphine almost died that day. When the flow of blood was finally stemmed, it had still seemed that she had no chance of surviving, but she continued breathing faintly in spite of everything. Louise and Blanche took turns in sitting with her by night and day, spooning nourishing liquids into her whenever there was a chance. Remembering Charles's firm belief in the helpful properties of pure water, Louise also gave her sips of it as often as possible.

Since it was obvious that Delphine would have no interest in naming her son, Louise decided he should be called Philippe after their father. Maria, whose full breasts had milk to spare, became his wet nurse and he thrived contentedly in spite of all his mother had done to herself to be rid of him. Blanche would have bound him in swaddling bands in the old belief that they helped a baby's limbs grow straight, but Louise would not allow it. She remembered that Charles, with his enlightened ideas, had been violently opposed to swathing in any form, sometimes telling her on a Sunday afternoon of yet another battle he had had with a midwife over it. So Philippe lay free in his cradle, a handsome infant in every way.

In a chair and propped up by cushions, Delphine passed the time when on her own by watching the comings and goings of the family and visitors from the window of her bedroom, but with little interest. It was taking a long time for her to recover her strength, and as yet she was only sitting out of bed for a short while daily. She never asked about her son and it was as if he did not exist. When the local doctor made a visit, he diagnosed melancholia and advised that she be allowed to take her own time to recover.

'She's young and her spirit will return,' he said sagely as he departed.

When Delphine finally felt well enough to rejoin the family circle, she still had a frail look about her, which gave some cause for concern, and had little appetite. Nothing would induce her to go near her baby. If he were in a room that she was about to enter, she would immediately go elsewhere until he was returned to his cradle in the nursery.

Then, after this had happened a number of times, there came a moment like a spark to gunpowder when Louise's patience finally ran out completely. She had come from looking in on Philippe, who had been crying most of the evening, when she saw Delphine going heedlessly across the hall to her room.

Darting forward after her, Louise seized her by the shoulders and jerked her round.

'You'll start caring for your son tomorrow!' she stated fiercely. 'No more excuses or evasions. He no longer looks like Pieter, but has your copper tint in his hair, and to my mind has a look of Papa in that painting of him as a boy that hung in the library at home. There is nothing to stop you taking full charge of him.'

Delphine looked panic-stricken. 'But he'll always look like Pieter to me.'

Louise was unmoved. 'Tomorrow I'll be at hand when you bath and change him. After that you'll manage him on your own, as you will every day after that until we leave here. Then you'll shoulder all responsibility for him in your new role as a widow.'

Delphine fixed her with a long and dangerous look before answering. 'You don't know what you're asking of me. I'll give you the truth, but you won't like hearing it. I don't go near him, because I can't trust myself. I'm afraid of doing him some violence!'

She turned on her heel and rushed into her room, slamming the door after her. Louise was left motionless in shock. In the parlour, Blanche and Alexandre, sitting by the fire, had been unable to avoid overhearing Delphine's high-pitched outburst. Blanche went at once to draw Louise into the room and to a chair with them by the fire.

'What am I to do?' Louise asked in despair, shaking her head. 'Even if I take on the responsibility for Philippe, which I'll do gladly, I must work, and I'll be afraid all the time of ever leaving Delphine alone with him. She's been totally unbalanced in her mind ever since Pieter deserted her. She was never like this before.' She covered her eyes with her fingers and spoke brokenly. 'It's been so long since I heard her laugh.'

Alexandre exchanged a significant glance with Blanche and then took his wife's hand, linking his fingers with hers before he spoke. 'I have a solution. If you'll agree, Louise, we'd like to adopt him.'

129

Louise let her hands fall to her lap. 'What are you saying?' she said incredulously.

'We want you to know that it would not be out of pity for Philippe or his unfortunate mother,' Alexandre continued, 'but because we want him to take the place of the son we can never have. I give you my word that we would love him and do our best for him always, as if he were our own flesh and blood.'

'Please say yes!' Blanche implored emotionally. 'I've been dreading the day when he would leave.'

Louise was deeply touched. She had seen for herself how much her friend had come to love Philippe, caring for him in every way, and invariably she was the first to reach his cradle whenever he cried in the night. Louise thought of the many times she and Blanche had shared a night-time drink in the kitchen until they were sure he had settled down again. As for Alexandre, it was natural that as a farmer he would want a son to inherit and to share his love of the land. He was a good man and Philippe could never have a better father.

Louise reached out a hand to him and to Blanche, and the three of them were linked as they had been in the past. 'For myself, what you are offering is all that I would wish for my little nephew. Loving parents, a good home and the wonderful chance to grow up in the country, as we three did in our childhood. I'm sure when Delphine hears what you're willing to do for her son, she will always be grateful to you both.'

'Naturally everything must be done legally,' Alexandre said firmly. 'I couldn't risk Blanche being broken-hearted if sometime in the future Delphine should have a change of heart and want him back. As soon as we've spoken to her in the morning, I'll take the sledge into town and see a lawyer about the necessary adoption papers, which will require her signature too.'

Next morning Delphine did not appear for breakfast. No notice was taken, as she frequently slept late, but Blanche was on tenterhooks, impatient for her to emerge. At midday, Louise knocked on her door, but when there was no reply she tried the handle and found it locked. Neither was there any response when she called her sister's name.

Feeling angry that her sister should be disrupting the household once again, this time through sheer selfishness, Louise took a cloak from a hook and went out on to the veranda. She intended to upbraid her sister through the glass panel of her veranda door if that should be locked too. But before she reached Delphine's door, she saw a trail of footsteps leading away from it in the snow.

Dashing into Delphine's bedroom, she saw that the bed had not been slept in and drawers to a chest stood open, the contents having been scooped up. A petticoat lay where it had been dropped on the floor. Throwing open the closet door, she saw that Delphine's cloak and a pair of lace-up boots were gone.

The search was started immediately. Horses were harnessed up to two sledges and Alexandre drove off in the direction of Albany and George turned towards Troy. At the farmhouse, the anxious waiting commenced. Louise knew that Delphine had some money to take with her and Blanche reported from the kitchen that she had food too, Maria having discovered that some bread, cheese and dried apple rings were missing.

It was evening before the men returned, the sledge lamps a welcome sight to Louise and Blanche watching from a window. George was first and had found no trace of Delphine, but Alexandre, arriving soon afterwards, had picked up her trail.

'She seems to have slept part of the night in a barn,' he said as he shed his warm jacket, the cold night air hanging about him. 'A tavern keeper told me that when she turned up at his door at five o'clock this morning she had some pieces of straw clinging to her clothes and brushed them off as soon as she saw them in his bar-room's candlelight. He had been getting breakfast for a traveller wanting an early start, but she said she'd eaten, so he gave her a hot punch. She sat at the traveller's table while she drank it and then they went off together.'

'Did he know where the man was going?' Louise asked quickly, trying not to think of the dangers that could entrap any woman travelling with a total stranger.

'No. The traveller had said he was on his way home, but

when he and Delphine were talking, the tavern keeper heard West Point mentioned.'

'We put in there when we came upriver,' Louise exclaimed. 'That's a long way.'

'Longer still with the river ice no longer safe. But the tavern keeper gave me the traveller's name. It's James Harrison, someone unknown to me.' Alexandre crossed to the fire and held out his hands to the blaze. 'Even if Delphine only went with him for a short way, we know the route she's taking and it shouldn't be hard to find her.' He smiled over his shoulder at Louise, firelight dancing up his face. 'Remember that my need in wanting her safely back here is as great as yours, because there's those adoption papers I want her to sign. Tomorrow I'll go prepared for a lengthy journey and I'll not return until I've found her.'

'I'll come with you,' Louise said determinedly.

'No, Louise.' He was adamant. 'I shall go on horseback and I'll do better on my own. You stay here with Blanche and trust me to bring your sister back to you.'

He was gone for four weeks. By then a thaw had set in, the snow had gone and the river was flowing again. Already the land was showing green. When he returned, he was alone.

'I'm so sorry, Louise,' he said heavily. 'The trail simply came to an end between Albany and West Point at a small town where I found James Harrison, a pleasant little man who runs a general goods shop with his son. He'd been visiting his sick brother on a farm that lies almost a day's journey from here, which was why he had put up at the tavern. Delphine gave him some story about being a maidservant leaving one place of employment in search of another. He took her home with him, where his daughter-in-law included her in a family meal and then she left.'

'Had she given him any idea where she was going?'

'No, except that as an émigré she knew of a French lady whom she was sure would take her in. I searched around, but nobody remembered seeing Delphine. It's likely that she managed to get a lift with some other traveller. I decided to continue on to West Point, but drew a blank there and everywhere else I tried.'

'Where can she be?' Blanche questioned in bewilderment.

'I can only conclude that somehow she has made her way back to New York,' Alexandre answered. Then he turned to Louise. 'Now that the ice has gone from the river you and I will take a sloop down to New York and look for her together. You'll know better than I where she's likely to have sought refuge.'

Louise sank down in a chair. 'I don't think she's gone to New York. I believe she'll have made her way to Boston.'

'Where your cousin lives!' Blanche almost breathed the words.

'By road that's a great many miles from here,' Alexandre put in doubtfully. 'I can't be certain, but it would take at least two weeks by coach in good weather over the log roads and I couldn't estimate it at this time of year, with the snow still melting in some places and the likelihood of flooding.' He frowned. 'Do you think Delphine would have attempted such a journey with no knowledge of what she might encounter?'

Louise nodded. 'It's been her ambition to get to Boston ever since we heard that our cousins had moved there. At least I can be sure of her being welcomed by Madeleine, providing she arrives there safely.' Although she spoke hopefully, her last words seemed to hang in the air. All three of them knew that anything could have happened to Delphine on the way.

Two days later Louise was ready to start her journey to Boston. It had been decided that she should go by road, following the route that Delphine was believed to have taken. She was leaving behind the trunks in which she had packed most of Delphine's clothes and her own, together with other possessions, which would be sent on to her when she had a settled address. She was taking only a large valise with all that she needed to tide her over for the time being. She sewed some of her jewellery, together with Delphine's sapphire necklace, into a hidden pocket in the short jacket that she would be wearing under her cloak, and the rest went into a false waistband.

If it had been necessary for Alexandre to accompany her, she knew he would have done, but it was one of the busiest times of the year on a farm and she had made it clear that she would be travelling alone. So, he had given her the adoption papers, which had been drawn up by his lawyer, and as soon as they were signed she would return them to him. He also gave her a pistol.

'Remember there are rogues here who prey on travellers, just as there are in France and anywhere else in the world, and you'll be travelling with some valuable jewels on you. Keep it available at all times.'

Before leaving the farmhouse Louise took Philippe up from his cradle and kissed him fondly. He gave a smile, still kicking happily when she laid him down again. As she tucked the covers around him she wondered when she would see him again.

Blanche and the two girls were waiting for her by the front door. She bade Henrietta and Betsy farewell before they went scampering off to play, leaving her alone with Blanche. They embraced each other.

'Au revoir, dear Blanche,' Louise said emotionally. 'Thank you again a million times for everything you and Alexandre have done for Delphine, Philippe and for me.'

'I wish you Godspeed.' Blanche's voice was choked. 'Come back soon.'

Alexandre was waiting with the two-wheeled carriage to drive Louise to Albany. Taking a last look before the farmhouse disappeared from sight, she waved again to the solitary figure on the veranda steps. There was a last flutter of Blanche's white handkerchief in reply and then she was lost from sight.

The coach from Albany departed on time and as the wheels began to roll, Alexandre kept level with the window for a few paces. 'Good luck! Write as soon as you've found Delphine.'

'I will!' Louise promised. Then as the coachman whipped up his team of six horses Alexandre was left behind and she settled back in her seat. She would need that luck, everything depended on Delphine having found a haven with their cousins.

It was a physically uncomfortable journey, even though the coach was well sprung and the upholstery well padded, for the road in most places had been given a surface of felled tree trunks. One child in the carriage, travelling with her mother, was as sick as if she had been on a rough sea. Louise took from her valise the sugar stick that Henrietta had given her as a farewell gift and offered it. The mother thanked her and gave it to her daughter. After the child had sucked it until it disappeared, the colour returned to her cheeks and the sickness went, to the relief of the other passengers.

At every stop Louise made enquiries about Delphine.

'A lot of young women come in here on their travels,' one tavern keeper's wife said to her. 'But – as you can see for yourself now – as soon as a coach-load arrives, we're mighty busy serving ale and hot pies and beans and all the rest, so there's scarcely time to take real note of anyone.' It was depressing information.

Louise found much to see on the journey, from open stretches of land where ferns and plants and early flowers were growing in abundance to densely forested mountain slopes. There were dark and mysterious groves that were richly green, fast-flowing rivers and creeks and, here and there, homesteads, crop fields and pasturage, small towns and rough settlements.

When the coach made an overnight stop, always at a tavern, which was sometimes the only building in a wide area of woodland, the older passengers alighted stiffly and even Louise found she seemed to ache in every limb. But a brisk walk after supper restored her suppleness and she welcomed the fresh air after the close confinement with others in the coach. She thought it was no wonder that Daniel preferred the stimulation of a coastal voyage instead of the torment of land travel on such roads.

Blanche had warned that Louise must have her own bedlinen for these overnight stopovers at wayside taverns, since it was not supplied, and had provided her with some that was old and much mended, which could be disposed of at the end of her journey. Louise was thankful for her friend's thoughtfulness when she saw the rough grey blankets that were provided in the primitively furnished bedrooms, usually under the eaves. After making up her bed and tired from the day's rough journey, she went to sleep swiftly and solidly until roused by a knock on the door in the morning.

At meals, which were usually wholesome and plentiful, Louise always scanned the faces of the serving maids just in case Delphine had needed to earn money by working along the way. It was the same when she took her walks whenever the stop had been made in a town or any other place of habitation, for she was always looking and searching in every direction.

It seemed a long two weeks before finally in the late evening's heavy rain the coach rattled over wet cobbles into Boston. Alighting, she found it impossible to hail a hackney carriage, each one that passed her being occupied. After making enquiries about the Bradshaws' address, she was relieved to hear it was not far away and set off on foot in the driving rain. As she had expected, her cousins' home was a grand house. It had a splendid two-pillared porch and a large door with a gleaming brass knocker shaped like an American eagle's head, but all the windows were dark. It was late, but not yet so late that everyone would have gone to bed, and she went quickly up the steps to jerk the bell-pull. At first nothing happened, so she tried again. Then after another wait the door opened. A footman, his wig awry as if he had just clapped it on his head, stood there with a candle.

'Yes, ma'am?'

With sudden dread Louise had the strangest feeling of déjà vu as she gave her name and stated that she had arrived to visit Mr and Mrs Theodore Bradshaw. The man's surprised attitude was all too similar to that of the footman at her cousins' former home when she and Delphine had called to see them there. As a result, his words brought no surprise, but intense disappointment.

'They went south for the winter after the master was not well in September. They're not expected back for a while yet.'

Louise's heart sank at this confirmation of her fears. 'Could you tell me if my sister has called here? She would have been on her own and made the same request.'

He shook his head. 'No, ma'am. I don't remember any young lady coming here.'

Louise became desperate. 'Please ask the other servants. Perhaps one of them answered the door to her. I need to know where she has gone. It's very important.'

He hesitated. This stranger looked respectable, even though she was somewhat bedraggled, and he could tell from her accent that she was a Frenchwoman like Mrs Bradshaw.

'You'd best come in, ma'am. I'll make enquiries.'

She was thankful to step inside. He lighted a candle on a side table and left her on her own. All the furniture in the large hall was covered with dust sheets. A large gilt-framed mirror gave back her reflection, a lonely figure with an anxious face, standing in the middle of the marble floor with her baggage on the floor beside her, rain water dripping from her cloak to make little pools in a circle around her.

He returned with a young maidservant, whom he addressed as Molly. 'Tell the lady what you remember.'

The girl bobbed a curtsey before speaking. 'A young woman did come to the door some time ago and asked for Mr and Mrs Bradshaw too, ma'am. She said they were her cousins as you have done, but in her case I found that difficult to believe, because her clothes were dirty and in a poor state, with torn lace hanging from her petticoat.'

'Did she give her name?' Louise demanded at once.

'Yes, but I don't remember it.'

'Was it Delphine de Montier?'

The maidservant looked uncertain. 'I couldn't say for sure. Yes, maybe it was that. I could tell she was a foreigner.'

'What happened when you told her Mr and Mrs Bradshaw were away?'

'She began to cry and begged for some food.' Molly cast

a nervous eye at the manservant. 'I couldn't help pitying her, and although I shouldn't have done it I sent her round to the kitchen door and gave her some leftovers. That was the last I saw of her.'

Louise drew in a shuddering breath. 'Thank you for showing her kindness. I'm extremely grateful. Did she have hand baggage with her?'

'I didn't see any.'

Louise's fear for her sister increased still further, for it was obvious Delphine had been robbed both of her money and her possessions. 'If she should return, please tell her that her sister is in Boston and looking for her. I've only just arrived here this evening and have yet to find a place to stay. Tell her I'll leave a letter at the post office giving my address.'

'Yes, ma'am.'

'Can you direct me to a good lodging house?'

The footman sent Molly back to the kitchen and came out on to the porch with Louise to give her complicated directions to a lodging house known to be clean and respectable. She followed his directions, but the wall-bracketed street lanterns had become few and far between and she soon realized that she had missed her way in the dark. Instead she had reached a dubious area where women were lingering in doorways and some sailors were emerging drunkenly from one of the taverns. Afraid of being accosted, she turned sharply away and, catching the reflection of a ship's light on water, realized she was near the harbour and most of the buildings around her were warehouses.

By now her valise felt heavier than ever before and rain had found its way in a trickle down between her breasts. A man suddenly loomed up in front of her out of the darkness and spread his arms wide to entrap her.

'Hi, there! I'm in need of company. Give me a good price, woman.'

She dodged past him, but with an angry yell he snatched at her cloak and it fell from her as she ran from him. His heavy footsteps broke into a run, but after a short distance he came to a halt, his swearing following her. When she paused to lean against a wall to get her breath and rest her arm from her burden her heart was beating wildly. It took her a few moments to see that she was opposite an office set in a large warehouse. A street lantern illumined the sign above the door in a yellowish glow. *Lombard, Silk Importer.*

Daniel's office! And a window on the floor above was brightly lit. Within seconds she was across the street and hammering on the door with her fist. If a conscientious employee was working this late, he could surely be trusted to give her assistance as an acquaintance of his employer.

Above her the window opened. She stepped back at once in order to be seen by the man silhouetted against the light. To her astonishment he gave a long, low laugh of surprise, cutting off the appeal she had been about to make.

'Louise! Why didn't you let me know you'd be calling?'

'Daniel! Stop joking and let me in!' she demanded wearily.

'I'll be down immediately.'

The window slammed shut and within seconds he opened the door to her, a candle-lamp in his hand, his grin fading as she almost fell in, letting her valise drop to the floor.

'Whatever has been happening to you?' He looked her up and down in disbelief. 'You're only in thin clothes and soaked through.'

'The ties on my cloak must have become loose and somebody in the street snatched it from me. The coach from Albany came in late this evening and my cousins are away. I've had a terrible time looking for a place to stay!'

'But how did you find your way here?' He led her into his office on the same floor. 'This isn't an area you should be in on your own at this time of night.'

'I lost my way. When I saw the lighted window I thought one of your clerks was working late and would give me some help. So, if you could just show me the way to the nearest hotel or a good lodging house, I'll be extremely grateful.'

'I know where there's comfortable accommodation that

should suit you and we'll go there without further delay. Just give me time to put the candle-lamps out upstairs.'

He came down again quickly, with his own cloak over his arm. 'Put this on and come with me.' Snatching up her valise, he led the way to the rear of the building, where a horse and a crimson high-wheeled gig stood under a roof jutting out above the door in a stable yard. He helped her into it and then left the extinguished candle-lamp indoors before locking up. After leading the horse out into the street he padlocked the gates after him before getting up beside her and taking the reins.

'It's sheer chance that you found me here tonight, Louise. I'd decided to take a look at some ledgers, because I was certain one of my clerks was fiddling the books and, unfortunately, I've discovered that I was right.' He glanced sideways at her. 'Why are you visiting Boston now, when the Bradshaws are spending the winter in Louisiana?'

'I didn't know that they were there. It's a long story, but Delphine ran away from where we were staying with friends and I've traced her here.'

'Where is she living?'

'I've no idea.' She looked at him with unhappy eyes and told him what she had heard from the maidservant. 'So, somewhere on her journey Delphine was robbed of her money and possessions; but what frightens me most is what else might have happened to cause her to arrive at Madeleine's home in such a pathetic state. I intend to start looking for her as soon as it's daylight.'

'Leave it to me. I'll make sure that she's found.'

Louise shook her head. 'Somebody else said that to me some weeks ago and she's still missing.' Her voice became unsteady. 'Now that I know that she's homeless and in dire straits, I fear the worst.'

She had taken no notice of where he was driving, except there were more street lanterns about and lights from windows were streaming down on to the wet cobbles. Now he was drawing up and she turned her head to see where he had brought her. It was a mansion even larger than her cousins' house, and a footman had opened the door as a groom came running from another direction to take charge of the horse and the vehicle.

'You've brought me to your home, Daniel,' she said wearily, no longer capable of protest as he helped her down from the carriage.

'Yes, because here you can have a hot bath to stop you shivering like a landed fish, a hot drink and anything else you want.'

In the wide hall a word from him brought the housekeeper, whose name was Mrs Carter, hurrying to take charge of the visitor. Louise, following her up the sweeping staircase, paused halfway to look down at Daniel, even more handsome than she remembered, where he stood watching her.

'Thank you for rescuing me from the rain,' she said seriously, thinking how, in spite of all her efforts to the contrary, Fate seemed determined to make their paths cross.

He gave her a warm grin, something close to triumph glinting in his eyes. 'Tomorrow the sun will be out and we'll find Delphine. Sleep well.'

He did not go to bed himself for another couple of hours. First of all he made a comprehensive list of all the possible places where Delphine might be found. Then he sat back in a comfortable chair by the fire, a glass of Madeira in his hand, and stretched out his long legs to rest his crossed ankles on a footstool. His luck had been in that evening. It was only on a sudden impulse after studying some business papers at home that he had gone to check the books and found the evidence that would nail the fraudster. But, far above anything else he could have wished for at the present time, he had the woman he loved under his own roof.

Eleven

D aniel had been out already in his search for Delphine
   when Louise came downstairs soon after eight o'clock,
having been given an early breakfast in bed. The housekeeper
had lent her a clock and she was ready to start on her mission.
Daniel was in the dining room, marking a map of Boston spread
out on the dining-room table, when he heard her footsteps
come tapping down the stairs. As he went into the hall to
greet her, she had just reached the lowest tread, her hand on
the newel post.

'Good morning, Louise! I hope you're well rested.' Then
he saw that the servant following her was carrying her valise.
'What's this? You're not leaving?'

Louise gave a nod. 'You've been very kind and I can't thank
you enough, but Mrs Carter has told me of a small hotel where
I can stay and my baggage is to be taken there now. I shall go
later, but I want to start looking for Delphine without delay.'

'But you can stay on here until she's found!' he protested.

'You've been very hospitable, but I have made my arrangements.'

He knew by the slight setting of her chin that nothing would
make her change her mind. Exasperated, he spoke more sharply
than he had intended. 'Then, before you go, come and look at a
map I have of the city. It will help you to get your bearings.'

Louise followed him into the dining room and leaned over
the map. 'Where are we now?' she asked.

'This is Beacon Hill and here is my house.' He indicated
the spot. 'The crosses I've made show where the homeless
and destitute gather.' His finger traced its way along a route.

'Now, this street leads to the State House. Then State Street takes you past my office building, which is not far from the Long Wharf, where my cargoes of silk are shipped in. Now, over here is the Faneuil Hall, another landmark if you should miss your way. In all these areas there are always plenty of people, which makes it a profitable area in which to beg. As you see, I've marked out three other streets too. And on this corner,' he added, indicating an inked cross near the wharfs, 'there's a charity soup kitchen. A handout of bread and hot soup takes place all the year round at nine o'clock every evening.'

'I can scarcely believe yet that my sister, with her pride and fastidiousness, has been reduced to such hardship.'

Out of the corner of his eye, Daniel saw her hand clench on the table. Glancing up, he met with compassion the bleakness of her expression. 'I'm sorry you have to face up to this situation, but from the description of the state Delphine was in, it's most likely that she had already been reduced to these circumstances before she even reached Boston.'

'I realize that. What frightens me so much is the thought of what might have happened to her on that journey, as well as what she may be enduring now.' She looked down again at the map with unhappy eyes, her words faltering. 'Perhaps I'm already too late in getting here. She may be—'

He guessed what she was about to say and seized her by the arms, giving her a slight shake. 'No! Don't even think it! She's somewhere in this city and she is alive. I checked at the morgue half an hour ago. There's been nobody of her description there during the past two months.'

She closed her eyes thankfully for a moment, but drew back from him, for his very nearness seemed to vibrate in her nostrils. 'That was thoughtful of you. I had dreaded going there myself.'

'I have to tell you that I questioned the servants last night and Delphine did come to this house too, but it was when I was away in New York. Here, as at the Bradshaws' home, I'm thankful to say she was given food, but when she returned

143

another day, she was sent away empty-handed and told not to return.'

'My poor foolish sister,' Louise said. Her voice sounded strangely dry and tired.

Daniel folded the map and handed it to her. 'Look for her among the beggars today. They come back regularly to the spots they consider to be the best for them. I have other places to investigate. This evening – if we don't find her today – I'll call for you at the hotel and, over dinner, we'll compare notes on our progress. Then, if you wish, you can come with me to the handing-out of the charity soup and we'll see if Delphine turns up there. That shall be our programme until she is found.'

Outside, it was not such a bright day as Daniel had predicted, and low clouds promised showers. Louise drew the hood of her borrowed cloak over her head as she and Daniel parted company at the porch steps, she going one way and he the other. He went first to a house of correction to see if any young women had been arrested recently, for he feared Delphine might have been reduced to stealing in order to keep alive. He was relieved to find she was not there.

At the poorhouse, Daniel was equally unsuccessful, as he was afterwards at both the fever and the city hospitals. With all these places eliminated, he took a couple of hours at his office, for having returned from New York only two days before, there were still matters that needed his immediate attention. After dismissing the clerk who had been defrauding him, he waited for a trader, who came promptly at the time arranged to bring him the first lengths of Lyons silk that he had received since the start of France's revolution. There were twenty precious rolls and, when the protective covering was removed from each, they proved to be in pristine condition and of such quality and magnificence that Daniel almost caught his breath at the sight of them, but his face gave nothing away.

'How did you come by these silks?' Daniel asked when the deal had been done to his private satisfaction.

'At the height of the Reign of Terror, a French aristocrat

smuggled them out of Lyons to use as currency when he escaped into Spain. There, brigands murdered the unfortunate fellow and these silks eventually turned up in Barcelona, where I was given a tip-off as to their whereabouts. I snapped them up at once.'

When the trader had gone, Daniel regarded the displayed silks radiating their splendour as if his office were bathed in the rich jewel colours of a stained-glass window. Some were patterned exquisitely with roses or lilies or sprigs of apple blossom, others were plain, but in vibrant hues of coral pink, ruby, pumpkin yellow, forest green and iris blue. As for the rest, one delicate parchment-coloured silk had vertical stripes in silver thread, an amber one was intricately patterned with gold, and a deep violet one had a pin-width stripe in a rich bronze that added magnificently to its lustre. Although the Chinese silks, in which he dealt in great quantities, were equally exquisite, there was an indefinable something about Lyons silk that he considered unique.

He cut a narrow strip from the end of each roll to use as a pattern. Then he summoned two of his experienced workers to stitch each one into a new protective cover of white cloth. The best rolls were to be put aside for Louise, but he knew that he would have to wait a great deal longer before she would accept anything from him. He had to find Delphine first.

Louise spent the day in the areas that Daniel had marked out for her. She had exchanged some dollars for small change with a banker and given one to each beggar she questioned. Some declared they had seen her sister, hoping to get more money, but further questioning proved they were lying. Only one old woman had something plausible to tell.

'Copper-red 'air, you say?' she croaked. 'Yes, I seed a young creature with curls that colour waiting at soup time more than once, but she was always losing her place and getting pushed to the back. It were this day last week I gave 'er a nudge and told 'er to use 'er elbows and shove to the front like me.'

'Did she?'

'She didn't seem to 'ave the strength, and so I grabbed 'er

at the waist and pushed 'er meself.' She cackled. 'We went through the rest of 'em there like a wagon team. When she ate 'er bread and soup like a starving bitch, I shoved 'er up again for another ladleful. Those charity folk never give more than once to anybody in an evening, but sometimes they're so busy they don't notice who's been afore. She were unlucky, poor little wretch, and they turned her away, but then that colour 'air ain't easily forgot. I should 'ave thought of that.' She frowned, compressing her lips in self-reproach. 'No, ma'am, I ain't seen her there since.'

Louise put several coins in the old woman's eager hand. 'If you do see her again, please tell her that her sister is staying at the hotel opposite the State Hall.'

'I will. The sooner you get 'er away from that man who 'angs about 'er, the better. He's real bad.'

With this additional information arousing new fears, Louise wondered exactly how deep the morass was that her sister had fallen into through running away. If only Delphine had waited until morning, she would have been told of Alexandre and Blanche's wonderful offer to adopt her child.

That evening at dinner with Daniel, Louise was able to report what appeared to have been a genuine sighting of Delphine, but she was relieved to hear from him that her sister was not in any of the grim places that he had visited. Then she gave him a full account of all that had happened between her sister and the Dutchman, as well as Delphine's total rejection of the baby and Alexandre and Blanche's wish to adopt him.

'Delphine isn't the first girl to be betrayed and she certainly won't be the last. Your friends have played their part in helping to solve the situation, and now it's up to us to continue ours.' He moved his chair back. 'It's time for us to go to the soup kitchen.'

He drove her there in the same two-wheeled carriage in which she had ridden the night before. When they reached the charity soup kitchen, a crowd of destitute people, some with children, had already gathered. But Delphine did not appear, even though they waited until the last stragglers to arrive had departed again. Louise and Daniel had both questioned those willing to talk to them, but without success.

When Daniel had left Louise at her hotel, he drove to the house of correction, where four volunteer keepers of the peace, their status shown by the cockade that each wore on their tricorne hats, were waiting for him as he had requested that morning. They were to accompany him in his search for Delphine throughout the brothels and other dubious establishments. All too often a vulnerable young girl arrived in Boston to be hoodwinked by a procuress and end up in prostitution, just as in cities everywhere in the world. Delphine, in her desperate straits, would have been easy prey.

As he set off in his carriage, the peacekeepers followed in a closed cart, ready for any arrests. As Daniel had expected, their arrival caused consternation at each brothel, with screams from the prostitutes, and men disappearing out of windows or hiding, but on the whole the madams cooperated. They made their girls line up and brought waif-like creatures, some only children, from chores in the kitchen to be thrust forward and scanned with the rest. After that, the whole establishment was searched in case Delphine was being concealed somewhere.

'She is not here either,' Daniel said to the peacekeepers after they came out of the last bawdy house designated for that night, dawn beginning to tint the sky. 'We'll be continuing the search at the same time tonight and every night until we have covered the rest of these hellholes.'

The pattern of Louise's hunt for Delphine continued daily without success, though she had extended the search after noticing that some beggars, often with the side trade of pickpocketing, only went to special places where people gathered closely in numbers, which took her into churches and meeting houses, open-air political speeches, the markets, and once even to the slave auction, where a ship from Africa had unloaded its human cargo. This latter sight distressed her so much that nothing other than her search for Delphine could have kept her there.

The evening came when Louise admitted to Daniel that she

147

feared time was fast running out, which had been in both their minds from the start. They were on their way back to the lodging house after their fourth visit to the soup kitchen. 'The only places left for me to look for her are the bawdy houses,' she stated frankly. 'But you'll have to mark them on the map for me. If I apply to work at them in turn, I can look for Delphine as soon as I've gained entry.'

'Do you know what you're saying?' he asked, astonished.

She shrugged impatiently. 'Indeed I do. There isn't a vice you could name that I didn't hear about at Versailles, so I wouldn't be going into these places with my eyes shut. I know that what I plan would not be without danger, but before I left the farm, Alexandre gave me a pistol and I'd not hesitate to use it, especially if it meant getting Delphine safely away.'

'You're prepared to take such risks for her?'

'Delphine's whole life is at stake.'

As he was about to leave, Daniel told her that he had already forestalled her plan. 'After I leave you now, I'm setting out for the fourth night in succession on a round of the brothels, with no less than four peacekeepers to help in the search. They ensure access to every part of an establishment, even to the cellars.'

She remained silent for a few moments in her deep gratitude. 'Thank you,' she said simply, and of her own volition rested her hand on his arm. He covered it with his own. Then, seeing the warmth deepen in his eyes, she bade him goodnight and went quickly upstairs. In her room she closed her door and leaned back against it. She had yearned almost overpoweringly to feel his arms reassuringly about her.

Daniel and the peacekeepers came out of the last place on their list. They were slightly later than they had been previously and daylight was beginning to lift the sky over the city, which was already astir. Although he had been unsuccessful in finding the French girl, the peacekeepers were well satisfied with the whole operation, having retaken an escaped prisoner who had killed a warden with his bare hands, a woman wanted for theft, two men wanted for mugging and another for rape.

This last night the haul consisted only of two prostitutes who had been trying to scratch out each other's eyes, but upon being thrust in the cart they had turned their venom on the peacekeepers. Their yelled abuse, combined with their hammering and kicking against the inside of the cart, echoed along the street.

Delphine, curled up between a low wall and a warehouse in the hideout she had made her own, paid no attention to the muffled shrieks as the cart was driven past. She was caught in a paroxysm of coughing and, each time, it left her exhausted. Having been lying there for several days, she was no longer fully aware of where she was, moaning softly from the searing pangs of hunger and the savage pain in her injured ankle. Sometimes she thought herself at home in France and at others in the Rousselot ballroom. It was her cough that had kept her away from other homeless people by night, for she had had missiles thrown at her for disturbing their sleep. After having been raped, robbed and abandoned at the roadside, and having been unable to find the refuge she had expected in Boston, her attempt to find work had been thwarted by the state of her clothes and her lack of references. She would have played her flute and begged if it had not been stolen from her with everything else.

Finally an old man who lived alone had taken her in, but it was not only housework he had wanted from her and she had left in a hurry. At least she had had time to launder her clothes, as well as bath and wash her hair, not knowing then that he was watching her through a crack in the door. She had also managed to steal three of his deceased wife's gowns without his knowledge, which she sold for food, but after sleeping rough again her appearance soon deteriorated.

She had not dared to go back to Daniel's house after her second enquiry, for a bad-tempered footman, recognizing her from before, had thrown her from the door with such force that she had fallen in a sprawl of limbs and hurt her ankle. It had left her with a painful limp, which meant she could no longer run. With this handicap, she had not dared to go again to the soup kitchen, where a brutal-looking man with bushy yellow hair had constantly harassed her. He had kept trying to grab her away with him into the dark and each time she had only escaped through speed.

At first she had hobbled to the Lombard office to ask after Daniel, only to be told he was still away. Sometimes all the nourishment she had in a day was on these visits, when a clerk gave her a piece of bread from his midday snack. When the pain had become too agonising for her to put any weight on her foot, she had decided that a complete rest would heal it. Instead, her strength had ebbed and she could no longer move from her hideout.

It helped that sometimes she seemed to be at home in France and could run wherever she wished, but now she was alone in the Rousselot ballroom and it was not as she remembered it. Only one candle was alight and it was burning low at a curious speed. In panic at being left in the dark, she rushed to get out before it extinguished itself, but the doors had vanished. Although she ran from wall to wall, constantly meeting her own reflection in the mirrors, there was no way out. Then, as the darkness closed in, she was aware of the yellow-haired man looming over her. Screaming, she hit out frantically . . . but firm hands caught her wrists and it was Daniel's voice that spoke to her.

'Delphine! You're safe now. I've come to take you home with me.'

Twelve

A s Daniel gathered Delphine up in his arms, her skeletal condition alarmed him. Previously he must have passed her at least twice in the darkness and it was only the early daylight that had enabled him to see from his high driving seat that someone was curled up behind the low wall.

As he carried her into his house he sent a servant running to fetch a doctor, another to summon Louise and a third with instructions to the housekeeper. Mrs Carter, who always had hot water ready for his bath when he returned from his searching, came hurrying with two maidservants carrying jugs. As soon as he had left the bedroom where he had laid Delphine on the bed, the three women removed her filthy clothes and washed her from head to foot. Her tangled curls were combed as gently as possible, although some strands were too knotted to be unravelled and would have to be cut away later. Finally they put her into a lace-trimmed nightgown that one of Daniel's almost-forgotten mistresses had left behind long ago.

When Louise arrived, Daniel came from the drawing room, where he had been watching for her from the window. She ran to him.

'How is she? Where did you find her?'

He gave her a reassuring smile. 'Not in a brothel, but behind a wall. As for her health, Dr Harvey is with her now. We shall have his report very shortly.'

She made a move towards the stairs. 'Which room is she in?'

'Wait!' He took her firmly by the elbow and steered her

into the drawing room. 'I want to prepare you for her changed appearance. Delphine is painfully thin and has a bad cough. She has also injured her right ankle and it is horribly swollen. I doubt if she has been able to walk on it for several days. But,' he added on a brighter note, 'she is here now and I'll ensure that she gets the best medical attention until she is completely well again.'

Louise had pressed her linked fingers against her trembling mouth, but lowered them as she spoke, her eyes full of gratitude. 'Both she and I will be for ever in your debt for all you have done for us.' Then she turned her head sharply as the doctor was heard coming down the stairs.

Dr Harvey came into the drawing room. He was in his forties, an alert, intelligent-looking man with a way of tilting his head slightly as if he were long used to listening patiently to those consulting him. He bowed as Daniel introduced him to Louise.

'Your sister is in a severely emaciated state, ma'am, and she has a fever from her inflamed lungs. I've left a bottle of physic that should relieve the coughing. As for her ankle, it is not broken, only badly sprained.' He flicked his hand to indicate that was only a minor problem. 'Her strength has to be built up again. She must have nourishing liquids, a little at a time and often.' He shook his head slightly. 'In fact, the next few days will be critical. She will need careful nursing around the clock if we're going to save her.'

Louise gave a cry of distress. 'Is it so serious? I'll do everything in my power to help her get well again!'

'I'm sure you will, ma'am.' He exchanged a solemn glance with Daniel. 'I'll call again this evening.'

Rushing upstairs, Louise found Mrs Carter sitting by the bedside. The woman rose immediately. 'I've already sent word down to the kitchen for a hot posset to be prepared for the patient. Dr Harvey gave me a list of nourishing liquids and light food that Miss Delphine is to be given.'

'Thank you, Mrs Carter.'

As the woman left the room, Louise took the vacated chair.

Although she had been prepared for her sister's appearance, it was still a severe shock when she saw Delphine's hollow-cheeked face, her closed eyes sunk in their sockets and her lips drained of colour. Reaching out, Louise lifted her sister's thin hand from the coverlet and held it between her own.

'You're going to get well again, Delphine,' she said softly. 'We've come through so much together and we'll get through this too.'

Delphine's lids fluttered and she opened her eyes. 'Louise?' she whispered.

'I'm here!'

'Don't leave me.'

'I won't. I'm here to stay.'

A maidservant came with the posset, which had been made with milk and a small measure of an extremely fine French brandy from a hoarded bottle in Daniel's cellar. Louise gave Delphine a few spoonfuls of it, afraid that she would vomit it up again, but this did not happen and she slept afterwards.

Daniel came quietly into the room and drew up a chair beside Louise. 'Mrs Carter's sister will share the nursing with you.' Then, as Louise would have protested, he added, 'You can't be at this bedside night and day, or else you'll be ill yourself. She is known as Nurse Annabelle and she is experienced in caring for the sick. I met her once when visiting a bedridden friend. She's a pleasant, competent woman.' He indicated a communicating door in the room. 'I thought you should have the neighbouring bedroom through there. Then you can be near Delphine by night as well as by day.'

'I'm imposing on your hospitality once again.'

'You could never impose.'

She did not meet his eyes, knowing what she would see there. 'Could one of the maidservants fetch my belongings from the lodging house?'

'It shall be done.'

From that time onward everything in the house revolved around the sickroom. There were days when Delphine hovered on the point of death and for forty-eight hours it seemed that there could be no saving her, but Louise and Annabelle were tireless in their ministrations. It was dawn when Louise emerged exhausted from the sickroom, knowing that the immediate danger was over.

Daniel, fearful of the night's result, was already up and dressed when she came slowly down the stairs. Tendrils of her hair had loosened during her night watch, her sleeves were still rolled up and she seemed unaware that the neck of her bodice was unbuttoned, which he guessed had been due to her exertions at the sickbed. To his quietly voiced query she gave a tired nod, her voice barely audible.

'We've brought her through this crisis. I pray there'll be no more.'

'Shouldn't you be taking some rest?' Her pallor and the shadows under her eyes concerned him.

'Not just yet. I'm going into the flower garden for a few minutes.'

He realized how she must feel after being cooped up unremittingly in the sickroom for such a long time. She seemed to glide along like a sleepwalker as he went with her. Outside, the sky was tinted gloriously by the approaching day and the air was fresh and sweet. She breathed it in deeply as she stood a few steps in front of him, crossing her arms, with her head tilted back while the dawn light seemed to glow about her whole graceful figure. It gave her such a tender, vulnerable look that he spoke her name as softly as if it were an expression of love.

She half turned, looking up at him under lowered lids, as if in her exhaustion the long lashes were weighing them down. As he put his hands on her slender waist and drew her gently to him, she did not resist, but raised her arms out straight to rest them across his shoulders. She closed her eyes and he kissed them, his lips travelling on to her brow, her cheeks, her ears and her long white throat. She leaned back, her spine arched, as if to give him easier access, and in her opened bodice, his kisses trailed down to her cleavage. Then his lips found hers in a kiss of adoration, without the violence or demand of passion. She responded submissively and gently as if in a dream.

'I love you,' he said softly. 'Ever since the moment I first saw you.'

She looked up at him, a half-smile touching her lips. 'Dear Daniel,' she said, almost in a whisper as she drew away from his embrace. 'My Good Samaritan.'

Then she drifted from him back into the house, the first rays of sun following to cast bronze lights into her hair.

He did not see her again during the day. Then, in the evening, refreshed by sleep, she was her usual spruce self once more. He caught sight of her from the hall as she was on her way along the gallery to the sickroom.

'Louise!'

She paused to look down at him. 'Yes, Daniel?'

'When can we talk?'

'Do we need to?' she asked, as if amused, and then added enigmatically, 'Haven't we reached the point of no return?'

He heard her laugh softly before the door of the sickroom closed behind her.

Slowly Delphine began to improve and Dr Harvey had hopes of her full recovery, although privately he was unsure whether her ankle would ever be completely right again. As a result she still occupied much of her sister's time, for Louise had insisted there was no longer any need for the nurse to remain. Daniel was constantly frustrated in his attempts to talk to her on her own. She always seemed to have a task to do when he waylaid her.

'Not now, Daniel. I'm busy. There'll be plenty of time to talk when Delphine is well again.'

As she took all her meals with her sister, not even dining with him after he had been out all day, his meetings with her continued to be brief. Then one evening he found her on her own in the library, choosing a book from the shelves. He slammed the door shut behind him with a force that made her jump. She spun round quickly, clutching the book close to her. Her laughter at her own surprise stilled when she saw how he was looking at her.

'It's hard to believe sometimes,' he said, coming towards

her, 'that you and I are living in the same house. You're like a will-o'-the-wisp, always disappearing through doors or whisking your way past me on some errand for the invalid.'

Somehow she seemed unable to take her eyes from his, such excitement beginning to pulse through her that she could feel her heart pounding against the book that she held against her. She did not move and let him take it from her to toss it aside on to a sofa. Then she almost fell against him as he drew her hard into his arms, moulding her body against his, and kissed her as long and as deeply as he had once in New York. She kissed him back with pent-up ardour, her whole body alive with passion as she drove her fingers into his thick hair, holding him to her.

'My love,' he said huskily when their kiss ended, both looking at each other breathlessly, her eyes wide and shining. 'Marry me, Louise. I want you for my own. For always.'

'This is not the time for talk of that.' She jerked herself free of his embrace and suddenly she seemed as self-controlled and elusive as ever. 'Everything I said in the past still holds good.'

Turning swiftly on her heel, she left him. That night, in spite of what she had said, he tried her door, but it was locked.

She heard him and turned on her pillow, aching for him. Slowly, almost from the start and without realizing it, she had fallen deeply and irrevocably in love with him, knowing only that he presented a threat to the way she wanted to organize her life. She could see now that loving Charles had been a refuge without demand on her senses or a threat to her freedom. Nothing could take the joy of having loved him away from her. Nobody could blot him out and he would have a part of her heart until the end of her days. Yet Daniel had the power to make her feel she was missing half of herself if he was not there.

Ever since Delphine had been able to receive visitors, Daniel had been to see her at least once every day. At first she lay weakly against her pillows, barely able to talk, but as soon as it was possible, Louise sat her in a chair every day, a plaid rug over her knees, and her foot resting on a footstool. Then Daniel would stay to play cards or backgammon with her. Louise always left them on their own together, partly to let her sister enjoy a complete change of company and also because it gave her the chance to take a walk and to explore a little more of the city each time.

Delphine always looked forward to Daniel's visits. He rarely came empty-handed, bringing her a box of caramels or some other candy that she liked, sometimes a nosegay of flowers or a book he thought she would enjoy, and he always had something to tell that made her laugh. As time went on she remained extremely thin and a slight cough still troubled her, but a glossiness returned to her copper curls and some colour began showing itself in her cheeks. Her provocative ways had quickly revived and she used her eyes and her smile as they chatted.

'I'm tired of being ill now, Daniel,' she said one day. 'I want to start dancing again and to get on with my life, but my ankle still hurts badly and your footman with the thick black eyebrows was to blame for that!'

'So Louise told me. Didn't you know? I dismissed him on the spot.'

'Yes, but you should have thrown him out as he did me!'

'What makes you think I didn't?' he asked with a grin, making her laugh again delightedly, and she clapped her hands together in approval like a child. 'How would you like me to carry you downstairs for a change of surroundings? You've been shut up here long enough.'

'Oh, yes! Now! At once! I've been longing to get out of this room. Dr Harvey is so afraid that I'll undo the good that rest has done to my ankle if I go downstairs. He seems to think I'll start walking about.'

'You can have a footstool downstairs, as you have up here.'

From then on Delphine was downstairs for most of each day. After the first time, she insisted on being dressed, for by now both her trunk and Louise's had arrived from the farm.

Although she had given Louise a brief outline of what had happened on her journey to Boston, there had always been certain details that she had kept to herself, unable yet to voice them. But feeling better in health gave her the strength to finally put the horrific experience into words. Even so, she found she had to lead up to it by repeating a little of what she had told Louise before.

She chose a moment when the two of them were on their own in the drawing room, Louise having been reading to her.

'As you know from what I've told you already,' Delphine began, 'I had lifts on my journey from some kind people. An elderly couple took me the greatest distance, saying I had made it a pleasure for them with my chatter and my company. They were so protective, saying they would do for me as they would for one of their grandchildren. I stayed ten days at their homestead before they found someone they trusted to take me on the next stage.'

Louise put her bookmark into place and put the volume aside. 'There's something I've been intending to ask you. Didn't all these people think it was strange you were travelling alone?'

'I told them I was on my way to stay with my cousins in Boston, because I'd been ill-treated by the couple I'd worked for, which was why I had no money for a fare.'

'A pack of lies!'

'But it worked.' Then Delphine's triumphant expression faded. 'There were only thirty miles left to Boston when a drover gave me a lift on the back of his cart. Five miles on, he stopped and pulled me off the cart and into the forest.' She drew a shuddering breath and covered her face with her hands. 'He hurt me cruelly when he raped me. I thought he would murder me too. But he left me in the bushes and drove away, taking my purse and belongings with him.'

Louise, full of compassion, moved to put an arm about her shoulders. 'Delphine! I had no idea that had happened to you.'

Delphine's hands slowly left her face and her lashes were

a-glitter with tears of self-pity. 'My clothes were torn and I was covered in bruises. Without any money, I had to walk the rest of the way to Boston, begging where I could and sleeping at night under bushes. Then I arrived at Cousin Madeleine's house to find they were far away. Even Daniel was in New York.' She hesitated briefly, her voice thick with shame. 'One morning before you came to my room, I asked Nurse Annabelle if that drover had given me any contagion, but she said no. She also assured me I wasn't pregnant, even though my moon circle hadn't returned. She said that was because I have been starved and ill.'

'I'm sure she's right.'

'It still hasn't come back and I hope it never does! I don't want any more babies. I would have died if I'd found you had brought Pieter's son here.'

Louise had waited deliberately over the past weeks for Delphine to become her normal self again before raising the subject of Philippe, giving her the last chance of a change of heart. 'But I've thought how we can manage to look after Philippe. When I start work again I could hire a girl to look after him during the day. The rest of the time we can both care for him.'

'No! Never!' She shook herself wildly in the chair as if she wanted to spring out of it and run physically away from the idea. 'Let him be sent to Pieter!'

'You know that is entirely impractical. And how can you be sure that Pieter would accept him? There is an alternative.' It was then Louise told her of Alexandre and Blanche's wish to adopt the boy. 'I have the necessary papers with me.'

Delphine answered at once. 'Bring me pen and ink. I'll sign them now.'

Louise despatched the papers the same day.

Daniel had thought that with Delphine downstairs he would see more of Louise. Although now she dined with him every evening, Delphine was always there too. He realized that it suited her that her sister's presence prevented any intimate conversation between them, and he was constantly irritated by it. He began to take up the social threads of his life again, spending evenings at gaming and cards with friends, attending balls and parties, and political gatherings. He would have taken Louise with him to many of these occasions, but she always refused, saying that the evenings would be long for Delphine without her. Finally he decided to pin her down with an invitation she could not refuse.

'You leave Delphine every morning when you go out walking. So come riding with me instead on Saturday. I've a horse that would be perfect for you. You sister won't be alone in the house.'

'I can't,' Louise answered calmly. 'I'm meeting someone.'

'Who?' he demanded fiercely.

Amusement showed in her eyes. 'Am I not allowed any private life?'

'Yes,' he replied impatiently. 'But you have all the week to meet this person, whoever he or she might be.'

'I can't cancel the arrangement I've made, but I promise you shall hear all about it afterwards.'

That evening he left the house to attend an evening of cards, hoping for some good play to banish his gloom. He was not used to being celibate, having a powerful sexual drive, and with Louise flitting about the house and the fragrant bouquet of her so often in his nostrils, he was totally possessed by his desire for her. If the library door had been locked that day he was certain she would have given herself eagerly to him.

He had just arrived at the venue when Theodore Bradshaw greeted him. 'You're looking well, Lombard.'

'So, you're back from Louisiana!' Daniel exclaimed. 'Yes, all is fine with me. Have you quite recovered your health?'

'Indeed I have.' Theodore was a man of immense dignity, quiet-voiced, with thick grey hair and aquiline features. 'We returned three days ago. I must say it's good to be back in Boston again.'

'How is Mrs Bradshaw? I have some important news for her concerning her cousins.' Briefly Daniel explained that they were staying with him after Delphine had injured her foot, but he left all details to be given by them.

'How soon may we call?' Theodore smiled. 'I know Madeleine would leave her bed and go this night if I told her when I get home.'

'Then why not tomorrow afternoon?'

When the sisters heard that their cousins would be coming to see them, their reactions were quite different. Delphine was wild with excitement in hopeful anticipation of what the future might hold for her now, whereas Louise thought only of the joy of seeing again the cousin of whom she had been so fond as a child.

Delphine chose to wear one of her best silk gowns and had arranged herself prettily in a chair where the June sun made a red-gold aureole about her hair. She had also had her chair turned to face the drawing room's double doors, which stood wide open, so she would be the first to be seen. Her pink dancing slipper revealed its tip on the footstool. Daniel had come home from his work to be there and tea was to be served in the lily-patterned porcelain cups that Louise liked best. Everything was ready when the doorbell jingled in the distant realms of the house.

'They're here!' Delphine exclaimed, levering herself up by the chair arms to catch a glimpse of the carriage drawn up outside. Daniel had already gone out to the hall and could be heard welcoming the visitors as they were shown into the house. Madeleine's excited voice, sweet and high, was music to both sisters ears. Then she appeared in the doorway, a short plump woman with a round, still-pretty face, bright blue eyes, silver-fair hair under a magnificent hat and a smiling expression that matched her voice. In spite of Delphine's careful planning, it was Louise whom Madeleine saw first.

'My darling girl! You are here with us at last!' Joyously, Madeleine flung out her arms and enfolded Louise in a bosomy embrace.

'You make me think the clock has turned back, Madeleine!'

Louise declared happily when they had kissed each other's cheeks. 'It's as if all those years between have condensed into yesterday.' Then, as Louise turned to greet Theodore, his wife saw Delphine for the first time.

'Merciful God!' Madeleine clapped a hand to her mouth, her face becoming ashen, and she swayed on her feet.

Daniel was swift to steady her. 'What is it, ma'am? Do you feel faint?'

'No, no.' She reached a hand behind her to seek her husband's and he clasped it tightly as they stood together, staring at Delphine, whose expression was becoming dismayed in her bewilderment at not knowing what was wrong.

'Why are you looking at me like that?' she cried in abject disappointment that she seemed to have made a bad first impression.

Her cry broke the couple's trance. Madeleine darted forward to cup Delphine's face lovingly between her hands, her eyes shining with tears. 'Forgive me, child. But you are the living image of our dear departed daughter, Mary Anne. She would have been just a few weeks older than you are now. You have the same eyes, the same nose and chin, as well as that wonderful bronze hair that comes from your mother's and my side of the family. You could be her twin sister.'

Louise, who had been watching in surprise, saw as nobody else did a slight shift in Delphine's eyes, and the smile curving her lips recalled the old adage about the cat having swallowed the cream.

'What a great compliment you have paid me, dear Cousin Madeleine,' Delphine breathed, radiating innocent pleasure.

Theodore was also deeply moved by her extraordinary likeness to the daughter he had loved. He could foresee this girl filling a gap in his wife's life and maybe becoming instrumental in easing out the problems that had arisen in their marriage since their bereavement.

As Louise poured the tea and they all talked, exchanging news and accounts of much that had happened in the intervening years, Madeleine could not take her gaze from Delphine.

'How did you injure your ankle, my dear?' she asked with concern.

'When I fell down Daniel's front steps!' Delphine answered merrily. 'Wasn't that a foolish thing to do?'

'I still don't understand why you or Louise didn't write to let us know you were coming to Boston. Your letter would have been sent on to us and we could have returned in time for your arrival.'

'My decision was made on the spur of the moment!' Delphine had prepared herself for the question. 'I have to confess that I became so bored with life on the farm that all I wanted was to come to Boston and stay for a little while with you and Theodore.'

Madeleine laughed delightedly. 'How impulsive of you and how sweet!'

Delphine, well aware that both Louise and Daniel had their eyes on her, knew that she had to tell the truth about what had happened next. Madeleine and Theodore listened in dismay and astonishment to her tale of how destitute she had become and of Daniel's rescue.

'You poor dear child!' Madeleine exclaimed. Then, having received Theodore's indulgent nod in answer to the appeal in her eyes, she spoke directly to Daniel.

'Would you allow us to take your two visitors away from you? Providing Louise and Delphine are willing to accept our abode as their family home from this day forward. After all, it's where they belong.'

'Oh, yes!' Delphine said eagerly. 'Daniel has been wonderful to us, but I've known we couldn't stay for ever. How did you guess that my secret dream has been for Louise and I to have a true home with our own kin? I never dreamt it would happen this way.'

Theodore looked across at Louise, who was almost bemused by her sister's guile. 'What do you say, Cousin?'

'I should like nothing better than to feel close to you and Madeleine, and I know I can always think of your home as my own, but I have made some plans that have yet to be consolidated. So, for a short time, if Daniel will forgive our departure, I should like to stay with you both to pick up the family threads again, which were severed for so long.' She met an icy look in Daniel's eyes before he turned with a smile to her cousins.

'I'm only glad I was able to be of service to my guests in your absence.'

Madeleine beamed at him. 'How kind and considerate you are!' Then to the sisters she added, 'How soon may Theodore and I expect you?'

Daniel spoke up in the same amiable tones as before. 'If they wish, this very hour. My housekeeper will supervise the packing of trunks and those shall be delivered to your house this evening.'

His words hit home to Louise and she realized the extent of his terrible anger with her, but there was nothing she could say to ease matters between them at the present time. She had to wait for the private plans she had mentioned to come into effect before she could tell him.

He did not look at her when the time came for leaving. She had been upstairs to collect her purse and Delphine's, as well as their capes. He sensed her coming down again, but he was paying attention only to the Bradshaws, as well as supervising the two footmen, who made a bandy chair with their arms to carry Delphine out to the carriage. As they bore her out of the door, she blew a kiss to him with her fingertips.

'Au revoir, dear Daniel.' She was pouting provocatively. 'I shall miss you. Come and see me soon.'

Louise paused on the steps outside and spoke to him, her words too quiet for anyone else to hear. 'I shall come to see you on Saturday evening if you'll be at home.'

He did look at her, but under fierce brows spoke rigidly. 'I'll be here. Dine with me.'

She gave a nod of acceptance and went down to the carriage. He stood watching as it drove away.

Thirteen

L ouise became as close to Madeleine as she had been in the past, her childhood devotion having turned to affectionate friendship. They often talked for hours on end, catching up on all the years between. But when Delphine came into the room or on to the porch or anywhere else they happened to be, Madeleine forgot everybody and everything else, having eyes only for her.

'Come and sit by me, dear child. Are you comfortable? Would you like the footstool nearer?'

Delphine revelled in the attention. Within two days of arriving at the Bradshaws' fine red-brick and stonework mansion, which a previous owner had renamed Independence House to celebrate the departure of the British, she declared her ankle had improved beyond measure. She had suddenly felt less pain and was managing to limp gracefully from room to room, even though she declared the stairs were still too much for her and she continued to be carried up and down.

Louise regarded her cynically. She realized she had been hoodwinked. While at Daniel's home, Delphine had deliberately hidden her ankle's improvement under the pretence of continual pain, which not even the doctor had been able to disprove. Clearly she had been determined to extend the time of her convalescence until the Bradshaws' return. Now at last she had achieved her long-awaited aim to come under Madeleine and Theodore's wealthy wing, and had been accepted by them in a way that must far exceed even her most optimistic imaginings. She had become a substitute daughter, with all the advantages that would bring her.

'Why did you go on pretending?' Louise demanded sharply when they were on their own, seated in wicker chairs on the porch, looking out over the flower garden with its leafy trees. Once again her sister's innate capriciousness had strained her tolerance to the limits.

Delphine made no denial of her deceit. 'Because I knew what would happen if I didn't. You are always so fiercely independent that you'd have dragged me away from Daniel's splendid home and off to some hovel, with talk of work and earning a living again. I've had enough of drudgery. I know there are dancing schools here in Boston, but now I only want to dance at grand balls with partners of my own choosing. Did you know that Cousin Madeleine is planning a great ball especially for me as soon as I'm able to dance again?' Her eyes sparkled excitedly. 'It's supposed to be a surprise for me, but I heard her talking about it to Cousin Theodore!'

'It could be held tomorrow as far as your foot is concerned,' Louise remarked crisply.

'Don't be so hard on me, Louise,' Delphine coaxed. 'Not when so many lovely things are about to happen. It will all start on Saturday evening, when there's to be a soirée for us to meet some of our cousins' friends.'

Louise was dismayed. 'But I've promised to dine with Daniel! Why didn't Madeleine tell me?'

'She will do when you see her later, but she only decided on it this morning after breakfast while she and I sat talking. You'd already gone out on another of your solitary walks. I helped her write the invitations and they've already been delivered. There'll only be about twenty of their close friends, as well as Daniel. He'll understand that you will have to be here.'

Louise bit her lip in exasperation. 'I'll go and see him now,' she said, getting up from her chair.

As before, on that rainy night, Louise stood looking up at the Lombard office building from the opposite side of the street. The windows were twinkling in the sunshine and it was far larger than she had realized when she had stood there in the darkness. Unlike the previous time, when the street had been almost deserted, there was plenty of traffic passing to and fro, which made her wait for an opportunity to cross it.

In the entrance hall of Lombard's, she glanced about her with interest, having been too exhausted to notice anything in detail when last there. A glass-panelled door led into a ground-floor office and she went in. Several clerks sat on stools at a row of high desks, their quill pens busy. Only one looked up, but an older, grey-haired man came from a table to meet her.

'Good morning, ma'am. May I be of assistance?'

'I wish to see Mr Lombard.'

'Yes, ma'am. I'll see if that's possible.' He sent an office boy running up the wide flight of stairs down which Daniel had come on that nightmare evening. Then she was shown into another room leading off the hall to wait. It was panelled and well furnished with sofas and chairs upholstered in yellow striped silk, which would have complimented any drawing room, and a Persian rug covered almost all the polished floor. Framed squares of richly figured silk, as well as etchings of looms, silkworms and ships in full sail gave clues to the business conducted in the building. There was also a watercolour view of mulberry trees, which she knew were called the *Trees of Gold* in the French silk industry, since the leaves provided the only diet on which the silkworms thrived. The door opened behind her and she knew with every fibre of her being that Daniel had entered the room.

'I see that the artist of this watercolour has a French name. Was it painted somewhere near Lyons?' she asked without looking round.

'Yes, it was. I came across it by chance one day at an auction.'

'It's exceptionally fine.' She did turn then and saw there was no welcome in his face, his eyes narrowed and glacial.

'So, you've come yourself to tell me that you're unable to dine with me after all.' His voice was dangerously soft. 'I received the Bradshaw invitation here this morning when it was brought to me with a more urgent message from my house. I shall, of course, accept it. I want to see for myself how quickly you have become absorbed into your new surroundings.'

Her sudden impatience with him glittered in her gaze. 'I knew nothing about the soirée until less than an hour ago. I had no idea that my cousin would arrange any event without telling me, but she is still so beside herself with happiness at having Delphine to fuss over and cherish that she scarcely knows where she is or what she is doing. I had my own reasons for choosing the last day of the week for our meeting, but if you'll be at home on Friday, I shall come that evening instead.'

He inclined his head sharply. 'A day earlier. All the better.'

There was no pleasure in his voice and she wondered what he expected to hear from her when Friday came. It was obvious that he had viewed her leaving his house as both desertion and a final severance, showing he had believed after that kiss between them in the library that she would never leave him. She must have revealed more of her inner self at that moment than she had realized at the time.

She made a move to go again. 'Now that our meeting has been rearranged satisfactorily, I'll bid you au revoir, Daniel.'

He saw her out. 'Until Friday then, Louise.'

She went away without looking back.

Instead of returning immediately to Independence House, she went to a lawyers' office on State Street. She would be early for her appointment, but she could wait there. When she emerged some time later there was a little smile on her lips. Now everything was in place. It had been like a game of chess. She had put so much thought into the secret moves that she had made prior to this day, all unbeknown to Daniel and Delphine. Neither had she said anything to the Bradshaws, who, had she wished it, might have been able to offer some advice. She was glad that this new venture would be entirely the result of her own efforts and she was prepared to work all hours of the day and night if necessary to make a success of it.

When she arrived back at Independence House Madeleine

came to the head of the stairs and beckoned to her. 'Come up, Louise,' she urged eagerly. 'You have such good taste and we've been waiting for your advice. I decided that our dear Delphine should have a new gown for the soirée. In fact, a new wardrobe altogether as she is so tired of everything she has worn during her convalescence.' Then she hurried back into Delphine's bedroom.

Reaching its doorway, Louise gazed in smiling amazement at the confusion reigning within. A portly seamstress with her three assistants seemed to have filled the whole bedroom with measuring tapes, swatches of silks, velvets, gauzes and muslins. There was a stack of London fashion plates and dolls in miniature versions of what could be supplied. In the midst of it all Delphine stood pirouetting in her petticoats, all pretence of a painful ankle abandoned, even though she had been carried downstairs again that morning. She was holding various lengths of fabric against herself, still undecided as to which she liked best. Seeing Louise, she waved happily.

'Isn't this wonderful! I'm to have everything in the very latest fashion. Waists are even higher! Right under the bosom now and flowing softly from underneath. Muslins and gauzes are now the most elegant. You can help me decide which of these lovely fabrics I should choose.'

'Which do you like best so far?'

'I love them all!'

Louise picked up the fashion plates and studied them. She thought the new styles wonderfully graceful. Her most recent gowns had followed the strong trend towards a higher waistline and a narrower silhouette, but she had had nothing new since leaving New York, having been too occupied ever since to give time to any sewing for herself.

Madeleine touched her on the arm. 'Come with me to my boudoir for a few minutes, Louise. There's something that I want to discuss with you in private.'

As soon as Madeleine had shut the boudoir door she sat down beside Louise, who had seated herself on the chaise longue. 'I know I'm being indulgent towards Delphine,' she began apologetically, 'but she is so delighted with everything she receives and both Theodore and I want her to be happy with us.'

'You need have no fear about that,' Louise said reassuringly.

'There's something else far more important that I have to say. Theodore is going to speak to you about it this evening, but I'm on such tenterhooks that I can't wait a moment longer to have some idea as to how you will react.' She drew a deep breath. 'First of all, I must tell you that we know about the baby. Delphine shed such tears when she told me how that Dutch villain in New York raped her and how your kind friends on the farm adopted the child. When I think how her one thought was to run away to me for understanding and comfort, I'm touched to the heart.' Madeleine's eyes filled with tears. 'As I told the darling girl, her terrible experience is all in the past now. She is making a new start in life with us.'

Louise thought how typical it was of Delphine to cover her tracks so skilfully as well as disguising the true facts for her own ends. 'You're very tolerant, Madeleine.'

'We love her as you do, my dear.'

'What was it you wished to ask me?'

'Theodore and I want you to let us take on full responsibility for Delphine, as if we were her true parents. She is not yet of age and we should like to adopt her officially. Not only is it our greatest desire, but you will be left free to enjoy yourself after years of putting her first, which I know you have always done, from everything she has told me.'

Louise thought how strange it was that for the second time she was being asked to agree to an adoption. Firstly the son and now the young mother. 'Have you spoken to Delphine about it?'

'No! Theodore said that we must consult you first.'

'Delphine has yearned for a long time to make her home with you and I know how safe and well cared for she would be, but—'

Madeleine smiled happily and made a dismissive little

gesture. 'Don't worry about anything, my dear. Delphine will be as much our daughter as if she had been Mary Anne's twin. She has brought youth and light back into our lives. As for you, at last you will have the chance to put your own wishes first and to live your life without any encumbrances.'

'I've never thought of my sister in that light. Anything I did for her was out of love, just as it always will be if ever she needs me.'

'I know,' Madeleine said softly. 'It shall be the same with us.'

Theodore and Louise discussed the matter at length that evening in his study. He made it clear that, unlike his wife, he was not deceived as to Delphine's true character.

'I think I know the problems you've had to deal with in taking care of your sister,' he said sagely. 'She has more mischief in her eyes than our own daughter had in her whole body, but I'm willing to shoulder whatever comes for my wife's sake. There were many times during Madeleine's terrible mourning when I was afraid to leave the house in case she should find some way to take her own life in my absence. Even after I brought her away from New York to Boston, she seemed unable to face life without our child and there have been many difficult periods as a result. But your sister has given her a purpose in life again. Madeleine has been transformed.'

'It seems to me in that way they are alike.' Louise commented. 'They both need to give love and to be surrounded by it.'

'I agree. So have I your permission to ask Delphine if she would like to become our legally adopted daughter?'

'I have no objection and can only thank you for fulfilling my sister's dream.'

When Delphine was told after dinner that evening, triumph radiated from her, but Louise could also see that there was genuine affection for both Madeleine and Theodore when she embraced them in turn. Once again Louise recognized her sister's ability to love generously.

When Friday evening came Louise dressed with care and

touched her throat and wrist with perfume from a bottle that Madeleine had given her as a welcome gift. Lastly she opened her jewel case. There were only a few pieces left, for she had sold them off one by one to cover the cost of many things. At the farm her good friends had made it clear from the start that she and Delphine were entirely their guests, just as Daniel had done, but she had forestalled him by paying Nurse Annabelle and settling Dr Harvey's account. But she still had her emerald necklace and earrings, which she would wear this evening. In the jewel case's secret drawer, her sister's sapphires and other inherited pieces lay untouched. Delphine had confessed they would have gone with her in her flight to Boston if she had known the case's secret mechanism, which had saved them from falling into the hands of the thief.

Daniel opened the door himself as Louise came up the steps, the glow from the hall behind him flooding on to her. It highlighted the pale oval of her lovely face upturned to him, her smile meeting his frown, and threw rich lights into her hair, which she had dressed in the latest mode, drawn back smoothly into a knot at the back of her head with short curls on her forehead. It suited her.

'Good evening, Daniel.'

He returned her greeting as she entered his house, swishing past him in olive-green silk with her fragrance drifting after her. Then she paused, looking over her creamy shoulder as she waited for him to reach her side. 'It's a perfect evening,' she said composedly. 'So warm, and I don't think I've ever seen the sky so full of stars.'

'That's why I decided we should dine on the terrace.'

'I was hoping that might happen.'

The table was laid for two, with tall candles held by a silver candelabrum, and the supper dishes were set out on a side table.

'I thought we'd wait on ourselves this evening as we've much to talk about,' he said, thinking that he had never before seen her in such high spirits, which was in marked contrast to his own sombre mood.

'An excellent idea.'

She thought the dishes looked more than usually appetizing. Curls of cucumber garnished the dressed lobsters, as if in the heart of a bouquet, the salads were crisp and bright, with edible flowers, and the collation of cold meats was arranged in fans, colour added delicately with tiny vegetables. Then she saw the heart-shaped dessert, set on a plate of celestial-blue porcelain beside a crystal bowl full of Chantilly cream, which was decorated with crystallized violets and rose petals.

'I believe you've acquired a French chef!' she exclaimed delightedly. 'I haven't seen a tarte Tatin since I was at Versailles!'

Daniel relaxed slightly at her show of pleasure. 'Yes, he's an émigré from Rouen. Mrs Carter took him on to the staff yesterday. She said he's a boastful fellow, so let's see if his cooking merits the praise that he seems to think he deserves.'

As they ate, Louise appreciated the chef's subtle use of herbs and his skill in bringing out the fine flavours. She sat opposite Daniel and by unspoken mutual consent they kept their conversation to safe subjects. It was after the caramelized apple tart had proved to be as delicious as it had looked that Louise rested her elbows on the table and her chin on her linked hands as she made her announcement.

'I've something important to tell you, Daniel. You're the first to hear my news. I've bought a shop with accommodation above it! I'm going to make and sell exclusive millinery. What have you to say? I hope you approve my venture.'

His gaze was on her wine glass, which he was refilling from a decanter, and he clenched his jaw slightly before he spoke. 'Where is it?'

'Washington Street. It's only small, but it's in a good position with plenty of people constantly passing by. Whenever it's been possible to get away on my own, I've been everywhere in the city to locate other millinery establishments and view their windows. I believe I can outshine them all.'

'I'm sure you will.' He set down the decanter and took up his own refilled glass for a toast. 'To your success!'

'Thank you, Daniel.'

'Have you ordered your shop sign yet?'

'No, I wanted to ask you about that. I need to find a good sign painter.'

'I know just the man.'

'That's most helpful. I've been to suppliers to order felts and straws, ribbons, feathers and beads, as well as English fashion plates. I've also purchased pressing irons, hat blocks and all else that I'll need. For a month I'll build up a stock myself and take on two workers to assist me. On Monday a decorator and a carpenter will start work on the paintwork and the alterations and fittings that I want. I wasn't sure that everything could be arranged before today, which is why originally I suggested meeting tomorrow evening.'

'Who's backing you in this enterprise?'

'Nobody. I raised the money myself by going back to the jeweller whom you recommended a while ago when I wanted to sell something. He was extremely pleased when I offered him the chance to buy my diamond parure.'

Daniel looked shocked. 'You didn't sell that! But those diamonds were superb. I've never seen anything to match them.'

'That's what he said. It was a wedding gift from Fernand, but as I eventually paid for it myself when I settled the first of his endless debts, I've never been at all sentimental about it. It would be a different matter if I had to part with my emeralds.' She touched her necklace lightly. 'They were my grandmother's and for that reason I treasure them. She died when I was seven and, although I remember her as being kind and loving towards me, my father always said she was a fierce old lady who ruled the family with an iron will. That makes me sure that she would have approved of my standing alone in my enterprise.'

'You're too much like her for your own good, Louise,' he stated unsmilingly.

She raised her eyebrows, laughing. 'But I take a comparison with her as a compliment! I'll need to keep that way if I'm to succeed in business.'

He sat back in his chair, shaking his head impatiently. 'I wasn't thinking of your ability in commerce.'

'Am I such a shrew?'

A smile curled his lips. 'You're stubborn enough.'

She flung back her head and laughed merrily. 'I don't deny it.'

'You mentioned accommodation being included in your new acquisition. Is that to be the workshop?'

'No, there's room behind the shop for that purpose. My new home will be upstairs.'

'I thought the Bradshaws wanted you to make your home with them.'

'You heard me say when they invited me that it would only be for a while.'

'They probably thought you had marriage in mind.'

'Then they'll discover that they were mistaken when I tell them my news.'

Daniel, losing patience, sprang up from his chair so quickly that the legs scraped the stones of the terrace. He stood looking out over the moonlit lawn as he questioned her bitterly. 'Did what happened between us in the library mean nothing to you? Have you even remembered what I said?'

There was silence for a few moments before she answered quietly. 'I remember.'

'So?' He heard her leave the table and the whisper of her skirts as she came to stand just behind him.

'I can't be your wife. I see marriage as a trap that would shut me in, no matter that I love you more than you could ever know. Instead, let us be lovers, Daniel!'

He turned in astonishment at her words. 'Do you know what you're saying? I want you with me for the rest of my life, not for some transient affair!'

'It won't be. I didn't want to fall in love with you. I fought against it for longer than I care to remember, but eventually I

175

realized you were part of my whole being and I was destined to love you till the end of my days.'

Stunned, he took her face slowly between his hands and bent his head to kiss her lips, lightly at first, as if memorizing their contours, and then with an almost savage joy as she began to kiss him frantically, clinging to him with her arms about his neck.

Together they left the terrace to go into the house and up the stairs, their progress slow, for most of the way they paused to kiss and kiss again, barely able to break apart. In the moonlit room that had been hers on her visit, he threw off his coat and stripped her with loving haste until she stood naked in a tumbled circle of her own garments. Exultantly, she raised her hands to comb the pins out of her hair before lifting her arms high, her head back and her spine arched as he kissed her throat, before his mouth moved slowly downwards to travel the contours of her breasts and make her nipples stand erect. Dropping to one knee, he continued his passionate exploration of her, cupping her buttocks in his hands and lingering at her most secret place until she clutched his head, scarcely able to bear such pleasure, and turned his adoring face up to hers. Her eyes were brimming with love.

It was then that he lifted her about the hips and carried her across to the wide bed, where he ripped back the covers to lay her down. He discarded his own clothes swiftly and then came to take his place beside her, his body in full power and she so eager in her longing for him that neither could hold back. She gasped with joy as he entered her with such a gathering of their love between them that it was a moment unlike any other she had ever known. He prolonged their passion until at last their shared ecstasy burst forth together, throbbing through her with a force that made her leap within his embracing arms and finally sealed the love that they had long held for each other.

There followed a night of loving that left each knowing the other's body as intimately as their own. Neither would ever forget those moonlit hours together. She was finally sleeping when he awoke in the dawn light and propped his weight on his elbow as he gazed down at her. Gently, he smoothed back some tendrils of hair that lay across her cheek, being careful not to disturb her, but she had been on the edge of wakefulness and his touch was enough to cause her to open her eyes and smile dreamily at him.

'I love you,' she whispered, reaching up her hand to run her fingers gently down the side of his face.

'My darling,' he answered in soft tones.

He moved over her and made slow and contented love to her in the dawn light.

Fourteen

L ouise was still sleeping when Daniel rose from their bed, put on a silk robe, and parted the drapes at the window. Then he jerked the bell-rope to summon breakfast on a tray. When the maidservant brought it, he took it into the room himself. By now Louise was awake and he set the tray on the bed between them before he fetched another robe and helped her slip her arms into it.

'You look beautiful,' he said, kissing her. She sat back against the propped pillows, her chestnut hair in lovely disarray, and he buried his face in it before kissing her again.

With a smile she pushed him gently back. 'Have breakfast now before you upset the tray. I must return to Independence House before I'm missed.'

He sat down on the bed to face her and drew up one knee to rest his arm across it as he gazed at her. The early rays of the sun bathed them in its warm, golden glow.

'There's plenty of time yet,' he said. 'And we need to discuss the future. In talking about your shop yesterday evening you mentioned wanting to outshine all the other milliners in Boston.' He helped himself to a slice of fresh peach. 'I hope you realize that you'll never get the clientele that you seem to have been expecting.'

'Why not?' She would have thought he was joking if it had not been for the seriousness of his expression. 'I know relations between our two countries have been deteriorating with French ships attacking American vessels in the West Indies, but personally I've never met any animosity.'

'That's not what I had in mind. I was referring to the scandal that you and I are going to create as soon as people find out about us.'

Louise looked confident. 'But they won't. Our love is a private matter between us.'

'It will be a secret impossible to keep. Already you've spent the whole night away from the Bradshaws' home, which will be known already below stairs there, and my household knows of your presence here. Servants' tittle-tattle travels like lightning along the grapevine and soon spreads out into the community.'

'That's true in a small place, but Boston is like New York, where people are too busy with their own lives to concern themselves with the affairs of others.'

'That's where you're mistaken. Boston isn't like New York in that way or any other. There is still a small-town mentality here in that everybody of importance knows everyone else on the same social level. You'll never get the Beacon Hill matrons crossing the threshold of your shop if there's even a whisper of gossip about us. They'll stop their daughters and all the rest of their female relatives and friends from buying from you, even though they might be drooling over your hats in the window.'

Louise raised her chin determinedly. 'Then I shall make elegant, but less expensive hats for those with smaller purses. They will enjoy coming to my shop.'

'But a lower pitch for customers whose interest in fashion is not all-consuming will put you on a level with all the other milliners and you'll lose your chance to use your creative abilities to the full.'

'Nevertheless I don't intend to submit myself to any kind of subterfuge in being with you. I'm not afraid of scandal. I'll face whatever comes.'

'It's of no consequence to me either, but that's not the solution. You have to think about your cousins. Any scandal about you would rub off on those two highly respected people. And then there's Delphine. She would suffer from having a sister with a notorious reputation. You could be responsible for ruining her chances of the good marriage that she's hoping to make. Believe me, the social importance of position and class and outwardly impeccable reputations for women is probably stronger here in Boston than anywhere else in the country.'

Her face was bleak. 'Does this mean that we must stay apart?'

'That's a sacrifice I'm not prepared to make and it's one too many for you after all you've done already for your imp of a sister. No, but I have a solution.'

'What's that?'

'We'll have a marriage of convenience by which you can live above your millinery shop and I'll continue to live here. People will think it strange, but since we shall be married, there will be no cause for gossip. We can be together whenever we wish. Otherwise, my dear Louise, I fear you'll end up bankrupt and your diamonds will have been sold to no purpose.'

She tossed her napkin down on the tray and swung her legs over the side of the bed to spring to her feet. 'You're trying to trick me into marriage!' Her voice was sharp and defensive. 'It happened to me once before and I won't let it happen again!'

He had not moved, but continued to look at her. 'Every word I've spoken is the truth. You have to make a decision.'

She stood for a few moments, her fingers pressed to her temples, wretched that once again her original aims had been thwarted, but in declaring her love for Daniel, she had crossed the Rubicon and there was no going back. She could not live without him and behind his words she had heard his desperate need of her.

Thoughtfully, she sat down again on the edge of the bed. 'Do you really mean that we could go on leading our separate lives?'

'I give you my word. You'll have your freedom and we shall go on being lovers just as you planned originally, but causing no harm to anyone. If we should have a child, he or she would not be illegitimate.'

'It's a bizarre arrangement!' she exclaimed in protest.

'But a practical one. You told me once in New York

that you always tried to deal with matters in a practical manner.'

'That's true,' she admitted.

He clambered across the wide bed to swing down his feet and sit beside her. He tilted her chin up to him and there was laughter in his eyes. 'I think we've found a way to keep married love alive. Maybe we should recommend it to others.'

She jerked her chin away, remote in her thoughts. 'If I should decide that marriage is the only solution,' she pondered uncertainly, 'it would have to be a quiet wedding. Just two witnesses and us.'

'That's easily arranged. Let's get married today! This morning!'

Once again she sprang to her feet, close to panic for the first time in her life. 'It's too soon! You're rushing me into this! I must think about it for a few days.'

'Take all the time you want, but don't expect wagging tongues to wait too.'

She clasped her hands distractedly, lifting them up and down as she paced the floor several times before coming to a halt. 'I see that I'll have to do as you suggest,' she conceded reluctantly. 'I can't let anything I do taint the lives of my cousins or my sister. If we are to marry, it might as well be today.'

He came to put his arms around her, speaking softly. 'You won't regret it. Maybe there will come a day in the future when you'll decide that the time is right for us to be together for the rest of our lives.'

She frowned, putting a finger firmly against his lips. 'You mustn't count on that, but you'll be the only one I'll love until my last breath.'

He drove her back to the Bradshaws' home to wait while she changed, for she was certain that no minister would marry her in her present gown, which had such a low décolletage. She ran up the steps and a servant admitted her. Nobody else saw her arrive or leave, for it was not yet nine o'clock and Madeleine and Delphine were still in their rooms. Theodore was always up early, but he was shut away in his study.

When Louise emerged into the sunshine again she was wearing a cream straw hat that she had made, and the amber-hued muslin of her gown flowed against her legs as she hurried down the steps. On the way to the church, Daniel stopped the horses and jumped out to buy her a posy of flowers from a street seller. She inhaled the scent of the blossoms as they continued on their way.

'It's just as if we were eloping.' She tilted back her head, laughing happily.

'I suppose in a way we are!' he declared, laughing with her.

The minister had called in his wife and daughter to be witnesses while he married Daniel and Louise in the otherwise empty church. The ring that Daniel slid on to her finger was a family heirloom of diamonds and pearls set in gold. They looked at each other very seriously before they kissed once the minister had pronounced that they were now husband and wife.

'Now to break the news!' Daniel declared with a grin, kissing her again on the church steps.

The Bradshaws were surprised, but pleased about the marriage. Delphine, after her initial disappointment at not having been a bridesmaid to outshine the bride, realized with relief that she would be free at last from her sister's eagle eye. Louise had always been able to read her like a book, whereas Madeleine only saw her in a rose-tinted light.

Theodore announced the marriage of Daniel and Louise that same evening at the soirée and there were congratulations and good wishes from all present.

Louise was to stay with Daniel all the time the alterations and decorations took place at the shop. There were several delays when it was discovered that the property had to be re-roofed and subsidence corrected in the basement. She visited Daniel's warehouse to select the silk fabrics she would need for her millinery. Afterwards, in a special storeroom, she had her choice of the exquisite Lyons silks to be made into high-waisted coats and gowns by the best seamstresses.

Neither she nor Daniel had ever been happier and they made love at every opportunity. It was as if their passion, long denied, could never be assuaged.

She called into the shop every day to see how the work was progressing. At her instructions the atelier and her office were the first to be made ready. Then she interviewed a number of women sent to her by an agency. Several were suitable, but she chose two older women with considerable experience in the millinery trade, as well as an apprentice, who showed she would be quick to learn the unique plaiting for the straw hats.

Finally she engaged a young woman of twenty, named Amy Saville, to assist in the showroom itself. She was the plainest of the applicants, but she was stylish in her simple summer clothes and wore her hat with flair. Louise intended to teach her how to show and display hats with the right tilt of the head, just as she herself had once done for Daniel at Miss Sullivan's. He had long since admitted that his purchase had been a pretext by which to meet her again, something she had known from the start.

To build up stock Louise took on four other milliners on a temporary basis and they and the two others were soon at work at the long tables, cutting and shaping and steaming. The hats they produced were from Louise's own designs, which she had started to sketch during her days at Miss Sullivan's and had continued periodically ever since. The latest London fashion plates showed that hats were gaining high crowns and narrower brims, some without brims at all, and even a bonnet shape that was all brim, like half a flowerpot.

By chance Louise met an American woman at a card party, Mrs Amelia Jackson, who was visiting her daughter in Boston after just returning from travelling with her husband on a diplomatic mission to Paris. She spoke descriptively of the neoclassical styles evolving there and of the hats being worn, which included spectacular turbans. Louise was delighted to know that, in spite of the war, fashion was rising again in France under the ruling Directory. Some of it sounded extreme, such as a daringly low décolletage, almost to the nipples, with the throat wrapped in a silk neck cloth. There were also bonnet brims extending to absurd lengths over the face. Yet it was through exaggeration that trends were set for the future.

Louise went to every social occasion that allowed her splendid eye-catching hats to be seen. Madeleine was delighted to have her company at any time and Daniel was always at her side at evening events and other important festivities. At the ball for Delphine and others that followed, Louise created a headdress for herself of pearls or plumes or ribbons. She knew that wherever she went women were starting to watch for her arrival to see what she was wearing.

'Why don't you make me a pretty hat?' Delphine pouted. She had no lack of male admirers herself and her coming-out ball had been an enormous personal success, but she had begun to resent the attention directed towards her sister. Men had always given Louise a second glance, a sharp turning of the head so often following in her wake, but now she was making her mark on Boston society in general and Delphine felt in danger of being overshadowed.

'I can't make you one yet,' Louise replied, 'because I need to wear my own designs exclusively to get them talked about. Then, when I open my shop, I hope everyone will come flocking to buy. But I have a special creation in mind for you and you shall have it on my opening day.'

By October, when the trees were in their full glory, Daniel had become convinced that Louise had dismissed all thought of moving into her own apartment, even though it had been furnished and ready for some time. So it came as a shock to him on the eve of the shop's opening when he saw her trunks being carried down the stairs. He went in search of her, flinging open doors and charging from one room to another until he finally found her with her writing box on her lap as she penned a letter. She looked up with a smile, about to tell him she was answering a letter from her aunt in England, and then saw his rage-congested face.

'Why?' he demanded furiously before she could speak. 'There's no reason at all for you to move out! You can be at the shop for opening hours like anyone else running a business. You don't have to live on site!'

She answered him quietly, putting the writing box aside. 'You've known from the start that this is what I planned to do. When the property became mine I told you that I'd move in on the eve of its opening. You agreed to it.'

'My God! I thought that once you were here you'd never leave. This house will be like a morgue without you. I want you here! I need to hear your voice and your laughter in these rooms.' He flung his arms wide. 'Your footsteps on the stairs. The essence of you in my breathing. To see you come through these doors. And I want you in my bed, to feel you there all through the night and to wake to the sight of you.'

She felt overwhelmed by this passionate outpouring of his love for her and rose to her feet, for he had been towering over her. During the past weeks her excitement over her shop had blunted her realization of what her absence from his house would mean to him, no matter how cheerfully he had accepted the arrangement originally.

'I would stay if I could, but you know only too well that I have this desperate need to achieve success independently, to prove to myself that I am a whole person by right and not just a chattel. Somehow it's the only way by which I can shake off the past that still haunts me. I want to be free. Not of loving you, but of all the old nightmares.' She caught up his hand and clasped it to her. 'I shall be here often, always with you when we entertain our friends or wish for an evening here on our own, and you can come to me and to my bed every night. Everything will be just as you mapped out when you suggested marriage and gave me your word that you would keep to our agreement.'

Her calmness had the effect of exacerbating his anger and he jerked his hand away. 'I never thought you'd keep me to such a promise! I believed you loved me enough to realize that we couldn't live apart. You're throwing me out of your life!'

'That's not true! All I'm asking is a breathing space in which to slay all my dragons. Is it so much to ask?'

'Indeed it is! You're driving in the thin edge of the wedge. This separation is only the beginning of the end!'

Her face became rigid with the gust of anger that swept through her. 'After all we have been to each other, do you still know so little about me that you believe I would be so devious?'

'I don't know what to believe any more!' he gave back fiercely, a desolate bitterness behind his rage.

'In that case, there's nothing more to be said.' White-faced, she swept furiously away from him and out of the room.

He ran a hand through his hair in exasperation before he slammed his way into the library and threw himself into a chair. He was shaking with rage and frustration. Louise was the most infuriating and stubborn and desirable woman he had ever known, but she was in his blood and his bones, the other half of himself, and there was nothing he could do about it. Half an hour later he heard her come from the stairs and across the marble floor of the hall to pause outside the library door. He thought for a few swift moments that she was coming to tell him she had changed her mind about leaving, but then she went on out of the house. He heard the door close after her.

That night, Louise spent a restless night on her own in her new surroundings, unable to put the quarrel from her mind. She was thankful when the first light of dawn signalled that it was time to get up.

The fresh flowers she had ordered arrived promptly at seven o'clock and she set about arranging them in the crystal vases that Theodore and Madeleine had given her, the scent banishing the last hint of new paint from the showroom. Then she stood back to get the effect. A dividing wall had been taken down during the alterations and the showroom was now a spacious area enhanced by cream wallpaper striped with green and supplied with plenty of gilt-framed mirrors and chairs. The whole place was unrecognizable from how it had been before. Everything was ready, even the specially made leaf-yellow silk turban that she had set aside as a gift for Madeleine, knowing how it would suit her.

Her staff arrived early, all of them excited by the importance of the occasion, Amy wearing the new russet velvet gown that Louise had supplied. For the winter, spring and summer collections there would be a gown for her in keeping with the main colour of the season, but for the present it had to be in tone with autumn. Louise herself had chosen bronze silk gauze, but had not dampened it to cling to her figure as Mrs Jackson had said many fashionable women were doing in France.

The shop window had curtains across it to hide the display until the opening at ten o'clock. Louise gave a final touch to the cream silk draped over the stand holding the solitary creation, a pumpkin-orange hat with a rolled brim and a sunburst of feathers in all the hues of the brilliant foliage that made the trees such a vista at this time of year. It was both spectacular and beautiful, a work of art that would enhance the looks of any woman, whatever her age.

Shortly before ten o'clock Madeleine arrived with Delphine, coming in through the staff entrance. 'There are quite a few carriages waiting outside, Louise,' Delphine exclaimed excitedly. 'And I saw Mrs Featherstone and Mrs Lucas chatting on the opposite side of the street, but they had one eye on this shop and I'm sure they're waiting to be first in.'

Her words proved to be right. They must have moved at the first ripple of the drapes being parted in the window, because, as Louise looped back the cream silk folds, they had already crossed the street to peer in at the window. When they entered the shop, both wanted the hat in the window. Louise, seeing there would be friction, explained that it was only for display at the present time, but she would show them other hats that were on the same theme. When they were seated, together with Madeleine and Delphine and several other women who had come from their carriages, Amy paraded in the various hats as rehearsed. More well-dressed customers arrived and the novelty of seeing the hats being shown in this completely new way proved highly popular.

In spite of their quarrel, Louise fully expected Daniel to make an appearance during the day, but he did not come. She had sold many hats and there was a long list in her order book when she took the special creation from the window and placed it in one of the new black and white striped hatboxes for Delphine.

It was then that Daniel came, tapping on the door as he looked through the glass panel at her. She shot back the bolts again and let him in.

'Did you have a good day?' he asked reservedly, making no attempt to take her into his arms.

'Yes, it was more successful than I dared hope. My milliners will be kept busy for weeks to come.'

'Congratulations. But you must be tired.' He made a conciliatory gesture. 'I've come to take you home to dine. I'll bring you back here afterwards.'

'No, stay here. I ordered a cold supper to be brought in for the two of us. It's ready upstairs.'

His reserve broke and he pulled her to him, locking her in his arms as he kissed her passionately, her head cupped in his hand, and she responded with loving abandon, tears flowing from under her lids at the mending of their quarrel, even though its cause still remained.

'I love you so much,' he declared ardently, drawing back to look into her face and smoothing away her tears with his thumbs. 'Have your two years and longer if it means you'll come home to me eventually. Live your own life. Follow your own way. But don't ever leave me.'

'Never!' she promised vehemently, unable to envisage anything able to take her from this man. 'Nothing shall ever part us.'

Fifteen

Two years went by during which Louise's shop became renowned for its beautiful creations, and her customers could be sure that they would never meet anybody else in the same hat. It also became the place for brides to order hats and headdresses, and Louise began a successful sideline of bonnets for babies, employing two lace makers.

Her relationship with Daniel had never been stronger. There was constant speculation in their social circles as to why they lived apart, some of the women privately envying Louise's independence, while most of the married men thought Daniel fortunate that he did not have his wife under his roof to check all his comings and goings.

By this time Louise felt ready at last to move back into Daniel's house. He had been saying that he wanted her to have her portrait painted, but in the meantime she had had a miniature of herself done for him, which she would give him on their first evening together. The two years of hard work had enabled her to prove herself and to feel at last a person in her own right, with all nightmares banished. Before the Revolution there had been a strong movement in France, by women in her social class, to gain equality with men. She had heard that it had survived with renewed force and she found it intensely satisfying that she had achieved that same equality here in her new country. Most important of all, it was the foundation of her marriage in a true partnership. Daniel had never asked her to return sooner than the time she had stated, but now that the two years were up she knew he was hoping that she would not extend it.

She had stopped using precautions against pregnancy. An understanding duchess at Versailles had given her certain advice during her first marriage, when she had become fearful of having a child by Fernand after being abused by him. Now every time she and Daniel made love she hoped to become pregnant. She was soon rewarded and he shared her joy.

'I'll be able to come home with you to stay very soon now,' she promised him when they met to go to a concert together. 'Today I appointed an experienced manageress, Mrs Saunders, who has been in millinery herself, and she will take over my workload. It means that in future I'll be able to concentrate wholly on designing and, most importantly, on taking care of our child.'

But their happiness over her pregnancy was short-lived and her homecoming not as expected. On her last day in her apartment she missed her footing at the head of the stairs while carrying one too many hatboxes. She had the sickening sensation of stepping into nothingness before she began to fall, crashing from one tread to another all the way down the flight. Mrs Saunders and Amy heard her cry out and ran to find her tumbled at the foot of the stairs amid crushed boxes and hats. She had knocked herself out on the way down.

'Fetch Mr Lombard at once!' the manageress ordered immediately, sending off one of the apprentices. 'And run!'

Then she and Amy carried Louise to a couch with the help of a customer. Daniel arrived in great haste and rushed to where Louise was lying. She had recovered consciousness, but a large bruise was already showing on her forehead.

'It was my own fault,' she said weakly.

'You haven't broken any bones,' he said consolingly. He took her home, where she was put to bed and a doctor attended her. But the damage was done and in the night she miscarried.

At first Louise was inconsolable and then deeply depressed for a long while afterwards. Eventually she recovered her spirits, taking heart from the doctor's reassurance that if she waited for a few months there was no reason why she should not become pregnant again. It gave her high hopes for the future and she looked forward to New Year's Eve, when Madeleine and Theodore were holding a ball to welcome in the new century. She hoped that the year of 1800 would bring the child that both she and Daniel wanted so much.

He had been extremely pleased with the miniature of her, but he had arranged the first sitting for her portrait and she had decided to wear the gown that had been made for New Year's Eve. As Louise was dressing for the occasion, helped by her émigré maid, Josette, she gave thought to her native France. She was glad that the old century was passing, with all the horrors of the latter years. Now a thirty-year-old Corsican, named Napoleon Bonaparte, was rising to heights of political and military power in France and, according to the latest newspaper report, he seemed destined to become a great ruler of her homeland. France had been at war with Britain and other nations for far too long, and she hoped fervently that eventually he would lead her homeland into more peaceful times.

With the last hook fastened at the back of her high-waisted, silver gauze gown, Louise sat down again at her dressing table. Then, just as she was putting on her pearl eardrops, she suddenly shivered.

'Is anything the matter, madame?' Josette asked with concern.

'No, Josette.' Louise replied quickly. How could she say that she had had a sudden sense of foreboding, as if a dark cloud had passed over her? 'Perhaps I felt a draught.'

Josette went to check the windows. She was a sensible, conscientious girl with a pleasing round face, silky black hair and long-lashed dark eyes. In spite of having had to flee for her life when her family was slaughtered in Paris, she could not conquer her homesickness for France. She had come to Boston about the same time as Louise had arrived in New York, but had never gained a good grasp of the English language. She had entered Louise's employ from an American household and was relieved to be able to speak her own tongue with her mistress at all times, as well as to the chef and to another émigré servant in the kitchen.

'All the windows are shut, madame,' she affirmed.

It was then that Daniel came into the room. Louise met his smiling eyes in the swing mirror in front of her. He stood waiting while Josette fastened a necklace of pearls around her throat, which with the matching eardrops had been his special homecoming gift to her.

'Are you ready?' he asked.

'Yes.' Louise rose from the dressing-table stool and took her fan from Josette. 'This is going to be a wonderful evening, Daniel!' she declared, deliberately dismissing that chilling sensation she had experienced. 'Welcome to 1800!'

Madeleine and Theodore had a handsome rectangular ballroom and over a hundred guests had gathered to dance in the iridescent sparkle of the crystal chandeliers. Louise observed that, as usual, Delphine had a wide choice of male partners. She had blossomed into full beauty during the cosseting of her adoptive parents, whose surname she now used. Twice she had been on the brink of becoming betrothed, but in her capricious way had changed her mind at the last minute. This evening, swirling around in the dances, her gown a flurry of apple-green silk, with ribbons in her coppery curls, her expression was smugly triumphant. She exulted in her social success and in drawing men to her like the proverbial bees to honey, and Louise thought it was not surprising that her sister had few, if any, young women friends.

During the evening Delphine snatched a few minutes on her own to draw Louise away from a group of people to whom she and Daniel were talking.

'I've met someone very special this evening, Louise,' she confided excitedly, forgetting how often she had made similar announcements in the past. 'His name is John Huntington and he's just returned to Boston after three years abroad. We've had only one dance so far, but we sat out a gavotte in the conservatory. Mama-Madeleine was furious with me over it, but he took all the blame so charmingly that I think she's forgiven us. After all, his family is the richest in Boston.'

'I don't think that aspect would have influenced Madeleine,' Louise commented dryly. His mother and sister, both pleasant women, were two of her best customers, and socially she knew them well.

'He's coming to meet you!' Delphine clasped her hands together in excitement, seeing that he was crossing the ball-room floor in their direction.

John Huntington at twenty-six was tall and lean with short-cut brown hair and an energetic face, his dark eyes very alert and observant. When the introductions took place he bowed over Louise's hand.

'I'm honoured to meet you, ma'am. I've heard from Miss Delphine that you know London well and I spent some time there before returning home.'

'I stayed with my aunt once in Mayfair before the Revolution and enjoyed every moment. There's so much to see and explore. One cannot take a step without treading on history. But setting that aside, how did you find the present situation there?'

'There is great fear of a French invasion. Defences along the south coast are being strengthened and regiments appear to be constantly on stand-by. But that doesn't stop a lively social round in London and Brighton and elsewhere. Now, if Miss Delphine will pardon us, I should like to have the pleasure of the next dance with you, ma'am.'

Delphine beamed her approval, able to see that Louise had liked him on sight.

John was leading Louise back to Daniel after they had danced a bourrée when a servant approached her. 'There is a French gentleman asking to see you, ma'am. He's waiting in the Blue Drawing Room. I requested his name, but he withheld it, saying he wanted to give you a pleasant surprise.'

She hurried from the ballroom, eager to see her visitor. Would it be Alexandre making a surprise visit, although he had never been yet and in any case that seemed highly unlikely at this time of year. Was it an old friend from France looking her up?

The double doors of the drawing room were closed and she opened them to the candlelit room, a fire blazing cheerfully in the grate. A tall, slim man stood gazing into the flames and he turned slowly to look towards her. Instantly she stood frozen on the threshold in shock. It was Fernand!

'Good evening, *Mrs* Lombard,' he said with sardonic emphasis. 'I must say I hadn't expected to find you had committed bigamy in my absence.'

The only movement about her was the dancing of her pearl eardrops and the shiver of her silver-striped gown in the candle glow. All colour had drained from her face. 'I thought you had died at the guillotine,' she uttered in a strangled whisper.

'That's what would have happened if fate hadn't intervened. Hell's fire! Don't stand there as if you'd seen a ghost! I'm very much alive. A servant at your home directed me here. Come in and shut those doors. I don't want anyone intruding and we need to talk for a while.'

Her immediate thought was that Daniel must not know of this awful turn of events before she had a chance to prepare him. After swiftly closing the doors she turned the key in the lock. Moving stiffly, she crossed the room to face her husband from the past. Tall, fair-haired and proud-looking, he was still a handsome man in spite of a bloating of his features by years of self-indulgence. His forehead was broad, his aristocratic nose long and thin, and his eyes a curiously light amber. Always alert to fashion, his coat collar and neck stock were so exaggeratedly high that his head seemed supported by them.

'What happened?' she asked, reaching for a chair and sitting down, for her legs seemed to have lost their strength. 'How did you escape the blade?'

'I made the mistake of staying on in Paris longer than was wise. The revolutionaries tried me in court and condemned me on the same trumped-up charge that sent so many other people to their death during the Reign of Terror. I was thrown into the Temple prison, but when I was with others in the tumbril on the way to the guillotine there was an accident. A runaway horse sent its cart crashing into us. I was thrown out by the impact and, apart from my shoulder, I was unharmed. So I scrambled to my feet and ran as I had never run in my life before, knowing a place where I could hide out for a while.'

'Weren't you pursued?'

'There was such confusion, with the tumbril horses rearing, the injured screaming and the cart on its side trapping people underneath, that nobody saw me go. Then, after several weeks and on a moonless night, a friend smuggled me down to one of the barges on the Seine and I hid under cover. It sailed down the river at dawn, taking me away from Paris into safety. Not that I didn't have several other narrow scrapes,' he added in case she should think it had been all too easy, 'before eventually I reached England.'

'I went home to Delphine,' she said in the same tight voice as before. 'Didn't you receive the letter I sent to Paris?'

He shrugged. 'No, but I guessed you'd gone home when you weren't with the Queen. Later in England I began to think that you must be still alive when neither your name nor Delphine's ever appeared on any list of the condemned.'

'How did you find me here?'

'It took a damnable long time,' he stated accusingly, as if she were to blame. 'I was still in London when I happened to meet an émigré from Bordeaux, who told me he'd heard you'd both gone to America.'

'We went first to New York. Not Boston. How did you discover my present address?'

'That took a hell of a time too. I'd remembered you had an aunt in England and I'd been trying to trace her, because I was in urgent need of cash. The allowance granted by the British Government to émigré aristocrats didn't meet my needs and I was sure that she would be generous to her nephew by marriage. When eventually I discovered her address she had been widowed and had moved through her own failing health from Mayfair to her country seat in Sussex. But when I arrived there the old bitch refused to see me!'

'Don't speak of her in that way!' Louise flared. 'She knew I had married again and would have wanted to protect me. She has never mentioned your visit in her letters.'

'I called every day until eventually I caught her unawares in the rose garden, where she was picking flowers. She had no choice but to hear what I had to say. I declared that I'd heard you were in America and the alarm in her face told me I was on the right track. That's when I explained to her that my sole aim was to find you again, and I was desperately in need of funds to continue my search.'

'What did she say?'

'Only that if I didn't leave immediately she would have me thrown off her property, and that you were well rid of me. But afterwards I waylaid one of her maidservants and I bribed her to find your address, which was how I learned of your new surname.'

'When were you at her house?'

'That was over a year ago. I'm living in France again these days. You must have heard of the amnesty that was granted a while ago, allowing certain émigrés to claim back property and land confiscated during the Revolution.'

'Yes, I read all about it at the time. But you have no property left. You'd gambled it all away before you married me, and your Paris apartment belonged to one of your mistresses.'

'That's true,' he agreed with a dangerous amiability that only increased her anxiety. He had rested an arm on the marble mantelshelf with one glossy-booted foot on the fender and he looked down at her where she sat. The firelight flickered across the planes of his face. 'But you are still the rightful owner of your château and its lands and forests.'

'You mean my home has not been destroyed?' she exclaimed thankfully. 'I feared it might have been burnt to the ground. That's what happened to Alexandre de Clement's château in the same district.'

'I went to see it for myself. It appeared to be in good order apart from a few broken windowpanes, but I was told that some looting took place before it was officially sealed. It was a great relief to me when I found it intact, because it's become fashionable to spend time in the country these days and a gentleman must have his roots. The château is ideal for that purpose.'

'So that's why you're here!' Louise shook her head in relief that his visit was purely mercenary. 'You want me to sign the property and land over to you!'

'All those acres, including the vineyard, are more valuable now than ever before and there's a great demand for timber.' Then he added bluntly, 'I need the château and the money, Louise.'

'I refused you often enough in the past,' she answered straightforwardly, rising to her feet, 'but circumstances have changed. I have a new life here and the château can never be my home again. I'm sure that eventually new gambling debts will force you to sell it, as well as everything else, and then, at least, I can only hope that the buyer will come to love my old home as much as I did when I grew up there.'

'So?' He raised his eyebrows questioningly.

'I'll do what you wish if you leave this house as secretly as you came and meet me at my lawyer's office tomorrow morning. My only condition is that you go back to France and never trouble me again.'

He gave a quiet laugh. 'You're in no position to make conditions, my dear wife. A word from me to the Boston police and you'll be in prison for your bigamous marriage. I have terms of my own to dictate. Claiming back sequestered property in France has to be done by the rightful owner or the legal heir in person, not by anyone who has bought it or obtained it by deed of gift.'

In spite of the warmth of the room, she felt herself chill at his words. 'Are you saying that you want me to go back to France with you?'

He nodded. 'Yes, as my wife.'

'No! Everything was over between us long ago!' She backed away from him. 'Get someone to impersonate me! It shouldn't be difficult!'

He shook his head. 'Do you think I'd be stupid enough to take such a risk? Others have tried it and ended up behind bars. You're coming with me and there's no way you can get out of it.'

'If you force me back to France I'll reclaim my property for myself! You shall never have it!'

'But you can't stop me living there with an adequate personal allowance. As for refusing to accompany me back to France, the law in this new country is no different from the old in upholding a husband's rights over his wife. Even if I kept quiet about your fraudulent marriage, I'd still have the law on my side in demanding that you return to me. The result would be your deportation in my charge as your lawful husband.'

At that moment the handle of the door was tried. They both looked sharply at each other. Then Daniel's voice was heard.

'Louise! Are you there? Have these doors jammed?' There was a rattling as he gave them a shake. 'It's nearly midnight. The new century is almost here.'

In anguish she turned to Fernand. 'Don't let him see you yet!' she implored. 'Give me a little time alone with him first.'

He cast a contemptuous glance at her and strode to the double doors himself, unlocked them and flung them wide. 'Come in, Lombard. I'm the Marquis de Vailly, and I've come to take my wife home with me to France.'

For a few seconds Daniel's face registered total disbelief. Then he looked beyond Fernand to where Louise stood, her tortured expression conveying the terrible truth of the announcement. In an explosion of fury he gave the Frenchman a violent thrust in the chest. As Fernand staggered back into the room, Daniel slammed the doors shut again before crossing the floor to Louise. With his eyes holding hers, he touched her cheek reassuringly before facing Fernand again.

'Now, sir,' he demanded dangerously, 'what is this fakery all about? If you think I'll surrender Louise to you or anyone else, you're entirely mistaken!'

Fernand, enraged by the thrust that had almost made him lose his balance, tidied his coat and smoothed his waistcoat buttons into a straight line again. 'You're the one in error, Lombard! But I'll let my wife explain the situation to you.'

Haltingly, Louise managed to tell Daniel all that had happened. When she had finished he turned back to Fernand. 'What is your price for returning to France and leaving us in peace?'

Fernand regarded him disdainfully. 'How crudely you Americans express yourselves! I've heard often enough how uncivilized it is in this country. In any case, you're wasting your breath. Not only do I want the château as a country seat, but also Louise will inherit a fortune when her aunt in England dies. My wife is worth more to me financially than anything you could hand out.'

'Try me!' Daniel had taken a step towards him, fists balled at his sides.

Fernand ignored him, addressing Louise. 'You have seventy-two hours in which to pack before we sail.' He took a folded piece of paper from his pocket and held it out. When she made no attempt to take it he placed it open on a side table. 'The time of sailing and all details are listed there. I'll collect you two hours beforehand on my way to the harbour. If you should take it into your head to go into hiding or attempt any other such foolery, I shall go straight to the authorities.'

'Get out!' Daniel roared in fury.

Fernand regarded him with narrowed eyes. 'I find your attitude extremely offensive. If we were in France, I'd run a blade through you, Lombard! And I shall do it if ever you dare to follow us to our château!'

'I advise you not to be overconfident about taking Louise away!' Daniel gave back fiercely. 'I'll be contacting my lawyer immediately. There is such a thing as extenuating circumstances to counter your proposed charge of bigamy. The entire world thought you were dead and that can be endorsed.'

Fernand opened the double doors to leave, letting in the

merry sound of music and voices from the ballroom, and he paused to regard Daniel mockingly. 'But, whatever happens, Louise will still be my legal wife. There isn't a court of justice here or anywhere else that would rule against my demand for the restoration of my conjugal rights.'

He went from the room. Daniel, unable to contain his wrath any longer, would have rushed at him for his final taunt if Louise had not hung on to his arm. 'Let him go!' she implored desperately. 'I can't bear any more.'

Contritely, Daniel took her into his arms. 'We'll find a way out of this mess! There must be a loophole somewhere. We have the new century ahead of us – our century! Nobody shall take it away from us.'

The Sèvres clock on the mantelshelf announced the imminence of midnight in its preliminary tinkling chime. At its first stroke Daniel kissed her lovingly, but Louise feared, no matter what he said, that their time together was drawing to an end.

Daniel's lawyer, Harry Tyler, was an old friend and, as he had also been celebrating the New Year, he was not yet in bed when Daniel arrived asking to see him immediately. He came downstairs in his dressing gown to find Daniel pacing up and down in the library. One look at Daniel's face told him that something extremely serious had happened.

'Sit down, my friend. I've some excellent cognac. We'll each have a glass.' When Harry had poured it he put one glass into Daniel's shaking hand and sat down himself. 'Now tell me what's brought you to this state.'

He listened attentively to Daniel's account of Fernand's reappearance. When it ended he spoke gravely as he summed up the situation.

'I have to say that Fernand de Vailly is entirely within his rights in demanding his wife's return, and she is still a French citizen. If there had been an annulment or a judicial separation, it would have been a different matter.'

'Couldn't we start legal proceedings for a judicial separation now?' Daniel persisted. 'We could aim for the lengthier proceedings of a divorce afterwards.'

'On what grounds?'

'Cruelty.'

'You have proof?'

'My wife's account of all she endured.'

'Madame de Vailly's account,' the lawyer corrected punctiliously. 'That would not be enough. You would need witnesses. Was Delphine ever present when this fellow struck her sister?'

'No, I asked Louise about that.'

'Is there any other émigré who could give evidence?'

'There's nobody.'

The lawyer sat back in his chair and shook his head slowly. 'I'd do anything in my power to help you and Louise, as you know. Even if we obtained an injunction to prevent her being taken from this country on the grounds of her wanting to become an American citizen, your enemy would immediately carry out his threat of accusing the two of you of bigamy. I'd fight the case and should be able to prevent a prison sentence for you both in view of the circumstances, but afterwards Fernand de Vailly would still demand that Louise be returned to him. I shall investigate and consult my partners, but I can't raise your hopes.'

'I refuse to believe that there isn't some solution!'

Harry regarded him sympathetically. 'I wish I didn't have to say this to you, Daniel, but I can see no way out for either of you.'

'Oh, my God!' Daniel buried his face in his hands. Harry poured him another cognac.

When Daniel arrived home Louise was in bed, but still awake with the candles lit. She knew the verdict without his having to say a word and slid from the bed to run into his arms. He held her tight, feeling the warmth of her body through the thin silk of her nightgown, and pressed his lips against her hair. Afterwards he ravished her with a passion born of love and despair.

In the morning, both deeply moved by their night of intense loving, they talked over the impasse that faced them. Louise dismissed all his frantic suggestions as to how they might delay the inevitable.

'It's pointless,' she said sadly. 'Harry gave you his best advice and we have to accept it. To try anything else would only result in the most dreadful scandal, which would harm the three people dearest to me in this city other than you, cheri. We married to avoid a similar scandal arising, and again I have to avoid hurting them.'

'But I can't let you go.' His voice was choked by anguish.

She took his tormented face between her hands. 'Nothing can prevent it. One thing I can promise you. I'll never let Fernand touch me. Nothing shall be as before. My time here in the States has given me the chance to realize my own strength and power. It also gave me you and a love that I'll cherish all my life.'

To her intense sorrow he broke down and wept. She cradled his head to her and wondered why she did not die from the pain of having to leave him.

Sixteen

The time for parting drew near. Louise felt as if she had passed the last hours of her liberty in a strange trance, carrying out every necessary task like a wound-up automaton. Daniel was to sell the shop on her behalf and if the purchaser continued in millinery he was to try to ensure that her present staff were kept on. She arranged financial matters with her bankers, settled all bills from her suppliers and also paid her seamstress for the three new gowns, still unfinished, which would be shipped to France when ready. Daniel had already secured a separate cabin for her on the ship.

Last of all Louise had to break the news of her departure to her sister and cousins. She let them know in advance that she would be making a special visit on Sunday afternoon on a matter of importance. When the time came she went to their home on her own, even though Daniel had wanted to accompany her, for she had a private request to make that she intended to keep from him for his own sake.

Theodore met her in the hall. 'Is it bad news?' he asked sympathetically.

She nodded, supposing that he assumed it would be of Violette's demise or some such distressing news. He took her gently by the elbow as they went together into the drawing room, where his wife and Delphine were waiting.

'Something totally unexpected and very serious has happened,' Louise began when she had seated herself. 'The whole course of my life has been changed yet again.' She paused, almost unnerved by the attentive silence in which they were listening to her. 'Fernand is here in Boston. He escaped the guillotine and has come back into my life.'

Madeleine gasped, but Delphine gave a little moan. 'Oh, no!'

Somehow Louise kept her voice steady. 'As I am still his wife, I'm compelled to return to France with him. Daniel has had the best legal advice, but there's nothing to be done that could counteract Fernand's demand.' She explained all that had happened while her listeners sat grave-faced. 'So I've come to tell you that I'm sailing back to France tomorrow morning.'

Both Madeleine and Delphine uttered cries of dismay, but Theodore took a practical viewpoint. 'Have all possible outlets been explored?' he questioned sharply.

Louise gave a weary nod. 'Harry Tyler has had endless consultations with his partners, but none has been able to offer a solution. There are no loopholes.'

At that point Delphine burst into a torrent of tears, throwing herself upon Louise and creating an hysterical scene that made everything worse for them all. 'You can't go! I'll never see you again!'

Madeleine spoke huskily. 'I can hardly believe that this is happening.'

'Listen to me, Delphine,' Louise said quietly, brushing her sister's curls back from the tear-wet face. 'One day when you are married your husband can bring you to visit me.'

'It would mean crossing that horrible ocean,' Delphine answered wildly, 'but I'd do it to see you again!'

'Then that is what I'll hope for in the future.' Louise hugged her comfortingly and disengaged herself from her sister's clinging arms before speaking again. 'I don't want the reason for my departure ever to be known by others. Daniel will never say a word and I implore you as my family to keep my secret. Otherwise there'll be the very scandal I want to avoid at all costs.'

Theodore spoke solemnly, his voice full of compassion for her. 'Your consideration for us is most thoughtful, but we would sustain any amount of scandal-mongering if it meant a solution.'

Delphine, alarmed by Theodore's words and only too aware of how such a scandal would harm her good name, was quick to make her promise to keep silent. 'I'd die before I ever spoke of it!'

'There will be plenty of gossip about why I have suddenly returned to France,' Louise continued. 'But since Daniel and I appeared not to live together for two years, it will be thought that we must have had some temporary arrangement. There will be plenty of women glad to know that he is a free man again.'

'My dear, he has eyes only for you!' Madeleine exclaimed in distress.

'I know, but with time he must pick up the threads of his life without me and find happiness again. That's why I've told him there must be no correspondence between us.'

'No, no!' Madeleine pressed her fingertips against her trembling mouth. 'The poor man! That's too cruel!'

Louise almost broke down and her voice faltered. 'It has to be like that for his sake, otherwise he'll always be looking over his shoulder at the past instead of ahead to the future.' It was for that same reason she had refused to let him arrange financial security for her from his own income for the rest of her life. 'Ties have to be severed. You may inform him of my well-being whenever he should ask you, but that is all. Yet for myself, I beg you to tell me everything about him in your letters. It will be my only comfort in the years ahead.'

'Even if he should marry again?' Madeleine ventured uncertainly.

Louise gave a nod. 'Then he will have the son that I've not had time to give him.'

At her words Madeleine began to weep so profusely that Theodore promptly took charge of the situation. 'This is no way to say adieu to Louise,' he said sternly. 'Dry your tears, Madeleine. As for you, Delphine, let's wish your courageous sister well.'

Delphine, curled up on the sofa, had been sobbing into a cushion like a child trying to shut out reality, but at his strict tone she looked up, red-eyed. 'I do! With all my heart!'

Theodore stepped forward and embraced Louise, who stood ready to leave, and spoke to her quietly. 'Let me know if ever I can assist you in any way. I'm well acquainted with our American ambassador in Paris. I shall give you a letter to present to him in the case of any emergency. It may be that you'll find yourself in need of an influential friend at some time.'

'Thank you.' She leaned her forehead briefly against his chest while she gathered strength to say farewell to her sister and Madeleine. Fearful of breaking down, she did not stay any longer than was necessary. Theodore had to restrain Delphine from running after her when she left the house and hurried away with her head bowed.

That evening Louise received Theodore's promised letter, which he delivered in person, wanting to have a few words about the finality of the situation with Daniel before her departure. She put it ready to take with her passport and other travelling papers.

Next morning Fernand arrived in a hackney carriage at the appointed time. He did not alight to enter the house, but continued to sit without a glance towards it while Louise's trunks and boxes were being loaded on to the roof. In the drawing room she and Daniel stood together in each other's arms, his face tortured as he pressed her to him. The final moment came and they exchanged a last long kiss.

'I'll love you always,' he said brokenly.

'As I'll love you,' she whispered.

She had begged him earlier to let her go from his arms without delay when the time came, knowing it could only prolong their torment, and he did as she wished.

As Louise went out into the chill January air asparkle with frost, she held her head high. Josette, who was going with her, having always been homesick, stood waiting by the open door of the carriage. Louise entered it, taking her place beside Fernand, who did not speak, and Josette took the seat opposite her.

From the steps of the house Daniel stood taking in this last sight of the woman he had loved since first seeing her. He had a final glimpse of her pale face turned tragically to him through the glass before the carriage drew away.

On board the ship, Fernand went ahead to the cabins, leaving Josette to supervise the luggage. He thought Louise was following him and did not see her being shown in another direction. When Louise entered her cabin she saw at once that Daniel had obtained the best accommodation on the ship for her. It was in the stern and, through the windows, reflected light from the sun-dappled water danced over the cabin. There were two sizeable bunks set opposite each other against the wooden panelling of the bulkheads and, in between, a table and two chairs that could be fastened down in rough weather. There were also wide leather straps to prevent her trunks from sliding around and a cupboard with a lid that opened to revealed a washbasin and a soap dish. Below this was what appeared to be a drawer, but the handle pulled out a necessary closestool. A candle-lantern, hanging from one of the low beams, would give meagre light at night, but Louise thought to herself that no admiral could have had better facilities.

She had removed her hat and gloves when Fernand suddenly appeared in the doorway. 'What nonsense is this, Louise?' he demanded angrily. 'I have taken a cabin for the two of us.'

She regarded him coolly. 'I'm sharing this one with Josette.'

'But there's a place for her with the other servants in the hold. She can sleep there.'

'She is staying here.'

'You'll do as I tell you!'

'No, Fernand,' she stated implacably. 'Never again. Those days are over. You must understand that I have no intention of ever being a wife to you again.'

'I suppose you're setting out with some misguided idea of remaining faithful to your American lover,' he replied scathingly. 'But he'll soon forget you. He'll fade from your memory too, when you're back in a civilized country again.'

She ignored his jibe, determined never to be drawn into any discussion with him about Daniel. 'Please go now.'

He stepped forward swiftly and seized her by the wrist, jerking her to him. 'I won't tolerate your getting high-handed with me!'

She gave him a blazing look. 'I've been informed that the captain has no compunction about locking passengers in their cabins if they disrupt the peace of his ship on what is always a dangerous voyage. I wouldn't hesitate to make a complaint if you should attempt to molest me.'

Taken aback by her attitude, he released his grip on her. 'I can see you've been badly influenced by American ways, but as soon as we're on French soil, I shall be fully in charge. You'll obey me for the rest of your life!' His angry face was thrust forward, his warm, wine-tainted breath fanning her face. 'I'll set you to scrubbing floors and washing pans if I've a mind to it!'

A wry smile skimmed her lips. 'I've had plenty of experience in doing such chores after you disappeared from my life. It's likely the need will arise again if we find the château in a poor state. Your threats don't alarm me. I'm no longer the young girl whom you married for gain.'

Outside the half-open door Josette, who had arrived at the head of the seamen shouldering the trunks and boxes, knocked and spoke. '*Pardon*, madame, the luggage is here.'

Fernand, unable to continue his verbal abuse in the hearing of others, left with his temper unabated and thrust past Josette with such force that she fell against the wall. She glared after him. It was aristos like him who had brought about the Revolution in the first place and cost the lives of all her family. Already she hated him.

When the ship set sail Louise stayed seated at the table in her cabin. Everybody else was on deck. She could have stood at the window for a last glimpse of the city she had come to know so well, but she wanted to link her thoughts solely with Daniel during these final moments of departure. Although she fought against giving way to despair, her desperate sorrow overcame her. As her arms slid forward on the table, she lowered her head on to them, and sobbed desolately.

Unbeknown to her, Daniel stood on the quay watching the ship leave. She had not wanted him or her cousins and sister to be there, but he had been unable to stay away. He stayed until the vessel was out of sight. No miracle had happened. Fernand had not relented. She was gone from his life, leaving it stretching emptily before him.

The voyage proved to be even rougher than Louise's previous crossing. Although neither she nor Josette was seasick, it was often too dangerous to venture on deck and a great deal of time was spent in the cabin. Whenever the tumultuous waves prevented any cooking in the galley, they ate dried fruits and other long-lasting food that they had brought with them. Often they were compelled to lie on their bunks for hours at a time to save being tossed off their feet.

The nights were the worst for Louise. Frequently she dreamed that she was back in Boston and whenever Daniel featured in her dreams he was always out of her reach. Sometimes she was searching for him through empty rooms in an unfamiliar house or else she could see him strolling far ahead of her. Although she called to him, he was always out of earshot and however fast she ran it was beyond her power to catch up with him. Then she would awake to the awful realization that she was truly far from him and not in the bed they had shared, with his arm around her.

During the voyage, Louise saw Fernand whenever passengers were able to gather for meals in the dining saloon and on deck, if it proved possible to walk there, well-clad against the cold. He always ignored her and she was thankful for it. She was sure he would have been more troublesome towards her if he had not gained the company of a young woman whom he had met on the first day of the voyage. A returning émigré, she was on her way home to her husband, who had survived the Revolution, but in the meantime she appeared to be totally charmed by Fernand. They were frequently on their own in her cabin.

It was a long eight weeks at sea for all the passengers before the last days of the voyage slipped away. The waves eased and everyone made the most of the better weather by being up in the open air most of the time.

On the morning of the first day of March, Fernand came to stand by Louise as she stood gazing at the smudge of land on the horizon that was France. 'So, we're home at last,' he said with a deep sigh of relief.

Louise's feelings towards her homeland were mixed. She had felt a deep rush of love for France upon seeing it again. It had warmed her heart with a forcefulness that had wiped out all that had sullied it for her in the time before her escape. But was it home any more? Surely that lay in the country she had left behind?

They landed at Toulon. Ahead lay the long cross-country journey to Bordeaux and the château. Louise felt no surprise in being addressed as *Citoyenne* instead of *Madame*, for she knew that many courtesies from the past had been wiped out in her absence. Fernand had no difficulty in hiring a coachman and an equipage to drive them all the way to the château, for transporting returning émigrés had become a profitable business and he had a choice of coachmen eager for the task.

As the coach rumbled over the cobbles through Toulon and other towns along the route, Louise watched to discover what changes had been made since she was last in France, but everything looked much as before, except that no scarlet Phrygian caps were being worn anywhere. After religion had been banned during the Revolution, it had not been unusual to see one of these caps on a church steeple, but since First Consul Napoleon had declared that the Revolution was at an end, the right to worship had been restored. There were signs of prosperity in fine new houses, grand carriages and well-dressed people, but the poor were still to be seen everywhere and, whenever the coach stopped for a change of horses, there were just as many beggars running forward for alms as there had ever been.

They stayed at hostelries every night. Louise paid for everything, as Fernand's purse appeared to have emptied. She guessed that the loan he had raised on the strength of fetching a rich wife home from America had finally run out. It gave her an advantage, as it enabled her always to take a room for Josette and herself and another for him without his being able to do anything about it. As Fernand would not eat with a servant, he always had a separate table, while Louise and Josette ate together. The coachman saw to his own sleeping and eating arrangements, which was usually in the stable-loft with others of his trade.

At last they reached Bordeaux, where they stayed overnight, for until the seal was removed from the Château de Montier they could not enter it. In the morning, Louise looked out at the familiar street below and was able to see the house where she and Delphine had hidden in the attic while they waited for a ship to take them to safety. It saddened her that their good friend was no longer there.

At the government office there were a number of other returned émigrés waiting ahead of Louise and Fernand when they arrived. She had known that he, as her husband, would be expected to accompany her, and she had to tolerate his presence. He was in a surprisingly amiable mood and several times he rubbed his hands together as if in anticipation of gaining a hold on the château at last. After a long wait their turn finally came. The official, a beak-nosed man with bushy eyebrows, was seated at his desk, and seemed harassed by all the work in hand. He waved them impatiently to two chairs.

'There are so many of you émigrés returning home these days that there's no end to applications,' he said to her, taking her papers from her to study them. 'There's a positive flood coming from England now. Were you there, Citoyenne? Oh, no, I see you went to America. A great number went there too.' The papers rustled as he went through them. 'Yes,

everything is in order. Now I have some declarations that
you must sign.'

Louise read each one carefully before adding her signature.
Everything was very straightforward in these more lenient
times. Then the official stood to study the labels on rows of
keys, before he located the right ones. He snipped off a large
label and held out the heavy ring of keys to her, together with
the important document that released her property and land
back to her. Although Fernand's hand had shot out to receive
both, the official ignored him and gave them to Louise as the
rightful owner.

She put them safely away in her purse as she and Fernand
left the office. The incident had been encouraging. In this new
France the official had not treated her as her husband's chattel,
but as an individual in her own right. So, women had kept their
first tentative claim on equality. It had shown itself prior to the
Revolution and the turbulent times had failed to destroy it.

At her bankers, Louise was given bad news. Her fortune,
which she had inherited from her father, had been forfeited
during the Revolution and there was no hope of her ever having
any of it returned to her. Fernand, who had been reassured in
Paris before leaving for America that his wife's fortune could
be reclaimed, had turned white to the lips. His disappointment
exploded into a terrible rage while Louise faced the fact that
all she had was what she had earned in America. It would mean
being careful in her spending until her land was productive
again. Before they left her bankers she arranged for Fernand
to have a modest income of his own out of what she had, but
he declared it to be totally inadequate and stormed out of the
building.

On the drive out of the town Louise was tense, not from
Fernand's exhausting show of temper, since she expected it
to be the first of many, but through not knowing quite how
she would find her beloved birthplace. She and Josette were
on their own in the coach, as Fernand had hired a riding horse
for his immediate use and, still in a livid mood, rode ahead.

When they reached the bend in the road that would bring the

château into sight, Louise held her breath. Then, as it appeared ahead of her in its setting of majestic trees and wide lawns, presently wildly overgrown, she gave a long soft sigh at its beauty. In spite of being sadly neglected, its old stone walls were still a pale amber in the sunshine, entwined sturdily by the curling branches of the ancient wisteria, which in a few weeks would be covered by a soft cloud of purple blossom. Although wooden boards had been nailed across the great double doors of the porticoed entrance and ivy had flourished unchecked to overhang the tall windows, some of which had panes cracked and broken, the grace and dignity of the house, with its high, sharply sloping grey roof, remained singularly untouched.

While the coachman unloaded the trunks, Fernand, who had come prepared with tools he had bought in town, prised off the wooden boards across the doorway and ripped away the seal. As soon as the doors were cleared, Louise went up the stone steps to try the largest key on the ring. It turned at once as if welcoming her return.

Thrusting open the doors, she swept in. The sunshine, flooding through to throw her shadow before her, became cloudy with dancing dust motes and set sparkling a scatter of fragments on the marble floor. She picked up a shard and realized it was crystal. Glancing upwards, she saw that the great chandelier had been viciously damaged and was hanging dangerously by a single chain.

Warning the others, she stepped quickly out of danger herself and stood looking about her, reflected many times over in the smashed mirror, under which a fine antique side table had once stood. All the carved chairs, which had been set against the hall walls for as long as she could remember, were gone. As her gaze travelled towards the stairs, she saw with a sinking heart that the family portraits on the wall had been slashed, the canvas hanging from some of the frames like pointed petals.

Behind her, Josette exclaimed in sympathy. 'Oh, *madame*!'

Turning abruptly, Louise went into the room that had always been known as the White Salon, because of the ivory silk of its panelled walls. In the gloom she dodged furniture to start opening the interior shutters and folding them back. Then she turned to survey the room. As far as she could tell, all the elegant chairs were still there, as well as the sofas, but some were broken beyond repair and the silk brocade of the upholstery had been ripped by knives, the stuffing sticking out. The paintings, mostly landscapes, were either slashed or had been kicked about the floor, light patches on the torn silk-panelled walls showing where they had hung. Louise clenched her fists, rage taking over from shock at the senseless vandalism. Fernand looked into the room, swore at the state of it and went out again.

Josette, previously instructed as to the layout of the upper rooms, had led the baggage-laden coachman up the stairs and was directing him as to where he should deposit the trunks and boxes. Downstairs, Louise went from room to room. Not a single musical instrument had been left in the music salon, and there were only empty spaces where the harp and the harpsichord had stood. She thought of how often she had accompanied Delphine's flute-playing there. Even the carpet had been taken, and a stain on the wall, similar to others she had already seen, showed where somebody had urinated. The dining room was equally bare of furniture, as was the Green Salon, where the lovely carpet which had given the room its name was missing.

It proved to be the same in every downstairs room. Even the kitchens had not escaped, the copper saucepans gone from their hooks, and cupboards left open where the hungry soldiers had searched for food. In the garden room, dead plants lay on the terracotta tiles amid smashed pots and scattered earth, but the charming furniture, specially designed for it, was gone.

She had left the library to last, cherishing a faint hope that the illiteracy of the looters would mean that the books had escaped their clutches. But, on the threshold, she halted in amazement while Fernand pushed past her to open the shutters. Even in the gloom, all the furniture appeared to be in place, and the red patterned Turkish carpet was soft under her feet.

But as light poured into the room, her hopes for the safety of the treasured volumes were dashed as the stark emptiness of the wall-to-ceiling bookshelves was revealed. Yet the library table was in its place, as were the antique chairs, and a portrait of her father as a boy of ten still gave a vibrant touch of life and colour to the room. Only the ebony clock and the silver candlesticks, which had always stood on the mantel, were no longer there.

'Why should the clock, candlesticks and the books have been stolen, but nothing else?' she asked in bewilderment.

Before Fernand could reply, Josette popped her head into the room. 'Good news, madame! Except for one of the bedrooms, nothing else seems to have been touched anywhere upstairs.' She vanished again to give further instructions to the coachman.

'It seems as if the looters were stopped before they wreaked further havoc,' Fernand remarked coldly as he strolled about the room.

Louise gave a nod. 'Perhaps, after an immediate orgy of destruction in the hall and the White Salon, the soldiers' minds turned to thieving until an officer arrived to put a stop to it.'

'Taking the clock and the silver for himself, perhaps.'

'But the books?' Louise shook her head despairingly. 'So many rare editions among them. There were hundreds. I suppose they were burnt.'

Fernand shook his head. 'I doubt it. Some of the revolutionary leaders had the foresight to make sure that the valuable libraries of our land were not destroyed in the mayhem. It's my guess that the books here were taken away en bloc and put into safe keeping. It's possible these days to apply to have a collection returned. I'll look into it next time I'm in Bordeaux. We should be able to raise funds by selling the most valuable volumes.'

Louise made no comment, only thinking to herself how different their attitudes were as to what constituted the value of a book. In the hall she found the coachman waiting to be paid. He was eager to get to Bordeaux in the hope of picking up more returning émigrés from a ship there before starting for home again. When he had gone, Louise went upstairs and along the gallery into the room she had first taken for her own after her flight home from Versailles. It had been her mother's room. Josette was already making up the four-poster bed.

'I found these clean sheets and blankets in the linen room. They're not damp at all, but I'm not sure about the mattress here or in the other bedrooms. I'll give them all a good airing tomorrow, so it will mean only a layer of blankets across the bed-slats tonight.'

Louise smiled. 'After the discomfort of the hostelries' beds, I won't miss a mattress for one night.' She went into the dressing room. All the garments she had left behind were still there. She took out a gown of green velvet and shook it from its folds. How dated it looked compared with the high-waisted gowns being worn now! After glancing at other garments and opening and shutting a few drawers to see what she had left in them, she came back into the bedroom.

Josette, smoothing out a sheet, glanced sideways at her. 'The Marquis has told me that he will have the neighbouring room to this one.'

Louise glanced across at the communicating door to what had been her father's bedroom. It was as spacious as her own and had the same fine view from the windows. Without a word she went to lock the door. She had difficulty in turning the key and thought to herself that it was probably the first time it had ever been used.

'I'll get help in from the village in the morning,' she said, brushing away a cobweb from the toilet table. 'The whole house must be scrubbed and cleaned from the cellars to the attic, although afterwards some of the rooms will have to be closed up again until they can be refurbished.'

'Let me find the right women for the task,' Josette requested firmly. 'I can meet them on equal terms. We don't know yet what the attitude of the local people will be towards aristos being back here, even though the Revolution is over.'

It was agreed. Various chores filled the rest of their day

while Fernand inspected the cellars. The looting there had left the racks bare, and emptied bottles lay smashed on the floor, but he found some superb wines in the darkest corner, which had been overlooked. He sampled one on the spot and took the bottle with him when he went to inspect the stables and decide how many horses would be needed for riding and carriage work. In the coach house he found two of the three carriages unharmed, except that the gold handles had been stolen from the doors, and there was a two-seater chaise that would be useful for driving into town in the absence of coach servants.

Finally he rode out to view the estate. Much of the land lay neglected, but work had been maintained in some areas and a section of the vineyard showed signs of having been carefully tended. He returned to the château with a tolerable report. Then he went down to the cellars again and brought up two more bottles that he intended to enjoy at dinner. Josette decanted it into crystal decanters, which she had discovered with some fine glasses in a library cupboard together with a number of other useful and quite valuable items that had been left untouched. Louise, using a couple of battered saucepans that looked as if they had been kicked about the kitchen, prepared the meal from a basket of food that she had purchased before they had left Bordeaux. As soon as it was ready Josette took charge.

'I'll serve you and the Marquis at the library table,' she said. 'That will have to be the dining room for the time being. I've laid it with a fine cloth that I found with others in the linen room, but there's no silver tableware left in the house. I've had to put out old knives and forks from the kitchen.'

'We can rectify that tomorrow. In one of my trunks I have some of the family silver that my sister and I took with us when we left here.' Louise realized that the homecoming journey was over and routine was being established. Even though she and Josette had worked together all day to do what they could to improve their immediate living conditions, the girl had reverted to the hierarchy of an established household as a natural right. With a smile to herself Louise wondered whether Fernand or

Josette would have been the most outraged if she had suggested eating in the kitchen.

Just before she and Fernand sat down to dine, a visitor came to see her. It was Pierre, looking much older, his once-dark hair thickly streaked with grey and his face ruddy and wrinkled as a winter-stored apple, but his grin and his dancing eyes revealed his pleasure at seeing her again. She welcomed him warmly, overjoyed at their reunion.

'How kind of you to come, Pierre! I was going to call on you and your wife in the morning! How are you both? Come in!'

'We are a little older, but that is all.'

She took him with her into the White Salon, where he stood to shake his head at the destruction before sitting himself down on a sofa while she took one of the chairs opposite him.

'It's good to see you home, madame. There have been some hard times during the six years you've been away, but I guess it wasn't easy for you either in a foreign land. I haven't come to spend more than a minute or two now, but I wanted you to know that I kept part of the vineyard going as well as was humanly possible in your absence, and there's some fine claret stored up for you.' He pulled a bottle from his capacious coat pocket. 'This is your own wine to welcome you home.'

She was touched by his thoughtfulness and took it from him. 'Thank you, Pierre. It seems a long time since you saved my life and my sister's, but I've never forgotten all the kindness you and your wife showed us in our hour of need. I reinstated you after my return from Versailles and I hope you've retained that authority in my absence.'

'All I can say is that I did what I could in the circumstances,' he replied dryly. 'Madness seemed to reign for a while, but things settled down again eventually. With nobody to pay any wages, people have been living off your land and selling whatever they could, myself included.'

'Does that mean those who worked for me in the past will agree to work for me again?'

'You need have no fear about that. They'll be glad if you'll let bygones be bygones and pay them regular wages again.

But strong young men will be in short supply. So many of them around here, who were boys when you left, have joined Napoleon's army, as there seems to be a never-ending demand for troops to fight all these foreigners we are at war with these days.' He glanced around the room again. 'The revolutionary soldiers did most of this, but there were those locally, whom I won't name, that did some looting of their own.'

'Few behaved normally in those evil days. It was like a sickness that affected everybody in one way or another. I'll bear no grudge.'

They talked for a while, he giving her a brief account of several terrible things that had happened in the district after her departure and also listing various returned émigré families who were back in their châteaux. When he left, it was with a promise that, if Josette called at their cottage in the morning, his wife would find all the cleaners that she would need.

When Louise went to bed she left Fernand getting steadily drunk downstairs, still seated at the table. As he did not try her locked doors when eventually he staggered past on his way to bed, she hoped it meant that he had accepted her independence from him.

Next morning Josette was up by dawn and went early into the village. When she returned she was accompanied by a trail of women, all wary of how they would be received, but Louise greeted them and later saw that they had food at noon. Throughout that day and the rest of the week, dust, cobwebs and spiders were banished, floors were scrubbed or polished, drapes and curtains washed and carpets beaten. Arriving with the women in the mornings were several local workmen called in to repair the damage that had been done to walls and woodwork, although, until more prosperous times, wallpaper had to replace every one of the silk panels in the White Salon.

While Josette supervised the work indoors, Louise rode out with Pierre to make her own inspection of the land. As before, his advice was invaluable. He had made a list of what was needed immediately for the spring sowing and other farm work, as well as essential repairs to be carried out on her tenants' cottages, the barns, the pens and the fences. She realized that she would have to raise a loan at the bank, which she had hoped to avoid, but the land had to be put back on to a financial footing.

As always, at the end of each busy day, Louise was tired physically and mentally when she went to bed, but she never failed to check that her doors were locked. Then, as she lay down, sleep was immediate and so deep that there were no dreams to disturb her rest, as on the ship, and for that she was thankful. There would be time ahead when yearning for Daniel would be almost beyond her strength to bear, but for a while at least tiredness was granting her much-needed rest.

Her deep sleep one night was the reason why she did not hear the communicating door between her room and Fernand's give a slight creak as he lifted it away. Earlier he had unscrewed the hinges on his side and, when Louise had checked the key, she had not noticed that the door was any less stable than before. He had been drinking, but he was not drunk as he went silently across to her bed, the moonlight through the windows giving a silvery gleam to his naked body.

He stood looking down at her, hard with lust and impatient for her. She had dared to deny him his rights on board ship, on the journey across land and here in what he now thought of as his own house. The time had come to show her that her defiance was at an end and he intended to punish her for every moment of it. With one hand he grabbed the coverlets and ripped them from her.

She awoke with a scream of horror as he fell on her, thrusting her legs apart to drive himself into her. As she beat at him with her fists, trying to struggle free, he caught her wrists and held them deep into her pillow as he rammed away at her body with his own, exulting in his possession of her at last. He gushed into her sooner than he had intended and as he collapsed across her she seized the chance to push him away and leap from the bed. Yet he had anticipated her action and his hand shot out to grab her nightgown.

Briefly she was held captive, but as he tried to snatch her back on to the bed, the fine fabric tore and she was free. But he reached the door to the gallery before she could unlock it and forced her back towards the bed. Although she screamed continually, clawing at his face as he beat her mercilessly about the head and body, there was no one to hear her. Their struggle excited him and when she lost her balance, causing both of them to fall, he took her again on the floor, viciously and brutally, and her screams were no longer just of outrage but of agonizing pain.

When he lifted himself away from her he gave her a kick where she lay, her cheek pressed into the carpet, her hair tumbled about her tear-wet face. 'There'll be no more locking doors against me!' he exclaimed fiercely, shaking a fist at her. 'You're my wife and I'll come to your bed whenever I choose. Remember that!'

He went back into his own room, but she remained huddled on the floor until she heard his bed creak and saw the candle-light extinguished. She rolled over and sat up. Unsteadily she rose to her feet and slipped on her silk robe, which had been left on a chair. Going out on to the gallery, she made her way slowly to the stairs that led up to the floor where Josette was sleeping.

The young woman awoke with a start as soon as her door opened and sat up. Even in the moonlight she could see at once that her mistress was in an extremely distressed state. She guessed immediately that rape had taken place and leapt from the bed.

'It's all right, madame! I know what to do!' Josette shoved her arms into her cotton robe and went to support Louise with an arm about the waist. 'There's an old hip bath hanging in the corridor by the kitchen. It will be quicker if I heat water for that one instead of bringing it in jugs upstairs to your own. There's a bottle of cognac in the library. I'll pour you a swig of that.'

Still talking in a reassuring tone, she took Louise down-stairs.

In the morning not all of Louise's cosmetics could have hidden her facial injuries. Her lip had been split, both her eyes blackened, and the purple bruises on her face and neck matched those hidden by her clothes. She was aware of the workmen's stares when they first caught sight of her and the cleaning women's whispers, but she carried on with all she had to do that day with her customary dignity. One workman was called from his task to carry out a special assignment for her.

When Fernand came in from riding and went upstairs to change he found that the communicating door between his room and his wife's had been bricked up and papered as if the aperture had never been.

He made no comment to Louise on what had been done, which she knew to be a danger signal. Josette would have stayed with her that night, wanting to put a truckle bed for herself at the end of the four-poster, but Louise sent her to her own room.

Fernand sat drinking until midnight before he came up the stairs carrying a heavy hammer taken earlier from a workman's tool bag. One blow would smash open the double doors that led from the gallery into Louise's bedroom. Pleasurable excitement was high in him. He was going to enjoy this night, with all he intended to do to her, and after it she would never dare cross him again.

As he reached her room he was about to swing the hammer against the door when he saw that it stood slightly ajar. Had she hidden herself somewhere else? Cowering in her maid's room perhaps? Or had she locked herself in another bedroom? Well, he'd find her wherever she was!

He kicked open the door, expecting to find the room deserted, but Louise, in nightgown and robe, sat facing him on the end of the bed. Surprised, he leaned a hand against the jamb as he set down the hammer and regarded her steadily.

'So, you've come to your senses, have you?' He gave a contemptuous nod towards the bricked-up aperture. 'But it's too late to regret your foolishness now. Tonight you'll pleasure

me exactly as I wish and then maybe – just maybe – I'll refrain
from giving you the further beating that you deserve.'

He slid off his jacket, the silk lining hissing away from his
shirtsleeves as he began to saunter across to her. Then he came
to an abrupt halt. From the folds of her robe she had raised a
pistol and was pointing it at him.

'This is the last time you are ever to enter my room,' she
said quietly. 'And you are never to touch me again. If you
take another step, I will shoot you.'

He gave a laugh of disbelief. 'Stop behaving like a fool!
These dramatics don't suit you. Give me that pistol.'

She ignored his outstretched hand and, as he took a step
forward, she cocked the weapon that Alexandre had given
her long ago for protection on her journey to Boston. At the
ominous click, Fernand came to a standstill again, his temper
soaring.

'That's a dangerous weapon you're holding! Put it down.
You haven't the least idea how to handle it.'

'You're wrong about that. Alexandre taught me when
Delphine and I stayed on his farm for a while. I shall not
miss my target when I shoot you in the leg, but neither will
I if I aim for your heart.'

Her set expression and the level tone of her voice showed
him she was not bluffing. Taken aback, he considered what
his next action should be. He was not near enough to wrest the
pistol from her, but if he could catch her off-guard it would be
easy enough.

'Very well.' He shrugged casually as if conceding to her
wishes. Turning away, he bent down and picked up his jacket
from the floor. A second later he had hurled it at her, blinding
her in its folds, and was on her at once. The explosion of
the pistol in her hand echoed throughout the house and he
staggered back as she threw the jacket from her, springing to
her feet.

'You stupid bitch!' he roared, clasping his hand to his upper
right arm, where a scarlet stain was spreading on his shirtsleeve
as the blood seeped through his fingers and dripped to the floor.

The wound was no more than a deep nick in the flesh, but shock and rage possessed him. 'You'll pay for this!'

As he went from the room he met Josette, white-faced, running along the gallery towards Louise's room. 'Get water and bandages, girl!' he ordered. 'There's been an accident.'

Josette, after reassuring herself by a glance through the doorway that Louise was unharmed, ran to do his bidding, but had to hide her grin of satisfaction as she bound up his wound, inflicting as much pain as was possible.

The next morning Louise and Fernand faced each other in the library, he regarding her with loathing in his eyes, his thoughts murderous. There was nothing he wanted more at that moment than to put his hands about her throat and strangle her. She spoke calmly.

'Both of us would prefer not to see each other again, but since we are compelled by circumstances to live under the same roof, we must make the best of it. You may go your way and I'll go mine, but for both our sakes we shall conduct ourselves civilly at all times. Are you agreed?'

He glared, but gave an angry nod. If he was to be accepted by the local nobility, whose lineage in some cases was superior to his own, he had no choice. He needed to be included in their country pursuits of hunting and drinking and gaming if he was not to die of boredom. Neither did he wish to be whispered about as a wife-beater by married women, who would otherwise be susceptible sexually to him. But when eventually Louise received her inheritance from her old aunt, who seemed to be taking a devilish long time to die, there would be nothing to stop him, as her husband, claiming it all. Then, he thought triumphantly, he would return to Paris and take up the pleasures of the past! But not before he had avenged himself on her for the humiliation she had wreaked on him that last night. He had mutilation of her beauty in mind.

On the last day the workmen were at the château, one arrived carrying two chairs. As he separated them Louise recognized the lyre backs and knew they were from the Music Room.

'I think these belong to the château,' he said, somewhat

uneasily. 'I happened to find them in my yard one day not long after you went away. I think looters must have dumped them there.'

She took his lie at its face value, only thankful to have them returned. 'If you hear of any more items taken from here, I'd be willing to give a reward for their return.'

He blinked in astonishment when she gave him a gold coin, which she hoped would encourage others to bring back their loot.

From then on several other pieces were brought back, but only three hall chairs ever reappeared and none of the smaller items, such as the silver, the clocks and many fine pieces of Sèvres porcelain, which must have been sold on. It was to be expected of starving people when even successive revolutionary governments had sold many of France's treasures internationally to raise money. It was said that countless numbers of the fine pieces and objets d'art from Versailles and other royal palaces had ended up in the stately homes of England.

When the small workforce departed from the château, it was left smelling of new paint and beeswax and dried lavender, with no sign left of the damage wreaked by the intruders. A number of rooms upstairs and down were then locked up. Those to be kept open were not as bare as before, for, as in any great house, furniture had been changed according to fashion throughout the decades and both the cellars and the attics had yielded up many good and useful pieces.

In the White Salon the sofas and surviving chairs had come back from Bordeaux, where they had been re-upholstered in some yellow-striped Lyons silk that Louise had found stored away in a chest. Pictures that had survived were rehung and others had been brought down from the attics to cover the light patches on the walls. Although two portraits of Louise's ancestors had been damaged beyond repair, there was a restorer of paintings, also in the town, who had been entrusted to work on the rest. By mail she had been informed that her application for the return of the contents of her library was being considered.

Her new domestic staff would have been by necessity only three in number, but Fernand insisted on having a valet, and she appointed one from Bordeaux, who doubled as a footman. Only two of the former twelve gardeners were re-employed, but although she engaged a gardener's boy to assist them, she could not afford a third man. In any case, the vegetables in the kitchen garden were more important than flowers for the time being. Fernand, who had an eye for a good horse, would have filled the stables, but Louise limited his purchases to riding horses for each of them and one for the chaise.

All these happenings took place while she and Pierre set improvements on the land in progress. It seemed to her that never before had every minute of her days been so occupied. If the thought came as to how joyous it would all have been with Daniel at her side, she drove it from her.

Seventeen

After what had seemed an endless time of waiting Louise finally received a letter from Madeleine. She read it eagerly. First of all, Madeleine wrote of how much they were all missing her and went on to give news of Delphine, whose romance with John had moved on to a more serious plane, with the possibility of a betrothal before long. The hat shop had been sold to another milliner and three of the staff had been retained, but the new owner's creations could not match those that Louise had made, either in style or charm. Madeleine also gave news of mutual friends and acquaintances, but did not mention the gossip that Louise knew must have erupted after her departure. *I know you are eager for news of Daniel*, Madeleine continued in her clear hand, *but there is little to tell.*

> He rarely attends balls and parties these days and I've only seen him once. That was this week, when he called on me in the hope that I had received a letter from you. I regretted having to disappoint him and we both agreed how much we wished mail could be speedier and more reliable, but that is just a dream when distances are so great and ships dependent on sea and weather. I have to say that Daniel is not the same man, very grim and reserved. Occasionally Theodore plays cards with him at their club, but he is more often at the gaming tables. Can you not show a little mercy and write to him? I have never seen a man more changed in such a short time.

Louise compressed her lips in anguish. She longed to write to him, but she had to keep to her resolve.

Gradually, as the weeks and months slid by, social life was re-established in the district as the returned émigrés began to feel settled again. Louise was pleased to renew old acquaintances as calls were made and returned. Almost without exception every landowner was like Louise in struggling to make estates profitable again, but there were dining and dancing, cards and picnics and hunting parties just as before, although nothing was on the lavish scale of the past. Yet there was private sorrow too, for there was not a family that had not lost one or more members to the guillotine, and none of the châteaux had escaped the looting, although some had fared better than others.

Louise and Fernand spoke very little to each other, but it suited them both and it lessened the strain between them. He played the role of host to perfection whenever they returned hospitality. He liked to give the impression that he was totally in charge of the estate and its gradual improvement, but he only questioned Pierre enough to talk knowledgeably in company about all that was being done. Except for hunting he was bored by country pleasures and the gaming was not for the high stakes that he enjoyed. But in Bordeaux he could find what he wanted and was often away from the château for several days at a time while he indulged himself at the gaming dens and brothels.

Now and again when he had a particularly good win he went to Paris, spending lavishly to make advantageous connections in his determination to gain an entrée into the high circles of the increasingly extravagant Napoleonic court. It pleased him to be addressed by his title again, which was not surprising since Napoleon had made princes and princesses of his brothers and sisters. It was obvious to Fernand that the First Consul appreciated lavish display and grandeur, which was to his own taste, for he had long missed the great days of Versailles. His current wish was to get an invitation to Malmaison, where Josephine Bonaparte, the great soldier's lovely wife, held sway. That might have to wait until he had his hands on Louise's inheritance from her aunt, when he could take up residence in Paris again, but in the meantime he was preparing the way.

Whenever Fernand returned to the château after his money had run out, he was always in a vile mood at having to come back to the dull countryside after a brief spell of living in the manner that he considered to be the inherent right of every nobleman, for the cause of the Revolution had left no mark on him, as it had on other thinking people in all ranks of society. All his life and in every circumstance, he had only considered what was best for himself.

Although Louise had written to Violette in England at the same time as she had to Madeleine, it took several weeks longer for a reply to reach her, which with the vagaries of the mail was not surprising. Violette wrote with compassion of Louise's having to return to Fernand after finding such happiness in America. She had hoped that Louise would never learn that he was still alive, which was why she had not mentioned his visit in any of the letters she had sent to Boston. Was there no chance of Louise ridding herself of her obnoxious husband through divorce?

Louise looked up from the letter for a few moments. She had thought of divorce many times and wished it was possible, but Fernand would never release her. Although he considered the estate to be essential to his social position, he had no wish to run it himself and, since he had no power to sell any of it for his own gain, he would continue to keep her tied to him until the end of her days. His infidelities would count for nothing, since he could counteract any accusations on her part by pointing out that he had forgiven her for taking another husband overseas.

Returning to the letter, Louise read the carefully phrased reply to her concerned enquiry as to her aunt's health. Violette explained that she had had a little trouble with her heart and her doctor had advised living in the country, away from the foul air of the city. The letter closed with the assurance that there was no cause for alarm and she sent her most affectionate greetings to her beloved niece while hoping for an immediate visit from her whenever the war between Britain and France should come to an end.

Louise folded the letter, hoping that opportunity would come soon.

Local châteaux owners had begun attending sales and auctions in Bordeaux and elsewhere in the hope of recovering furniture and other family items that had been looted from their homes. Louise was among them, but so far she had not found anything that she recognized. Then one day she discovered a large painting in oils of Alexandre's old home, which she remembered had hung in his library. Triumphantly, she purchased it to keep until such time as it could be returned to him in a traveller's safe keeping, not wanting to risk it being lost. She had written regularly to Alexandre and Blanche, although she knew some letters would never arrive, but she hoped that they would receive this special news of her discovery, knowing how pleased they would be. In the meantime she hung it in the music salon to remind her of the happy times she had spent at the château before it had become no more than a fire-blackened ruin.

On a January morning in the New Year of 1801, Louise sat looking over the accounts she had kept since taking charge of the estate after her homecoming nearly ten months ago. She saw again how her American assets had drained away, even the proceeds of her shop having gone towards paying off the high interest on the loan she had had to shoulder to meet the many expenses incurred by the estate. Fernand's gaming debts were another problem. Whenever he owed money locally he borrowed from her. He had repaid a loan only once, when, in an attempt to humiliate her, he had thrown the money at her feet as if scattering alms to the poor.

On the credit side of her finances the wine harvest had been far better than either she or Pierre had expected and the corn had grown tall and golden, selling for a good price. The woodland had also yielded some good timber, which had been shipped to a naval dockyard, the need for ships to replace those sunk by the British Navy being acute.

There was still much to be done in the way of further improvement to her estate, for many fields had been left fallow for far too long and it was essential that a large area of the vineyard, long neglected in her absence, was revived. But as she considered all that had been achieved since her return, she allowed herself to be optimistic about the estate's future. Hard work was her opiate for the yearning for Daniel that never left her. She had heard only twice from Madeleine since the letter received after her return last year, and it was obvious that some had gone missing in between. There had been almost no fresh news of him, for there seemed to have been no change in his withdrawn mood or in his solitary living.

One summer morning a newly returned émigré called to make herself known to Louise. Upon being told that the mistress of the château was out, she chose to wait. Two hours passed before Louise, who had been on an inspection of the vineyards with Pierre, returned home. She saw at once from the chaise parked in the forecourt that she had a visitor. Dismounting swiftly from her horse, she went indoors to the White Salon, where her visitor was waiting.

Rose de Torré, whose age was close to Louise's own, rose to her feet immediately, a smile of greeting lighting up her finely featured face. Tallish, with soft blond hair, her violet eyes large and expressive, she had a warmth and friendliness in her attitude that made Louise take to her at once as they introduced themselves.

'I was widowed two years ago in America,' Rose explained as they sat down on a sofa together. 'I longed to come home again, but my late husband's spinster sister, a rather helpless creature, was living with me and since she had no wish to return I felt unable to leave her. Then, quite unexpectedly, she met someone and married him, all within six weeks!' She laughed merrily. 'I started packing immediately! Now I've come home to live with my own sister, Celestine de Danville, and her husband, Adrien, your neighbours, whom you know well.'

'Indeed I do!' Louise knew them to be a kindhearted couple, older than either Rose or herself, who had suffered greatly through the Revolution, having lost all three of their grown sons to the guillotine.

'I took ship at Boston,' Rose continued. 'My American home lay fifty miles north of the city, but it was the nearest port. Prior to sailing, I stayed with an American friend on the city's Beacon Hill and through her I met three members of your family, Mr and Mrs Bradshaw and your sister, Delphine.' She paused, seeing colour rush to Louise's cheeks in pleasure.

'Are they all well?' Louise asked eagerly.

'Yes, indeed. They looked as delighted as you do now when they heard where I should be living in France. Mrs Bradshaw and your sister asked me at once if I would bring letters and gifts to you.' She dived into a basket on the floor by her feet and produced them. 'One is from your sister and the other from your cousin and her husband.'

Louise took the letters gladly, for she knew there would be news of Daniel too, and the gifts had been prettily wrapped with ribbons. 'I can never thank you enough for bringing these to me,' she said, her voice choked. 'Did you meet Daniel Lombard as well?'

'The silk merchant?' Rose shook her head. 'No, I didn't. Your cousin was most anxious to arrange a meeting, but he had gone South to a family funeral and was not expected back for another three weeks.' She had heard the eager note in Louise's quick question and, sensing her keen disappointment, wondered how close this beautiful woman and the silk merchant had been. Louise's relatives had said nothing to her, but since coming home she had heard from Celestine that Fernand de Vailly had gone to Boston specially to bring his wife back to France. For herself, his name was one she remembered from Paris at the height of the Reign of Terror, before she and her husband escaped. What she had heard might only have been rumour, and for that reason she had never repeated it, but if it were true, she pitied Louise for being his wife. 'Your sister and her charming husband, John, invited me to dine, and they have a beautiful home on Beacon Hill with everything on a most lavish scale.'

'So, my sister has married John!' Louise exclaimed, her brows raised in surprise. 'I hope she will be very happy. The last I heard was that there was a betrothal in the air. It's been so long since I last had a letter from Boston.'

'They had heard from you only once in many months, and I know from what was said that Mrs Bradshaw has been writing frequently to you. I'll leave now and allow you to read such long-awaited news at leisure.'

'Don't hurry away! It's such a pleasure to have your company and you've had no refreshment!' Louise would have gone to pull the bell-rope, but Rose reassured her.

'I was well looked after in your absence, with a pot of hot chocolate and sugared ratafias. But let's meet again soon. Next Tuesday perhaps?'

It was arranged. Together they went out of the house. As they faced each other, both having recognized the birth of friendship, Louise spoke from the heart. 'Thank you for bringing me news. It means more to me than I could ever express.'

'Next time I'll describe your sister's magnificent home to you and try to recount all that was said to me that may be of further interest to you.'

'I shall look forward to that so much.'

They kissed each other's cheeks as if they had been long acquainted. Louise waved to Rose as she drove away.

Although Fernand had been in Bordeaux for several days, Louise took the letters to the privacy of her bedroom, for she never knew when he would return and she did not want to be interrupted. As she read, she found that Madeleine had wisely rewritten much of what she had told in the previous letters, explaining that, since she was certain Louise's correspondence had gone astray, she was assuming that it had been the same with her letters too.

I shall write first of Daniel, since news of him will mean

so much to you. He is in the best of health and has picked up some threads of his social life again. Yet he seems very restless. He was twice to the South before his recent departure for his uncle's funeral and prior to those visits he had two visitors from Charleston staying with him. I met them on several occasions, a pretty widow named Sarah Jane Delafield, and her brother, Thomas Thorpe, both of them friends of his since childhood. It is said that he was betrothed to her once, but at the last moment she turned him down for someone else. Whether that is correct, I do not know, but since you wished for all news of him, I offer it for whatever it's worth. I have to say that their visit seemed to do him a great deal of good, and since then he has looked more himself again than he did for a long time after you went away. It is not that he has forgotten you, for there is always that same haunted look in his eyes when he asks about you. Once he pressed me to tell him more about you other than that you were well, and I had to admit that you had forbidden me to reveal anything else. He looked both angry and hurt, but not surprised. With this recent change in him I have been wondering if it is possible that he has begun to look to the future instead of the past, which was what you wished for him.

Louise lowered the letter and drew in a shuddering breath. It was what she wanted for him, but that did not lessen the desperate anguish she felt at the thought of another woman in his arms. In all the time they had been together he had never mentioned Sarah Jane, although she had sometimes wondered if a woman had been the reason why he had left his Southern roots and moved north. All he had ever said was that the silk business had interested him and he'd had the chance to buy the property in Boston. Perhaps time had healed the breach with the woman he had once wanted to marry and now they were able to reconsider the relationship that had been between them.

Louise forced herself to read on, trying to take everything

in. There followed a long description of Delphine's wedding day, but Louise knew she would have to read the letter again later before it made sense to her. Firstly she had to come to terms with all that Madeleine had written about Daniel. She knew it had been done as a kindness to prepare her for what might happen in time to come, but it was tearing her apart.

Delphine's letter was a joyous paean of praise to luxury. John had given her some wonderful jewels, a carriage of her own with four matched greys and so many gowns that all her closets were full. He was advancing politically and she had made him promise that if he should become a senator they would have an elegant home in Washington to rival the White House. There was much more in the same vein. Delphine wrote as she spoke, a lack of punctuation making the letter an echo of her chattering. Yet not once did she mention loving John – but then she had once declared she could never love any man again after Pieter. It made the letter a sad one to read.

Slowly Louise unwrapped her gifts. Delphine had sent her a sugar rose from the wedding cake and a stole of finest cream lace. From Madeleine there was a book on the early history of America that Louise had long wanted to read, but had found it impossible to obtain when she was in Boston. Both gifts touched her deeply.

After their next meeting, Louise and Rose saw each other often, never running out of lively conversation, enjoying each other's company and sharing laughter. Louise had not felt so completely in harmony with a friend since being with Blanche. Rose confided that she would like to marry again, for her late husband had been chosen for her and, although now she was in her early thirties, she dared to hope that one day she would find the love that had eluded her marriage.

It was for this reason that, when Rose came to dine with her sister and husband, Louise also invited a widower, whom she liked for his good humour and intelligence, together with other guests. Fernand had not met Rose before this evening, although he was well acquainted with her brother-in-law as they rode with the same hunt. Since she was a fine-looking woman, he was prepared to give her his special attention, having cultivated a way of looking at women that was admiring and predatory and sexually aware. Women were flattered by his ability to make them feel beautiful and desirable, but Rose, whom he treated to the full force of his charm, met his eyes with such a shaft of cold dislike that he was taken aback by it. There flew through his mind the uncomfortable thought that she might know something about him from the past that he had hoped would never come to light. Then he dismissed the troubled thought. His conceit was such that he decided she was piqued because he had been closely attentive to a younger and prettier woman among the guests before welcoming her.

Although Rose and the widower talked together for a while, Louise saw that her attempt at matchmaking would come to nothing this time. That same evening, Rose told her that she would be going to Paris to see an old friend, Ginette, whose husband, Antoine de Beauclaire, believed there was a chance that she could reclaim a piece of building land in the city, which had belonged to her father.

'Paris!' Louise breathed nostalgically. 'It's so long since I was there.'

'Come with me! It will only be for a few days at most. I'll write to Ginette today. We can see the latest fashions, go to the theatres and you can buy yourself a new gown!'

A week later they set off in Louise's carriage, Josette and Rose's maid going with them. Although Paris would be full of painful memories for Josette, she had a longing to see her old home again and perhaps find a friend or two still living nearby.

There was a silk-blue sky on a day steeped in sunshine when the carriage rolled through the gates of Paris and Louise saw again the city that had been through so much since she was last there. Although there had been a considerable amount of rebuilding, the Louvre and the Palace of the Tuileries still stood aloof in their history-enhanced magnificence, the city remaining mainly mediaeval in its narrow streets. Coffee houses, chocolate houses, cafés and taverns all seemed to be doing brisk business, people thronging everywhere. Soldiers, now in the smart uniforms of Napoleon's army, eyed the young grisettes delivering parcels and hatboxes, who hurried past. Street traders shouted their wares while entertainers and beggars jostled for attention. In the wide cobbled square where once the guillotine had stood, all was peaceful, but the cracked paving stones showed how many of the heavy-wheeled tumbrils had rolled across there with their victims in the not so distant past.

At the house where Rose's friends lived, the door was opened immediately the carriage drew up and Ginette de Beauclaire came out on to the steps with her arms outstretched in welcome. Louise was ushered indoors amid the excited greetings being exchanged, for Ginette and Rose had not seen each other since the time of the Terror.

It was a happy household. Antoine was a rotund, red-faced man who laughed a great deal and always slapped his large thigh prior to his extra-loud guffaws. In contrast, Ginette was slim, pale in complexion and quiet-voiced, but just as good-natured. Their five children, ages ranging from twelve to two, had angelic faces and mischievous eyes. Louise half-expected to find a frog in her bed that night, but Rose was the unlucky one.

Louise had Ginette for company when her husband took Rose to see various government officials about the land. Afterwards the three of them went to the shops and fashion houses while in the evenings there was always a social event arranged. When Ginette heard that Louise had been one of the ladies-in-waiting to the late Queen, she suggested that the three of them drive out one afternoon to look at the old Palace of Versailles. When they arrived, Rose and Ginette remained in the carriage, letting Louise alight on her own. The great gates still stood wide as they had done when, having rusted on their hinges through long disuse, they had proved impossible to close against the mob on that fateful day when everything had changed.

Louise walked slowly into the great courtyard. A solitary

figure in that vast area, she stopped to gaze up at the balcony of the Royal apartment. There the King had courageously addressed the bloodthirsty crowd and the Queen had made a brave appearance on her own, even though she had known herself to be the most hated woman in France and would have been an easy target for a pistol shot.

The Palace had been reopened for some time, but not to hold glorious functions as in the past. Most of its furnishings and fine works of art had been sold to foreign buyers or transferred to the Louvre and elsewhere. In the beautiful Hall of Mirrors, where once three thousand candles had given light, not a single one of the marvellous chandeliers still hung from the ornate ceiling. Napoleon seemed to have no liking for the place, although he had been there from time to time, and many of the rooms were used as offices or for equally mundane purposes, while the rest were closed up.

Louise turned away and went back to the carriage, keeping her memories to herself. She would never go there again.

Louise and Rose left Paris two days later. The piece of land had been given over to Rose, and Antoine was to sell it for her, which would bring her some much-needed money.

In the following year of 1802, to the relief of innumerable people, a treaty, known as the Treaty of Amiens, was signed in March between France, Britain, Spain and Holland. To Louise it meant that at last she could visit Violette in England. She would have liked to make the journey without delay, but spring was a busy time on all the estates and there were financial matters she had to deal with that could not be left in Pierre's hands. She wrote at once to her aunt, promising that she would visit her after the wine and corn harvests were in. At that time she could stay for much longer than if she came in the immediate months ahead.

Those who did not delay an immediate journey across the Channel were the English aristocracy. Paris had always been their favourite foreign city and they flocked back to enjoy its variety of pleasures, with its theatres and gaming houses, its exotic diversions, its splendid wines and its fashion. There was also an exciting new dance known as the waltz. Never before had couples danced face to face in what was virtually an embrace and it was as intoxicating as the champagne. Among the visitors were the nouveau riche who had made fortunes during the long war. Paris was almost afloat with the outpouring of golden guineas.

There was a joke going around that, since the treaty had been signed, the same amount of spies had come to France as had gone to England. Louise became convinced that Fernand was one of them as he had begun to be away from the château for lengthier periods, with no talk of Paris upon his return.

French officers, who had been prisoners-of-war in England, were being released if they gave their word as gentlemen never to take up arms against Britain again, but many felt unable to give it, remaining in liberal custody with the hope of eventually joining invading French forces on British soil. One of the wounded, Jerome Colbert, whose loss of his right arm prevented any further service, came home to his nearby château, which had been opened up by his two sisters. On an evening when Fernand was away, Louise held a dinner party to which Jerome and his sisters, whom she knew from childhood, were invited. She welcomed him warmly. He had never been handsome, but he had a kind face and quiet grey eyes.

'Thank you, Louise,' he replied, with the ease that comes with old friendships renewed. 'It's good to be home again.'

Then she saw how his eyes met Rose's clear gaze as she introduced them. There was instant attraction between them. Louise hoped that perhaps Rose had found the man she had been wanting in her life

Before the summer was out there was a letter from Madeleine that brought Louise disturbing news.

Before you left here you asked me to tell you everything about Daniel and I have done my best, but that chance will soon be taken from me, as he has sold his house and his business and is leaving Boston. He is going back to live in the South, but what his plans are there I do not know. He has said only that he will be visiting his sister for a while in Charleston before he makes settled arrangements. I asked him to keep in touch. Perhaps he guessed the reason, because he made a strange reply. He said that he would have taken another hat as a gift for his sister if you could have chosen it for him.

For the first time since sailing out of Boston harbour Louise broke down completely and shed despairing tears. By now Daniel would have moved South and the last link with him was broken. She did not know how to bear the pain of it.

It was late October when Louise, accompanied by Josette, crossed the Channel and landed at the old naval city of Portsmouth. From there it was only a few hours' drive into the county of Sussex. Her aunt's home nestled in the countryside not far from the ancient city of Chichester. Violette, having sighted the arrival of the carriage from an upper window, came hurrying down the wide staircase as Louise entered the hall.

'My darling niece! You are here at last!'

'Tante Violette!' Louise rushed forward to the foot of the flight and they both laughed in joy at their reunion as they held each other in a long and emotional embrace. When they drew apart they gazed at each other happily.

'I thought this day would never come,' Violette declared blissfully. Her hair had lost its rich flame colour and turned snow-white, but her classic facial bones still made her a pretty woman, and there was the same perky brightness about her that had always been part of her charm.

'You are looking so well, Tante!' Louise exclaimed, having feared she would find her an invalid.

'That must be due to the sea-fresh air of Sussex,' Violette declared, determined that nothing should spoil their time together. 'And you're to call me by my Christian name in future. It will make me feel younger. How lovely you are, my dear. From the pretty girl that I remember, you've become a beautiful woman.'

While they had been talking, Louise's trunks had been carried upstairs and they began to follow, Violette still talking. 'I can hardly believe that you've been half across the world and back again since you were last here! There's so much to talk about! So much for you to tell me about Delphine and Madeleine! And how are you, my dear?' She paused on the stairs to take Louise's hands into both her own, her expression revealing her deep concern, for never having had a child of her own, her pent-up maternal love had always been directed towards her sister's firstborn.

Louise smiled. 'I'm fit and strong! My life is well organized. Fernand and I keep out of each other's way as much as possible. Running the estate keeps me busy and I have renewed old friendships with neighbours who have come home again.'

Violette thought to herself that it sounded a bleak existence for a woman so deserving of the love that she had been forced to leave behind in Boston.

Upstairs, Louise met Marie, plump and grey-haired, who was Violette's lady's maid. She had come from France with Violette at the time of her marriage and, as Violette joked, they had grown old together. Louise soon realized that Marie also fulfilled the role of nurse, being meticulous in seeing that Violette took her pills and physic daily as the doctor had ordered. Sometimes they could be heard quarrelling cheerfully when Violette was in a rebellious mood.

For the first week, Violette abandoned her usual social activities, wanting to keep Louise to herself until they had caught up with all that had happened in the years since they were last together. After that she allowed the local society to meet her niece and invitations flowed in. Violette, who had always loved company, entertained in her turn.

The last leaves of the October trees fell. November passed by bleak and cold, and when Christmas came Louise and Violette attended a service at Chichester Cathedral. Then came the New Year parties and when the first snowdrops of

February were in full flower Louise began to think of going back to France.

Violette had dreaded this time of parting. 'I'd ask you to stay on with me if I thought it were possible,' she said sadly.

'You know how much I would want to do that,' Louise replied quietly, 'but Fernand would only come looking for me, as he did in Boston.'

'Would you do something for me?'

'Anything!'

'Let me travel back to France with you. I want to see Paris once more before I draw my last breath.'

Louise hesitated. During her stay she had not been deceived by her aunt's excuses about needing to rest or to take a little nap, able to see that she was not as well as she tried to appear.

'Will your doctor agree to a trip?' Louise asked with concern.

Violette threw up her hands in exasperation. 'That old fool would keep me in bed all the time if he had his way!' she scoffed. 'I'm not ending my days like that! I want to live my life right up to the last moment. So, what do you say?'

Louise nodded smilingly. 'We'll go! I shall escort you there and back.'

Violette laughed with delight. 'When you described those few days in Paris with your friend, Rose, such a yearning came over me to be with my fellow countrymen again, to talk my own language and to see once more all that I remember so well.' She clasped her hands together, her voice merry. 'A Parisian doctor will prescribe champagne and oysters – not that ill-tasting poison that my English doctor gives me! I shall feel young again!'

They sailed for France a week later. When Violette stepped ashore her eyes swam with happy tears. 'I'm home!' she exclaimed huskily.

It was dawn in Bordeaux when Fernand finished a night of gaming with a heavy purse of gold in his pocket. He sat back in his carriage as it began to roll along in a homeward direction. Sleepily he glanced out of the window as they passed a hostelry where a traveller had alighted from a coach and was waiting for his baggage to be unloaded. Fernand sat forward abruptly. It was Daniel Lombard!

Drawing back quickly to avoid being seen, Fernand swore to himself. The American had come looking for Louise! There was no doubt of that! It was sheer luck she was far away in England, but if Lombard appeared at the château he must make sure that the search for her was nipped in the bud!

Arriving home, he ordered the senior staff to come to him in the library. Their number had increased since the château had first reopened. He gave them strict instructions regarding the possible visit of an American. The housekeeper, whom he had appointed in Louise's absence and who came willingly to his bed whenever he had need of her, was given special instructions on her own.

Daniel arrived at the château late that morning. He had chosen to ride, for the March morning was full of crisp sunshine, with a sky the colour of a duck's egg. As he came up the drive, he reined in for a few minutes to view the château that Louise had described to him when she had talked of her childhood. With its old walls and the slumbering look of its fine windows, the shutters open to the sun, he thought it as beautiful as she had described.

Excitement gripped him. He was not far from her now! He had no idea if she would be angry that he had come seeking her, but he would explain that he could not go on any longer without seeing for himself how she was and if she had investigated the possibility of divorce. Madeleine had been almost fanatical in refusing to give him any information about her, even though he could see that she was always longing to tell him. He had gained a few snippets from Delphine, enough to let him know that Louise was coping courageously in spite of enormous difficulties. Although his move South had opened a new life for him, he had found it impossible to continue with it until he could be sure that, since Louise's return to France, no loophole had revealed itself that might be used to enable them to be together. Coming here was like the last throw of the dice and his future and hers depended upon it.

As he dismounted, a stable boy came running to take his horse. He tugged the bell-pull and after a few moments a manservant opened the door to him.

'I'm here to see the mistress of the house,' he said in French.

'Madame la Marquise is not at home.'

'I prefer to find that out for myself.' Daniel strode past him. Catching sight of a maidservant near the head of the stairs, he spoke sharply. 'Tell your mistress that she has a visitor who will not leave until he has seen her.' He had had the sudden fear that Louise might have been locked away.

'She is not here, monsieur.'

'What's your name?'

'Isabelle.' She was highly nervous. This stranger, with his dark, frowning brows, was frightening her as much as the master.

Daniel took a gold piece from his pocket and held it out to her. 'Where can I find her, Isabelle?'

She drew back, her hands behind her, shaking her head. Then she turned and scuttled up the rest of the flight out of his line of vision. Fernand spoke lazily from the library doorway, his voice echoing slightly in the large hall.

'Put your gold away, Lombard. My servants have told you the truth. You'll not find Louise here.' He was leaning a shoulder against the jamb of the open library door. 'If she had been, I suppose it would have ended up with my rapier blade going through you, but in her absence there is no need.'

'Has she left you?'

Fernand laughed without humour. 'That would suit you, wouldn't it? No, my dear wife is dutiful in all matters and you have become a distant memory.'

'I dispute that! Is she visiting her aunt in England?'

'No! She went there as soon as the Treaty of Amiens enabled her to travel and stayed three months,' Fernand lied glibly, determined that this American should not seek her out there. 'Did you suppose she would delay going to see the old woman of whom she is so fond?'

'No, that's why I'm sure she's here now.'

Fernand lost patience. 'You're wasting your time and mine.' He stepped forward aggressively. 'Leave my house now! You have come in vain to make another attempt to take my wife from me, and I'll tell you why you'll never find her. A maidservant on an errand in Bordeaux this morning told Louise afterwards of a foreigner from the New World staying at her brother's hostelry. Maybe Louise has always been afraid that you would reappear one day, because as soon as the young woman gave a description of him, she knew it must be you. She made her servants start packing immediately and she left the château within the hour, taking off in the carriage at high speed.'

'That can't be true!' Daniel glared in disbelief.

'Ask any of the servants. Take a look in her bedroom if you wish. I doubt if there's been time for it to be cleared up yet.' Fernand looked towards the stairs, where the maidservant had reappeared. 'Guide this visitor to your mistress's bedroom.'

When Daniel stood on the threshold of the bedroom, he saw all the signs of a hasty departure. Drawers stood open, discarded gowns were flung across the bed and a single shoe lay on its side near the bed. A slim woman in dark blue, whom he guessed was the housekeeper, was picking up a petticoat from the floor and raised her eyebrows in surprise at seeing him.

'Where has your mistress gone?' he demanded, entering the room.

'I do not know, monsieur.'

'Speak the truth! I have travelled far to get here and if you have any compassion you will tell me where she is to be found.' When the woman only tightened her lips he dived into his pocket and drew out a handful of gold coins. 'Would these help you to recall? Something must have been said to give you some inkling as to where your mistress can be found.'

She took the coins from him. 'I speak honestly when I say

I truly do not know her whereabouts, but unknown to the Marquis de Vailly, she did give me a message to pass on to you. She wished you well and implored you not to attempt to look for her.'

He stood quite still for a few moments, as if he had been dealt a physical blow that had knocked all the breath from him. Then he gave a nod and turned slowly away. She smiled behind his back as he left the room. Fernand's tactics had worked well. If there had been any advantage for herself in revealing that Louise was in England, she would have done it, but if Fernand ever rid himself of his wife, he would never marry a servant. She opened her hand to count the gold coins she had been clutching and smiled again. Fernand would not have paid her extra to untidy the room and then put everything to rights again. This money was a welcome bonus.

Daniel went down the stairs and out of the château without looking to the right or left. Fernand followed him to the steps and watched him ride away. It had been a totally satisfactory encounter. The American would never come back.

Eighteen

In Paris Violette was back in her element, buying hats and gowns and gloves for herself and wanting to get as much for Louise, who was content with the one beautiful hat she had chosen. It was brimless with cream plumes, a fashion rivalling the wide-brimmed bonnets that many women were wearing.

Violette had taken a large elegantly furnished apartment on the prestigious Rue d'Anjou. They ate in all the exclusive restaurants, sat in the best box at the opera and at various theatres, as well as visiting the most elite gaming houses, where Violette played extravagantly and won more often than she lost. She met several former émigrés, whom she had entertained in London and Sussex during their exile, and old friendships were renewed.

She still suffered the occasional cramp in her chest, but no more than in England, and she began to believe that living in the country had really done her no good at all. Yet common sense did tell her that it was sensible to continue to set aside two hours daily to lie on her bed. It did not stop her arguing with Marie about how much and how often she should take her medicine, and their clashes had become more explosive than before. Sometimes Josette took over this duty to relieve Marie, and perversely Violette took the dose without a murmur, since there was no fun in annoying this firm-faced lady's maid.

Although Violette liked Louise to be with her wherever she went, there was one visit she made on her own. It was to her Parisian lawyers, who had always handled her French interests, finding ways of corresponding with her throughout the war by a personal courier, except at the height of the Revolution when everything was in turmoil and they themselves had had to lie low. She was received with courtesy and consideration by the grandson of the man whom she had always seen in the distant past, who had long since retired.

Frédéric Terain was in his early thirties, sharp-eyed and intelligent. She liked him and was particularly pleased at the way he paid meticulous attention to her wishes, explaining ways to her by which they could be carried out. Two days later she went to sign the new will he had drawn up for her, for although her niece would still be the main beneficiary, as in her previous will, certain conditions had been introduced.

After three weeks in Paris, Violette told Louise that she had decided to stay on in France. They were on their way back to the Rue d'Anjou after visiting Ginette and Antoine, whom Louise had wanted her to meet, and it had been a great success.

'I've come home to my roots, Louise. I have friends here to visit and entertain, including the couple I've just met, and already it feels as if I've never been away. I shall continue renting the apartment until I find a suitable place to buy and I'm going to live in Paris until the end of my days. It also means that, although Bordeaux is a long way from here, there'll never be a sea or an ocean between us ever again! You can visit me whenever you like.'

'I'm so glad!' Louise exclaimed. She was thankful to know she would always be able to reach her aunt, for nobody knew how long the Treaty of Amiens would last, rumours rumbling on all sides.

'If it hadn't been for you, I would never have made the effort to come here again,' Violette continued. 'Something went out of me when I followed that stupid London doctor's advice and moved from the city to the countryside. Now I feel alive again!' She wagged a be-ringed finger at Louise with a flash of rubies. 'But don't ever invite me to your château, even though it would be full of memories for me of your dear mother, because I never want to clap eyes on that husband of yours again!'

'I won't,' Louise promised. 'But I shall soon have to return there, even though I left a clerk to deal with the accounts. My bailiff, Pierre, will want to consult me on any number of matters to do with the estate.'

Violette sighed. 'We've both known that this time together in Paris would be short. But you will return soon?'

'At the first opportunity.'

'Why not bring Rose with you next time? I'd like to meet her. After all, she is responsible in a way for my being here. If she hadn't invited you to Paris, you would not have conjured up for me the wonderful and exciting atmosphere of this city, which made me yearn to see it again.'

Louise thought it would be a good idea to bring Rose. There had been no proposal yet from Jerome Colbert, even though he and Rose saw each other frequently. Rose believed his sisters were the cause, for they were jealous of their domestic reign over the château, and did not want him to take a wife. But he would miss Rose when she was away. Perhaps that would make him realize what his life would be without her exuberant personality to counteract the dullness of living with his sisters.

Later that day Louise sat down with pen and paper as Violette began to list all that she wanted sent from her Sussex home, which included the French furniture that had gone across the Channel with her when she married. Her housekeeper there and her lawyers in Chichester would organize everything and there should be no need for her to return to England.

In the evening they went to the theatre again. As they stood in their box to leave at the end of the performance, Louise, glancing down at the departing audience, happened to see a tall man, who had just left a seat immediately below. He was already making his way up the aisle and she could only see the back of him, but in the way he held his head and in the breadth of his shoulders he was so like Daniel that spontaneously she cried out. 'Daniel!'

He did not turn. In any case, he could not have heard her in the buzz of conversation and the orchestra was still playing. But still she stood, looking after him until he was lost from sight.

Violette had turned from leaving the box and came to her side. 'What is it, my dear?'

Louise smiled ruefully. 'I saw someone who reminded me of Daniel. It was stupid of me to even think he could be here. It's not the first time I've been reminded of him in a stranger's physique or a turn of the head.'

'That's natural when you're finding it so hard to live without him.' Violette took her hand and patted it comfortingly.

Outside the theatre, Daniel decided to walk back to his hotel, although it was raining hard. It would be a long wait for a hackney carriage and he wanted to finish his packing for an early departure to take ship at Calais. His week in Paris had gone quickly, but he had not wanted to leave France without seeing the city and the Palace of Versailles, which Louise had spoken about many times. Although he had lost her, he had still wanted to add to his memories of her by following the paths she had trodden. He bent his head against the rain, which pattered against his hat, and the shoulder-cape of his coat billowed as he joined the dispersing crowd of theatregoers making their way along the street.

In the darkness, with the rain pouring in rivulets down the window, Louise did not see Daniel as the carriage overtook him and bowled past. She was trying to pay attention to Violette's opinion of the play they had just seen, but she was still overwhelmed by the agonizing rush of love she had felt in being reminded of him.

Louise left Paris with Josette at the end of the week. She was thankful to know that capable Marie would always be at hand to care for Violette, who would never be lonely as so many old acquaintances had already been renewed.

Arriving home, Louise met Fernand, dressed for travelling, as he came through the hall.

'So, you're back from England at last,' he greeted her. 'Is the old hag on her deathbed yet?'

Louise flushed angrily. 'I've forbidden you to speak of my aunt in such a way!'

'Forbidden?' he laughed mockingly. 'I can say whatever I choose about that tight-fisted bitch. But don't keep me in suspense. How ill is she?'

'Violette has moved back to live permanently in Paris and is already enjoying a social round almost as if she were a young woman again.'

His face tightened and he spoke viciously through thin lips. 'If you'd had any sense, you would have pressed a pillow over her face one night!'

Thrusting past her, he kicked a piece of her baggage out of his way, and went swiftly down the steps to his waiting coach.

From the first hour, Louise was back into the routine of the estate. The clerk, who also worked for Rose's brother-in-law, had done well, and Pierre had been his usual reliable self in all matters. As yet, Louise could not foresee when the estate would start making a profit. It was still running on a loan from her bankers, for although debts incurred in reviving the husbandry of the land had been paid off, they had been replaced by others that she could not yet clear. There were worrying moments when she had to decide which bill needed payment most urgently. In her absence Fernand had far extended their hospitality budget. She did not know whom he had entertained in her absence, but the stock of wine in the cellar was severely depleted.

In May the Treaty of Amiens, which had been no more than a truce, ended as many had feared and hostilities were resumed. Louise read all she could about the war and, although she loved her country, she had begun to fear that Napoleon's ambition was French domination of Europe, with the crushing of Britain as his ultimate aim.

When Louise went next to visit Paris her aunt had bought a mansion on the Rue d'Anjou, having liked the location. Violette had settled back into Paris as if she had never been away and held soirées that gathered a circle of intellectuals around her, including writers and artists and patrons of the arts.

A letter from Madeleine late in November showed that once again some previous correspondence had gone missing. Louise thought that her cousin had written coolly, almost as if displeased with her, but she could not imagine why. First of all Madeleine cast doubt on the wisdom of Violette's move to Paris when France was too aggressive for its own good and blamed Louise for influencing her.

> There are times now when I have to doubt your common sense, as I never did before. As I wrote last time, your action still puzzles me, but perhaps you are adjusting to life with Fernand. If that is the case, what you did is understandable and nobody wishes for you to have contentment in your life more than I do.

The rest of the letter followed the usual run of local news as well as announcing that Delphine and John would be moving to Washington, as he had just won an important election. They had already paid a visit to the capital and been received by George Washington's successor, President John Adams and his wife, at the White House. At the end of the letter there was a brief reference to Daniel.

> It was considerate of Daniel to write to me from his sister's home in Charlestown, but I do not expect ever to hear again now that all that was between you really is a closed book.

Louise found the letter upsetting. Her cousin had never written in such a tone before. Puzzled, she shook her head as she put the letter away in her bureau.

It worried her that Fernand had become even more unpredictable in his behaviour. Somehow he had managed to gain an entrée into the Napoleonic court and had begun inviting acquaintances from Paris to visit his country home. Some, who he wanted to help his advancement, usually came with their wives, and took part in all the local country activities. Yet one day he brought others, men who were hard drinkers and reckless gamblers, accompanied by dubious women. That night they quarrelled fiercely in their cups, overturning the card tables and breaking chairs. Against all the rules of duelling, two men took up pistols against each other in the rose garden, but both were too drunk to aim straight and missed each other.

After this incident Fernand did not invite them or their kind again. It was not Louise's anger or her outrage over the damage caused that made him take action, but the protection of his local reputation. If the duel, without the presence of a doctor and two responsible, sober men as seconds, became public knowledge, it would result in a terrible scandal. It might taint his name as far away as Paris and, locally, it was all too easy to be dropped by the country society that he secretly despised. He needed their goodwill, for he wanted always to impress his Parisian guests of importance with his good standing in the neighbourhood. So, whenever he was in the capital and well away from the château, he joined in orgies with his wild friends, some of whom he met daily in their courtly roles at the Palace of the Tuileries. But in spite of his good looks, impeccable manners and his ability to charm women when it suited him, he still had not managed to gain an invitation to Malmaison. It had not occurred to him that Josephine might not like his sly-eyed handsomeness.

'He reminds me of a snake,' she had remarked to a friend.

She had spoken in Napoleon's hearing. Usually he was intolerant of women's opinions and disliked politically minded women who exerted their influence at the soirées that they held, but what Josephine had said about Fernand de Vailly stuck in his mind. He reminded himself that the fellow had done some good work for France when spying in England during the truce, but personally he did not like spies any more than he could endure traitors. Mentally he crossed off Fernand de Vailly's name for any position of importance.

It was not long after Louise had received the disturbing letter from Boston that Rose and Jerome were married. Rose did not expect to have an easy time with his sisters as the new first lady of the household.

'But I'm starting as I mean to go on,' she told Louise determinedly. 'I shall be kind, but firm.'

It took until spring the following year before her sisters-in-law accepted her true position at the château. Then it was only because one married an elderly widower and the other went to live with them in Bordeaux. Louise visited Violette as often as was possible. Although she had written to Madeleine that her letter had puzzled her, no explanation was given in subsequent months-old correspondence that sometimes managed to filter through the hazards of war.

It was early December and Louise was sitting with Rose by a cheerful fire in the music salon, discussing a book they had both read, when a maidservant brought in a letter.

'A messenger has come from Paris, madame. He will await a reply.'

'See that he has food and a hot drink,' Louise said as she took the letter. Then, seeing it was from Violette's lawyer, she was alarmed and tore it open.

I regret to inform you that on December 2nd at half past seven in the evening, Madame Violette died of a seizure of the heart. Earlier she had arrived at Notre Dame for the crowning ceremony of the Emperor Napoleon and Empress Josephine, when she collapsed and was taken home. Although her doctor did all possible to save her, it was in vain. Pray accept my sincere condolences. I await your instructions.

Louise, her face white to the lips with shock, looked across at Rose. 'My dear aunt has died! I can scarcely believe it! I must leave for Paris at once.' She dropped her face into her hands, unable to hold back her sudden flood of tears.

Rose darted forward from where she sat to put a comforting arm about her shoulders. 'I'm so sorry. Such a lively lady! You shall not travel to Paris on your own. I'll come with you!'

The journey and the days that followed were steeped in grief for Louise. It should have been some consolation to her that the last two years had been among the happiest her aunt had ever known, but her personal sense of loss blocked out all else. The day of the funeral was bitterly cold, snow having fallen in the night. Yet the church was full, many among the mourners having reason to be grateful for the hospitality and generous help Violette had given them in their émigré days. She was buried in a churchyard in the heart of the city she had loved.

It was as Louise turned away from the graveside, wiping her eyes under her black veil, that her arm was gripped painfully. Even as she gasped with shock and surprise, she was wrenched about to face an aristocratic-looking woman in her mid-fifties, well dressed in black, who was completely unknown to her, but whose eyes were blazing with fury and hatred.

'How dare you mourn your good aunt when you've never mourned your evil husband's victims!' She hissed her words in her wrath.

Louise wrenched herself free, wondering if the woman was mad. 'I don't know you, madame!'

'But I remember seeing you at Versailles with the Queen! Your husband is that monster, Fernand de Vailly!'

'Why should you call him that?'

'He murdered my family!'

Rose, who had been near enough to overhear the woman's first accusing words, had been quick to turn and divert the mourners leaving the graveside out of earshot and had signalled to Antoine and Ginette that they should take over from her. Then she turned back to Louise's side. 'Go away!' she ordered the woman. 'You've no right to make such accusations!'

'I have every right!'

Louise intervened fiercely before Rose could speak again. 'Allow this lady to speak, Rose! I want to know what grounds there are for this accusation against Fernand and me.'

The woman became a little calmer, but was no less furious. She drew herself up, holding her head high. 'I'm the Duchesse de Roget. My two sisters, their husbands, and seven of my nephews and nieces, all under the age of thirteen, went to the guillotine. They were caught as they tried to flee to safety in England, because your husband betrayed them!'

'But that's impossible! He was also condemned. Everybody knows that his life was saved only because of an accident with the tumbril on his way to the scaffold.'

'Do you truly believe from all you must know of him that he is innocent of the crime I have related?' The question was rapier-like in its directness.

'I should need absolute proof before I would believe anybody guilty of such horror.'

Rose intervened, aware of curious glances being cast in their direction. 'It's very cold and very public standing here. Would it not be better to discuss this matter in a carriage?'

The duchess gave a vague nod to show she had heard and continued to address Louise as they went side by side towards the nearest equipage, which was the one Violette had bought for herself. 'I can see my accusation has come as a great shock to you, Madame la Marquise.' Her tone had become easier. 'I had believed you knew of your husband's crimes, but clearly you did not.'

As soon as the three of them were settled in the carriage, Louise clasped her trembling hands in her lap as she faced the duchess, Rose seated at her side.

'Tell me what you have to say,' she said, keeping her voice firm.

'It was during the Reign of Terror that Fernand de Vailly was a spy in Paris and elsewhere for the traitor and regicide, the Duc d'Orléans. Because your husband was a fellow aristocrat, other nobles trusted him when they were desperate to escape with their families to England. He would profess to know a secret route with safe houses along the way to the coast, one he declared he would follow himself as soon as he could locate you. He would say that he could not leave France without taking you to safety too.'

Louise shuddered inwardly at Fernand's duplicity. 'How were those unfortunate people entrapped?'

'They were allowed to get halfway to the coast before an ambush was sprung. To my knowledge only two people ever escaped, each on a separate occasion, and they were both young men travelling with parents and siblings, one with his betrothed as well. The two youths met each other during exile.'

'Why have they not denounced my husband?'

'Because one eventually died in England of the wounds he had sustained during the ambush. He was lying bleeding in the bushes when a peasant woman and her husband found him. They took him into their hovel and the woman nursed him until he had recovered enough to get away, but his physical strength was never the same. The other young man was my nephew. He married in England, but a fever took him. His young widow is English and has no wish to live in France, but I visited her during the time of the Treaty of Amiens, and it was she who related the treachery that had sealed the fate of those dear to me.'

'Why were you not with your relatives in their attempt to escape?'

'My husband and I had taken our only child to southern Italy for her health's sake before the Revolution started, and we decided to stay on till all was well in France again. Then our daughter married an Italian, so we have settled there permanently and this is only my second visit home.'

'I still don't understand why you haven't spoken out against my husband.'

The duchess shrugged. 'Without witnesses?'

Rose turned to Louise. 'I know that it's hard for you to accept all you have been told, but I heard in my exile from another émigré of an aristocrat, bearing Fernand's name, who had deliberately betrayed his own kind.'

'Has that émigré returned to France?' the duchess demanded sharply.

'I have no idea. It was a chance meeting and I never saw him again.'

Louise still felt it only fair to continue to protest on Fernand's behalf. 'But my husband was imprisoned and destined for the guillotine, or else his name would never have appeared on the list of deceased!'

'Agreed,' Rose endorsed. 'Maybe he fell from Orléan's favour and Fernand's account of his escape is the truth.'

Louise accepted it was the most logical explanation. Many supporters of the Revolution, as well as the ringleaders, had risen high and fallen again during those tumultuous times. She also believed she knew what had caused Fernand's treachery. It was greed. Not for money then, but for power and position in the new regime. But eventually Orléans had gone to the guillotine, as so many of his victims had done before him, and Fernand had escaped to England just in time to give himself an alibi as an innocent émigré. It was then that he had been able to visit her aunt. She no longer doubted that the Duchess de Roget had told her the truth.

'We have met through a tragic and treacherous event in the past, Madame la Duchesse,' she said. 'Pray accept my most heartfelt sympathy on your terrible bereavement.'

The duchess inclined her head in acknowledgement as she alighted from the carriage. She was too arrogant to show pity, but it was obvious to her that Fernand de Vailly's wife was in torment over what she had learned.

Most of the mourners invited back to the mansion on the Rue d'Anjou had already arrived by the time Louise and Rose joined them. There were several curious glances sent in Louise's direction as those present wondered about the altercation they had witnessed in the churchyard, but nothing was said and they left none the wiser after wine and refreshments had been served. Ginette and Antoine left too. They had asked no questions, but had seen that Louise had been deeply affected by the encounter, on top of her deep grief for her aunt.

Going into the lilac-hued salon where Violette had written her letters at a magnificent boulle desk, Louise found Frédéric Terain waiting for her with her aunt's will. As they sat down together he thought how drained and pale she looked in her black gown, her eyes so full of sadness that he wondered if she would be able to concentrate on all he had to tell her.

'You have inherited richly from your aunt's estate here and in England. Apart from a generous bequest to her servant, Marie Mallet, and another to a charitable home for orphaned children, plus some minor amounts to other of her loyal servants in England, all else is yours. The will is somewhat unusual, but I believe you will know the reason for it.'

He read the will aloud to her as a formality. Except for a few treasured possessions and her late aunt's jewellery, all of which was bequeathed to Louise, everything else was to be sold. This included hundreds of acres of land and some fine properties both in France and England, and certain business premises in London and Paris. The resulting fortune would be secured in trusts tied up legally in such a way that Louise could draw funds for herself at any time, but no other person could lay claim to it.

'In other words,' the lawyer added as he folded the will to hand it to her, 'it means that, although you are a married woman, your husband cannot acquire your fortune, no matter if he does take the matter to court.' He gave a slight smile. 'Your late aunt was an astute woman.'

Louise managed to respond. 'My aunt could never be turned from what she wanted when her mind was made up.' She paused slightly. 'There are two other matters I should like to discuss with you.'

'I'm at your service, madame.'

She spent so long with the lawyer that it was almost suppertime when he left. After telling Rose of her late aunt's generosity towards her in the will, she also told her what else had been discussed. Nobody else was to know of it until the time was right.

The next day Louise wrote a long letter at the boulle desk, while Rose went shopping. When it was closed and sealed she went to the American Embassy. Theodore had told her that, if ever she were in need of a friend, the Ambassador would help her. She had to wait for half an hour before he could see her, but her name had been given to him together with a reminder of her relationship with Theodore, and he greeted her with a welcoming smile. Her request was simple enough, but when he had heard her explanation, he understood the importance of it.

'It shall be done exactly as you wish,' he promised as he escorted her to the door and bowed over her hand. If it had not been for her intense grief in her bereavement, she would have left the embassy with a lighter step.

On the journey home, with Rose dozing next to her and Josette fast asleep on the opposite seat, Louise sat thinking over all she had learned about Fernand as she gazed unseeingly out of the window. She recalled how in rare, tolerant moments towards her he had talked with something close to exultation about the power of Napoleon and how he believed he had made a good impression in showing the great leader that he was a loyal supporter of his aims for France. She supposed he had impressed the traitor Orléans in the same way. The difference was that, if he had spied for Napoleon during the truce, it would have been for information against France's enemies to help save French lives instead of slaughtering them on a scaffold. Now that France had her first Emperor, it was certain that Fernand would be even more eager to forge ahead in what was said to be the most dazzling court in Europe.

After leaving Rose at her home, where Jerome hurried out of the house to meet her, Louise arrived back at the château to find to her relief that Fernand was still away and had not returned in her absence. But there was a letter waiting from Madeleine. Only one paragraph of it stayed in her mind afterwards.

> Delphine met one of Daniel's Southern acquaintances in Washington, who told her that at the end of the month he is to marry the widow, Sarah Jane, to whom he was betrothed once before. They will be living in a small town in Alabama, where he has already taken over his late uncle's vast cotton plantation. By the time this letter reaches you, they will have been husband and wife for many weeks.

Louise sat for a long time as if frozen, with the letter lying on her lap. Outside, the daylight faded. A servant came in to light the candles. It was still a long time before she moved.

She was in Bordeaux at an auction, having recognized a harpsichord looted from the music salon, when Fernand returned from Paris. As soon as she re-entered the château she was informed that he was home. She left the manservants to help carry in her purchase, which had been brought by a carter following in the wake of her carriage, and went in search of Fernand. Since he never spoke to servants except to give them orders, she guessed he would not know of her bereavement. She found him writing at the library table. He did not look up as she entered.

'Close the door when you go out,' he said, dipping his quill in the ink without taking his eyes from the letter he was penning.

Ignoring what he had said, she went to stand in front of his desk. 'Ten days ago I returned from Paris,' she began.

'Fortunately our paths did not cross.' His quill scratched on.

'While there I met the Duchesse de Roget.' She drew in a deep breath. 'Her family went to the blade through your treachery, Fernand!'

Still without looking up, he stopped writing and put down his quill. Then he sat back in his chair, crossing one leg leisurely over the other, and eyed her coldly. 'I don't remember the name, but it's possible.'

His bland acceptance of her knowing the awful truth about him caused her to take a step back from the desk in revulsion. 'Have you no conscience about their lives, and others that were lost – some of them children – through your actions?' she exclaimed incredulously. 'No repentance?'

'Of course not. It's all in the past now. I began giving my support to the Revolutionary cause as a precautionary measure when the future of the monarchy began to be in doubt. If I hadn't taken that step and afterwards proved my worth by doing what was required of me, I'd have gone to the guillotine with all the rest. As it was, I had a lucky escape when eventually something I did upset someone in power. If that accident with the tumbril had not happened, I'd have been in an unmarked grave somewhere now, minus my head.' He took up his quill again, raising an inquiring eyebrow. 'Is there anything else you wish to know?'

She put a hand to her throat and answered him in a voice taut with horror. 'How am I to endure living under the same roof with you?'

He grinned. 'We can solve that matter when your old aunt dies. There will be a fortune that you'll not be able to keep from me and I'll be off to live in Paris for the rest of my days, visiting this château only when it suits me. You can stay here and rot!'

His laugh followed her out of the room. Out in the hall, she shook her head wearily and went slowly up the stairs. The duchess had described him as a monster. It was an apt description.

Although Fernand returned to his writing, something about Louise niggled at the back of his mind. She had looked very pale, but their confrontation could have caused that. No, there was still more that had not been as usual. Then realization hit him. She had been in black, a colour she never normally wore by day or evening, and black ribbons had been fastened to the coil of her luxuriant hair high at the back of her head. She was in mourning!

He flung down the quill and knocked his chair over as he sprang to his feet. Out in the hall, he shouted to the timid little maidservant, Isabelle, who was adding water to a vase of flowers, 'Where's your mistress?'

She gulped at his red-faced rage and pointed upstairs. He charged past her up the flight and along to Louise's bedroom. Flinging open the door and then slamming it shut behind him, he faced her where she stood, halfway across the room.

'She's dead, isn't she?' he snapped angrily. 'That's why you were in Paris this time! The old bitch has finally gone. Why didn't you tell me in the library instead of raking up the past?

How great is her fortune? How much land? What properties? Answer me, damn you!'

Louise spoke quietly. 'She has left a large fortune, or it will be when everything is sold, because, apart from her jewels and some other small things kept for me, that is what she wanted.'

'What about the mansion on the Rue d'Anjou? I went specially to take a look at it one day when I was in Paris. It will suit me very well as my city residence.' His anger had subsided and, rubbing his hands gleefully, he began pacing about the room with a buoyant step.

'That is to be sold too.'

'No matter. I shall buy it. Quite apart from it being one of the finest houses in Paris, it will amuse me to live there. It will be my revenge on the old bitch for not giving me as much as an English penny when I called on her in need.' He stopped to face Louise with his feet apart and his hands resting low on his hips in a triumphant stance. 'How long did the lawyers think it would take to settle the estate?'

'It will take quite a while, but nothing is yours, Fernand. My aunt left her fortune to me, for which I'm intensely grateful. Debts can be paid, the vineyards expanded, and improvements to the land will provide much-needed employment for more people in the area.'

He dismissed her words contemptuously. 'You're my wife. You can't make any decisions about the money! It becomes mine by right of the laws of marriage. It was only the craftiness of your father that stopped me acquiring your inheritance when we married. But it is different this time.'

She steeled herself for his wrath, which she knew would come. He was between her and the table by the bed where she kept her pistol, and she could not reach it. There was nothing else within reach by which she could defend herself if he should react violently.

'No, Fernand. My aunt's will prevents you from having a single franc. When all is sold, the money will be tied up in trusts that you cannot touch.'

The ugly colour had soared back into his face, his eyes narrowing into glittering slits. 'That's not possible! You are lying!'

She shook her head. 'It's the truth.'

'I shall contest the will in court!'

She shook her head. 'My lawyer assured me that it would be pointless for you to even try.'

He was shaking with temper, his fists balled at his side, his voice thick with rage. 'You dare to speak to me of conniving with some crooked lawyer behind my back! I, your husband, who could throw you out of this house now with only the clothes you're wearing.'

She ignored his threat, for the château was hers to live in or to dispose of as she wished, but she was desperately afraid of what he might attempt in his rage. 'I have told you how some of the money will be spent, and I have other plans too!'

'You'll do nothing with it! You will sign everything you have inherited over to me!'

'I refused to do it in the past and neither shall I do it now.'

'You had the Queen's protection then, but that's gone long since. You'll do as I say!'

'No!'

He lunged at her, seizing her arm and twisting it behind her, making her scream with pain, his face close to hers. 'I've had enough of not being the true master in this house, with your locked doors and penny-pinching ways! From now on you'll do what I want, even if I have to beat and starve you to my will!'

She screamed again as he twisted her arm still further, holding her in such a grip that she could not escape. Kicking and struggling, she beat and clawed at him with her free hand, but he grabbed it. Thrusting it behind her, he was able to hold both her wrists in the iron grip of his left hand, and he punched her hard in the left breast, grinning savagely as she shrieked out, almost fainting from the pain. He was not going to disfigure her face. That had been a mistake last time and had sent rumours circulating. It would be an even bigger error now, for she was friendly with too many people of importance in the district and he had his own reputation to consider. Better to cause her pain where bruises were hidden, and he knew many other ways that would pleasure him as much as they would torment her. He punched her again on the other breast, followed by another in the stomach, before releasing her as she sank to her knees on the floor, almost fainting with pain.

He put a hand under her chin and tilted her agonized, tear-wet face upwards as he looked down at her. 'Now you've had a taste of the treatment you'll receive if you don't sign your aunt's money over to me as soon as everything is settled.'

Her head sank down again. As yet she could not move, holding a hand to one throbbing breast while her twisted arm hung limply. She feared it was broken. Before leaving the room he went in turn to the small tables, one at each side of the bed. He found her pistol and ammunition in the drawer of the second one.

'I'll take charge of this, Louise. You'll have no need of it. I shall not come to this room again until your aunt's estate is settled. But if you fail to sign immediately the papers that my lawyers will have ready, that is another matter. Think about it carefully. You have a desirable body. It would be a pity for it to become one that no lover would ever want.' He went from the room.

For a while Louise could not move. Then she managed to crawl across to the bell-pull by her bed and reached up just high enough to tug it.

It was Isabelle who heard the bell ringing in Josette's room, but knew the lady's maid was outside in the grounds, so went to find her. Recently a new good-looking gardener, named Barnard, had taken the place of an elderly one who had retired, and he and Josette had become attracted to each other. As Isabelle had expected, she found them together, Josette watching him as he worked.

'You're wanted!' Isabelle called as soon as she was within earshot. 'Madame is ringing her bell.'

'At this time?' Josette questioned in surprise as she and Isabelle fell into step in the direction of the château. 'Perhaps she has lost something.'

'The master has been with her. He went up to her room in a terrible temper. I was as scared when he shouted at me as I was on the day the foreigner came. He was in an awful mood then too.'

Josette had increased her pace, certain there had been trouble. 'I don't remember any foreigner coming.'

'It was when you and Madame were in Paris. Not the last time, but one of the times before. It was a gentleman from the New World.'

'An American?' Josette came to an abrupt halt, taking Isabelle by the shoulders and giving the surprised girl a shake. 'Think now! What was he like?'

As she listened to Isabelle's description, she was certain it was Daniel Lombard who had come in their absence. She almost groaned aloud. What a cruel trick of fate that he should have come so far and then her mistress had not been at home. But she could not tell her. It would be too cruel on top of all else that the poor woman had had to endure.

She flew into the house and up the stairs. Louise was still lying on the floor, unable to move, but raised her eyes gratefully as Josette rushed to her.

Nineteen

L ouise's arm was not broken, but so badly strained that she had to wear a sling until eventually the pain subsided. Fernand made a visit to Paris, where he went first to consult his own lawyers, who emphasized that his wife's signature on a document surrendering everything to him was the simplest solution. Otherwise there could be months of costly litigation in the courts, with no guarantee of success unless he could prove that his wife was mad. It gave him food for deep thought. There were ways of making a woman appear out of her mind that were sufficient to make a bribed doctor certify her for an asylum. But he hoped it would not come to that, for she did manage the château and its estate most efficiently. He might be swindled by anybody else.

He estimated that it would take some months for everything in the will to be sold and settled. After three months he did not absent himself from the château again for any length of time, determined to be at home whenever Louise's lawyer should come to see her. He had his own document, drawn up by his lawyers, ready for her signature.

Louise found Fernand's constant presence a daily ordeal. They passed each other on the stairs without a glance and, since his brutality against her, they had never again eaten in the same room, except, under some social obligation, in the presence of others. When she entertained, it was to hold all-female gatherings for card parties, musical evenings and literary afternoons, when a chosen book was read aloud. Most people guessed that the marriage was in crisis, but it was not an uncommon state of affairs and little notice was taken. Only

Rose knew the cause. Had others known of Fernand's betrayal of his own kind, all doors in the district would have been barred to him.

After four months, a courier from the American Embassy in Paris arrived to deliver a letter to Louise personally, refusing to give it to a servant. As she directed the messenger towards the kitchens for refreshment, Fernand came hurrying to see what she had received.

'Is it from your lawyer?' he demanded eagerly.

'No, it's a letter from Alexandre,' she replied calmly, letting him see it was from America while ensuring that he did not snatch it from her. 'When I was in conversation once with the American Ambassador in Paris, I said how often letters were lost between our two countries. He kindly agreed to include correspondence from me in the next diplomatic bag carried to Washington by one of his couriers, who would arrange personal delivery. So, I gave him a letter for Alexandre. It was most kind of the Ambassador to have the reply given right into my hands.'

Fernand gave a grunt. He had already lost interest and turned away. She went swiftly up to her room and locked the door before she opened the letter. After reading it through, she gave a sigh of satisfaction before putting it away in the secret compartment of her jewel case.

Three weeks later, when Monsieur Terain arrived just before midday one morning, Fernand was the first to greet him.

'You have had a long and tiring journey, monsieur,' he said, anxious to get the lawyer out of the hall and into the library before Louise was informed of his arrival. 'A glass of wine while we discuss business?'

'Thank you, but I stayed overnight in Bordeaux and I'm not in the least tired. Nevertheless, a glass of wine would be welcome. But I'm here to see the marquise.' Then his face lit up as he saw her appear at the head of the stairs. Turning away from the threshold of the library, he went to greet her, bowing over her hand when she reached the foot of the flight.

'I have no objection to my husband being present,' she

assured him as Fernand stood stolidly in the doorway of the library. The lawyer showed no surprise, having been forewarned what to expect in a letter from her. He sat at the library table, since he had papers to show her, and she and Fernand sat opposite.

'How much?' Fernand demanded at once, tapping his fingers impatiently on the wooden arms of his chair. 'What's the total figure?'

'All in good time,' Terain replied coolly. He then proceeded to go through receipts and papers dealing with the sales of everything Violette had owned. Fernand became more and more elated as the total figure rose in leaps and bounds to culminate in a fortune beyond even his expectations.

All the time, the lawyer had addressed Louise as if they were on their own. 'That is the total figure,' he concluded, indicating where it was written down.

Fernand thumped a triumphant fist on the desk. 'Well done! Now all that remains is for you and one of the servants to witness my wife's signature on this document drawn up by my lawyers!' He took a key from his pocket and reached forward to unlock a drawer on his side of the library table. Taking out the document, he handed it to the lawyer with a flourish.

Terain read it through carefully before he looked across at Louise. 'Have you agreed to sign this or any other document?'

She shook her head. 'No.'

The lawyer pushed the document back across the table to Fernand. 'I advise you to tear it up. There is a clause in the will that, if you should contest it, your wife would lose everything and the trusts would be held instead for the progeny of any marriage other than yours. As it is, Madame la Marquise is willing for you to have the house of your choice in Paris, other than that of her late aunt, who would never have wanted you to live there, and an income that should keep you in comfort for the rest of your life. If you wish to have a country estate, it will be purchased for you, but it will not be on the scale of this château and its extensive vineyards. In all, I think that is an extremely generous arrangement.'

Fernand narrowed his eyes in disbelief. 'You speak as if the Marquise were no longer my wife!' he exclaimed in outrage, half rising to his feet and thumping the table as before but in rage instead of jubilation. 'I've no intention of having a country estate anywhere other than this one!'

'That will not be possible, since it is already bespoken to a new owner and your wife will relinquish the property at the end of next month.'

'What? I can't believe what I'm hearing!' Fernand, purple with wrath, swung round to Louise. 'What trickery are you attempting?'

She met his eyes. 'It's not a trick. Alexandre told me long ago that he and Blanche had always hoped to return to France one day for their children to grow up here in this lovely countryside. After he heard from me that his château had been destroyed and his land sequestered, that hope died. I have been able to rekindle that chance. The American Ambassador understood how important it was that my letter to Alexandre and his reply to me should not go astray, which is why both my letter and his reply travelled in the personal care of an American courier. I offered Alexandre this château, which he knows as well as his own lost home, for the token sum of one dollar. He accepted at once and the dollar duly arrived in his letter, which you saw me receive a short while ago.'

Fernand sank down again in his chair, his face frozen. 'I shall refuse to leave,' he stated implacably. 'No court will accept a wife selling the roof over her husband's head.'

Louise exchanged a glance with the lawyer that showed she wished to take over from him now. 'It's only fair to tell you, Fernand, that, when I was in Paris for my aunt's funeral, I instigated divorce proceedings against you on the grounds of incompatibility. Monsieur Terain assured me there should be no difficulty. Josette would bear witness to the brutal way you have treated me.'

'Any husband has a right to chastise a wayward wife!'

Fernand roared. 'You're married to me and so you shall
remain!'

Terain felt it time to intervene, for he had something to tell
that Louise herself had not heard yet. 'I have not been idle
since your wife first spoke of divorce to me. She also related
in confidence her meeting with the Duchesse de Roget. Now
that our Emperor has raised up again the glory of the ancien
régime, with all its splendour and titles and fine manners,
there is a great loathing of those responsible in the past for
sending the innocent to the guillotine. Unbeknown to your
wife, I have had extensive enquiries made and a witness to
your crimes has been found. He was a clerk in Orléans's
employ and still has a list, endorsed by your signature, of
those who died as a result of your treachery. No court would
keep a wife tied to a husband with blood on his hands.' He
saw how he had astonished Louise and stunned her husband
with his information. Fernand was gripping the arms of his
chair, his knuckles as white as his face.

'Lies! You've paid the fellow to forge it!'

Terain raised his eyebrows. 'The list has been proved genuine. So, I suggest you do not contest the divorce, Monsieur
le Marquis, and then your past will never come to light.
Otherwise it could have terrible consequences for you. Without
a doubt, you would be challenged to any number of duels by
those wanting to avenge the deaths of those known to them.
Accept the generosity of your wife and be thankful for her
magnanimity.'

Fernand sprang to his feet, breathing heavily, and glared
down at Louise for a few tense seconds in concentrated hatred.
'Your aunt would never have left such a will if you hadn't
plotted it together!' He almost screamed the words.

'No! I knew nothing that was in the will until after the
funeral,' Louise replied.

But Fernand was not listening. He grabbed her by the neck,
wrenching her to her feet, and shook her violently as his grip
tightened. 'Don't lie to me, you scheming whore!'

The lawyer was on him at once, hooking an arm about his

throat and forcing him back to break his hold. Both men were well matched in height and strength, but Terain had gained an advantage. Fernand lost his footing, sending them both crashing down together and Louise was left coughing and gasping. She reeled across to open the window for air while Fernand sprang to his feet only a moment before Terain.

Fernand shook a fist in Louise's direction. 'I want all that has been offered to me!' He gave Terain a great thrust in the chest, making him stagger back. 'My lawyers will contact you as to my terms regarding the income I intend to receive!'

'You'll take what has already been decided or nothing at all!'

Fernand slammed out of the room. Louise was never to see him again, for he left for Paris within an hour, leaving instructions for his possessions to be packed and sent on to him.

Next morning Louise talked with Terain, who had stayed overnight in one of the guest rooms at her invitation. Her throat was still extremely sore, making it difficult to speak, and she was wearing a chiffon scarf around her neck, tied with a soft bow to hide the purple bruises.

'Where are you planning to live?' he asked her. 'Shall you move to Paris?'

She shook her head. 'There is nothing to keep me in France any more. By now Alexandre and his wife and children will be halfway across the Atlantic. I shall wait to welcome them here. Then, when my bailiff and I have made him familiar with all the workings of the estate, I shall take ship for the United States. I have cousins in Boston and my sister lives in Washington.'

'A wise decision. Meanwhile, the monies you have decided to invest in the estate will eventually give your returning friends rich rewards.'

'I'm the one reaping the main reward in knowing that my home and land will always be loved and cared for.' She did not add that the family ties with the château had not been broken, for Delphine's blood ran in young Philippe's veins and it would be his inheritance.

Louise was disappointed, but not surprised when Josette felt unable to return to America with her.

'I never wanted to leave France last time, madame. If your friends will employ me, I'd like to stay on for a while. You see, Barnard, the gardener, will be entitled to one of the new estate cottages being built, and then we shall be married.'

'That's splendid news, Josette. I wish you every happiness.'

It was a memorable day when Alexandre and Blanche returned. Louise ran from the château to hug Blanche while Alexandre put his arms around them both as they laughed and talked together. Then Louise turned to the children. Henrietta at twelve years old was as bright and friendly as before, eager to see everything around her. To Louise's delight when she spoke to Philippe, a sturdy, handsome boy, now eight years old, he put his hand into hers to lead her back into the house.

'Papa says we've come home,' he told her.

'Indeed you have, Philippe.' She could see a likeness to Delphine in the hint of copper in his brown curls and in the colour of his eyes, but otherwise – as so often with children adopted from birth – his features seemed a blend of both his foster parents.

In the hall, Blanche and Alexandre stood together to look up and around at the place they remembered so well.

'It's wonderful to be here again,' she declared.

Alexandre took hold of Louise by her arms. 'We can never thank you enough for giving us the chance to come home again.' His voice was full of emotion. 'You've made a dream come true.'

She put her forefinger against his lips. 'It is I who should be thanking you. You have set me free to live my own life again in America, where I most want to be.'

It seemed to Louise in the days that followed that the château had come alive again. There was the laughter of the children and the clatter of their feet, Alexandre's booming voice echoing throughout and Blanche moving gracefully from room to room, overseeing household matters with a contented smile that never seemed to leave her lips.

Louise received the date of the divorce proceedings from Terain and set off to Paris to arrive the day before the case was to be heard. Although he had reassured her in his letters that nothing should go wrong, she was uneasy. She could not be sure until the last minute that Fernand would not find some way to delay the divorce or complicate matters in some unforeseen way simply out of revenge. She had arranged to meet Terain at the court and he was waiting for her when she arrived, coming to her immediately.

'There will be no divorce proceedings today,' he said seriously.

Her heart sank. 'What has happened?'

'Prepare yourself. Fernand de Vailly was shot and killed last night in a drunken quarrel over cards. Your marriage has ended in a way that neither of us expected.'

There were many farewells to be said in the neighbourhood before the day of Louise's departure came. Rose was particularly affected by her going away. Both knew that it was highly unlikely that they would ever meet again.

It was for the same reason that Blanche shed tears when the moment came for Louise to leave the château for the last time. The servants had lined up in the hall and she said goodbye to each in turn.

Outside, the coach was waiting, her baggage loaded. She and Blanche embraced and Alexandre put his arms about them both as he had done before, binding the three of them again in lasting friendship. After Louise had kissed the children in turn, Alexandre handed her into the carriage. As soon as she was seated, both Henrietta and Philippe each held out a tiny bunch of wild violets that they had picked earlier.

'For you,' they chorused eagerly.

Emotionally, she waved the family out of sight. Then she waved again to the peasants who paused in their work to wave her on her way. When all were left behind, she selected one of the violets from Philippe's bunch and put it carefully into her purse to press later as a memento of her childhood home and its future master.

Twenty

S even weeks later and, after a smooth voyage, Louise stepped ashore in Charleston. She had given a great deal of thought to whether she should go to South Carolina before travelling to Boston, knowing how it would tear at her heart. Daniel would have been married and settled in Alabama long since and she had no hope that it could be otherwise, but she had long wanted to see the house where he was born and the town in which he had grown up. He had talked of Charleston many times and had planned to take her to visit his sister in their family home, but pressure of work, on her side as well as his, had caused postponement until it was too late.

She took a room in a new hotel in the centre of Charleston and then went out to start exploring the town, with its wide streets and shady trees, its brick mansions and carefully watered flower gardens. Every kind of trade was represented in the shops, workshops and stables. Slaves in smart livery carried parcels and drove fine carriages, while every woman, on foot or as a passenger, held a parasol, all in a variety of pastel colours that protected them in tinted shade from the strong sunshine. As always, Louise paused to look with interest in the windows of any milliner's that she happened to pass. Each time, she was reminded poignantly of the hat that Daniel had bought for his sister after she had displayed it for him.

She knew the address to which it had been sent, for after she and Daniel had married, Elizabeth had corresponded with her from time to time. Although she was eager to see the house, it was too soon yet. She needed time to adjust emotionally to being here.

By the end of the week, Louise had picked out several places that Daniel had mentioned from time to time. She went to a comedy at the theatre where he had seen his first play and strolled across a small square where he had played as a boy, for it had been ideal for bowling a hoop. When he had spoken once of the rustling of the palmetto leaves in the ocean breeze, it had sounded so alien to her, but now she was hearing them for herself and it was one more memory to take away with her.

After three weeks, and on the last day before sailing north to Boston, she made her way to the avenue where Daniel's family home was located. She found it set in green lawns and stood to look up the short drive at the large, wide-fronted house. Built of red brick, sun-weathered to a mellow hue, it had many windows, which were presently shaded against the sun. Its paintwork was a gleaming white and six steps led up to the entrance porch. She stayed long enough to take in every detail of the house before she turned sadly away.

She had taken no more than a step or two when a woman's voice called out to her.

'Louise de Vailly?'

She swung round to see a woman older than herself, dressed to go out and hurrying down the steps. 'Elizabeth?' she replied uncertainly.

'Yes! Surely you weren't going to leave without calling on me?' Elizabeth hurried to her. 'We meet at last!'

'How did you know me?'

'From the miniature that Daniel showed me! Your hair is dressed differently, but its beautiful colour is unmistakable. If I hadn't come out of the house at that exact moment, I should have missed you. Come in!' She linked her arm through Louise's and led her towards the house. 'My appointment can wait! I'll send someone to say I'll come another day. How long shall you be in Charleston?'

'I leave tomorrow for Boston.'

'So soon!' Elizabeth exclaimed as they entered the house. 'Then we must not waste a single moment of today. Gregory, my husband, will be home later and he'll be delighted to meet you too.' She discarded her hat and then held it for a moment before handing it to the waiting maidservant. 'Do you remember the hat you advised Daniel to choose for me?'

'Very well indeed.' Louise smiled. 'I can see now that it would have suited you very well.'

Elizabeth, whose hair was as dark as Daniel's, had a creamy complexion and a smiling mouth. She led the way across the hall to a large drawing room. As Louise sat down she could no longer hold back the question she most wanted to ask.

'How is Daniel?' Her voice faltered slightly.

Elizabeth gave her a direct look. 'He's well and settled in Jonesville in Alabama. The past is behind him. He has made a successful new start to his life. I should not want anything to spoil it.'

They continued into the drawing room with its sofas and chairs upholstered in rose-patterned silk. Above the fireplace was a portrait of Elizabeth that must have been painted when she was about eighteen, dressed in a cinnamon-hued gown with a fichu such as had been fashionable at that time.

'That's a very fine likeness,' Louise said admiringly as she and Charlotte sat down opposite each other. 'I would have recognized you from it just as you knew me from the miniature. Please don't think I'm inquisitive, because I've been looking around me at everything, but it means a great deal to me to be in Daniel's family home.'

'I'm sure he felt the same when he visited your château.'

'He was never there!' Louise replied.

'Indeed he was! Afterwards he went to Paris to see the city that you had known so well. He told me all about it.'

'He was in France?' Louise's cry tore from her. 'I never knew! I must have been visiting my aunt in England at the time!'

Elizabeth was regarding her steadily. 'No. You were in France, but you chose to absent yourself from the château as soon as you knew he was in the district. I realize you did it for the best,' she added quickly, 'but it would have meant so much to my brother just to see you again, even if a divorce

on your part was still out of the question. It was a final blow
when your housekeeper gave him your message.'

Louise had turned white and she clasped her hands, raising
them up and down in her despair. 'I left no message! I never
knew he had come!' Then she shut her eyes as a terrible
realization hit her. 'Did he say if he went to the theatre
in Paris?'

'Yes, two or three times, I believe.'

'Dear God! Then I did see him there one night! I even
called his name, but he did not hear me and I thought I'd
been mistaken! Fernand must have made sure that I'd never
be told!'

Elizabeth was touched by Louise's deep distress. 'I'm so
sorry that you failed to see each other. It would have meant
so much to him.'

'Why did he come looking for me? We had agreed that we
should not even correspond.'

'He wanted to know if anything had changed in your
marriage and some loophole discovered that might still give
a chance for you both. I warned him not to be too hopeful,
but he said he had to find out for himself.'

'My poor Daniel,' Louise said softly.

'You haven't told me yet the reason why you'll be visiting
Boston after leaving Charleston. I hope your relatives there
are well?'

Louise nodded. 'I'm widowed now and I have come back
to live in the States again. After visiting my cousins in Boston
and my sister in Washington, I may settle in New York, where
I have friends.'

'Does Boston have too many memories for you?'

Louise nodded. 'I could never live there again.'

'It was for the same reason that Daniel decided to sell up
and move back to the South. Our late uncle and his wife had
always been fond of Daniel and it was to be expected that the
Alabama plantation should be bequeathed to him one day.'

'Daniel told me about his boyhood vacations with them and
how he still thought of their house as a second home.'

'That's right, but he has built a fine new mansion there now. Gregory and I visited a while ago.' Elizabeth paused, looking down at her hands in her lap, as if deciding what to say next, before her eyes met Louise's gaze again. 'He has changed, Louise. I saw a great difference in him when he first came to stay here after leaving Boston, but since returning from France he seemed shut away within himself and no longer the brother I knew.'

'But you said yourself he had made a successful fresh start.'

'So he has done commercially, but emotionally is a different matter. After what he thought to be your total rejection of him in France, there was so much hurt in him that I believe it shattered him inwardly.'

Louise shook her head despairingly. 'I'd try to heal that hurt if it were not for Sarah Jane.'

Elizabeth raised her eyebrows. 'What has she to do with it?'

'Are they not married?'

'No!' Elizabeth made a dismissive gesture. 'I don't doubt he shared her bed when it suited him while he was here, but that was all. Rumours of a possible marriage flew around as gossip always does in Charleston.' Then what Louise had said seemed to hit her and she sat very straight. 'Do you mean what you said? You'd go to see him?'

'Yes!'

Elizabeth looked doubtful. 'You could be greatly hurt in your turn.'

'I'm willing to risk anything!'

'A great gulf has widened since the two of you were last together. There may be no bridging it now. Have you faced the fact that his love for you might have died?'

'I realize that is a possibility. But all my life I've had to fight for what I wanted, not always successfully, and this time it will be the most important venture of my life.'

'I wish you well, but I'll give you the same warning as I gave Daniel when he left for Europe. Don't raise your hopes too high.'

*   *   *

On the long journey to Jonesville, Louise saw vast cotton plantations, for such was the great demand from the textile industries. The sight of the slaves working on them disturbed her. Slavery had always been abhorrent to her and it was encouraging that politicians in England were fighting to get it abolished, which made her hope that this country and others would soon follow suit.

Overnight halts were made on the way and she arrived in Jonesville on a late May afternoon in a coach covered with red dust from the rough roads and found the little town gloriously clouded by magnolia trees in full bloom.

The only accommodation available was a room in a modest hotel on one of the smaller streets. After soaking in a cool hipbath she felt refreshed as she put on a lily-green gown with a new yellow straw hat of her own making. The landlady gave her directions how to find the address that Elizabeth had given her.

She walked slowly, exploring and observing everything. There was an air of prosperity about the place, with plenty of shops, a courthouse and two banks, both with a columned frontage, a library and streets of fine mansions that were evidence of the fortunes and trade generated by cotton.

Daniel's house was large and white with a long columned porch that stretched the width of the house and a flower-lined drive with wide lawns. She did not stay at the gate as she had at his childhood home, but took a deep breath and went straight up the drive. After mounting the wide steps up to the porch, she lifted the shining brass knocker and banged it twice. A butler opened the door to her.

'I'm Madame de Vailly and I'm here to see Mr Lombard,' she said, stepping inside.

'He's not at home, ma'am.'

'When is he expected back?'

'Not for an hour or more. He is at a business meeting.'

'I'll wait.'

From the large hall with its sweeping staircase, where magnolias filled tall vases in the wall niches, Louise was shown into a spacious drawing room. The fashionable scroll-ended furniture made her wonder if somehow it had been imported from France. There were more magnolias here, arranged in a Sèvres bowl on a round rosewood table, their porcelain-like petals seeming to add to the refreshing coolness of the window-shaded room.

An ormolu clock ticked the time away, but Daniel did not return. She became restless, trepidation mounting, and moved about the room to study the paintings on the wall. Double doors into the next room had been folded back, letting the cool air drift through into other rooms beyond. She wandered on and went through a dining room into another fine drawing room, where glass doors led to the flower garden and lawns at the rear of the house.

She opened them and stepped out, closing them after her. It was just beginning to get dark, the magnolia trees standing pale and fireflies already darting here and there like tiny stars. There was a garden seat under the nearest tree and she drifted to it, taking off her hat and setting it beside her as she sat down. In the house, candles were being lit and chandeliers had begun to glow. There was no dusk in this part of the world and almost at once she was in darkness, with only the light through the glass doors falling across the grass and etching her where she sat. Gradually she felt at peace, for this flower-scented setting was almost dream-like.

The glass doors opened and Daniel stood silhouetted, looking towards her. 'Louise,' he said quietly, as if unable to believe she was there.

She stood and went towards him. He drew her into the candlelight and held her gently by the arms as he looked down into her face. She was no longer afraid. Whatever difficulties lay ahead, they could be overcome. There was a deep look in his eyes that told her that all her long journeys were over at last.

1

hf 1.17(0)   bcl 2.24
rc 10.19 (1)
ha 2.22(1)
NNS   A-85   NC